λ

D1336964

C800368416

Living Souls

ALMA BOOKS LTD
London House
243–253 Lower Mortlake Road
Richmond
Surrey TW9 2LL
United Kingdom
www.almabooks.com

Living Souls originally published in Russian as ЖД by Vagrius in 2006
This translation, edited and abridged with the author's consent, first published
in UK by Alma Books Ltd in 2010
Russian text Copyright © 2006 by Dmitry Bykov
Translation rights into the English language acquired via FTM Agency Ltd,
Russia, 2007
English language translation © Cathy Porter, 2010

Dmitry Bykov asserts his moral right to be identified as the author of this
work in accordance with the Copyright, Designs and Patents Act 1988

Printed in Great Britain by CPI Antony Rowe

ISBN: 978-1-84688-098-8

LIVING SOULS

DMITRY BYKOV

TRANSLATED BY CATHY PORTER

ALMA BOOKS

Contents

Part One: Departure   3
Chapter One: In the Camp of the Russian Warriors   5
Chapter Two: The Kaganate   80
Chapter Three: Maugham's Way   140
Chapter Four: The Joe   201
Interlude   231

Part Two: Arrival   235
Chapter One: Bella Ciao   237
Chapter Two: The Bath Hut   247
Chapter Three: The Town of Blatsk   271
Chapter Four: White Power   283
Chapter Five: The Pentameron   288
Chapter Six: The Monastery   305
Chapter Seven: The Gates   321
Chapter Eight: "Vasilenko Syndrome"   337
Chapter Nine: Parents' Day   345
Chapter Ten: Treason   374
Chapter Eleven: The Final Battle   381
Chapter Twelve: The Village of Degunino   402
Chapter Thirteen: A Tale of Three Towns   407
Chapter Fourteen: The Village of Zhadrunovo   415
Chapter Fifteen: The Soldier on Leave   426
Epilogue   435

Living Souls

A Poem

Part One

Departure

Chapter One
In the Camp of the Russian Warriors

All go unto the same place; all are of the dust and all turn to dust again.

Ecclesiastes 3:20

1

By evening Gromov and his unit had recaptured the village of Degunino. He had had to hurry, he hadn't enough men to attack at night and they were all exhausted, and if it dragged on to the next day it might have cut short his leave. He had to take it by the evening of 17th July, and he made it, with practically no casualties. The architect Krasnov sprained his ankle on the slippery clay of the famous Hill 16 and limped to the medic, who bandaged him up and sent him back. The rest were uninjured and already shacked up in their usual billets: it was the twelfth time they had taken Degunino, and they all had a woman there.

It had poured with rain for three days without stopping, just slowing to a drizzle every so often to gather strength and throw it down again. The river Dresva had burst its banks and was a foaming torrent, and it sickened Gromov to have to wade across. Normally it was just a trickle, too shallow even to swim in and cool down from the heat, and they would simply have jumped it: now it meant a whole fording manoeuvre he would have to put in his report.

Lance Corporal Gannushkin distinguished himself during the operation by bursting into song to raise company morale. "He set off at night on the night train!" he bawled raucously, slithering around the bottom, and continued with a lewd version about his testicles.

"What's wrong with you, Gannushkin?" snapped Gromov. He was in a foul mood.

"I'm laughing, Captain!" Gannushkin grinned. "I'll be tucked up in bed with her soon, ready for some action!"

"Never mind that, I'll give you action. Company, keep tight!"

The last time they were driven out of Degunino was a week ago, in a surprise attack by Ataman Batuga and his Cossack Eagles – plump, well-fed youths smelling of hashish, home brew and meat, who

5

galloped up early in the morning, silently dispatched the patrols and drove the sleepy soldiers from their familiar haunts with whips. Most of Gromov's men didn't have time to grab their weapons – Batugin's boys just burst into the cottages and yanked them by their collars from their stoves and beds. It was humiliating. Gromov hadn't been asleep. For two months he had been plagued by insomnia, waiting for his leave which could at any moment be cancelled, and he had acted bravely too; in other circumstances he would have received a mention in the bulletin.

But they ended up looking like a bunch of idiots. He had taken out two, but they had to retreat and the Cossacks hadn't even chased them, and he had dug in three kilometres from Degunino in a flat field of sunflowers to plan his counterattack. He had no idea how many men Batuga had, and the Command hadn't sent reinforcements. There were fifty left in his company, theoretically enough to drive them out, but who knows how many Batuga had conscripted from the neighbouring villages.

On the 17th, his scout Redkin reported that after five days of revelries and firing rifles in the air the village was quiet. "They're knackered, boss," he said, with the familiarity of a friend. "We'll take them with our bare hands, they're too pissed to move."

Gromov pondered. He didn't like the quiet. In war things were never based on calculation, always on intuition. His leave was in three days, and he knew his men were sick of sitting in their dugouts in the rain, and they had to take the village before the Cossacks sobered up. But he hung on another day, playing beggar-my-neighbour in his tent with his orderly Papatya, and only at twenty hundred hours gave the signal to attack.

In the mauve half-light of dusk, under pounding streams of warm rain, they scrambled up Hill 16 a line abreast and advanced to the village, and discovered not one of Batuga's men there. The Cossacks had had their fun and galloped off.

Gromov was glad it hadn't come to a battle, but he knew Batuga wouldn't have simply retreated; it was a fair bet his boys had polished off all the meat and alcohol in Degunino and moved on to raid Khabarov or Pereyaslov, leaving Gromov and his men to suck their paws. After the Cossacks, as with Astrid Lindgren's Karlsson, there was never anything left.

He sat on the board bed in his room, under a portrait of a fat whiskery peasant bearing an uncanny resemblance to the Bolshevik hero Marshal Budyonny. "What a cock-up, eh, Redkin?" he asked his unfortunate scout in a weary voice, pulling off his muddy boots with a grimace of pain and pleasure.

"It was all quiet, comrade Captain!" his young friend said, forced out of embarrassment to address him more formally.

"All quiet," he mocked him. "When will we learn to fight, Sergeant? Are we going to be Muscovites all our life?"

Men from Moscow were despised in the army, but they fought no worse than the others; after three years of war the Federal Guard was in a pitiful state and anyone could send them packing.

"Government rabble. What shall I tell the Command – that the village was taken without a battle in the absence of the enemy?"

"Can't we just say we drove them out?"

"Better say we turned them into toads, they're more likely to believe us. Right, shove off, get out of my sight."

Redkin shuddered. He had a lovely girl in Degunino, plump, silly and playful, with a golden plait like straw, and he worried that Gromov would punish him by sending him off on night patrol and put paid to their romantic meeting. But instead he picked Gannushkin, who he couldn't stand. It wasn't fair, of course, but he made up for it by writing him up in the report.

Gannushkin was also looking forward to spending the night with his girl, Travka. She wasn't fussy who she went with, because she was nothing to look at, and she lived next to Degunino's church, a bizarre architectural construction covered in onion-domes, like a tree stump covered in mushrooms. No other village – and Gromov had seen plenty during the war – had such a hideous church. Travka worked as a cleaner there, and according to some even filled in for the priest who had been called up – a sure sign of the country's collapse: never before had a woman been known to serve in the Orthodox Church.

"Someone on the line for you, comrade Captain!" his orderly Papatya said, handing him his mobile.

"Dawn, Dawn! Earth here, do you hear me?" Colonel Zdrok's shrill voice shrieked in his ear.

"I hear you loud and clear. I'm in Degunino, comrade Colonel."

"What the hell are you doing there, Bonaparte, playing war games? We've captured the locality and we're in Degunino? I order you in plain Russian to advance on Baskakovo, rendezvous with Major Volokhov's Flying Guards and take the locality of Bobra in a joint operation, and they're sitting in Degunino mating for their weddles?

I'll give them the Medal of the Haemorrhoids First Class!" (Zdrok tended to mix up his consonants and pronouns when angry.)

He raved on, and the call was on Gromov's phone, which he hadn't topped up for a week.

"I had no such orders, comrade Colonel—"

"You didn't?" Zdrok rose slowly to the boil. "Well you have now, you Red Army clown, that's why I'm calling you. You're to advance immediately on the locality of Baskakovo! Silently, at the double, under cover of darkness, you hear me, Captain?"

"It's night, comrade Colonel, the men are tired," Gromov protested in vain.

"What, you're questioning me? It's a bloody shambles! Court martial in twenty-four hours!" bawled the Chief of Staff. "Snivelling pansy, dragging them to Degunino to get out of the rain!"

"I had orders to clear Degunino."

"He had orders! He has a woman there..." Zdrok had reached his climax and trailed off, and was quickly roused again. "His men move three metres and they're tired – you'll be too tired to wipe your own arses soon! I'm giving you peasants an hour's rest, and in five hours I expect to hear Captain Gromov's unit has reached Baskakovo under cover of darkness and made contact with Major Volokhov!"

"Right then," said Gromov lifelessly.

"Right in the neck! I'll give you medals!" Zdrok was off again, but at that moment the line crackled and went dead, and he was spared another dose of military folklore.

Gromov loathed Zdrok. It was because of men like the Chief of Staff of the Thirty-Sixth Guards that the army was a shambles. The rot had set in as soon as the war started and had spread exponentially, and there was no chance of military action taking care of him: people like Zdrok were never killed. This man took the most senseless decisions with idiotic stubbornness, and as well as his strategic incompetence he liked to cause maximum grief to his men. How on earth was he to move them fifteen kilometres at night and link up with the mythical Volokhov? The rain had stopped, the sky was clearing, it was enough that they had taken Degunino for peace and harmony to be restored. The roads, however, were mud. Gromov cursed through his teeth.

"Konyshev, get me Baskakovo," he ordered his signaller.

Konyshev was one of the few educated men in the regiment; he had all the codes in his head, and quickly dialled the twenty-digit number.

"Duty Officer of the regiment here," said a groggy voice.

"Put Selivanov on the line," Gromov said.

The duty officer flicked a switch. "Captain Selivanov," grunted Gromov's old mate from Kalashnikov classes.

"It's me, Gromov. Tell me, is Major Volokhov with you?"

"We've been expecting him for two days. He's supposed to liaise with someone and attack somewhere." The Captain stifled a yawn. "He's attacking everywhere with his Eagles, he'll never get here. Elite scum, they're never on time. Volokhov this, Volokhov that – what exactly has Volokhov done?"

"It's me he's liaising with. I'm on my way to you now."

"Where are you?"

"Degunino. I've just cleared it, for your information."

"Well you won't go hungry then. Cleared it of who exactly?"

Selivanov could be heard picking his teeth in his Baskakovo headquarters.

"Batuga's Cossacks. You know him?"

"I'll say," Selivanov sniggered. "He's been with his Marusya since this morning in Litmanov, the next station from here. How did you do it, Grom? You must mention it in the report – how he scarpered and turned up in Litmanov this morning. Mighty Gromov, conqueror of space and time, driving Batuga out with his shrieks!" He expanded at length on the subject; apparently it was the talk of the army.

"Knock it off!" Gromov interrupted him. Selivanov was cackling unpleasantly, imagining Batuga galloping from Degunino at the speed of light, with Gromov chasing behind in an ox cart. "He sent his men in – I never said he was there himself. I'm advancing at dawn."

"Advance, advance, no point hanging around if you've eaten."

"Right, over and out."

Gromov wondered gloomily how he would break the news to his men. They had already turned in for the night and were dreaming around Degunino's warm stoves, with their equally warm landladies, who bedded and boarded each of the warring sides in turn, and had already dragged up from their cellars what was left from Batuga's revels.

At the thought of the march ahead and the general grumbling, he felt sick to his stomach. He decided to say nothing that night, and to raise the alarm at three in the morning. There was no point in him sleeping; it would be easier to stay awake than have to drag himself out of bed after a few hours.

"OK, pack up in the next room and if there's anything urgent call me." He dismissed his signaller. "Papatya, tell Galya to get me something to eat."

He always stayed in the same squat, stout, spacious cottage, with stout, squat, middle-aged Galya, and he could never get over her endless supplies. No matter how many armies, bands and hordes passed through Degunino, she always brought pickled cucumbers and cabbage from the cellar for all of them, and various infusions and mysterious gruels the Muscovite Gromov had never tasted before, along with Degunino's thick sour cream and ice-cold milk, and there was always a pot of potatoes on the stove and a pie. "Eat, liberators, I put them on when I heard you were coming," she would say.

It was all the more remarkable too in a village in which a quarter of the homes were burnt to the ground and a good half had been pulverized in battles, with windows smashed and the whole side of one cottage missing.

Gromov knew quite well why all the armies liked to take Degunino. Despite countless lectures by Political Instructor Ploskorylov about the strategic importance of the area, and the wedge the masculine North was driving into the feminine South at the very point where Hitler was driven back in '42 – and the outcome of that last war would have been very different otherwise – it was clear everyone had just one thing in mind: stuffing their faces. It's a major factor in war, and none of the neighbouring villages offered the same opportunities to sleep, guzzle and cuddle peasant women by the fire.

In three years he had taken no less than fifty localities, survived outside Oryol, and surrendered Trosno four times and recaptured it, and for the past six months, circling in the Degunino cauldron, his company had blessed their fate. In other villages people cursed them or welcomed them grudgingly, after suffering at the hands of the Federals or Khazars, but nowhere else had he encountered the docile compliance with which Degunino welcomed its successive soldiers like an easygoing mistress.

All in turn were fed and given beds to sleep in and the delicious local mint vodka to drink, and however much Ploskorylov demanded that everyone who collaborated with the enemy be shot, even Zdrok turned a blind eye to this state of affairs. It seemed to Gromov (he was drifting off to sleep now, with a pleasant heaviness in his stomach from Galya's smoked bacon and potatoes) that even if Ploskorylov's lousy plan to shoot every woman in Degunino was carried out, and by some miracle

one of them hid in the orchards and survived, she would still have
vodka and bacon and potatoes for the next happy heroes and would
take them all on the stove, muddy and stinking and desperate for love.
  Gromov knew he mustn't sleep, but he slept anyway, with his head
slumped on the hefty, scrubbed-clean table – nowhere else had he seen
such enormous tables, they seemed designed for a giant's banquet, and
were an essential feature of every Degunino cottage. And as he dozed
off, he could hear Galya talking in the next room with her neighbour
Panya. No one knew Panya's full name, she was just Panya, a jolly
snub-nosed woman who could have been thirty or forty, or even older,
only in his dream she was different, sadder and more serious, and it
was as if Galya, away from people and on her own with her friend,
had discarded her squat stout body and become young and slender
again, almost like a child.

  They were talking in the bedroom she had shared with her husband,
who she said had been conscripted (although according to Gannushkin
all the peasants from Degunino were partisans in the surrounding
forests, and their wives were feeding them). She slept alone there now,
and Gromov didn't bother her: what would he want with this burly,
uncommunicative forty-year-old woman, whose only words to him were
"eat" and "stove"? And in his sleep he heard Galya and Panya quietly
complaining and consoling each other in their high, girlish voices, just
as girlish it seemed to him as their magically altered bodies. It was
definitely Russian they were speaking, but he had only a vague sense
of what it was about, although he could hear them as clearly through
the thick log wall as if there was nothing between them. He couldn't
make out what was so special about their language, only that it was
extraordinarily powerful and precise, without Ploskorylov's bombast
or the soldiers' smut, or the sprawling jargon of the official reports, as
if they had had total command of it since childhood and were giving
each thing its proper name. Some words he couldn't understand, others
were familiar to him but used in unfamiliar ways, but he could guess
their meaning just from the sound of them: calling oven tongs "a little
moon" for instance, or a chicken a cauliflower, seemed so appropriate
and natural he couldn't think why he hadn't used them himself. Oven
tongs had an unpleasant angular ring to them, and the heavy casserole
was always placed so readily on the table, gleaming in the moonlight.
He smiled in his sleep as he heard them call a formation of soldiers
a "buttock" for some reason, and there was something friendly and
comforting about the chicken-cauliflower. He couldn't make out the

actual subject of their conversation though, just that life wasn't easy for Galya and Panya, and as they poured their hearts out to each other, it was as if they were bracing themselves for endless new captures and surrenders of Degunino.

It seemed to him too that what they were talking about was the earth's capacity to thrive. There had been no one to farm it since the start of the war, yet miraculously things seemed to grow even better now, without all the authorities that had wrecked it with ploughing and chemicals and incessant commands, crushing its will to survive. It seemed so obvious to him in his dream – there was no need to do anything, tons of fruit and crops would grow all by themselves, like the magic stove and the apple tree in the fairy tale saying "eat my pies" and "pick my apples". And talk of this inexhaustibly fertile earth became a song whose meaning he couldn't quite grasp: he just followed its mood of melancholy joy, as when two people are saying goodbye before a long parting and things don't turn out as they expected. Galya took the melody, and Panya wove the second part around it, and there was so much age-old joy and grief in it that his heart followed it like a sunflower turning to the sun.

He could make out separate words, all two-syllabled, with the stress on the first – rowan, nettles, sorrow – and at the sound of them a soft green light soothed his tired eyes, and he saw an overgrown graveyard opening onto an orchard, and the abandoned parks he had seen in the liberated towns of Central Russia, and he wanted the rowan and the nettles and the sorrow to be braided into a plait and never end.

But already Papatya was shaking him, and with each shake the correct beautiful Russian words for things flew out of his mind. He woke and threw off his dream, remembering only that Papatya was the proper word for a sort of thyme, and glanced at his army watch. It was ten to three.

"Raise the alarm!" he grunted at his orderly, going out to the porch to splash his face with cold water from the bucket.

"Alarm!" Papatya shouted, tearing down Degunino's main street, firing wildly in the air in accordance with the Rulebook, gleefully anticipating the delightful spectacle as he dashed into the cottages with deafening cries of "Get up!"

Gromov's company, remembering their recent disgrace at the hands of Batuga, hurtled from their stoves and beds and jumped into their boots without tying on their foot-cloths, not wanting to be chased out again with whips.

Gromov waited in front of the village shop, where they always lined up, and five minutes later (six, to be accurate, but even double the three-minute norm was a big improvement), his men stood sleepily before him in two columns.

The sky had cleared, a few wispy clouds drifted over the roofs, and the night air smelt of grass, earth and woodsmoke – he could have stood there for ever. He remembered his parents' dacha, marvelling at the power of smells to evoke memories. So much had happened, for three years there'd been nothing but war, and still he remembered the dacha, and suddenly he was five years old again, kneeling on the old bentwood chair by the open window and looking out at the stars, his freshly washed feet stung by nettles and mosquitoes, and they were the same stars and the same smells, and soon his mother would read to him and he would feel the cool linoleum under his heels as she shooed him to bed – he should have been under the covers long ago, instead of staring out of the window…

"Company!" he barked.

They all stood to attention.

"Very sloppy," he said, inspecting them with a practised disdain. "Look at you Voronin, button up your shirt. Barannikov, you think the Rulebook doesn't apply to you? Ogureyev, you haven't cleaned your boots. Two penalty points!" Lanky Ogureyev coughed nervously. "Our orders are to rendezvous in two hours with Major Volokhov's detachment near the village of Baskakovo for a joint strike at the enemy in the appointed place, to be indicated to us later. It's fifteen kilometres from here to Baskakovo, the roads are a swamp. What enemy, you ask? Who knows. We'll be informed by the relevant people at the relevant time." He ironically rapped out the stock phrases from the military Rulebook. "Look sharp, take it on the chin, march briskly, bear all hardships bravely. All clear, my little Eagles?"

The men laughed. They all liked Gromov and knew he was all bark and no bite.

"Le-eft…" He paused for effect, ending with a flourish. "Turn!"

The men turned two abreast in the darkness, in the direction of Baskakovo.

"A one two three! A one two three!" he commanded, noticing with pleasure his Eagles' bulging gas-mask bags: their hostesses had evidently sent them well supplied with bacon, bread and apples from their fruitful, uncultivated earth.

They marched off at a brisk pace. Far away in the eastern sky, the dense night was beginning to fade, like a blocked nose slowly clearing when someone turns over in the night.

* * *

"Panya, Panya!" called a hoarse familiar voice.

Panya, who had just returned from Galya's and was about to go to bed, jumped up and ran to the window.

"Misha!" she whispered.

"Let me in, Panechka!"

She dashed to the door and quickly slid back the lock. Her husband grabbed her in his arms and embraced her, grunting with pleasure.

"Oh Misha, I didn't heat you a bath—"

"It's not a bath I want, I want you, sweetheart," he murmured. "Has everyone left?"

"All of them!" Panya nodded happily. "First the Cossacks, now the others."

"I wanted to come yesterday, but I couldn't risk it," Misha explained, still holding his wife. "Wait, darling, I'll give the signal."

He went to the street and fired three shots from the pistol hanging at his belt, and soon bearded men in quilted jackets appeared from the forests around Degunino, and the male population made their way back to their homes.

The Degunino peasants had been inspired to become partisans by their strong aversion to joining the army. Each new wave of liberators rolling through the village had orders to conscript the locals, and the women would tell all of them that their husbands had already joined up. If anyone asked why so many were pregnant, they would bashfully explain that there were a lot of soldiers, and if they found some attractive they wouldn't say no, and the men would spit and throw up their hands.

"We're used to it, Panechka, it's as if I was born in the forest," her husband said, gulping down his noodle soup. "If only you were there, it would be heaven."

"I missed you, Misha," Panya smiled.

"Oh my darling," he sighed. "Let's lie by the stove. Tomorrow we can sleep..."

2

Major-General Paukov, whose name derives from the Russian for "spider", was proud of his resemblance to his great idol in the last war, Marshal Zhukov, or "beetle". He saw the connection as highly symbolic, and the difference in their names seemed to sum up the difference in their tactics. While Zhukov had rolled the dung-ball of the masses to the gleaming heights of victory against Hitler, General Paukov had woven a vast web of spies and agents throughout the land in which to trap the enemy. This new enemy was cunning, and came exclusively from within; it was a long time since foreigners had invaded Russia's bewitched landscape, for fear of being caught in Paukov's web. The internal enemy had to be monitored, encircled, immobilized and smashed: these were the four main points he had formulated in his new Rulebook, which he and Priest-Captain Ploskorylov knew by heart.

Paukov regarded Ploskorylov as the ideal political instructor. Twenty-seven years old, plump and inclined to breathlessness, he understood the sacred, or, as he put it, the sacramental significance of every letter of the Rulebook. Most of it would seem gibberish to a civilian, and it was indeed gibberish, but this was a secret known only to the few. The great systematizing power of gibberish was truly understood only by soldiers, and Ploskorylov was a true soldier, with his civilian demeanour, his soothing expressive voice and his inability to fire a shot.

His grandfather had been a staff-officer, and his great-grandfather a White general who had gone over to the Reds, successfully surviving Stalin's terror and dying in a hunting accident, mauled by a wild boar: the perfect death for an officer, thought Ploskorylov, who considered death in battle unworthy of a general.

Ploskorylov also knew the Philosophy of the Common Cause, the supreme staff discipline taught only at the theological faculty of the Military Academy and inaccessible to Paukov, although Ploskorylov assured the Major-General he had an instinctive grasp of it. All Paukov's commands so manifestly served the Common Cause that Ploskorylov blessed his own foresight in having invited himself to join the former's staff; undoubtedly there was only one brilliant Russian general in the army now, and this was Paukov.

Paukov was definitely brilliant, with his expensive aftershave and his square bristling tunic on his square, slightly lopsided figure. He spoke abruptly, and gave orders with the ferocity of someone who had loathed his officers and soldiers all his life. In this he was a true Teuton, a natural Northerner, whose purpose was not so much to expel the enemy and grab land as to exterminate his own men with maximum efficiency.

Ploskorylov was twenty years his junior, and had only just received his priest-captain's stars, and although he felt slightly awkward about knowing more than his divisional commander, Paukov seemed to know things even he hadn't grasped yet at his Sixth Level.

The Seventh, final stage of the initiation was very rare in the military, and few achieved it even at the highest levels of government. Ploskorylov had recently made friends with one who had, Military Inspector Gurov, who would visit from Moscow from time to time for a personal inspection. The Inspector would chat frankly with him when they met, and had clearly singled him out. He wore spectacles and dressed casually in a service jacket, and like all Seventh-Level Teutons he had a shaven head and a small goatee beard. Ploskorylov was looking forward to growing one himself, but wasn't allowed to yet at his level.

Gurov had promised to put him forward for initiation to the Seventh at the beginning of August, and Ploskorylov was as happy as a child at the prospect. He had no idea what it entailed, but he expected wonders. He imagined the world pouring into his open heart and sharing its secrets with him, revealing the full majesty of its starry brilliance. Before his eyes would appear ice mountains and sharp crystal needles, the crunch and the glitter, and the violet aura of the polar brightness. And at the end of the world at the magnetic pole, raising his hands to the black velvet of the heavens where the lines of force meet, the starry Teuton and Supreme Prophet, Father of the peoples of the North. And for him they would conquer the earth and the seas and lay at his feet all the flags of the world, replacing them with one, the black-and-blue one, and tell of the End of Days and a new age of Titans...

Ploskorylov knew he would live to see this black-and-blue day, but for now he merely hinted in his lectures at the tasks of the army and the purpose of the war, and those who understood him would be discreetly promoted to the Academy. Sadly there were few true Teutons in the army now. It wasn't that they were wiped out in the first three years of war: the elite didn't perish in battle; in critical situations an officer must always think first of his own life. There are many men, and only one officer; this summed up the classic relationship of the occupying forces with the natives, and was best expressed in the Varangian motto: "You are many, I am One. Our God is One, there is no other." (The Varangians liked to stress words on the first syllable, and it pleased them that the mighty Norse god Odin was the same as the Russian word for "One" if pronounced this way.)

In fact there were only two numbers in the ancient Russian language, One and Many, the leader and the led. The Varangian, born to lead the masses, hadn't the right to risk his life and abandon the wretched flesh beneath him, and Ploskorylov liked to illustrate this to his officers with a children's story:

"A mother walks at night with her child through a forest full of dangers, and they are attacked by wolves. What should she do? Throw herself to the wolves, so her child can escape from the forest full of dangers and run to safety? But with no one to protect it the child will be lost, and if it did survive how would it manage without its mother? Whereas if the mother threw it to the wolves and saved herself, she could escape from the forest full of dangers and go on to serve her country. In the same way an officer has no right to leave his men alone in the world, and like a true mother must put his own safety first to preserve the integrity of the officer corps. Think how much the state has spent training an officer, and what a waste it would be if he sacrificed himself according to some Christian notion of morality!"

No, the reason for the Varangians' present low morale wasn't that they were being killed; in almost every war Russia had fought, the population of the North remained virtually untouched. The Varangian, a true warrior of Odin, tended to meet his end feasting, hunting or womanizing, but dying in battle would be more shameful than ploughing – or, heaven forbid, darning his socks. Alas, the fact was that the men of the North had for too long been frivolously mixing with the native people, whose weak will had entered their blood, and they had become decadent. A nation is generally renewed and purified by war, but this war was radically different from those preceding it, in that the officers not only had trouble kicking their men into battle, they had no appetite for it themselves.

It wouldn't do for a political instructor with a higher military-theological education to take up arms, but, observing manoeuvres at a distance through his telescope, Ploskorylov was appalled. He had tried to boost morale with regular public executions, and could boast over twice as many of his men killed in the first year of war by his firing squads as by the Khazars and the mountain people. But they had had no effect. The Khazars' propaganda leaflets spoke of Russians being slaughtered by their own brothers, but he laughed at them. How could the feminine South, trembling for its wretched existence, defeat the titanic Varangians, for whom a soldier's life was worth no more than an ear of barley!

Yet in the past year the Varangian strategy had been hard to achieve; there weren't enough men even for the catering detachment, and the executions could only be carried out on the holiest of holidays. The army was no longer the same, and with each passing day morale declined inexorably. Only Paukov could rouse the troops with his menacing oratory, and even Paukov wasn't the man he used to be.

* * *

Although Major-General Paukov had changed, he strove to maintain the manners and decorum of a brilliant officer in the best traditions of the Varangian General Staff.

On the morning of 19th July, he rose as usual at 6.30, ordered a bowl of cold water from the Baskakovo well, did some light exercises from Appendix 5 in the officer's manual – twenty stretches to the left, twenty to the right, arms out, arms together, the "swallow", the "wings", fifteen sit-ups. Then he shaved himself with his blunt Neva razor, splashed himself with aftershave, put on his uniform, ironed for him by his orderly, and left for his regular morning visit to the actress Guslyatnikova.

Plump forty-year-old Guslyatnikova was in Baskakovo with the actors' brigade. During this lull at the fronts, the men of the Thirtieth Division had been entertained by a stream of actors, sent by Moscow as part of its education programme. The first to arrive were "Full House". Then the writers came, another entire brigade, seconded to Paukov for some reason, followed by several tours of the Nizhny Novgorod Theatre of the Russian Army. It wasn't the army any more, just an endless mass-education programme. For all he knew they'd get a brothel next, and there wouldn't be a virgin left in all the villages, and the soldiers would neglect their soldierly hygiene and come out in boils. But the actors were sent with specific instructions from Moscow to feed them and watch the plays. They were hungry of course. In Nizhny, as in the rest of the province, theatres were closing due to lack of audiences, and the only way to survive was by entertaining the troops.

Most of them were frankly atrocious, but not "Full House". You could tell by the name. To begin with they read the soldiers some fables about the bear and the fox, then they performed a specially reworked version of the story *The Loaf*, about the greasy Yds with their briefcases, then an act from the play *The Soldier's Mother*, about a deserter running home to mummy, who hands him over to the Military Commissariat and they pack him off back to the Front. The play's political message was excellent, and Guslyatnikova as the soldier's mother was a big hit with the men, with her juicy curvaceous figure. This produced some unhealthy responses from them, and many were heard making lewd comments that they would like such a mother and would show her a good time, so the play didn't entirely have the desired effect.

The actors did their three shows, and it was time for them to be off, but they were keen to stay; there had been no food in Nizhny for months, and they were on army rations here. The stage manager, Guslyatnikova's son, was the most shameless of them all, shovelling down tinned meat until it came out of his ears. Paukov complained to Ploskorylov, who called Moscow, but Moscow insisted they must keep the actors or it would wreck their educational programme.

And so they stayed and ate with them another week and performed the entire classical Russian repertoire, and the night before they left Paukov happily ordered glasses of vodka all round and ended up prancing like a hussar. It was shameful to recall. The brilliant Russian officer drank from a shoe, not a very clean one, size thirty-nine, then went down on one knee before Guslyatnikova and picked the damn woman up in his arms, clicking his heels and almost collapsing from the strain. He regaled them with more treats, reciting poems from the *Officers' Anthology* ("The jasmine is a lovely flower, its smell is very nice"), then at the actors' request from the *Officers' Alphabet*: "David played the harp like a god, bored of wanking on the bog." He cracked jokes and flashed his officer's wit, and that night Guslyatnikova gave herself to him, and when the others left she stayed on.

At first Paukov was flattered to have a real actress quartered with him, even one from Nizhny Novgorod, and that after three years away from his fat wife and two ugly daughters he had his own field companion, as he read was proper in a real war. Guslyatnikova would put on her velvet concert gown every evening, wring her sweaty handkerchief and recite poems in the villages where the troops were quartered, and they would listen to her instead of watching the news on television: "Touching the great oceans she lies…" Only now they didn't snigger about where they would like to touch her, because Guslyatnikova wasn't the soldier's mother but General Paukov's mistress, and the General didn't like jokes. The news would have been more interesting, in fact, but she evoked memories of civilian life, and women in summer dresses eating ice cream…

In the past month she had performed several times in all the villages around Baskakovo, and Paukov had appointed a young soldier named Tulin as her batman. The first half of the day she would bask in the cottage where she was quartered, putting on her make-up and lamenting her fate to Tulin and her landlady. Paukov hadn't slept with her for two weeks. In the sober light of day he found the soldier's mother flabby and repulsive, and she was also utterly insatiable. It was hard for forty-eight-year-old Paukov to satisfy her, and it embarrassed him to be seen by his men with this harpy, so he merely visited her once a day.

At first he was perfection in her eyes, then she was hurt and offended with him for avoiding her, opening wide her eyes and berating him in a low breathy voice for seducing and abandoning her.

Paukov was desperate to get her as far away from him as possible, but a Russian officer couldn't shout at a woman and simply throw her out.

On the morning of the 19th, he went to her as usual and rapped softly on the door of her room with a curled finger.

"Wait, I'm not dressed yet!" she murmured.

He waited five minutes. "What's she doing, putting on her gas mask?" he muttered irritably, rapping again.

"I'm ready!" she called at last with a rustling sound, and he went in.

She was lying on her wide peasant bed in an alluring pose, wearing a brightly coloured dressing gown and surrounded by artfully scattered garments. He was shocked by her immodesty.

"Good morning, General," she said languidly. Despite the earliness of the hour there was a thick layer of greyish make-up on her face. "I'm flattered by your visit, I so rarely see you these days – does duty call?"

"It's war," the General said curtly. "War is our duty, Katerina Ivanovna, and demands our unceasing attention."

"Yes, yes, as you say. But when do you think this frightful war will end?"

"As a military man I'm unable to disclose this information," Paukov said, repeating his formulation from the new Rulebook. "A military man with secret intelligence must disclose it to no one. The date of the war's end can be divulged under no circumstances, likewise the numbers, equipment or designation of the likely enemy or its whereabouts." He couldn't resist dazzling her with the Rulebook.

"I'm so afraid for you," she whispered.

"Can't be helped, that's how it is. But a Russian actress shouldn't be afraid for a Russian general. From our first meeting I was impressed by your fortitude," he said, paying her his mandatory morning compliment.

"In the Russian classical theatre we call it bearing," she nodded.

"Ah yes, the classic feminine fortitude. You mustn't give in to womanly fears, Katerina Ivanovna. We soldiers must take it on the chin and so must you. It's our Russian duty."

A pause hung in the air. He had exhausted his stock of officers' compliments and paid his respects to the Russian theatre and was keen to be off to his men, but she was still gazing at him with her moist, cowlike eyes.

"Couldn't you at least tell me where the enemy is and if an attack is expected? You must give me plenty of notice, I'm dreadfully afraid of shooting. Your company is precious to me." She lowered her eyes significantly. "And I've grown so fond of your men."

"Yes, yes, of course," Paukov barked. "The soldier's an instrument of love for his country and so forth, we're guided by subtle lofty emotions and force fields." With the mention of force fields he had finally exhausted his civilian repertoire. "We appreciate your courage, Katerina Ivanovna," he went on in an abrupt tone, with the icy politeness of an old soldier. "But I recommend that you leave your quarters immediately. War is an unpredictable business. None of us can tell today what tomorrow will bring." This was another fine military phrase he intended to popularize later in his communiqués.

"As you never tire of repeating," she said, peevishly wrinkling her nose. "One would think I was a burden to you."

"Absolutely not, nothing of the sort," he said, forcing out the last reserves of his military eloquence. "Just as the flower isn't burdened by the bee, the soldier isn't burdened by the presence of a member of the fair sex, that splendid bouquet which adorns the loaded table..." (Without realizing it he had slipped into the standard officer's toast:

if a man could repeat the phrase with its treacherous sibilants, it meant he wasn't drunk yet.)

"And to think I left someone I cared for," she went on. "A saintly man, a selfless servant of the arts. You say only an officer knows how to treat a woman – but see how you treat me! You promised to care for me and stay with me, and I never see you! Because of your duties, you say! What duties can you possibly have between operations? You're probably drinking with the stupid native girls because you can't manage an educated woman like me, and feel like a boor in her presence. Yes, a boor! I'm locked in this dirty cottage for days on end with stupid Tulin for company – it's no fun, I can tell you! You can't even make your soldiers sit still when I perform. I bare my soul to them and they're darning their socks in the back row! I simply don't understand, I demand—"

"Silence woman! Stand up when you talk to me, I'm a general!" screamed Paukov, flushed with rage. He had been brilliant and courteous with her long enough, and every man has his limits. "I'll show you touching the oceans, you old tart!" And with this he threw a bucket at her and ran out to the street.

3

Meanwhile Ploskorylov was preparing to give his first lecture of the day to the officers of the Divisional Staff. In the yard, the men were sweeping for the third time and repairing the fence under the watchful eye of their sergeant, while inside the officers had gathered for their geopolitical-studies class.

Ever since he was a child, Ploskorylov had loved the Varangian fighting spirit, the officer's upright bearing and his contempt for work and his men – essential to the Norse conception of the Great Sacrifice. The idea of a professional army was anathema to him, and an insult to the ideal of war. A soldier's thoughts must be not of his family or financial reward, or even his country, but exclusively of posthumous glory, the kind Ploskorylov was called upon to bestow.

He worshipped the dead warrior. Only the dead soldier on the plinth in the square, referred to as the Unknown Warrior, and mentioned in his prayers, was the absolute embodiment of the Norse spirit, for he had lost his personality, which he didn't need in war. The commanders needed one, and the political instructor, and it was essential to agents of the Special Services, or Smersh, but the soldier's personality was superfluous to the Varangian notion of valour. The sole purpose of the ugly little figure in his grey greatcoat and clumsily tied foot-cloths (this was Ploskorylov's rather touching image of the typical soldier), was to march as quickly as possible to his end. The enemy wasn't defeated by heroism or acts of initiative (what initiative could there be if the command was given correctly?), but by this living mass of men, who fulfilled the dual task of enslaving the opponent and reducing their own numbers. The road to victory must be paved with bodies, as all the best commanders realized, including Paukov and his idol Zhukov. An action was judged a success or failure in terms of the quantity of blood spilt – not elite Varangian blood of course (Ploskorylov himself traced his lineage to the personal Boyars of the sons of Rurik), but the black blood of earth, the oil of war, the juice squeezed from the ranks. The ranks were like a vineyard that withered if it wasn't harvested, according to the collected sayings of the venerable Arch-Colonel Dalnevostochny of the Far East, from whom few returned alive, even in peacetime.

Reducing the population to its ideal size was never easy, however, and after each war people always managed to increase their numbers. Stalin's purges had made it easier to breathe in Russia, and as a boy studying history he had loved reading about the Big Clearout. But things had soon become cluttered again with children and old people whinging in corners, and the life of the masses returned to normal. The elite, called to lead them and bless them, became lost in this blind stirring human herd, hungry for procreation, and lording it over the whole putrefying substructure were the inexterminable Khazars.

And so reasons had had to be found for another great campaign, and there was the build-up to war. Yet the more time passed between battles, the more unwilling people were to mobilize. The Yds would write anyone medical notes if they were paid enough, and it wasn't easy to explain its necessity to the ordinary officers, most of whom hadn't graduated from the academies but from military departments in civilian colleges, where they didn't teach the correct worldview. Ploskorylov had tried all sorts of approaches with his students, but had drawn a blank in the face of their boredom and indifference. He couldn't tell them the truth yet: the reason for the Varangian occupation was taught only at the Fifth Level – until then they genuinely believed Russia's native population to be the Russians.

Despite all this he enjoyed giving lectures. He saw himself as the father of these men, and even their mother. All thinkers construct the world according to their own temperament, and Ploskorylov was born to bless those going to their death. He loved the dead, with a tender, delicate love, and he loved being in their presence; they weren't bored by him and didn't answer back, and he prided himself on his flowing womanly voice with them. In his voice spoke the Mother in the famous poster, calling the next generation of her shamelessly multiplying sons to the grave, and as he imagined his officers dying bravely in the name of the Russian Cause, he even mourned them a little, sitting in their still-imperfect living state in the stuffy hut he had kitted up as the Russian Room.

He had hung portraits on the walls of Spengler, Weininger, Nietzsche and other great Norsemen dear to his heart, and on the blackboard, expropriated from the abandoned school, he had sketched a chart of the battle between North and South. The subject of today's lecture was the anniversary of the great tank battle of Kursk in the Second World War. He had to be careful in depicting the Norse concept of this war – they didn't understand yet the true tasks of the opposing sides, and the Norse spirit that united them. He merely alluded to the base role of Britain in stirring up discord at the last minute between the two titans and their pact of eternal love, choosing his words in such a way that the more thoughtful of them would understand him and the others would notice nothing. (The Yds were in cahoots with the British of course, knowing this alliance between the Aryan peoples would be the end of them.)

"Gentlemen, please!" bawled Warrant Officer Kruglov, on duty in the Russian Room.

The officers stood up. Ploskorylov, in his flowing cassock and gold peaked cap, held out his moist hand for Kruglov to kiss, then blessed everyone and felt a flood of warm feelings come over him. It was extraordinarily pleasant, although a huge responsibility, to be ministering to them at the age of just twenty-seven; there was stiff competition for places at the theological faculty of the Military Academy, and only one in twenty was accepted.

"Dear brothers, I want to discuss with you today the idea of the North," he began, in his musical, priestly voice. "For years Khazar propagandists have distracted us from the main battle, between North and South, foisting on our Russian consciousness the wholly artificial one between East and West. No, a deep consanguinity linked the combatants, these two titans of the North, great brothers who had become crowded living together on the same planet, colliding like clouds in the sky to produce thunder and lightning. The Russian spirit blocked the path of the mighty German, and the Russian brother planted a deadly kiss on his Teuton foe, who expired in his steely embrace. The enemies of both regimes tried to exploit the fruits of Russia's victory, and the Khazars rejoiced, but the far-sighted Leader deported them to a distant reservation, and the Russian-Teutonic work continued for forty years. Much was accomplished in those years – space travel, man's first steps into the icy abundance of the cosmos – but the Khazar revenge halted the triumphant march of Fate. The South is now striving once more to rob humanity of its civilized values and replace them with a primitive, animal lust for life, which is aimed above all at us, the last bastion of the world spirit. History is being made here today in the Degunino cauldron, where North and South come face to face. Degunino is the geopolitical heart of Eurasia, and whoever controls it will be master of the world…"

He spoke for exactly twenty minutes, leaving the last ten for questions. The officers were always astonishingly inventive with these. If there were none, Ploskorylov would inform HQ and they would get a carpeting, and it would be goodbye to their leave.

"Can you please explain the United States' war against Islam in terms of the North-South battle, and how it ended and who won?" asked Captain Selivanov. "My men would like to know."

"Your little soldiers would do better to study their marching drill as the basic military discipline of the Russian spirit," Ploskorylov said severely. "If you allow them to ask general political questions, I recommend you tell them they'll find all they need in the Rulebook. A thorough reading of the Rulebook will provide answers to any question, from the practical to the theological. I refer you to Paragraph Fifteen of the drill ordinance, from Paisy Zakavkazsky: 'Whosoever doubts his military might in fear of the advancing foe, may he suffer the shame and curses of his comrades and three penalty points.'"

Selivanov was frightened into silence. Ploskorylov had no way of answering this tricky question. Islam had suffered much, but was now our ally and outpost in the East, although it wouldn't do to say so publicly. Islam hadn't stood a chance ever since Phlogiston was discovered and the rest of the world no longer needed the black blood of the earth, and Russia's complete isolation let it play out its splendid mystery unhindered.

It was hard to believe that a country God had so richly blessed with hemp, oil, blubber and forests could have missed out on this invisible substance which mysteriously powered the rest of the world. Cars ran on it, and smokeless factories, and people made crazy money from it, and Russia still ran on petrol, which it had plenty of now that no one was buying oil any more. Phlogiston had been discovered everywhere – in the United States and Africa, even the Antarctic; the Khazar Kaganate had so much of it you couldn't move for boreholes. The only places without it were the Muslim East and the vast territory of Russia, right up to its borders. By a cruel trick of nature it started just over the border in despised Poland. The damn thing had put paid to America's promising wars in the Middle East, where it was now hopelessly bogged down, and Islam had already been demoted from a major religion to something parochial and harmless, even vegetarian. Ploskorylov detested Phlogiston, and thought it was probably another evil Yd hoax, though he had no way to explain how it fuelled cars.

He knew his reply to Selivanov was vague and evasive, but the basis of Varangian counter-propaganda was precisely its vagueness. It wasn't information his officers needed, it was power. It was a weak counter-propagandist who answered questions about the enemy's successes or the Khazar way of life with facts and figures; the political instructor should either kick the questioner in the balls, or if he was squeamish like Ploskorylov, who was prone to asthma, he would hand him over to Smersh, where soon all became clear, since a man understands everything before death, even if he has no one to share it with.

The officers knew they must phrase their questions carefully. Ploskorylov wouldn't report them in so many words of course – an officer must be protected, as he himself had taught them – but it would be easy to fall under suspicion if he let something slip to the commanders; any excuse would do. So after Selivanov no one asked anything interesting, apart from whether it was right to punish the men by banning their letters home or if this merely encouraged desertion. Ploskorylov was pleased to report that the number of deserters had almost halved in the last year, and that the head of the Mothers' Committee, Strelnikova, had been captured at the Chinese border after escaping from jail, and was now in a hard-labour camp in Chita.

He saved this happy news for the end, but there was something even better in store for them, and this was the Maiden Ira.

Maiden Ira had been doing the rounds of the divisions for over six months now. Until the age of fifteen she had developed normally, but in the third year of war she started seeing visions and hearing voices.

She left home and lived on the streets, where she was arrested and questioned, and she soon came to the attention of the General Staff, who couldn't resist the chance to meet her. Ploskorylov had attended her first show in Moscow, in the clubhouse of the theological faculty. Unlike Maiden Zhanna, Maiden Ira was no beauty, with her thin adolescent figure, her small features and mousy hair, but all this was redeemed by her huge grey eyes and her cracked metallic voice – the voice of a patriotic child and true Varangian. She sang nostalgic popular songs she heard on late-night radio programmes, such as 'Little Fire', 'In a Sunny Glade' and 'Dark Night'. Ploskorylov didn't think much of these songs composed in the trenches, so different from 'The People's War', with its Teutonic beat. But in Ira's rendition they acquired a wild, almost Dostoevskian pathos. So might a Varangian child sing, spilling her last tear before being immolated by the Khazars. Ira didn't bother with complicated musical arrangements, she just twanged the strings of an old guitar. Anything else would have drowned out her weak tinny voice, like a jangling weathervane. Yet there was such power and emotion in it: in such a voice someone might shout their last words as they were executed, or cry "Fire!" as they shot the enemy within.

This sacrificial image expressed perfectly the Varangian ideal, and she knew it instinctively; there was nowhere you could learn it, certainly not at the Academy. Only voices could transcend the icy world of absolute beings, and Maiden Ira's excruciating childish alto had been recorded on three hastily released discs that flew around the country for the entertainment of the troops.

After singing she would fall into a trance: "I see... I see..." She would see all there was to see – the velvet blackness of the sky pricked with stars, the pole of magnetic power, the jagged tops of the pine forests against the rosy sunset, the deserted mountains and the soaring eagle, ancient people praying in a frenzy of rapture to inscrutable stone idols of extinct giants...

Maiden Ira could have been speaking directly from the great Aryan philosophers, who she hadn't read, of course, and their visions of a time when earth was populated by Titans who spent their days in mighty single combat, striding across the bristling undergrowth, laughingly sprinkling lakes and juggling mountains – and we see the remains of their games today in the Alps. Then came the geopolitical catastrophe of the Great Freeze, and the people of the North were forced to move South, where they died out in the warmth and their legacy was debased by the low people and the dull servants of profit.

"We conclude our discussion today with a true wonder, gentlemen," Ploskorylov said, in the tone of a loving nanny about to present a child with a treat, a barrel of sturdy birch rods soaked in brine perhaps. "You have doubtless heard of this wonder, but few of you have witnessed her with your own eyes. Today a Russian marvel will sing for us, a young muse of the war and the voice of the Russian resistance, Maiden Ira!"

The officers rose noisily to their feet as Ira's mother Efrosinya opened the door clutching a small child's guitar, and pushed pale Ira in on her bowed legs.

Efrosinya was a stiff heavy woman of indeterminate age, with a grey face and a grim mournful mouth, the ideal of the Varangian widow. Ira's eyes wandered round the walls before she fell into her trance. Efrosinya pushed her to the blackboard and Ploskorylov obligingly moved his chair to the corner, waiting for the holy music to begin. She distractedly plucked the strings of the guitar a few times and shook her head, then started singing:

"A soldier of wa-ar,
Beside the sho-ore,
A grey army coat he wo-ore..."

Ploskorylov closed his eyes and saw the boundless Russian landscape, the grey river and the grey sand of the shore, and the infinitely small grey figure of the soldier marching along, an insect of war. The soldier was doubtless marching to his death, and he was moved by a sudden unexpected pity for him, consoled only by the thought that he would soon acquire granite immortality.

Ira's voice gathered strength:

"The soldier marching knows no fe-ear,
Saving the land he holds so de-ear..."

She paused (the officers tactfully didn't break the silence by clapping), and twanged her guitar with her thumb:

"From the birch tree flutters a yellow le-eaf,
An old accordion plays 'Autumn Dre-eam',
The soldiers listen, fre-ee of gri-ief..."

While she sang, Ploskorylov pictured himself in an autumn clearing with an accordion for some reason, playing 'Autumn Dream' (although he had never played an instrument in his life) and, as he played, his men left the clearing and melted into the yellow foliage, leaving a slightly musty smell behind, disappearing in silence like true soldiers, without even crying "For our country!" at the end. He played on, his music dissolving in the air like Haydn's *Farewell Symphony*, taking them to a state of sad ecstasy, fewer and fewer of them with each note, and as they vanished into the yellow autumn light he finished playing, and was alone in the clearing.

Twilight crept on, and the leaves lost their colour, and the priest sat alone in the gathering darkness with his silent accordion, the last memory of his men who had died so heroically, and he felt so sorry for himself two tears rolled down his round cheeks.

The officers tactfully averted their eyes and put their hands to their temples. The girl's singing had a nauseating, depressing effect on them. It would be different if they fancied her, but she made them long for tea and bedtime, anything not to have to listen to her cracked patriotic wailing.

She had more for them though, and there was nothing to beat the poignant bravura of 'Stars of the North':

> "What stars are these that shine so bright
> At the threshold of the polar night?
> The princess sits on her silver throne,
> Jewels flashing in her icy crown.
> Oh pampered children of the So-outh,
> Nothing is lovelier than the distant No-orth!"

Ploskorylov imagined the Hyperborean North – its severe vertical majesty, its pine trees and rocks, a man with an eagle – and a shudder of ecstasy ran up his back and made his hair stand on end, and he had an urge to jump up and salute. But the officers would have followed suit, clicking their heels and breaking the mood, and he wanted her to sing on.

"Comrades!" she cried suddenly, jumping from her chair, her unseeing eyes fixed on the far corner of the Russian Room. "Comrades, we must all die! We must die for what is holy! We must die for what is pure! We must all die! Steel... pierced by steel... Bliss..." And with that she fell unconscious on the floor.

4

For the past two days Major Evdokimov of Special Services had been interrogating young Private Voronov. Voronov was thin, dark and terribly nervous, which was why Evdokimov had picked him. There was no point questioning the dim peasants, who were incapable of wriggling out of things. Voronov was perfect, and was wriggling like a grass snake.

Evdokimov didn't have much on him, he was simply interested in what he came up with himself. It was the most fascinating part of his work with the intelligentsia, the way they incriminated themselves. Voronov knew of countless offences he had committed, and was feverishly trying to decide which was the least serious and which to confess first. For the first ten minutes of the interview Evdokimov had been friendly and affable, but he knew he might turn violent at any moment. It was already their third session, and neither the Major nor his patient had any idea how things would turn out.

Evdokimov's basic Smersh tactic was to lead his victims to recognize their own guilt. Having them shot was easy, there was time for that. It was necessary to trample on them first, and convince them that their punishment was deserved. Voronov would have the chance to betray everyone, disown his mother and denounce his commander, and only then would he go to his death, convinced he was unworthy to live. It was doing him a favour in a way: it would have been unforgivable to kill someone convinced of his innocence. Before sentencing his victim and sending him to the wall, he had to make him sentence himself, and in this Evdokimov had no equal in the Staff of the Thirtieth Infantry.

He was one of those old Smersh hands of which legends are made, a graduate of the Dzerzhinsky Academy and heir to the Bolshevik Cheka, who could force a confession out of anyone, and turn a healthy young man into a broken wreck in three days – all this practically without physical violence: Evdokimov liked subtlety.

He had spotted Voronov as soon as the new recruits arrived. For a fortnight he had bided his time and sent an informer to spy on his conversations, and Voronov was exactly what he needed – he missed home, complained of his foot-cloths, and once said he couldn't see the point of the war and what they were fighting for. Others would have let this go, but not Evdokimov. Morale was low after the rains, and Ploskorylov had ordered another public execution. This was his chance.

He had asked to see the Private in his office, on the pretext of giving him a letter from home, and he received him warmly. He knew what a letter meant for someone like Voronov. He had made a careful study of the recruit's background, and knew he had been brought up by his mother and didn't know his father or like manly sports, and that despite his pleasant appearance he was just a snivelling girl at heart. He had written two letters to his mother, both of which he had intercepted. There was nothing special in them, just a lot of soppy emotions and assurances that he was fine and she shouldn't worry about him.

Russia was a strange country. Most of its history had happened within its borders, and its main wars were internal ones; a soldier's biggest battles weren't with the likely or unlikely enemy, but with the sergeant or some other commander (the sergeant was closer, almost like family). It was said that the sergeant, and the whole pyramid above him, including the inevitable Smersh man, would make a man of a soldier this way. But they squeezed the last drop out of the real man, like a slave, and instead of the material from which men are made, they poured into his veins a rotten swill that paralysed his spirit of resistance. The soldier formed like this could only fight Varangian-style, more afraid of his own side than his opponent's. This was because neither the commanders nor the Smersh men were soldiers and never could be, having been born for other things. An officer required to do a soldier's job would run away, and if fate put a Varangian manager in a position where he had to manage, he would be unable to do anything but make tea. A Varangian boss was no example to others and had no leadership skills, running with the same incompetence a bank, an oil-barge, a military unit or hospital. He couldn't build houses or construct defences, he knew only how to make subordinates, preferably in order of size. Varangian bosses were born, not made, and the only people fit for the role were those incapable of doing anything but trampling on others.

Evdokimov was a born Smersh man, the elite of the elite, who knew how to do nothing. He looked as if he'd been hacked out of wood, broad-shouldered and filthy – a piece of shit frankly. Few were worse than Evdokimov, which was why the commanders loved him.

When Voronov arrived to collect his letter he suspected nothing, since all letters went through Smersh, and Evdokimov was looking forward to breaking him. A proper army psychologist must painstakingly research his subject's past and present life, so he could ignore the secondary incidental crimes and focus on the main one, and Voronov was already so conveniently guilty that after two days the Major had a bunch of death warrants in his hands.

"Private Voronov present at your request, sir!" the victim said smartly.

"Right, right," Evdokimov drawled. (This was a basic Smersh ploy, dragging things out to make the victim feel uneasy). "Let's see, Voronov is it? You've come for your letter?"

"Yes, sir."

"From whom, may I ask?"

"From my mother, comrade Major."

"Your mother, that's good. You live with your mother?"

"Yes, sir."

"I see. And why do you think your mother's writing to you?"

Voronov blushed. "Because... because she worries about me, comrade Major."

"Worry? Why would she worry? Have you written anything to her that might worry her?"

"Absolutely not, comrade Major," Voronov stammered. "I just... I thought she might worry, it's war..."

"Did you tell her you were in the area of military operations?" Evdokimov's voice was suddenly steely. Soldiers at the Front were forbidden to disclose their location. It was a Jesuitical ruling of the General Staff that families could know only the number of the unit, and any information in a letter referring to a soldier's exact whereabouts was punished as treason.

"No, comrade Major, I just wrote that we'd arrived."

"So why would she worry? Does she suffer from nerves? Is she ill?"

"No, comrade Major."

"Comrade Major, comrade Major, I know I'm comrade Major! You think we're idiots in Smersh?"

"No, com... No, I don't think that."

"I see. So what do you think?"

"I don't think that about Smersh, sir."

"You should call me comrade Major, you're in the army aren't you? Have you forgotten your rank?"

"No I haven't, comrade Major."

"I know I'm comrade Major!" yelled Evdokimov.

Voronov was panicking. Evdokimov had timed his change of tactics perfectly. "So first we worry our mother and possibly give her a nervous breakdown, then we turn up at Smersh for a letter?" (This was another favourite tactic, to state in a threatening tone some innocent fact from which unexpected and lethal conclusions might be drawn.)

"I didn't just turn up, comrade Major, I came at your request—"

"I know I called you, I'm not senile!" Evdokimov interrupted loudly. "Do you think we're all senile in Smersh? Answer me!"

"Not at all, comrade Major!"

"Not what?"

"Not at all senile in Smersh, comrade Major!"

"How do you know what we're like in Smersh? Perhaps you've been here before?"

Major Evdokimov played with Voronov, waiting to trap him, and by the end of the second day he was finally rewarded. Flapping against the Major's net, longing only to rest for an hour (Evdokimov had had meals brought in for himself twice, and hadn't let him use the lavatory), the Private became hysterical and ready to confess to anything. Evdokimov referred to his conversations with his fellow recruits about the hardships of military life and the mindless repetitions of the Rulebook, and he threatened to bring in Private Kruzhkin, who had reported his remarks about the war being pointless.

"So we don't see the point of the war, is that it?" he said testily.

"No, no, comrade Major!"

"So we don't, do we!"

"No, I mean, yes we do, comrade Major!"

Evdokimov jumped up. "Are you mocking me? Are you mocking an officer at the Front, you little shit?" (Evdokimov was singing inside; he had never been at the Front himself, of course, Smersh men were too valuable). "I've had broken men sitting here who did nothing compared to you, and you mock me? Do we or do we not see the point of the war?"

Voronov tried wildly to make sense of this, but his brains didn't let him down. "Yes, we do see the point of it, comrade Major!"

"Who does?"

"We do!"

This was the slip Evdokimov needed.

"Did you record that?" he said to his secretary Babura, a tall languid young man who looked like a pederast.

"Yes sir!" Babura replied cheerfully; he was in his element, knowing Voronov wouldn't survive.

"So who are these 'we'?" Evdokimov addressed him in a gentle ingratiating voice.

"All of us, comrade Major, all of us see the point of it."

"How can you speak for them? Are you a mind-reader? I put it to you that you're in a secret organization conspiring with the enemy to weaken the men's will to fight! Confess!"

"No, comrade Major, no!" Voronov jumped up. "There's no secret organization!"

"You've said as much though," his interrogator said, looking sadly down at the table, as if disappointed by his treachery. "You've betrayed yourself and conspired against your commander and betrayed your mother. Who are you? You're nothing. But your mother, how could you betray your mother?"

"I haven't betrayed my mother!" Voronov protested, summoning up the last drop of his courage.

"Really? Isn't the Motherland your mother? You're recording this, Babura?"

"Yes, sir!" Babura grinned.

"He's renounced his country! Where did you grow up, Voronov?"

Evdokimov had moved from the informal to the formal "you" mode of address, as if the Private had irrevocably crossed some secret line separating a citizen of the Motherland from a traitor unworthy to be called a man.

"In Moscow, comrade Major."

"Moscow. What is Moscow, according to the Rulebook, please!" he bawled.

"'Moscow is the capital of capitals, the historic heart of the Russian land, the nationally purified hero city of red-and-white stone, mother of all Russian towns, who has repeatedly defended her honour against the alien foe!" Voronov babbled from Chapter Two of the Rulebook, on Russia's history and population.

"Correct," Evdokimov nodded, and hope sprang in Voronov's tormented breast. "The mother of Russian towns you say, yet you renounce this mother, create a fighting organization and discuss in the ranks whether the war your country is fighting makes sense or not. Merely to ask this question is state treason, Private Voronov! You know what awaits you, and what will happen to your family. You can save their lives only with a full disclosure of the members of your organization, by name please. I'm waiting."

Voronov said nothing. Evdokimov stood up and wrenched his tunic so the buttons flew off, then punched him lazily but painfully in the stomach a few times. "I can keep this up," he told him.

Voronov said nothing for the rest of the day and all that night, while the Major's three assistants worked on him. But when Evdokimov showed him the names and addresses of his entire family and an arrest warrant for spreading defeatist propaganda (printed on a special form signed by the General Staff), he finally confessed the existence of the secret organization and named everyone in his regiment as members; he couldn't remember all of them, and had to ask for the list.

"Everyone?" Evdokimov asked, delighted by his success.

"Yes, sir, everyone."

"You're mocking me again?" he shouted. He punched him again, until he almost fell off his chair, then Babura recorded his confession, after which Evdokimov could have him shot.

"Stand up!" he roared. "All of them, the whole regiment? What sort of scum betrays his comrades?"

Voronov didn't reply.

"You know they'll all be arrested because of you? Here, today! They have mothers too!"

Voronov had imagined his ludicrous evidence would provoke another fit of rage from the Major, but that at least in the half-hour it took him to dictate all the names they might stop beating him and give him some water. He knew of others from his regiment who had named everyone when interrogated, hoping to overload the punishment machine with so much fodder. But the machine could digest all of them many times over, plus their children and family members, and might want to prolong the pleasure and not stop there. Most of all it liked telling the fodder how worthless it was, and that it wouldn't have been broken if it had tried just once to defend itself...

"Remove this filth," Evdokimov said curtly, and Voronov was led off to the shed by Babura and Evdokimov's batman, the convivial Starostin, a brilliant masseur, whose foot massages were better than a blowjob.

"We'll use the darling tomorrow," Evdokimov told himself. Now came the main pleasure he had been looking forward to all day, the pleasure that surpassed all others. Taking Private Voronov's last letter from a folder, he read it again from beginning to end: "Dearest Mother, I love you so much, please don't worry about me. Everyone's being very kind to me and I'm busy all the time. No military actions are expected, and if only I didn't miss you all my darlings, things would be perfect here. You mustn't bother with food parcels, I have everything I need and more..."

A shudder of pleasure ran through Evdokimov's body – not erotic pleasure – but something more like the paroxysm the great amphibians feel at the moment of climax – a sort of mental belch, a sense of fullness and the consciousness of a job well done. The victim lay in the shed. The shed would fill like a stomach. Major Evdokimov had exposed one hundred and thirty-one members of the internal enemy.

5

Ploskorylov sat at the scrubbed kitchen table in the cottage of the young soldier's wife, Marfa, preparing tomorrow's lecture, an introduction to the theme "The Nordic Path".

He smiled as he remembered his youthful errors at the Second and Third levels, when he saw an almost evangelical subtext in people like Marfa. It would have touched him that she took such trouble cooking for him, putting his food on the table with her shy smile and listening attentively to his lectures on poultry-keeping, although she clearly understood nothing of the subject: how could a simple native woman grasp the spiritual aspects of poultry-keeping? Now he understood the Khazar legends better, he saw how tawdry and tasteless they were, compared to those of the Great Cold. The Christian ceremonies have a certain fascination for hot hearts and young minds, and in days of old the wise Varangian King Vladimir had been forced in a hostile land to mimic them and adopt their faith. It was for the more mature Varangians who followed him to cast off this delusion, and to do so one had to understand their impressively monolithic culture and the way they reared their young.

Ploskorylov thought it best to teach the next generation from the cradle to hate their environment, and that they were superior to others. He himself had been a neurotic child, beset by a mass of fears and premonitions, and it was to this he owed his wunderkind career. His relationship with Christianity now was that of a true Khazar: he observed its pieties but deep down he despised it, which was why he wasn't touched by Marfa as he would have been seven years ago, and didn't say, "Oh Marfa, Marfa, you have chosen the wrong way!" Today's Ploskorylov didn't waste his wisdom on the natives.

The Nordic Path was the cornerstone of the officer's worldview, and fortified him against all privations and hardships, especially the cold. To begin with, he had to explain why the army used the word

Nord for north, rather than the Russian *Sever*. The vulgar, almost abusive-sounding *Sever* was fine for the common people, but not for the military aristocracy. *Nord* derived from a fine Sanskrit root, *Nar*, meaning "flowing water". *Nara* was Sanskrit for river, and *Nary* a Sanskrit bed, presumably dating from the times the Aryans had slept in their boats during their long sea journeys, and Nar-cissus was the youth who fell in love with his own reflection. The warrior must be a narcissist, and love himself with a tender passionate love. Ploskorylov never missed the chance to glance at himself in the mirror, and even had a private notebook in which he recorded his successes – who said what to him, and how and when he was praised; he didn't bother with the rest, there was no point dwelling on the negative.

Nar and *Nor* were the heritage of the Aryans and the race of the Norsemen, with their strict military norm. Russia's ancient people, the Rus, were a great Nordic race driven from the North by the sudden cold. But Nature had a purpose for this (Ploskorylov liked to refer to Nature in his Aryan lectures, rather than the alien god of Christianity). The real cause of the Freeze was that those living in the South, in the heart of the mainland, needed enlightenment, and the Aryans arrived to provide it – tall, fair-haired warriors, who spent their days perfecting their magic rituals and their fighting skills. Led by the commander Yar, mentioned in the book of Veles, the Rus left the Hyperborean North for the fertile lands inhabited by savage tribes who had cultivated them without knowing why, or rather for whom.

"Distant Tula," he wrote in neat round letters, pushing out his tongue and admiring his plump hand and his plump notebook, "was the patrimony of the Northern weapon-makers. Having settled in these abundant lands, they forthwith set up their Tula, renowned then and to this day for the forging of arms. As legends tell, Tula was the land of the famed bandit-hero Solovei the Nightingale and his followers, wise men and priests of a superior race who preached Hinduism, and after leaving the Far North had founded first the Slavic then the ancient Greek and Hindu civilizations..."

Inspector Gurov as always slipped in unannounced, as if from nowhere, without giving him the chance to present himself at his best.

Although he had every reason to think of the Inspector as a friend, almost as an older brother, so clearly had he singled him out, he was careful to observe strict military etiquette with him. Catching in his eye signs of approval and even admiration of his worthy pupil – in some respects he outranked him, although he didn't always act this way – he would be the humble political instructor in touch with his men's needs, a quiet worker at the Front exposed to constant risk and danger. He would salute smartly and shyly give Gurov his hand to kiss (despite his Seventh Level, Gurov was obliged as a civilian to greet the Priest-Captain this way), then after a brief report on recent events they would exchange three brotherly Varangian kisses.

Gurov generally didn't bother with any of this; perhaps at his level he didn't need such rituals, or his own were so complicated that Ploskorylov wouldn't have understood them. The Fifth allowed things forbidden in the First, and the Fourth ordained what was banned in the Third, and this combination of mutually exclusive rules, in which one person was allowed one thing and another something completely different, seemed to Ploskorylov the Varangians' finest achievement. He had even written his first paper at the Academy on the subject and won a free trip to the pagan stones of Arkaim, where Russia's druid community gathered for their rituals.

Gurov had appeared silently, without knocking or creaking the floorboards, and always seemed at home in the peasants' hovels, almost like a member of the family.

Ploskorylov adjusted his cassock and jumped up, adopting the "Subordinate" position from the Rulebook, and prepared to salute. "Never mind, Priest, at ease," Gurov said, cutting him short. "Are you well?"

Not knowing where to direct his moist eyes, Ploskorylov stretched out his hand, which Gurov bent over and kissed.

"I'm glad," he said, with tears in his voice. "Glad and touched, I thank you. I came to the Front as soon as I could. I haven't been idle. I'm glad, very glad."

Ploskorylov couldn't help noticing the Inspector was frowning as he spoke, as if the words were being forced out of him, however glad he was to see his young friend at his labours.

"How's work?" the Inspector said, taking a seat at the table as if he had lived at Marfa's all his life. He had a special way with the natives. With Ploskorylov they were reserved and deferential and gave nothing away, but they loved Gurov as the workers had loved Lenin, recognizing his innate right to lead them. Now, as Marfa came in, she bowed from the waist and started laying the table for him. Ploskorylov quickly moved his notebook.

"Don't bother, I've eaten," Gurov said. "So, Marfa, how's our Priest treating you?"

"All right." She cast her eyes down.

"Any news of your husband?"

"He wrote. Seems he's alive," she nodded.

"Good. God, my bones ache. What a ding-dong, eh, Marfushka? The ram's up the mountain and the cat's down the well."

She bowed again and left the room. Ploskorylov was mystified by Gurov's fondness for these peasant sayings, which seemed to sum up the whole idiocy of their life. Perhaps at his level he was ordered to play with them a little and pity them from his great height. Ploskorylov himself adhered strictly to his priestly code to be lofty, gracious and distant with them at all times.

"So, Priest, what's our Smersh man up to?" the Inspector said with wonderful military directness: while the Sixth demanded efficiency and diligence – what the soldiers in their vulgar way called "getting their teeth in" – the Seventh promoted a more free-and-easy approach.

"Good news, I'm glad to say. He's a simple fellow, but first-rate, he's just exposed a provocateur – turned out he was a Khazar agent! Nothing to look at, but a textbook defeatist, sorry for his mother, blubbing like a pacifist and so on. We'll dispose of him tomorrow."

Gurov purred like a cat after a big meal, but Ploskorylov knew the steel in him, ready to strike when he heard the call to battle that only he could hear.

"Nice work. A provocateur, you say – the snake. When did he catch him?"

"About four days ago. Took a while to break him, but you know Evdokimov."

"Any special measures?"

"No need, he has people for that. At the end he was licking his boots."

This expression was popular in Varangian circles, and knowing Gurov's liking for traditional idioms, Ploskorylov always tried to slip a few into his conversation.

"Good, good, I'll see him later. Do you think we should put Evdokimov up for initiation?"

"I see him as more suitable for the Fifth," Ploskorylov said in a confidential tone, lowering his voice. It was inexpressibly pleasant to be discussing promotions and career levels with this Initiate as his equal. "You see, he hasn't had the Higher—"

"Smersh has no need of that. You think the ones up there" – Gurov raised his eyes to the ceiling – "have the Academy behind them? They made it on their own, through sheer will-power and hard work. Anyway, he's long past the Fifth by now. Any thoughts about your own initiation, by the way?"

Ploskorylov cursed his tendency to blush like a virgin when excited. "Our duty is to the Nordic Fatherland, Inspector. The rest is in the hands of the Almighty…"

"Fine, fine, you're with friends here," Gurov checked him. "Prepare yourself and you'll be clicking your heels soon like Paukov. I came for a reason, Priest, you get me?"

Ploskorylov gazed at him with worshipful, doglike eyes.

"You're no fool, I've been watching you. You know how valuable men like you are? There's a real Varangian spirit in the ranks, we don't often see that now. You've obviously trained your men well. Don't worry, I'll see that you'll teach at the Academy, you won't be in Baskakovo for ever, you just need some military experience. Don't blush, it's nothing. We'll be initiating you in August, the best month for it. Guess who'll perform the ceremony?"

"Oh, I couldn't!" Ploskorylov smiled, assuming it would be Gurov.

"Korneyev," the Inspector said with a conspiratorial wink.

He almost passed out from the shock. Korneyev was the eternal orderly, a big lump of a man with huge fists, thick as a Siberian boot and utterly incapable of military study.

"Private Korneyev?" he asked.

"Who else?" Gurov said with a fatherly smile. "It's not as simple as you think, old chap, we need the Seventh everywhere, even in the ranks. Who else will look out for the officer? How else do we learn about insubordination? Don't spread it around, but keep in touch with Korneyev, he's our Initiator here, all our best people pass through him."

"Not you?" Ploskorylov asked dully.

"Me?" Gurov smiled. "Me – well, it's not what I do, you'll find out soon enough. You must get ready, Captain, we'll do it on the eighth. Now there's something I want to ask you. Have you seen a new girl around here, one of the natives?"

Nothing in Gurov's voice or expression changed, but Ploskorylov sensed with his usual special sense that his inner steel was finally revealing itself through his casual manner.

"No, I haven't, why?"

"Just keep an eye out for her," Gurov continued, without going into details as befits a Varangian commander. "She probably won't be alone, we're expecting a man of about forty-five to be with her. I'll leave this with you." He reached in the breast pocket of his jacket, and a photograph of an imposing grey-haired man stared back at Ploskorylov, with the mysterious authority seen in senior federal-level civil servants that outshines any European lustre. "We have no mugshots of her yet, but I'm chasing them up. If she turns up here she'll definitely come to you first. If she comes to Degunino I'll take her myself. There's a colonel's star for you if you catch her."

For the second time in an hour Ploskorylov felt dizzy with excitement. "Is she a black-widow terrorist?" he asked knowingly.

"In a way," Gurov nodded, but Ploskorylov knew him too well not to realize she must be something far, far worse than a Chechen suicide bomber. "Terrorism on a scale undreamt of by your common terrorist. They may come separately, but I'm expecting them to be together. On no account let them go. I'm counting on Evdokimov, but a special instinct is required. You must be vigilant, Priest."

"Perhaps you could tell me a little about them, and what to expect..."

"Expect nothing. Just let me know the minute you see a new girl here and lock her up, you hear me? With a strong key. Maybe she's pregnant, maybe not. If she's pregnant, get me on my mobile. If you see him I give you leave to strangle him with your bare hands. You've killed a man before, haven't you?"

He stood up and pushed his face close to Ploskorylov's, and Ploskorylov peered into his grey birdlike eyes behind their steel-rimmed spectacles and felt hopelessly flustered.

"I see," Gurov said. "Well, you have to start somewhere, you won't be a colonel without blood on your hands. Just keep it to yourself, who knows how many friends they have here. That's an order, Captain."

"Yes, of course!" Ploskorylov said ardently.

"Not 'of course'! By the Rulebook!" Gurov suddenly raised his voice.

Ploskorylov jumped up, and after hesitating a shameful second, threw up his arm: "Yes, sir!"

"You fool!" the Inspector burst out laughing, and Ploskorylov didn't know if he was serious or merely testing him. "No, you're a sharp boy, I admire you, my son, you're a soldier to your bones, a real Varangian..." He looked away, clearly embarrassed by this display of fatherly feelings, and Ploskorylov loved him so much at that moment he would have gladly sent him to his death.

"Let us pray together, Inspector," he said, choking with emotion; praying was the best thing he could offer his guest at this moment.

"Really? Now?" Gurov looked up. "Fine, let's go."

* * *

Ploskorylov had had a church built next door to HQ. Paukov organized the masses at lightning speed, and they had put it up in three days from his plans. It was plain and bare, in the military style, with a sweeping arctic roof and a little cross, purely for appearance's sake, but without the hideous onion-dome that normally adorns Orthodox churches. Ploskorylov would have loved to see his beloved swastika up there, and had even fixed little hints of it to the tips of the cross – there was nothing to stop him going the whole way of course: the peasants wouldn't have cared if he stuck a red star to the roof, and the Stalin style had virtually demanded them, but it wouldn't do yet. He just had a small hut built adjoining the church for his Aryan treasures, to which he alone had the key, and he would have lost his mind here without them, with the dull peasants and their dull food and the never-ending rain.

Since his initiation to the Third Level and his ecstatic study of Aryanism and all things Aryan, he wouldn't have dreamt of praying to the vulgar Christian god and its suffering figure on the cross. Now in his hut he kept the swastika he had made from a piece of tin plate, in conditions of strict secrecy, along with twelve Aryan deities – virtually the entire pantheon except Veles, the Slavic spirit of the underworld, who had been gnawed by the hungry Baskakovo mice, and he had nothing to make another with. Also the skull he took everywhere with him as a memento, a handkerchief soaked in Khazar blood (a precious relic entrusted to him at the Fourth Level), and a crystal weight with sharp icy prisms and a little image of the North Pole inside, and the message "Greetings from the Arctic!"

Gurov headed out to the church with a shuffling unmilitary gait. It was drizzling again, and Ploskorylov shivered after the warm cottage.

"How often do you take services?" the Inspector asked him, staring straight ahead.

"Three a week at most," the priest confessed guiltily. "Tell me where I'm to find the strength—"

"You don't find strength, it comes from within," Gurov frowned.

"Oh but it does, it does!" the Priest said, regretting his mistake. "It's just that there's nothing to read, no one to talk to – I'll be growing fur here soon!"

"You're in the middle of the country," Gurov said didactically. "Why does the monk live in a cell? Why did Christianity adopt this Vedic practice? In your soul you'll find an inexhaustible source of wisdom. You think you're wasted here at the Front? You're being hardened for greater tasks ahead!"

Ploskorylov would drum these words into his officers every day, but didn't take kindly to hearing them from Gurov. "I know, but in practice—"

"For that you must read the Rulebook!" Gurov raised his voice again. "You must be a diamond, a diamond, do you hear me? In you alone I see my equal, but if you had to do a batman's job in the regiment you'd be up a gum tree, right?"

"Are you joking?" Ploskorylov said, hurt. "I knew the Rulebook when I was twelve! I slept with it under my pillow in my sixth year at school and drew a map of the battle of Kursk – I won first prize in the district for my essay—"

"Well, you don't win first prize with me," Gurov said coldly, and once again Ploskorylov didn't know if he was joking or serious. "Tell me the duties of an Orderly, in the Subordinate position please."

"The Orderly is a soldier of war," Ploskorylov began confidently, "whose chief duties are to supervise, monitor and report back, and furthermore to maintain order tirelessly in the Officers' mess. The Orderly is the property of the table which is the property of the mess. The Orderly's duty is to wipe the taps and surfaces, stand in the Subordinate position while awaiting a friendly guest, to salute the friendly guest and fire three shots – of notification, monitoring and warning – in case the friendly guest is in fact the enemy. When the Orderly withdraws, the guest may proceed—"

"You're lying," Gurov said calmly. "You left out the Duty Officer."

Damn, Ploskorylov thought, why did he always forget that one?

"The Orderly's duty is to notify the regimental Duty Officer as to bedding and seating, packing and processing, loading and unloading..."

"Yes?"

"Sorry, forgive me, Inspector, I don't remember—"

"Counting in, counting out," the Inspector said carelessly. "The Orderly is his chief assistant and right hand, and an inanimate object... Right, that's it. Next time I'll question you on the patrol towers, and if you don't get *quantum satis* it'll be three penalty points, washing the walls in the kitchen and mopping floors, do I make myself clear?" He chuckled. "You don't know the Rulebook and I'm promoting you! Terrible lapse of discipline! Fine, let's pray."

It was damp and chilly in the church, and Ploskorylov was inspired by the wonderful smell of fresh pine and living nature, even though it was just the smell of rain and muddy floorboards. He scurried around removing the Christian knick-knacks, the tatty paper icons and plywood crucifix, carved without love by a local craftsman, and fetched his holy objects from the hut.

As he laid them on the altar, Gurov looked around. They had prayed only once before, on his first visit, and Ploskorylov had fond memories of the occasion. He was impressed by the Inspector's precise, austere delivery, and the way he mumbled the prayers with an almost complete lack of expression. This workaday approach was an important aspect of his style, and for a while the Priest had tried to imitate it, but it didn't suit his more damp, feminine personality.

It was a matter of youth, he thought indulgently. Gurov had seen everything, he knew the natives and their way of life and had spent time with them, and he had lost his purity. Ploskorylov was still pure, and although he didn't dwell on it, he felt it gave him an advantage. He was tender and delicate, and nowhere was it written that the Varangian couldn't be tender and delicate. Some of us are moist, some are dry, it was all part of life's richness and diversity.

He arranged the relics – the skull, the swastika and the crystal – and drew from his vestments an old prayer book, spattered with wax and blood, then fixed the candle in its holder, placed a cup under it to catch the precious holy wax and furtively put the cross in the special pocket he kept for the hated Christian symbol during his private prayer sessions. Everything was ready.

Gurov ran a hand through his beard, straightened his spectacles and composed himself. "Will you say the prayer?" Ploskorylov asked him.

"With pleasure," the Inspector said curtly. Then, placing his right hand on the crystal, he began to recite without flourishes, pauses or any variation in tone 'Prayer for the Victory of the Aryans over the Sons of Ham':

"Almighty Father, the One True Father of the Nordic Race, chosen by the sons of Shem and Japhet, who hast made Man in Thy image and proclaimed Thy ascendancy over the tribes of Noah through Moses and the other prophets and raised the German at the end of days, may it please Thee to be called YAHVEH, and command us not to mix with the cursed Sons of Ham, for it is foretold that the Chosen Ones will smite the collective Antichrist and have spiritual Dominion on earth. We pray to Thee, Lord, to gather the tribes of Israel unto the Promised Land, that we may raise once more the Holy Swastika, the ancient symbol of the everlasting Spirit. For Thou art the God of warriors and Thy sword will deliver us from our foes. To the end of time. Amen."

"Amen!" echoed Ploskorylov fervently. The prayer, even in the Inspector's wooden delivery, had an almost narcotic effect on him and made his eyes well up. At the words "the Nordic Race" he experienced such a flood of feelings that he forgot the vile weather outside and the stupid villagers, and an inviolable truth shone before him in the words "It is foretold that the Chosen Ones..." How dare the Yds claim Israel as theirs! At such moments he could have torn them to pieces with his teeth.

"Say the prayer for Those Entering Battle," Gurov smiled gently at his young friend, observing his exalted state.

"Adonai, YAHVEH, Mighty Veles, great Lord and Father," Ploskorylov began in a trembling voice, fighting back the tears. "I beseech Thee to reveal Thyself and lead Thy people out of Egypt, and protect Thy servants Anatoly and Pyotr, and guard them night and day." (He almost shouted Gurov's name, and felt the special bond between them.) "Thou hast sent Moses to the land of the Canaanites and ordered Gideon and the three hundred to drive out the Midianites and slay Zebedee, father of James and John, and all their disciples, that we may be blessed with Thy life-giving force. Now and for evermore, to the end of time. Amen."

"Amen Yahveh, Mighty Veles, stinking pot-bellied heretical Varangian idol!" Gurov suddenly broke in, in a high mocking tone.

Ploskorylov gazed stunned at the blaspheming Inspector. "What are you saying, Petya?" he whispered.

"Keep your nose out of things you know nothing about," he said icily. "The Canon of the Great God Veles is the Seventh and Final one, it's not for you until your initiation. Don't teach your father to pray."

"But you never—"

"Didn't I?" shouted Gurov. "You've got to know things, you fat careerist! You'd better study and take notes, I shan't promote you until you've learnt the Garrison and Sentry code, the long and short version. Now clear up your trash."

Ploskorylov stood rooted to the spot.

"What's wrong? You think I tricked you into a test? I love you, you idiot!" Gurov said with a short staccato laugh, flapping an arm at him and noisily kissing his cheek.

"In a church..." Ploskorylov gasped, barely able to breathe.

"Forgive me Father, I've sinned," Gurov grinned. "Right, fuck off, Priest, I'm going to inspect our troops."

6

While this was going on, the mother of a recruit named Gorokhov was sitting with Commander Funtov in the cottage in Baskakovo where the Sixth Regiment had set up its office. She was about fifty, of that social status that retained traces of the old cultured professional class, wearing a bright embroidered Kashmiri shawl such as women used to wear during Russia's friendship with India in the Seventies. The petitioner, terribly anxious, clasped her hands on her knees and her face was full of entreaty.

The office was an exceptionally depressing place, with its scuffed yellow stools, scruffy ledgers and gloomy portrait of Marshal Zhukov on the wall, and anyone entering it instantly lost all hope. The floor was scrubbed three times a day but was always filthy. From the ceiling hung three flypapers thick with dead flies, and at the window was a withered cheese plant. The orderlies watered it regularly, but some power beyond them seemed to hang in the air, sucking the moisture from it and feeding it to the flies, leaving the window sill covered in dust. A white curtain was nailed to the window, yellowing from hopelessness, and an endless hopelessness filled Funtov's voice, which was as monotonous as the buzzing flies, although no flypaper had yet been invented to catch Commander Funtov.

A short stocky man of twenty-seven, he looked twenty years older, dozy and lethargic, as if he too was covered in dust. It was hard to imagine what the soldier's mother would discuss in the ten minutes she had with him. He liked to make dirty jokes about women, accusing the younger ones of being lazy sluts, and would say: "If I had a load

of money I'd pay some peasant bitches to slap them around a bit."
There was absolutely nothing else in him. It's unbearable to be with
people like him when you long for an understanding glance and a kind
word, and Funtov was like wood in that regard. Deprived of emotions
since birth, he had slept through school, and was known only for the
efficient way he could twist the heads off birds. As an officer he was
sluggish and indifferent to his men's lives, which made him invaluable
in the eyes of his superiors, and Zdrok would refer glowingly to him
in his interminable Castro-like speeches at the officers' meetings. He
understood nothing of his geopolitical studies, was useless in battle,
and barely understood who he was fighting or why, yet he had an excess
of the main thing an officer needs, namely stupidity, which filled him to
the exclusion of anything else, and even Paukov revered him.

"It's the third time you've come," he droned. "Your son must be
disciplined, basically. The milk's not dry on him, he's not a soldier
yet, he's a greenhorn, a cabbage. No one likes it, but their mothers
don't keep coming all the time. Why have you come?"

"Well you see..." she began nervously, sincerely believing that if she
could find the right words he might go easy on her son – not release him
of course, it was war, and each time she visited they made things harder
for her, phoning all her contacts and speaking to a former classmate
of hers who answered more and more reluctantly, to her shame and
humiliation – just perhaps find him some quiet job at HQ or in the
rear, closer to home. Surely Funtov must have a soul, she just hadn't
found it yet. It was her third visit to Baskakovo in four months, because
she was tormented by her son's letters and couldn't help him, and there
was another year of this torment left. She had aged twenty years in the
months before he was called up and in the four months of his service,
and her face was etched with the wretched, beseeching expression of
someone who has long ago abandoned her personal dignity.

"He writes that he has blisters and can't march, and he's made to
run—"

"They all say they have blisters and it's a lie," Funtov boomed. "No
one's made to run and they've got plimsolls, and there's a medical
room with all the facilities. You didn't raise him right, basically. If
you had, he wouldn't be writing. So he writes and you come. Why
have you come?"

"He wants to know if he can wear socks," Gorokhova said in a
rush. "He can't tie his foot-cloths properly. Couldn't he wear socks,
to begin with at least?"

"The foot-cloth lets the air in and allows the foot to breathe, basically," explained Funtov. "The foot sweats, the sweaty foot rots in the boot, you get me? So the foot doesn't rot we use the foot-cloth, as prescribed in the Rulebook, from the word foot and the word cloth, a special army cloth that lets the foot breathe. Look at our forebears."

"What forebears?" the soldier's mother said wildly.

"All of them, basically," he said with a wistful sigh. "They all fought in foot-cloths, even Suvorov. The Battle of Stalingrad was fought in foot-cloths, and the battle of Kursk. There's nothing you can't do in a foot-cloth, marching and shooting and so on. Follow the Rulebook and you'll win honour and glory. But you have to put them on right. What's the trick? I'll show you. Put the foot in a corner, the whole foot, then wrap the cloth tight so it doesn't wrinkle, then pull it round again, making sure the foot is covered and the sweaty foot can breathe. Then the other one. Takes an average of fifteen seconds, simple as that." He lazily wound one stubby hand over the other, showing the soldier's mother how to do it, as if she was about to put on foot-cloths right there in his office and run off to drill. "Then walk around a bit to wear them in. The sock doesn't let the foot breathe, basically. Sores and funguses and so forth." (Funtov himself had worn socks during his training and was punished for it; he had never got the hang of foot-cloths.) "They're a Russian invention, if you're a Russian soldier you wear foot-cloths, basically. Everyone knows this. Europe, Australia..." He paused and cast around for somewhere else. "Africa."

"But not everyone can manage it," she jabbered. "And he's no good at running either. He has lovely handwriting, he does calligraphy – perhaps you could find him a job like that? Or something to do with biology? He's a biologist, in his second year at college..."

"He doesn't need biology, he needs a general grounding," Funtov said flatly. "He can get his general grounding, then do his biology. We've plenty of clever people here, we've a warrant officer who knows words your son's probably never heard of. The modern army's a family, basically. They eat together, sleep together, if one gets a cold, they all get a cold. When it's drill they've all got colds, then it's teatime and they're off singing and dancing."

"Teatime?" the soldier's mother asked numbly.

"They have their own tea shop," he explained. "Very nice, with sugar and cakes and so on. We've nothing against it, but your country comes first. You run around all morning in the fresh air serving your country, then it's tea and an evening stroll. And what sort of soldier do you make if your mother keeps coming with her pots and pans? Especially in war."

At this Gorokhova had finally had enough and snapped out of her numb state. "War!" she shouted. "My son's been serving for four months and says he hasn't even done target practice! Your soldiers peel potatoes and scrub floors and run round in circles in their foot-cloths – what are you training them for? You've been fighting for four years and what have you achieved? How dare you say we haven't raised our sons right! My neighbour's boy was an officer and was killed in the second month! You just need dumb cattle to do whatever you like with!"

She realized in an instant that she had robbed her son of any chance of being transferred to HQ, because she had committed the unforgivable sin of raising her voice to an officer. She slipped from her chair and knelt before Funtov, beating her head on the floor of the regimental office.

"I'm sorry!" she howled. "Forgive me, I beg you. His father's ill, he's bedridden, I'll do anything. Forgive me, for Heaven's sake, I can't go on—"

"Get up, woman, it's a military office, not a circus. They all say their fathers are ill and it's a lie."

"I'll do anything," she cried. "I'll clean your boots, I'll give you money, I beg you—"

"Orderly!" bawled Funtov.

Fat Dudukin came in, with his usual expression of dull joy on his face. Despite being overweight, Dudukin was a model soldier. He couldn't run, but he loved housework, happily washing floors and wringing the cloth and tidying all day. He was also a master of shaving, cutting hair and whittling, and could carve a peasant and a bear from a piece of wood.

"Captain Dudukin at your service!" he reported merrily.

"Right, remove this woman and give her some water. Leave the papers for the shift on the table. It's not an office, it's a bloody knocking shop."

The soldier's mother felt terribly afraid for her son. She knew now that this appalling man had no feelings, which was why he was in charge of her son, and she realized how dreadful it must be for him, surrounded by this inhuman mass, sleeping and eating and tying their foot-cloths together. It was how the fly must feel, pointlessly appealing to the conscience of the flypaper. Sometimes people had to kill, but her son had never learnt to kill, and she knew he must become part of this mass to survive. She left the office; there was no reason for her to return a fourth time.

Her son still knew nothing, but was hoping for the best, annoyed with his mother for taking so long, and with himself for being unable to fit in like the others. Mainly though he knew she had brought pies, and had gone straight to the office with them. In civilian life he would never have dreamt that while she was deciding his fate with the Commander he would be thinking of pies, but he could think of nothing else. If Funtov refused her requests, which was most likely, even though she could be very persuasive, he would at least have the consolation of food. He must eat them quickly though, on no account would he take them inside. He could bear anything but the thought of his comrades tucking into his mother's pies.

He didn't know that she was at that moment stumbling through Baskakovo to the bus stop, with the bag of pies flapping against her legs. She hadn't the strength to see him again, to look into his eyes and promise things would improve, knowing they wouldn't.

The bus arrived in an hour and took her to the district capital, from where it would be another day to Moscow on the only train. The bus howled. Gorokhova howled. The sodden landscape howled outside the window.

7

Back at HQ, the eight-man writers' brigade was being drilled on the waterlogged parade ground.

They had been packed off from Moscow to the Southern Front to write articles for the *Red Star* newspaper and were stuck there after the start of the battles, and the High Command had given orders not to send them back. There was no risk of them being killed of course, but too many writer scum had run off to the Khazars, seduced by promises of freedom and a better life, and the High Command didn't want that. They obviously got nothing of the sort with them, the Yds being generally suspicious of ethnically alien elements in their ranks; there was even a TV programme on Channel One about deserters being made prisoners-of-war. But some of the more useful writers had to be preserved, and as a result Paukov had had his patriotic scribblers hanging round his neck for three weeks, eating army rations and hobnobbing with his men.

At first they were billeted with the Staff, then a directive came from Moscow to embed them within the ranks, so they moved their guests to the cottages, and the commanders were told to introduce them to the bravest of them. The commanders were in a dilemma: it was hard to find heroes in Paukov's division worthy of appearing in *Red Star*, occupied as they were with square-bashing, geopolitics and cleaning their weapons, occasionally breaking the monotony by taking potshots at each other.

"Talk to Private Krasnukhin, he's a good one," Platoon Commander Kasatkin said with an embarrassed smile. "He's done nothing heroic yet, but on sentry duty he didn't shoot an individual who forgot the password, and just fired a warning shot."

"Hello there!" the writer Kurlovich said pleasantly a little later to ginger-haired, red-cheeked Private Krasnukhin, sitting before him in the Lenin room with his big hands on his knees. "Tell me please about your brave deed."

"I dunno, I'm standing there on patrol and I think no, better not!"

"And what were you patrolling?" Kurlovich said, eagerly scribbling away.

"You know, the mushroom tower."

"Ah, I see," he nodded, keen to show his familiarity with army terms. But his article must be scrupulously accurate, and he hadn't the faintest idea what a mushroom tower was.

"Forgive me, what are these towers actually like?" he pressed him after a short silence.

"You know," Krasnukhin said reluctantly, fearing he was being grilled on the Rulebook. "According to Point Five of the Sentry Code, any rural location where a platoon, company, regiment or other military formation is stationed must be guarded night and day by patrol towers built at intervals of fifty metres, in the dimensions of a mushroom. These dimensions must be five metres long, three wide and two metres high, for the purpose of sheltering the sentry from wind, rain, snowstorms and hail, and guarding the personnel from colds, rashes and other *force majeure* eventualities."

He drew breath, and Kurlovich wrote it all down.

"That's the mushroom, see, we put them up ourselves. It's pouring with rain, and we're snug inside like we're at home with our mothers."

"Do you love your mother?" Kurlovich asked him with a friendly smile.

Krasnukhin suspected another trick. "I don't know…"

"I know! Aren't I Russian too!" (In fact he was half-Khazar, but a loyal government man.) "I just wanted some living detail, to imagine you standing in the rain thinking of your mother."

Private Krasnukhin had thought rather a lot about his mother last night, although she had born no resemblance to his own mother, a big strapping woman from a village outside Voronezh.

"She's a nurse in a hospital," he said bashfully. "My dad left. She's OK, she writes."

"So what do you think of when you remember her?" Kurlovich persisted. "The smell of frying cutlets perhaps? Don't be shy, cutlets and home life are part of our little country too!"

"No, mainly potatoes," Krasnukhin said. "You know, potato-cakes, fritters."

"Yes, of course!" The writer nodded happily; fritters were reassuring and familiar, and at least they weren't mushrooms.

"And stuffed cabbage too sometimes," he added after a pause.

"Tell me, do you think of your mother's hands?"

Krasnukhin thought of her long fingers with their swollen joints and flat nails, and suddenly felt sorry for her, although he had had little love from her. But he bore her no grudge. She had never beaten him, although he deserved it. He had frequently been hauled into the young offenders' room at the police station for his scrapes. He had robbed a market stall once with his friends and it was a wonder they weren't arrested, and if it wasn't for the army he would be in a prison camp by now. His mother was his mother. Why was this spectacled scumbag pestering him with his questions?

"So what if I do?" he said. "What's she got to do with it?"

"You simply said—"

"I said the towers shelter us from God's rain!" he repeated angrily.

"So you believe in God?"

"God?" Krasnukhin asked. "God has chosen the state of Holy Rus, which covers a sixth of the earth's surface, pleasingly and symmetrically arranged and blessed by the Father, the Son and the Holy Spirit, whose defence is the sacred duty of the Orthodox fighting force created to preserve, defend and guard it ceaselessly."

"Did you think that up yourself, out of your own head?" Kurlovich asked excitedly.

"What do you mean?" Krasnukhin blushed. "It's from the Sixth chapter of the General Military Rulebook by Sofrony the Anchorite. Haven't you read it?"

"Of course I have!" Kurlovich said in a panic. "I just... you said it so sincerely I thought you might be a writer. Perhaps you write poems and verses?"

"No, I don't, I'm in the Patrol Platoon. In the Rulebook that's washing floors, darning and erecting mushrooms—"

"Fine," Kurlovich said hastily. "So you're standing there, then what happens?"

"I hear a rustle," Krasnukhin replied slowly. "So I shout 'Who goes there?' according to the Rulebook, and the password is 'horse in a blanket', but I don't hear the password, so I load my rifle and say again 'Who goes there?' The third time I don't hear it I fire in the air, then I see Sergeant Glukharev and he gives me the Subordinate command but not the password. So I load my rifle again and ask for the password and Sergeant Glukharev gives it and I lay down my rifle and salute."

"So what would have happened if Sergeant Glukharev hadn't said the password?" Kurlovich asked, feeling increasingly alarmed.

"Well then," Krasnukhin said, baffled by the question, "I'd have shot him in the chest area according to the Rulebook, until the latter was dead."

"But you knew him, he's your sergeant!"

"So what," Krasnukhin said in the same baffled tone. "Maybe he's the enemy in disguise or he forgot the password – that means he's shot, see? I asked him three times, I fired my weapon. What if he was a zombie? Have you seen *Night of the Living Dead*?"

"Yes, I have," Kurlovich said with a sinking feeling. "But surely he would have been coming from the village?" He explained in the wordy manner of the Rulebook: "The individual was in your locality, signifying that he was from your unit, not the enemy's, and he posed no threat."

"I suppose," Krasnukhin nodded, not seeing the relevance of this; it was obviously of no interest to him.

"So why would you have killed him?"

"Makes no difference where he's coming from. He broke the rules see, I was following orders."

"And what if you had?"

"They'd have given me leave!" he said, stretching his rubbery lips in a wide grin.

* * *

After the writers had spent a fortnight asking such questions, Paukov and Zdrok got sick of them living with the soldiers and getting up whenever they felt like it in breach of army rules. They had been told to embed them with the men, but it was more like bed-rest. Then another directive came from Moscow to hold literary evenings and question-and-answer sessions for the Staff, but the Staff hadn't read their works, so the questions dried up on the first day. One asked how much they were paid and why, and another about their creative approach, but there were eight of them, and there had to be an evening for each of them.

They would obviously be around for a while and something had to be done with them, so Paukov took a decision the Yd Solomon would have admired. For the first half of the day he had them sweating like soldiers, and for the second half, when the men were studying geopolitics or being drilled, they resumed their writerly duties, meeting them and answering questions about their literary work.

After a week the writers had all fallen out with each other. They hadn't got on from the start, thanks to their filthy trade, but after their first taste of military life they began to loathe each other in earnest.

They marched and put on their gas masks and did their cross-country runs with their kit, gasping after the first hundred metres, while the sergeants encouraged them with fatherly kicks. But when the distinguished Osetrenko fell to the ground gasping that he couldn't go on, the others had to carry him off, and afterwards they began to bully him like the sergeants and generally to display a healthy Varangian spirit.

In the afternoons, as soon as they returned to their quarters, they would meet the Staff and answer questions from the same sergeants who had bellowed at them on the parade ground, and thus a sort of equilibrium was established between their services to the Muse and to the military.

Sergeant Gryzlov was now drilling them in the playground of the Baskakovo school, next to the tilting basketball posts and Swedish walls.

"Move your arses, pansies! It's the army, not a collective farm!" he bawled, as if the writers had spent their lives gorging themselves on farms. "Attention! Right turn! Left shoulder forwards, march! One, two, stop! Right leg up, down! Stop scuttling like a crab, Strunin! Is that a leg or a piece of piss! Answer me!"

"A leg," said the elderly Strunin, trembling on his stumps.

"I don't see a leg, I see a piece of piss!" Gryzlov repeated cheerfully. "Second-Level crab Strunin, do the command on your own! Lift your leg and push it out, now stand there, you little monkey!"

Strunin swayed on one leg and collapsed in the mud. The others looked away squeamishly and didn't help him up. Strunin was a lousy writer, to be honest, and his colleagues disliked him; his sketches about Russian writers in the army, *Nightingales of the General Staff*, were considered too grovelling even by this patriotic crowd.

"Get up!" roared Gryzlov. "What are you, crab Strunin? What would your wife say if she saw you? Do you fall off her in bed too?"

* * *

"God knows what we're doing here, we should be back in Moscow by now," said the haughty patriotic Grushin later as the writers ate their thin salty borscht with a few bits of beetroot and old cabbage leaves floating on top.

"So who dragged us here in the first place?" the thin, bilious sketch-writer Gvozdev snapped.

Grushin shrugged. "As you know, I always said a Russian writer's place was in the ranks—"

"So what are you complaining about? You're in the ranks now!"

"Each serves in his own way. I serve with my pen."

"You can shove it up Zdrok's arse then!"

Grushin looked disdainfully at Gvozdev and resolved to report him for this. All the writers wrote reports on each other. Evdokimov had a whole file of them, and they were the pearls of his collection. The writers could write, they expressed themselves in a flowery, complicated language, and Grushin was the best of them, calling Gvozdev a chained hyena and a maddened fox. The script-writer Shubnikov was good too, with his punchy style honed by writing TV serials. His words were almost all one-syllabled – "toad", "slime", "snake" and so on. Two-syllabled ones had become a rarity on TV, and the three-syllabled ones were simply crossed out by the producers.

After dinner the writers assembled as usual to answer questions, and the same Sergeant Gryzlov who had called Strunin's leg a piece of piss and asked what he did in bed with his wife now enquired with the utmost civility: "Comrade Second-Level Crab, kindly tell us about your creative approach!"

He was quite sincere in this. Sergeant Gryzlov was what is called in the army a "tooth", who served by the Sergeant's Code in the Rulebook to win honour and glory. He would spend the morning humiliating the writers like young reservists, and in the evening he treated them as an honoured delegation. Although he hadn't the vocabulary to articulate it, he knew a sergeant's job was precisely this role play, in which all relationships apart from those with his superiors cancelled each other out. He would probably have been quite nice to his mother if she visited on so-called Parents' Day, but if she arrived with the young recruits he would have made her march and pull herself up on the bars.

Ploskorylov thought highly of Gryzlov. He wasn't of the Varangian caste of course, and he was ignorant and uneducated, but he had the army in his guts – not his bones, Ploskorylov insisted, only the Varangians had it in their bones. Gryzlov could adopt any form into which he was poured, or sometimes pushed; not many of the natives had this talent, and it was worth using what remained of the more alert flexible ones.

Strunin generally answered questions about his creative approach; others were practically never asked. He cleared his throat and began in a weighty voice.

"The Army has always played a major role in my work. I think if we compare an officer with a teacher, say, or a manager, the officer proves superior in every respect, with a special style and decorum. I plan to write a book about the officer class, and how the Russian military aristocracy was formed since the days of Ivan the Terrible. I would like to pen a group portrait, a wreath to lay before the Russian officer who has forged a path through Russia to the sea and defended with his body the brotherly Slavic nations, and is distinguished by an exceptional decency. If I consider myself worthy, I plan to start immediately on my book, and General Paukov, Commander of this division which has welcomed us so hospitably, occupies an honourable place in this gallery of brilliant officers. Have I answered your question?"

"Abso-lutely!" said Gryzlov. "Let more questions com-mence!"

"Comrade Second-Level Crab," said Private Saprykin bashfully, "tell us please about your creative approach."

Strunin cleared his throat. "The Army has always played a big part in my work. I think if we compare an officer with a doctor, or a magician, the officer proves the better teacher. The officer has been trained to know everything and has a special intelligence, a special skill. I'd like to write a book about these Knights of the Sword, and weave it into a wreath to present to the officer, who has defended the Slav nations and is distinguished by an exceptional fragrance. If I have the strength, I plan to start my book soon, and General Paukov, entrusted with our little brigade, will have an honourable place in it. Have I answered your question?"

"Oh yes!" Gryzlov replied for Saprykin as his superior. "Co-ompany, more questions!"

"Your creative approach, Comrade Crab!" rapped Private Sukhikh, evidently a sergeant in the making.

"What's the magic word?" said Gryzlov crossly.

"Please!" Sukhikh grinned.

Strunin cleared his throat. "The army plays a big part in my work. If we compare an officer with a mother, or a camel, the officer is the better teacher. The officer has the training, there's a special homeliness about the Russian officer. And where would we be without General Paukov? Yes indeed! We writers are all indebted to him. Have I answered your question?"

"Yes!" Sukhikh said cheerfully, waking from a brief sleep; all the soldiers learnt to nap in their free moments.

"Co-ompany exit!" commanded Gryzlov. "One at a time please! Thank you, Comrade writer!"

* * *

That evening before bedtime the writers were quarrelling again.

"Already in '99 you were—" Grushin began.

"Here we go again," yawned Gvozdev. "Remember what you wrote about Banana?"

"Of course I do. What I wrote and what you wrote, and what Mr Strunin here wrote – remember, Strunin? I should show the magazine to Special Services…"

"You've always envied me, always! You're filthy, your feet stunk!" Stunin flared up, forgetting he wasn't that clean himself after falling in the mud.

"What about you? I know your real name's Stein!"

"Gentlemen, please," Kurlovich tried to reason with them. "We're intelligent people, creative people—"

"Shut up! Stay out of our Russian quarrel!" Grushin shouted. "I'll report you for what you wrote about the Khazars—"

"Stop it, you should be ashamed of yourselves!" said Kozev, one half of the creative tandem KozaKi, who wrote bestsellers about the adventures of Special Agent Sedoy.

"We're at the Front, after all," nodded his co-author Kirienko.

"At the Front with your potboilers," sneered Grushin. "Purveyors of trash…"

KozaKi ignored him and went off to their cottage. They had to knock out their sixteenth novel about Smersh man Sedoy by morning. "We're government officials, we serve the state," Sedoy would say as he stamped out another slimy act of sabotage. The book should have been with the publishers a week ago, and they might lose their rations for being late.

Grushin, Gvozdev and Strunin cursed and argued, and the Baskakovo dogs barked and scratched themselves in the darkness.

8

All day Ploskorylov had been looking forward to a special treat, which he carried deep in his heart for fear of sullying it. The fact was, there was something there he was afraid to look at, because he could find no explanation for it that would let him respect himself.

Bidding farewell to those sentenced to death was one of his duties, and fulfilling them honourably was always a pleasure, but none gave him this shameful, secret pleasure. Each time someone was sentenced he was moved to a feeling of ecstasy he didn't fully understand; it was the same feeling he had when Maiden Ira sang, and it was unambiguously sensual, which was why he was afraid to analyse it.

He had first felt this dark attraction to the condemned during the trial of a young soldier named Kalinin, arrested for shooting himself in the foot to avoid his duties. Kalinin had cried out to the court that his rifle had gone off accidentally, that he would serve his time and he was his mother's only son, and for a moment he dared to hope that he might, just might, escape death. It was a relatively peaceful time, a lull between battles, he had no previous convictions, and was known for his valour – there was the famous time he had made one of his juniors eat shit, and he was all set to be promoted to sergeant.

Ploskorylov had been stirred by the handsome insolent youth in the dock, with his full mouth and his wide-set eyes. But when Kalinin sobbed like a professional, swearing to serve honourably and make amends, the Priest experienced a powerful sense of anticlimax; Kalinin's pardon would deprive him of an important and edifying experience. He wanted to keep the brave soldier alive for future work of course, but somehow a dead Kalinin seemed to him better than a living one. So he used his prerogative to address the court, arguing that even if Kalinin had shot himself by accident, as he claimed, this was actually worse than if he had done it on purpose. What sort of soldier let his rifle shoot the foot of its owner? Was it a proper use of army property? Wasn't it right that Kalinin should pay for his single so-called accidental shot with the standard single shot through the heart? Such aesthetic symmetry was vital in an execution, and it would be an appropriate punishment. "Let he that has sinned be purged of it, and woe to those who seek pardon. Woe I say, woe!" he chanted, quoting from the eighth book of the Code of Psalms, 'Thou Shalt Not Forgive'. And as he uttered these words in his flowing voice, like molten steel, it became clear to Kalinin and the judges that there was nothing to hope for.

Such exalted pleasures were in short supply in the army, and Ploskorylov couldn't let one pass. And now this evening he was to administer the last rites to young Private Voronov, sentenced for lack of Varangian spirit. He hadn't managed to do much damage, thank Veles, but he was a rotten soldier and would be a lesson to the others.

Ploskorylov got ready. He changed into clean vestments and sniffed himself, finding it a healthy Varangian smell, then splashed on some "Junkers" aftershave. It was time to read the last rites.

The Varangian faith differed from the Christian fairy tales in that the dying man was offered not bread and wine but useful information. Each received this in his own way. Kalinin, for example, had almost wet himself with shock, and was so impressed by the Sacraments that he went off to be shot in a bovine daze. If he hadn't, he would have met death without dignity, squealing like a pig, and it was clearly better to die like a cow than like a pig. Some said they had known as much all along; others understood nothing, and thought the Last Revelations were merely a figure of speech. But as a Godfaculty graduate Ploskorylov knew better.

* * *

It was all at the level of instinct for the Varangians, Voronov thought. They didn't think in words, they despised people's words, because words suggested something beyond instinct. The highest human morality for them was to overcome their human mortal nature, cracking jokes before the firing squad and laughing as they fell, and a reprieve would leave a cold empty place where the soul should be, because the soul was repellent to them. They wanted to turn the whole world into this cold empty place, and everything human – love of family and friends, caring for the sick – was vile to them and must be exterminated, which was why they made allies with the lunatic Hitler, babbling about being superhuman. Yet neither the Varangians nor the insane German understood that to be superhuman meant being human to the highest degree: the mother sitting up five nights in a row with her sick child, the grandfather searching the city to buy it a toy. And since they didn't understand this, the Varangians never achieved anything, rampaging around the country that couldn't or wouldn't resist them, murdering and torturing people, their own and others, and it was a hideous distortion of humanity. And the psychological torture was even worse for people like Voronov, because the victim dared hope he might say something that would spare him, and that the torture wasn't an end in itself, which it often was. And so it would go on, until he felt at last that he shouldn't live, that the machine had picked him, checked him for taste and stuck a fork in him, before shovelling him down its iron gullet, and nothing he said or did would change anything. The fodder could repent and squirm, or meet death with courage and dignity, but it was still fodder.

So as not to surrender to the power of the machine, Voronov tried to remember what was human in him, his home and his family, everything the Varangians despised – his mother and his sister in Moscow, and his mother's brother who lived there too – and he imagined their life going on while he lay in the shed, guarded outside without a care in the world by Private Pakharev, and he was horrified to think that these two worlds could exist simultaneously.

At the moment he was being killed (he had read that it wouldn't happen at once, it would take nine minutes or so while the brain was in agony), his mother would suspect nothing, or if she did she would try to ignore it. He was her boy, dreamy and gentle, and she never let herself give in to despair or she would have gone mad, imagining him far from home with strangers in a strange place. At home they thought of others and shared their food with them. All the dogs in the yard used to wait for him to leave for school because he would have titbits for them, and it wasn't done for show or pride, but because it was right. And there were the mice. They had these velvet toy mice that were worn and darned, but they didn't throw them out, because even a velvet mouse had feelings, and without noticing it he began to give feelings to inanimate things, just as now he addressed the machine that was about to devour him. He couldn't imagine not pitying someone who was suffering, he was sorry for everyone. Why didn't Pakharev outside think of his sad fate, instead of pacing up and down wondering when he could get off, and whether to sleep or eat first. After you eat you don't want to sleep, then you want to sleep more, and if you sleep first you want to eat less. The world was made for Pakharev, and there was no place in it for Voronov, who had betrayed his mother and his sister and his uncle, a kind doctor who cared tirelessly for the children at his hospital. The authorities had warned him that he must teach them to endure pain bravely and not spoil them with painkillers, but he regularly raided the emergency supplies for them and was eventually sacked; painkillers were reserved exclusively for the top brass, and it was a miracle he wasn't arrested.

Of course dying in hospital wasn't the same as dying in battle, but the machine needed sick fodder too. The only thing Voronov didn't know was what would happen when the machine had devoured everyone. Perhaps when only people like Pakharev were left it would reach its optimal state and stop devouring, and occupy itself with its main task. But his soul shuddered to think what this was.

At that moment the bolt of the shed clattered, and he realized he couldn't get up. What a disgrace. However much he struggled he couldn't stand on his own two feet.

The door swung open, and into the shed swept the tall, corpulent figure of the Priest-Captain. Voronov had always thought of him as a pleasant man who enjoyed talking to the soldiers, it never occurred to him that he simply liked the sound of his own voice.

"At ease, at ease," smiled Ploskorylov, patting his damp robes and giving Voronov his hand to kiss. "I have come for our final conversation. Now you will expiate your sin, Private Voronov, and return to the ranks of our glorious soldiers, and I am charged with the pleasant duty of counselling you. But why do you lie there?" He spoke like a father, as if his tenderness could raise him from the floor. "Do we not rise before our superiors, especially a priest? Pray rise, Private Voronov, be of good cheer. Why do you lie like a princess before your superior? Will you lie when you are shot?" He enunciated the word very clearly. "No, dear Voronov, you earn the right to lie like a princess before your superiors only with your death. Until then you must stand. Pull yourself together and stand like a soldier. Now I want to tell you," he murmured, stroking his shoulder, "that the sins of those weak in spirit such as yourself may be redeemed, and you may reflect on saving your soldierly soul. Tomorrow at dawn you will be led outside the village to a pure Russian field. A Russian field is a lovely sight in the sunrise, and you will have the chance to enjoy it. The field is saying farewell to you as it takes you into its pure Russian heart, and you were born for this moment, Private Voronov. Then the guard will utter the words 'May God's servant Private So-and-so be eliminated for lack of military virtue'. I will be there, and you will kiss my hand as a sign that you are ready to repent, and I will bless you and wish you good health on this beautiful day, and the guard will give the command to fire. You may experience some discomfort, possibly pain, although shooting is the most humane punishment available. But you have earned this pain, Private Voronov, and it's happening for a reason. And now I will give you the Holy Sacraments. These are two in number. The First states that all is as it seems, despite the fact many have doubted it. The Second, more important one, is that the path of the soldier is the path to death, and his purpose is to perish, and thus you will have fulfilled your purpose, Private Voronov. These are the Holy Secrets, that you may know now that you can reveal them to no one."

Voronov didn't understand.

"Did you hear me, Private Voronov? Have you understood the Sacraments? Are you imbued with their fragrance?" he persisted. "It's my duty to make sure you do. Do you realize that tomorrow you will atone for your sin and fulfil your destiny? I congratulate you, tomorrow at dawn you will become the ideal soldier!"

Voronov remained silent, numb with fear.

"What I'm thinking, comrade Priest-Captain," he said at last, so quietly that his voice was barely audible above the rustle of the rain on the roof, "is that I've lived my life and hurt no one, and your people came and I had to serve somewhere and die somewhere, and I've taken nothing from you and you're taking everything from me, and I don't understand, comrade Priest-Captain."

"Shooting's too good for you!" exclaimed Ploskorylov, feeling his groin grow hot and tense. "Your life only has value when you're dead! Death is the start of life, and you'll be a maggot, and a beautiful butterfly will fly from you to the icy flowers of Valhalla! Are you Aryan-born, Private Voronov?"

"I don't know. I was born of my father and mother," he said. "I don't want icy flowers, I don't understand why you decide if I live or die."

"Because it suits the commanders that you do!" cried Ploskorylov, raising his plump arms to the roof.

Voronov wasn't a proper victim. He should have wept and slobbered over his hand, or even his boots, as Kalinin had, and he would have felt that shudder up his spine and the feelings he loved and was ashamed of. But Voronov was no good at it. Ploskorylov hurried out into the rain, banging the door behind him. Pakharev slid the bolt and could be heard noisily kissing his superior's hand, and Voronov was alone.

He thought of home again, and for some reason he remembered the little spice box in the kitchen that used to contain his children's shoes. He remembered waiting in the warm square space under the orange lampshade for his mother to return from the school where she taught; she had had to work two shifts to support him and his sister now his father had left. In November it was already dark by five. His sister was out with her boyfriend, and the windows were steamed up, with teardrops streaming down the glass. He heard the key in the door and his mother coming in, and the world made sense again.

It had all been a dream. Even then the future Private Voronov knew his life was just a dream. The reality, as stated in the First Sacrament, was the shed and the rain and Pakharev pacing outside, wondering whether to sleep or eat first. And nine-year-old Voronov, waiting for his mother to get home, was protected from this reality only by the bright kitchen and the shoebox full of spices and handwritten recipes. These recipes had been passed down through generations of his family and there were so many of them, and no one needed them any more because they were just a distraction from the main task of the true citizen, which was death.

Voronov knew this now, but he didn't want these to be his last thoughts before dying, he had to find others to replace them, because the spice box and the recipes had more right to live than Ploskorylov and Pakharev and the shed. But he couldn't finish the thought, because at that moment the bolt clattered again and the door fell open. The night seemed to have passed so quickly, but it hadn't passed, and a bald stranger in little glasses came in. Voronov could see nothing else of him in the darkness.

"You're waiting to die?" asked the stranger. "Don't worry, it's early, we've still things to do. Here, drink this." He handed him a jug.

"Drink it, it's not poison. We can't just throw people away, Private Voronov, I hope the experience was a useful lesson for you. Now listen to me carefully, Roly-poly!"

Voronov thought he was going mad. Anyone could have entered the shed at that moment, but as the spectacled stranger spoke he recognized the Ministry of Education psychologist who had tested his class at school seven years ago. It was a basic aptitude test, which involved solving a simple equation, drawing a circle without a compass and answering a children's riddle: "A ring, a ring, a hoop and a swing, round and round – what is it?"

"I know, Roly-poly!" twelve-year-old Voronov had told the Inspector, quick as a flash. He had no idea what it meant. He must have read it in a storybook without understanding it, and for some reason he was the only one in his class to get it. Another boy in the parallel one had guessed it too, he didn't know from where either. Then the boy left the school and he never saw him again, or the Inspector. But he remembered his appearance, and it wasn't every day you heard riddles like that.

9

Captain Gromov woke in tears from a dream, which hadn't happened for a long time. He had dreamt of a poem, which also hadn't happened for a long time. Not one of his, thank God, someone else's: "Remember, in our sunny bay…"

He lay there in the darkness, picking out the dismal sounds of the village night, the ticking of the grandfather-clock, his landlady snoring quietly in the next room, the rain beating against the window, and it was terrible to think such poems were possible.

He had written poetry too once, in his other life, of which nothing remained now after two years of war, apart from Masha and his fleeting correspondence with her. He had banished all other memories of his past. All his thoughts now were reduced to practicalities about his men – whether they were alive and fed, whether the commanders were angry and threw them into battle and cancelled their leave. But in the dark depths of his soul everything had been ransacked, like a ransacked house – or, as he would put it now, in the language of the Front, an encircled area deep in enemy territory. The army had retreated and forgotten about those stranded, and still they fought on, trying to reach their side and sending meaningless messages that got lost on the way, because all communications had been cut.

It was best not to think of his doomed regiment, without reinforcements or supplies, yet sometimes voices broke through from that other world: "Remember, in our sunny bay..."

Gromov had forgotten what the poem was about, but he woke in tears. He couldn't have said why, it wasn't the words he was crying for, or poetry in general, but these barely decipherable messages coming up from under the terrible red-black crust of his life.

And there were the swallows, the poem in his dream had something to do with the swallows. He sat on the bench and smoked, and as his lungs filled with smoke, the world acquired its soothing, hideous features again. Everything insufficiently hideous maddened him, like a jewelled bandage on an open sore. He had no time for sentimentality. The torturer weeping over his victim was obscene, and since even before the war there were only torturers and victims, he had long ago banished poetic feelings. For some reason sadists were always sentimental, he thought, not just the Nazis with their carols and Christmas cards, but those sweet Soviet children's cartoons from the Sixties about bunnies and hedgehogs, when the human mask was pulled over the iron fist. He hated this mask, and had learnt over time to see the jewelled bandage even in the flowering lime trees, their leaves glistening in the lamplight. Everything seemed a cover to him now for something rotten and swarming with flies. The world was just steel and decay, and steel was all he had; everything else was a lie. You couldn't stop the body enjoying itself; the body enjoyed mealtimes and breaks, and wanted to live and be safe from danger. But at night the soul came to life, with its poetry and memories of childhood.

Intolerable, disturbing memories, like the swallows. Two summers running they had built their nest at the dacha, hatching their young on the porch of the outdoor kitchen, and he and his mother had watched the fledglings grow and had drawn pictures of them. Then his parents had built a door to the kitchen, and when the swallows flew back to their usual place the door frightened them, and they abandoned the nest. Where had they gone? They must have gone somewhere, or their atoms were scattered somewhere, and for some reason he found this idea more frightening than if they had simply vanished without trace – for that might mean there was some gap through which they had escaped. But there was no way to escape from this vast enclosed space; the same material passed from decay to flesh and decay again, like snow in the Antarctic, drifting endlessly from place to place, because new snow almost never falls and there's no room for it.

The dacha had probably disappeared by now. He had forbidden himself to think of it, but suddenly, he didn't know from where, a memory of an insatiable childish sadness broke through, which he could suppress only by hating it, gulping in his squalid surroundings like beer for a hangover – the damp grey linen, the rustle of mice or perhaps cockroaches in the corner, the rain and the endless muddy roads beyond the window.

It reminded him of when he would wake terrified in the night as a child, and would calm himself by thinking of school. It was a terror of death that woke him, a terror of who he was, something he had no words for, no way to share with his parents, which made it more frightening. He could read things in books and discuss things with friends, yet here he was, and this was who he was, and every second he would sink deeper into the terror. A nightmare could be remembered and forgotten, but there was no escape from this, knowing it was all happening to him and there was nowhere to go, and he would grab at memories of school, which he hated by day and loved at night because it was less frightening.

The dacha brought a flutter of forbidden memories: yellow clouds in a rainy sunset, the smell of currants and strawberries warmed by the sun, with little pink marks where the ants had nibbled them. The dacha must be still there, it couldn't have vanished, although the strawberries were probably overgrown with weeds by now, not that it mattered. All that mattered were this night and this cottage and the grey days stretching ahead, and this war that no one needed, to which he had given himself with some notion of honourable service.

The demands made on the soldiers and junior officers were far harsher than the samurai code. The samurai despised death, consoled by the greatness of his personality, worshipping honour and letting no one treat him like a dog. If the feudal lord insulted him he could cut off his head, saying "I am full of resolve, sir!" The men here were being told to risk their lives, follow any order from their commanders and not fear the enemy, and they soon discovered they had more to fear from their own side. The enemy was evil and cunning, but they shot far fewer prisoners, and the only reason soldiers weren't deserting in droves was that their families would be arrested: no one would have fought if the army hadn't had these hostages.

The hotheads from the Legion of Honour party had covered Russia with youth training camps, where heathen sports were played in honour of Perun, the god of thunder, and they preached a programme of universal conscription. If the conscript served badly, he lost his rations and his family would be sent to jail. If he tried to escape, their sentence would be doubled and he would be shot, or better still there would be a public execution. People were divided into soldiers and prisoners, with a small block of specialists at the top who controlled the flow. They just didn't know what to do with the childless ones. With no sons to conscript, they couldn't be sent to jail or to do farm work, and would be more mouths to feed. One hero from this block of specialists had even smashed through the barrier and suggested liquidating people for childlessness, as an act of sabotage that aided the Asiatics. Then when the Muslim threat receded it was aiding Europe, although Europe was dying faster than Russia.

Everything connected to the war seemed worthless to Gromov now, and the people who served it worse than honest idlers. There was something heroic about those who refused to work, even if it killed them, and he had loved Masha for her refusal to be part of all this bogus activity.

In fact no one had worked before the war. She had had a series of pointless jobs for starvation wages like everyone else, and had lost all of them, and it wasn't in her fierce nature to put up with things. She was made redundant from one after a week, and walked out of another after three days, and in the end she decided to do nothing and die honestly, she said.

When he met her she was living in a wretched way, although he wasn't doing much better. The difference was that he worked; he had a passion for order and discipline, but finding no jobs compatible with human dignity, he ended up joining the army and had gone off happily to war.

He thought of Masha, the only compromise between this life and his soul, which he had almost suppressed, apart from his love for her. It was a strange love. He didn't really know the girl that well, which was probably why he had loved her for four years, two of them mainly apart. It seemed he meant something to her too, and not just for want of someone better, and she had visited him and written to him and kept him in touch with her woes and her frequent changes of address.

He loved her because he didn't feel sorry for her; it was impossible to imagine her humiliated by life. It could grind her down, but that only made her happy. Like himself at her age, perhaps even more so, she felt the pain of things so deeply that when she met him at the age of twenty, it seemed nothing would ever make her happy. She was bored by the company of her young friends and hated listening to their conversations and compliments, and even with Gromov she allowed only occasional meetings, always at her initiative. She didn't want to be tied to him and he didn't press her, and it was precisely this freedom that bound them. And it seemed they both realized this on their last night together, before she saw him off.

They had met in the spring on Moscow's Tverskoy Boulevard, the year before the war started. He was walking past the Literary Institute of the University, which he had never had anything to do with, thank God, and he was drawn into conversation with a bunch of rather drunk people on a bench. Everyone knew each other, and who had written what and said what, and as he was in no hurry to go anywhere, he sat down with them and joined in the shouting and arguing. The reason was Masha, of course. If it hadn't been for her, he would never have got caught up in this mindless drinking, of which he had done far too much in his youth. But he noticed her at once, amazed that every passing man didn't fall at her feet, and to his joy none of them seemed to notice her beauty. It seemed to him an ideal beauty. Everything about her was large, with her big green eyes, her straight nose and her full, rather chapped lips that never wore lipstick.

It shocked him to see where she was living, in a yellow two-storey barrack block in Medvedkovo in the middle of nowhere, with a leaking roof and obscene graffiti on the walls. Her drunken neighbours upstairs had taken over the place by sheer weight of numbers, moving their innumerable relatives into her flat without asking her, and they lived there without permits or documents, cooking and washing and using the bathroom. But he was touched by the love between these people. Kolya visited, and sat with his brother Misha in the kitchen gazing affectionately at him in silence, and he went in at regular intervals on the pretext of washing a cup or fetching jam, and saw them sitting opposite each other without moving, with just the vodka going down in the bottle. "Brother!" Misha nodded proudly at his guest. "Kolya!" Kolya gleamed like a samovar. His pregnant wife, all brown and yellow in a cotton dressing gown, kept bumping into Gromov in the corridor, tenderly showing him her big belly.

They never fought or had rows, and their meekness simply encouraged the louts above to bully Masha and her mother, the most defenceless people in the building. Once one had phoned the police, claiming she had attacked him and slammed the door in his face, and they came round and demanded to see her papers. Gromov arrived in the middle of it after she phoned him, and found her sitting pale-faced at the table with piles of documents while her mother lay ill in bed, and the neighbours went on brawling upstairs and the cops didn't raise an eyebrow.

The bath had a rusty bottom, and above it a reddish stream of water seeped from a mildewing pipe down a crack in the wall, and he would wash under a forest of cotton knickers and dressing gowns in lukewarm water, because the geyser didn't work and no one could fix it. After ten minutes people would start banging on the door; he and Masha would share their food with the relatives, but one morning when her mother came back from the dacha where she was babysitting, someone had complained that the strange man staying with her daughter had stolen his pickles from the kitchen in the night.

He remembered those nights with her in her room when her mother was away, with the affectionate brothers next door and the drunks upstairs who were friends with the police, and the teenage rock bands howling from the neighbouring flats until three in the morning. The scent of lilacs, wet earth and rain wafted through the open window, and they huddled on a little handkerchief of happiness, besieged on all sides and taken to a place of unimaginable fullness. "I missed you, I missed you," she would moan, burying herself in him, and his soul howled as he remembered the building burning down after her hasty evacuation from Moscow.

For so long she had expected the world to end, and she was afraid of nothing, yet she was afraid when the war finally started. Hundreds of people in those early days were evacuated to the Caucasus, and she left with her mother for Makhachkala in Dagestan, three thousand miles away on the shores of the Caspian. From the happy newspapers it was obvious there was no danger in the capital, and life there was going on as normal. But after leaving she couldn't get back, because her housemates had set fire to the building, as if she had protected it by living there.

He remembered cutting through the courtyards to visit her, past a strange red building behind a high concrete wall. She had lived there for six years, but had no idea what went on behind it, and once he suggested she slip in through a gap. He followed, and the secret was revealed; it was a home for disabled children. When they reached the yard of the red building, the children ran out and crowded round them in identical blue sweaters, one with a runny nose, another with a harelip, gaping and howling at them and shaking their heads, desperate for love from these friendly strangers, and she would have fainted if he hadn't caught her.

Why hadn't they married? They had never considered it: it seemed a sacrilege when everything was ending. They both lived with this feeling, and the war proved them right. The lovers in dying Pompeii were beautiful, but not a wedding in the ashes. He rented a room near his parents and lived alone and could take her there – but marry her, turn her into a housewife? Rub along together like other couples? He wanted to see her now, and had got his leave to see her, and he was saving himself for her and wasn't visiting his parents in Moscow, although Moscow was on the way to Central Asia. But brief meetings on leave weren't the same as living together.

She could fastidiously, almost contemptuously, take his money, and he understood her childish defensiveness. But she would never marry him and he felt the same, because it would mean lying, and she was so incapable of lying she had snatched her hand from his once and run off when she heard a slightly false note in his voice. It never occurred to him to be angry with her, especially as he usually got his way. A petty man might think it was just the usual thing, with the rest thrown in free – and what if it was, at least it wouldn't have been a lie. Pretending they were living a normal life was a lie, swapping news and discussing friends. But their rare meals out at the Maki café weren't a lie. When they had money, Masha loved to eat. She ate a lot and without embarrassment, and he admired her for it, and when she ate or bought clothes, again when they had money, or darned his shirts, he would see how she could have lived if she had something to live on and somewhere to live – in a bigger sense, in a world that wasn't dying every second, in a way more worthy of her.

The problem was that the worse people were at things, the better, these days, and she was good at whatever she did, which was why she did almost nothing. Being good at things merely hastened the destruction of the world, ripping the worn canvas from its frame, instead of prolonging the agony of this half-life.

She liked good clothes and hated dressing within her means, and she preferred living without money than having to fight for it. Others pontificated about all or nothing. She just lived this way, like an exiled queen, he told her, forbidden by ancient protocol to drink carrot coffee and drinking tap water if there was no proper coffee, from the last cup in the family tea set.

He was rewarded with a rare smile when he said this. In general she didn't talk much. As he was then, before he developed a samurai hardness, he would get angry with her for disdaining everything and everyone. He had even shouted at her once, and she wasn't offended and hadn't run away from him, because his anger was genuine and he wasn't being some half-person, going to work every day and seeing honour in his slavery.

They were walking in the Sparrow Hills, and he had given her some trousers he bought from a market to surprise her, and she angrily refused them, saying she didn't wear clothes from markets. He lost his temper with her – who did she think she was, she didn't work and she didn't dress from markets! And she explained with a sudden seriousness that she couldn't, it was better to have nothing, and he stopped being angry with her and understood it really was better for her to put nothing on her nakedness than second-hand rags.

He threw them over the railings of the watchtower, and they were picked up by a local Joe, as homeless men were called, who made money taking bottles to the bottle banks that appeared before the war, like a dying man rummaging through his wretched inventory of shirts and blankets to make sure he had something left at the end. The Joes lived from old recycled things, and were old and recycled themselves, then they all vanished from the city. Some escaped, some were arrested, and on that day in the Sparrow Hills, Gromov said something about the horror of this human debris, and how he was afraid of becoming one himself.

"Don't be," she said firmly. "They're the best ones."

"Why?"

"Because they're pure, they don't lie."

"And me?"

"You lie sometimes. We all do, don't be angry." She added. "It's like the castes in India. At first there were three – the Brahmins, the warriors and the others, who worried about the necessities of life. Then the traders and merchants got together to make another caste because they didn't want to be lumped with the Joes, so there were four, the Brahmins, the warriors, the ordinary people and the Joes. It's fair in a way, the upper castes and the untouchables can think about life, the rest of us lie. It sounds false, but it's true."

She worried all the time about being false. He had thought of himself then as a leader, a Brahmin, because he wrote a bit and was in touch with events, then he realized it was time to be a warrior. It wasn't that he had lost faith in his Brahmin skills, it just wasn't the time for them – people didn't divine from the stars in Pompeii when the ashes came down.

Before the war it had seemed so pointless to do anything that anyone with a computer either wrote blogs or played Solitaire all day. Gromov couldn't stand these vacuous outpourings on the net, but played a huge amount of Solitaire. It was as if everyone was searching for answers, but the answers were always different, shadowy insubstantial essences floating and colliding in the air, from which something concrete always seemed about to emerge. But nothing emerged, and it was clear something sad and bloody was taking shape before his eyes.

There was no time or energy for a full-scale terror, and instead it would be something clumsy and illiterate, ridiculous for torturers and victims alike, as they faced each other at the wall of death. The actors knew their lines but were sick of them and knew no others, and you had either to smash the theatre or grow a holy rage in yourself and go to war, no matter how wrong and degrading it was. The rage grew, and now the theatre was crumbling and the rot had nowhere to go.

Gromov knew he must play his part to the end, a minor actor in a failing show repeating, "Dinner is served" night after night, knowing the star was drunk and the hero had forgotten his lines, while the audience brazenly made off with the seats and curtains. His role was simple: stand up, sit down, right shoulder forwards, die when he was ordered to or at his own command.

Masha had written very little from Makhachkala, in her small straight hand. Life clearly wasn't easy in the mountains, near the border with Chechnya. But her mother had relatives there, and she used to visit Dagestan as a child and got on well with her Dagestanian relatives, and although the local people hated the Russians, they didn't attack them. She even had work, a hack editing job for the local prince, who was being immortalized in his lifetime. Her mother suffered from the heat and couldn't work, and if it was only a matter of her own survival she would never have taken on *Forty Teachings of the Stay-at-Home Nomad* for all the Turkish delights and watermelons in the world, and would have preferred to die of hunger with a smile on her face.

He had known the moment he set eyes on her, from the first word she spoke, that she would have the strength to smile at the end. Careless with her mindless jobs and with small things, she was steadfast in the main one, and however hard it would have been to live with her, there was nowhere he would rather die than in her calm disciplined presence.

He listened to the ticking clock, his snoring landlady and the rustling mice, and he thought of her and called out to her for the thousandth time, knowing everything would be different when they met, and that she too would be different. She had sent him a photograph of herself, and he had torn it up because it was a compromise, and they both hated compromises. Her cropped hair was bleached from the sun and she was dark and very thin, wearing a garish cotton robe. The photo was faded, as if from the heat, and the lines round her mouth had become more pronounced, with that expression he knew so well, as if saying, "Let's see what you come up with next!"

He remembered the day they met on Tverskoy Boulevard and, in the middle of the usual drunken discussion about careers and prospects, she had gone to him and taken his hand and said, "Let's go," and suddenly careers and prospects no longer mattered.

He remembered her tense back as she drew the curtains, and the way she would slip off silently at dawn, without kisses or notes. He would wake sometimes and pretend to be asleep, and after she left it was hard to believe she existed, and he would wait impatiently for the nights when he could see her again. Then sometimes she would vanish for a week, or even a month, reappearing to explain in a few words that she had tried to live without him and people in general, and she couldn't, but next time she would manage it.

He was trying to prepare himself for this, but it terrified him. They were too similar for him to lose her. He liked her taciturn melancholy nature, her unsociability, which released him from the petty jealousy that, although not as keen as it used to be in the early days, still hadn't disappeared completely. He liked her clothes – not many, but all of them good. He liked her low modulated voice, the voice of a singer; she had studied music seriously until she was fifteen, but she concealed her musical talents from him and never sang to him, because once she dropped something she dropped it for good. He liked the way she would resist him, then grudgingly, gradually drop her guard and surrender and laugh, and at night, when she couldn't stop herself, she would cling to him in her sleep.

He remembered her and knew he wouldn't get back to sleep. Perhaps it would come later, but now it was only three. He pulled on his boots and went out to check the posts.

* * *

It preyed on him that he would lose his leave, and perhaps his dream was an unconscious expression of this. He still hadn't fully mastered a samurai resilience. He had learnt to be unafraid of death, and the battles had often been so sickening that death would have been preferable, but he was afraid of losing his leave and the humiliation that went with the denial.

Zdrok liked nothing better than to turn an officer back at the door. "Wait, what's this, comrade Captain?" he would say. "I see from your membership card for the Stormy Petrel Sports Club that you haven't paid up since January. You're an officer, do you take us for children? About turn, I'm giving you a penalty point and you'll spend your leave standing in for the duty officer for letting your membership lapse!" (An officer would often stand in for the duty officer these days, gargling his name at the morning meetings.)

Gromov inspected the wet little soldier guarding the munitions dump, who would have jumped like a rabbit if there was an attack. Then he checked the guard at the supplies hut, and was heading for the punishment shed at the edge of Baskakovo when he noticed someone was already there before him. Outside the hut, his bald head shining in the rain, stood Inspector Gurov.

"Ah, Captain," he yawned. "Can't sleep? Afraid you won't get your leave?"

Gromov shrugged.

"Don't worry, you'll get it," Gurov nodded distractedly. "You're from Moscow?"

"Yes."

"You're seeing your parents there?"

"No, comrade Inspector, I'm seeing my girlfriend in Makhachkala."

"Makhachkala, excellent." Gurov peered at him with sudden interest. "Look here, why don't you go via Moscow? I could get you five extra days, how does that sound? God must have sent you, my dear chap, I've a little job for you. Go on, beat it, you're dismissed." He turned to Private Pakharev guarding the shed.

"Abandoning my post, comrade Inspector..." he said nervously.

"Smart arse! Talking back to a Seventh-Level inspector! You'll do five, six, fifteen sentry duties for me over your normal shifts! Name!" Gurov said in a thin voice.

"Pakharev," he said, offended.

"You think some old walrus-face has come from Moscow? Answer me!"

"No, I don't!" he said.

"Thank God. Am I your wife or mother or your comrade-in-arms? Do I sleep next to you and fart in my sleep? Stand to attention when a Seventh-Level inspector addresses you, don't slouch!" Gromov automatically straightened up and threw back his shoulders.

"No, you aren't!" he whimpered.

"About turn, on your knees!" Pakharev flopped down into the mud. "March on your belly! Do the leopard's crawl to the patrol hut! If I see you get up, you'll clear an entire section of the trench!"

Pakharev crawled off in the rain with his scrawny backside in the air.

"Varangian thug," Gurov muttered incomprehensibly. "Are you one too? Did you do the courses?"

"No, I'm not," Gromov said. "Firstly, comrade Inspector, I'm not a thug; secondly, I'm not a Varangian; and thirdly, I'm not one of your Pakharevs who shits himself when an inspector insults him. I'm an officer, and you know where you can go, you Moscow rat!"

If he hadn't dreamt of poetry and thought of Masha he would have said nothing of the sort to the Inspector. But remembering Masha made it impossible to put up with his oafishness. He was carried away by the same emotions he felt in battle, and was afraid of nothing at that moment, especially as there were no witnesses and Gurov couldn't prove anything, and the Staff would always take an officer's word over an inspector's.

He looked at him with new respect. "Well said, Captain, a reply worthy of an officer," he smiled. "An inspector tests people in different ways, not many people understand that. A soldier who disobeys orders is a bad soldier, but an officer must stand up for himself, even to an inspector. You've earned yourself those five extra days. Now tell me, does the wheel go round the well?"

"I beg your pardon?" said Gromov.

"I'm telling you, stop the wheel, but don't break it!" he said sharply, and suddenly it seemed to Gromov that he was hearing again the strange language he had heard in Galya's cottage that night in Degunino.

"I don't get you, comrade Inspector," he mumbled.

"So be it. Trust everything and test everything. You're just what I need at the moment," said the Inspector. "The Varangian son of Odin as he is today is a mongrel, don't you agree? What about you, Captain, are you a mongrel?"

"I still don't get you," Gromov frowned.

He stared at Gurov; he looked drunk and spoke like a drunk, but he didn't smell of drink.

"Never mind, you don't need to, it's not for everyone to know. Why do you think the army has so many inspectors? Now listen to me carefully. In a minute I'll bring Private Voronov from the shed, who Major Evdokimov has prepared on my personal orders – my personal orders, I repeat – for a special assignment, and you are to escort him to the village of Koposovo in the Plakhotsky district, fifteen kilometres north of Blatsk. Don't take notes, I've printed the instructions for him and will give them to him myself. If these are carried out correctly you can then accompany him to Moscow and deliver him to his family. Afterwards you have no further duties and your time is your own. Is all that clear?"

"Perfectly," Gromov said, understanding nothing.

"It's vital you make it, Captain," Gurov said, lowering his voice. "You must be in Koposovo no later than 12.40 a.m. the day after tomorrow, Voronov can't do anything after that. It's twenty-four hours on the train. You'll be met there by this man and a girl."

He pulled out the photograph of the man he had shown Ploskorylov earlier and held it carefully in front of him, shining a torch at it and protecting it with his sleeve from the rain. "Come closer, take a good look. Now I'll explain your assignment. You're escorting Voronov for me personally, not as part of your regular duties, and you'll answer to me for him with your life. You're key to the operation. If Voronov comes back and says sorry, comrade Captain, can't do it, you must shoot the girl and the man yourself, do you understand?"

"No, comrade Seventh-Level Inspector," said Gromov. "As an officer I don't kill civilians."

"Oh yes you do, Captain," Gurov said with a level voice. "You certainly do, or I'll send you to Zhadrunovo. Have you heard of Zhadrunovo? No sheep graze where you'll go." He stood very close to him, with his shiny head and his little glasses. "You'll do it and I'll sign the papers to get you promoted, or I'll find you in hell and string you up by your nuts and hunt down your girlfriend in Makhachkala, and there'll be nothing left of Makhachkala by then. Or don't you know me, Captain Gromov?"

"I don't kill civilians, comrade Inspector," he repeated.

"You took the military oath, didn't you?" Gurov asked, pulling himself up to his full height and adopting the "Command" tone from the Rulebook. "Locate the individuals in the village of Koposovo and, if necessary, at the signal of Private Voronov, shoot them. That's an order, Captain! Now wait here while I get him. You must go at once to the station. I'll send my car. The train leaves at 6.53."

He paused for a second and stared at the ground while the rain beat down. "There aren't enough of us, you see, five per cent at most. If there were more we could do without you. Fine, I said nothing and you heard nothing."

He went into the shed and Gromov stood in the rain, unsure if he was dreaming or not.

Five minutes later he came out with the skinny, dishevelled Private, who was missing his belt. He handed him a bag. "Your documents are signed, there's all you need in there, you can get dressed at the station. Afterwards stay in Moscow and sit tight. If things don't work out in Koposovo, report directly to him, he's your first line of defence." He nodded at Gromov. "Good, off you go! Onwards to Excalibur!"

"Your good health, comrade Captain!" the Private grinned at Gromov.

"My driver's at HQ," said Gurov. "March there and I'll send him to collect you."

Gromov and Voronov trudged off in the rain.

"People call me Lyosha," said Voronov, still dizzy from his miraculous escape, forgetting the proper way to address his superior.

"People call you Private Voronov," said Gromov. "Be good enough to follow the Rulebook."

* * *

The train waited two minutes at Baskakovo station. The compartment was empty apart from a few little peddlers and black-marketeers huddled on the luggage racks, hugging their wretched belongings to them.

Voronov couldn't contain himself for joy, and longed to talk. Gromov glared at him; he knew in his heart the lad had done nothing wrong, but it didn't mean he had to be friends with him.

"Are you from Moscow yourself, comrade Captain?" he asked.

Gromov wanted to tell the Private to mind his own business, but he just nodded curtly.

"I've been away six months, I haven't seen my mother, or my girl," Voronov said dreamily, hoping to impress the gloomy officer and melt his heart by mentioning his girl.

Gromov said nothing. He didn't see why he had to waste his hard-earned leave dragging this jabbering pipsqueak to Koposovo, where he definitely didn't intend to stop.

"I'll shut up in a minute, comrade Captain," Voronov chattered happily. "I just... You see, I just met this extraordinarily good man. I'd forgotten people like him existed, I thought they were all like this..." He tapped the wooden seat. "Don't talk if you don't want to, but I know you're not one of them, that's why I can say a human word to you."

Gromov was taken aback by his familiarity, and shot him a withering commander's look, but Voronov held his gaze, as if his brush with death had knocked all fear of earthly commanders out of him. Gromov had seen plenty of this in the first year of war, when there were real battles. You could only command those who hadn't been shot yet, because the ones who had weren't afraid of being shouted at, only of incompetence. Which was why he didn't shout at Voronov now, he merely said, "You see, Private Voronov, being almost killed doesn't make you a hero. If you'd been at the Front I could talk to you like a soldier, but all I know about your heroism is that Inspector Gurov needs you for some reason, and he's above you in rank."

"Yes, of course!" he cried eagerly. "Of course I'm not a hero, but people can talk sometimes, can't they? Or do you only talk to heroes?"

"With a civilian it's one thing, but you're a soldier, only you've done nothing to show me you're one yet, apart from wear the uniform. You see what I'm saying?" he said, enunciating clearly.

"Yes, I do," Voronov said, feeling all his happiness drain out of him. He thought the officer escorting him would be warm and human, like Gurov. But it turned out Gurov had simply picked some random officer, not an animal exactly, but not a living soul, just a good working machine, a rarity among the rusty unoiled machines of the Varangian army.

The train juddered and moved off and it grew light, and behind the window drops of rain made flowing rivulets on the glass. Hills and valleys flowed past, and gullies and embankments, and a long grey river with sandy shallows.

"Permission to go out for a smoke," he said.

Gromov looked him up and down. "Put your belt and cap on, civilians will see you."

Voronov went to the corridor and banged his head on the window. He had no tobacco, he just wanted to be alone with the fields and the river flowing past.

"Not alone in the field, little road,
Not alone…"

He didn't sing the song out loud, just murmured it to himself. A man smoking in the corridor with black hair and a big beard covering his face stared at him suspiciously, and he sang on in silence. He didn't know where he had heard it – on television probably, in an old film about people travelling on a slow train through a grey landscape, with little boys waving at them from the cuttings.

"Not alone in the field, little road,
Not alone weeping, not alone sleeping,
Not alone in the field, little road…"

Chapter Two
The Kaganate

1

Waking next to Zhenka, lying straight and still on her back in a state of absolute repose, so unlike her normal exuberance when she was awake, Volokhov thought he might as well die right now. For so long death had been the constant background to his thoughts, whether it was a premonition of the impending war, or because as a historian he was in the habit of taking stock of his life. What guarantee was there that he wouldn't die tomorrow? Each year you lived through the day of your birth and the day of your death. This thought had come to him as a child and kept surfacing in Moscow, where there hadn't been a proper life for a long time. Death waited – twenty-eight was too young to die; he wanted to know how it all ended. But here, lying next to Zhenka, he wouldn't have minded dying now, so as not to spoil the moment. He had a horror of compromises, agreeing to this or that instead of what you wanted, clinging to the idiotic hope you might live to be authentic – and then what?

"Your place or mine?" she had said the evening he arrived, when they were finally alone together after a long noisy dinner with friends. They were sitting on the street at an outdoor café, arguing about the new borders, joking that someone passing looked like a terrorist, until someone mentioned a friend who had died or was injured in the last bombing, and the joking stopped.

They noticed each other at once. He couldn't believe she had chosen him, but her every look said "That's right, you've got it!" She laughed at his artless jokes, and when she told her stories about her work as a journalist concisely and well, she seemed oblivious to the general admiration and to be talking exclusively to him.

"Right boys, I'm off to show our new guest the town," she said. People whistled and winked, and Volokhov caught a look of hatred from a talkative youth who had evidently been trying to impress her; he smiled at him as if to say, sorry, these things happen.

"My place," he said, and she liked that, but after that first night they moved to hers, where she had her computer and books and cameras.

Her work involved constant trips away, and he quickly became part of her insane rhythm, with its unpredictable absences and night departures. He didn't push things with her, and spent a lot of time on his own working, turning up late to see her and not asking where she had been. "Aren't you jealous?" she would ask him, and he would say, "Yeah, you're driving me crazy."

At night, and sometimes in the morning, at that blissful lazy hour when time melted like a sticky dribble of Turkish delight, he felt so blessed he couldn't imagine her wanting anyone else, and he would wonder if such an abundance of life wasn't too much for him and he would have to pay for it later – unless of course he had already paid for it in his past.

Life was almost unbearably fierce and intense here, and all he needed to be completely happy was to know he had a right to her. Perhaps he should try simply to enjoy things like a tourist. At any moment he might be hit by a stray bullet or blown up at a bus stop, and people here behaved as if the endless bombings were the least of their worries. You're bombing us? For Heaven's sake, we go to extremes ourselves all the time! As a teenager Zhenka had ridden motorbikes and run wild, and it was this wildness in her that he loved; the longer he spent with her (he had two months here in all, and three weeks left), the more sorry he was that God hadn't made him a Khazar. Of course he was proud of his difference and wouldn't change who he was, but with these people all feelings were sharper, even their feelings for their country, perhaps because it was smaller.

He promised himself to consider the reasons for this when he got home. He was already getting used to the idea that he would soon be flying back to autumn Moscow, and she would be sharing her low folding bed with God knows who, with the same abandon as she had shared it with him. It was a beautiful promiscuity, and it wasn't for him to moralize, and he thought with sadness now of Moscow and the Institute and his fellow Alternatives, his friends from the grim days, for his country had become a place now where sticky half-truths ruled.

Sometimes he thought he would gladly have packed it all in and moved here. But emigration shouldn't be confused with tourism; they had welcomed him wonderfully, and could just as wonderfully do without him. Not Zhenka of course, but Zhenka had a simple rule: to live each minute as if it was the last. It was a good rule, but selfish: you wanted someone, and a month later you wanted someone else.

It was curious how similar the Russian Alternatives were to the Khazars, although none of them here studied Alternative history and the official version ruled. He was keenly aware of this: the newspapers and the Knesset and every gathering Zhenka dragged him to cursed the government and squabbled constantly, but unlike in Russia it all seemed to him something sweet and friendly and parochial.

There's a Japanese sauce with no taste of its own that makes fish taste more fishy and meat more meaty, and it was like that here in the Kaganate. The sun was more sunny and quarrels were more quarrelsome, and even death, spilling constantly into the air, was more deathlike. And when Zhenka's mobile rang in the night and she would jump up and run off somewhere (he remembered her hopping barefoot on one leg, cursing as she wriggled into her jeans, clearly proud of her professionalism as she dictated something in a language he didn't understand), it seemed to him that life here couldn't be more alive.

At the time he thought this was simply because he was with her, although what made her this way he had no idea. Sometimes a wild passionate girl was born, and there weren't many of them. Even her temperature was always a little above normal, and when she fell ill at the beginning of July and stayed at home with a temperature of thirty-nine it suited her: he had never seen her so calm, languishing in bed, gazing dreamily at him with her hands folded behind her head, telling him about her early childhood in the Urals.

It was strange how little she remembered of Russia, and how wonderful she imagined it to be. Sometimes he dreamt of taking her home with him, journalists like her always found work. Then he would pull himself together. She was brighter than the average scribbler, that was all; her knowledge of Russia was zilch. But to begin with he could support her while she looked for a job; she couldn't endure more than a week or so without one. And sometimes he felt sure she would agree to come with him, but he was afraid to suggest it because a rejection would throw him into despair, however sincerely he tried to tell himself she was a free agent.

He had had a girlfriend in Moscow, whom he had lived with for two years, until he ran away from her meekness and her perpetual sadness. She was a strange girl, who always went with the flow and never argued with anyone. He had almost forgotten her – what was her name? Valya. She was in his year at the Philosophy Faculty, a philologist and folklorist in the Humanities department on the floor above him. They had lived quietly and comfortably together, but he didn't want to go on living like that, he could never understand what was going on in her head. Sometimes she would come back from her field trips with little rhymes the peasants had told her which she would repeat to him: "Cobbler, cobbler, mend my shoe, stitch it up by half-past two." "Up the ladder, down the wall, a bag of buckwheat will feed us all."

He had heard something like these rhymes before, he couldn't remember where, in Bulgaria or another of the Southern Slav states probably, and he understood her folktales even less, in which good never flourished and was always beaten down and suppressed. He remembered one about an old couple who had a little magic mill that ground things by itself, and a rooster, a useful rooster who took care of them and was the breadwinner.

One day a nobleman passed the cottage and stole the mill. The rooster flew at him and sat on his collar, crying, "Gentleman, gentleman, give me back my mill, my darling golden mill!" The nobleman ordered it to be roasted, but it escaped from the oven and again flew at him, crying, "Gentleman, gentleman, give back my mill, my darling golden mill!" The nobleman put it in water to be boiled, and it drank all the water, and the sad thing was that it went on asking for the mill – not threatening to peck out the nobleman's eyes or burn his house down, just praising his darling golden mill...

He listened to her stories and fled, overwhelmed by their humility and sadness. Ever since childhood he had been prone to these feelings himself, and if he hadn't conquered them they would have consumed him in these sad times.

Zhenka was different. She was the first woman he knew whom he wasn't afraid for, and three weeks before he left, he finally asked her with an embarrassment he had almost forgotten here, where people said yes and no and were so direct, "Hey Zhen, why don't you come back with me?"

She stared at him with a baffled smile that grew wider. "You mean marry you?"

"I guess," he mumbled.

"I'm terribly flattered darling, but I'm a Yd. Most of us are here, didn't you know?"

"You mean an actual Yd, in terms of nationality?"

His first urge was to comfort her and tell her not all Russians were fools, and if anyone called her one he would punch them. But his masculine desire to defend her vanished, and she was laughing at his slow-wittedness.

"That's right, by nationality. How come you didn't know?"

He disliked this patronizing tone from someone five years younger than he was. "I know as much as I need to, Zhenka. That's where the historian differs from the journalist."

"Please don't be angry. I can't marry you or anyone else now."

"You mean until the Messiah comes?"

"Not that, until the Mission's finished. Now it's just the beginning."

"The beginning of what? A Khazar plot?" he scowled. The truth was that he was hurt. "Why didn't you tell me?"

"Sweetheart, I assumed you knew and were tactfully avoiding the subject because you're not native, it's not in your genes, even though you're so clever and you've got such a big nose! I'll definitely come and see you later Vol, but I'm afraid by then you won't want me."

"Why? Because you'll be ninety?"

"No, no, not as old as that. Wait till this evening, we'll talk then."

She hurried off to her shift at the newspaper, which always made him wild with jealousy, because he never knew whom she had slept with there or was planning to sleep with when he left, and before she got back he decided to ask his colleague and fellow historian from the Museum of Atrocities about the Yds.

* * *

His name was Misha Everstein, and he was described by a mutual friend of theirs as "so Khazar it's indecent". He belonged to a common type here, who took every opportunity to parody their Khazarness. He even imitated the local accent, although he himself spoke a rich beautiful Russian without a trace of an accent, and Volokhov found this more attractive than growing a long beard and speaking in a weighty solid tone like a rabbi. He was small, dark and bird-nosed, with a thin black beard and quick brown eyes, fussy, messy and talkative, gobbling his food and constantly rubbing his nose, digging wax from his ears and scratching his armpits, as if merging his own features with the comic stereotype. But he had the sharpest mind of anyone Volokhov knew. Volokhov formulated his ideas more carefully; Everstein would seize them the moment he uttered them and refute them in passing. From his articles, which he read with respect and often envy, he knew he was capable of thinking slowly and deeply, and he very much wanted to get to this level with him, but he always kept him at a distance. He felt he liked him, but that there was something conditional about his friendship, and that he was avoiding discussing anything important with him.

After making small talk for a while, Volokhov asked with studied casualness, "By the way, Everstein, I keep meaning to ask you to tell me about the Yds."

He had expected an immediate change of tone from him, but if he was surprised he didn't show it, and comically clutched his head: "*Oi vai*, they've got him! Are they after you, Volenka?"

"I just don't know anything about them, I'm ashamed to say."

"My God, don't be ashamed, I'll tell you about us, but your Zhenka should have kept her mouth shut. Didn't you know anything when you came here? Didn't some granny from Zhitomir tell you about them? Grannies from Zhitomir are always very talkative with goys, it drives them to such verbal incontinence you have to punch them in the mouth. When I leave this stupid country for Russia, will you defend me from the skinheads on the streets?"

"I think you exaggerate," frowned Volokhov, who was sick of stories of Russian Khazarophobia. "If we punched you all for chattering you'd have taken a twenty-year vow of silence by now."

Everstein yelped with laughter and leant back in his chair. They were sitting in the cool white room of the museum. Behind the window a huge sun melted and spilt into a puddle of gold.

He explained with his usual grimaces that Zhenka was a radical, whereas he was just a humble historian, and when he finally reached the nub of his argument, Volokhov at first took it as just one more local theory of which he had heard so many at the Institute. He was about to say "Yes, I always knew you were a wonderful Alternative!" but something stopped him. Everstein sat with his back to the sun and his face in shadow, and as he talked about the Khazars, his local accent disappeared and his vocabulary became more precise, and Volokhov was glad later that he listened seriously to him; if he had laughed, it would have shut him up.

And it was worth taking what he said seriously for a moment, not just as some faddish theory, but as a picture of an unrecognizably different world. He had studied Alternative history for twelve years and knew that every event was known in countless retellings, and an hour ago he would never have dreamt he would be sitting with Everstein in the cool white room in the sunset, noticing suddenly how he had stopped clowning and was speaking like a prophet.

Perhaps what he was saying was true, perhaps not. Each person picked facts to suit their own convictions. The Moscow Institute of Alternative History existed to classify the main versions, and Everstein's was better than most. What surprised him was that he hadn't heard it before. Now, just ten minutes after he began explaining it, he wasn't sure he hadn't secretly guessed it all his life. His simple, harmonious theory was that the Russians weren't the native people of Russia.

"By native I don't mean the ones who settled it first, or that it's defined simply by numbers," he added hastily, taking the words from Volokhov's mouth.

"Agreed," Volokhov nodded. "No one knows who the Rus were, they were just a dozen ancient tribes in the north, south and east."

Everstein nodded cheerfully. "But it's when you look at Russian life in the last fifty years that you see how they've always behaved like occupiers in a foreign country," he said. "How they've colonized and killed the native people so there can be no progress, like the colonizers in North America who brought nothing but fire-water and human bonfires, killing people and rooting out all traces of their culture so they had no strength to resist. The country's not yours, and only your conqueror's pride stops you admitting it. But what have you to be proud of, Volenka? No one ever resisted you." He was clowning again, with more winks and grimaces.

"So who could have resisted us?" asked Volokhov.

"Who?" Everstein was surprised. "The ones whose land it is, of course. You're a clever boy, Volenka, you know there was no Mongol Yoke. Yoke, shmoke, it's just another nationalist myth, there's a mass of evidence in the chronicles contradicting it. Which Mongols? Where were they from? It was the Khazars they were fighting on Kulikovo Field!"

"Well I suppose that figures, if you're the native people."

"Don't be sarcastic with me!" Everstein said with unexpected anger. The room had grown dark in an instant, as it always did in the South, but he didn't switch on the light. "It's the cry of the wounded patriot who hates his land and can't be free of it! Remember our Pales of Settlement, those reservations where your governments sent us under the pretence of protecting us? And when we broke out, you dreamt that up for us…" He looked out of the window at the deepening lilac night. "To our wilderness, the land of our fathers! Remember the first version of it in 1936, when you tried to exile us to Birobidjan in the Far East? Then you sensibly realized we'd be under your feet and the whole thing would start again, so you sent us to die in the desert with the Arabs! But it didn't work out that way, did it?" he chuckled. "We destroyed their olive groves and built towns and got on with them and gave them work – we didn't need olive groves on Mars! Then you made the mistake of creating Arafat. But it's too late, my friend, we're not leaving now."

"I see. Very elegant," Volokhov said, choosing his words carefully. "But I'm a bit of a historian too, Misha, and I know the old Kaganate was just a small state on the Volga where a few ethnic Khazars practised the Karaim version of Judaism. There are almost no memories of their culture left, apart from a lot of fairy tales about Ilya of Murom defending Russia against them, and we don't even know if Ilya really existed or not. So if you're saying the Russian state started with them—"

"No, of course not!" cried Everstein. "Who said the Khazars were necessarily ethnic? Do the Sephardi resemble the Ashkenazy? Does Zhenka look like a Khazar? And our culture's disappeared because you wiped it out! Even now you're trying to demolish the last of our fortresses, imagine the stubbornness! Forgive me Volenka, you know nothing of this new Varangian empire of yours that teaches everyone to unite against the Yds. I suppose you studied Marxism too?"

"It stopped with us. They abolished it in the mid-Nineties," he said gloomily. "It's a shame, there were some good things in it, especially the idea that everyone makes history according to their own interests."

"Well of course, we Khazars have our interests, to make your women sad and destroy your state, why deny it!" He laughed. "Do you ever wonder why you hate ours, and why you turned your beloved Revolution into a bloodbath?"

"But it was your people who made the Revolution," Volokhov said. "There were plenty of you in the government then—"

"Yes, I know!" Everstein said. "We were purged later, just before and after the war. Tell me Volodya, if you were lashed with whips for twenty years by the Cossacks, wouldn't you want to kill the Cossacks? If for fifty years you weren't allowed to work your own land, wouldn't you want to throw out the people who ruined it with their incompetence? Have you heard of the Jewish farming communes on the Volga after our Pales of Settlement were abolished in 1919? Of course you haven't, they don't write about them in your history books," he said with inexpressible contempt. "And when there was famine on the Volga the communes always had bread and meat because they knew how to farm them! They were burnt down in

1922, and again in 1929 – you think the people who destroyed them should be given medals? Then during the war you handed hundreds of us over to the Germans, and when Jewish girls were taken off to be shot, the villagers would howl, 'Kill the garlic-eaters! The place reeks of garlic!'"

He dropped his head and fell silent.

"So why won't she come with me?" Volokhov said after a pause.

"You asked her?" Everstein blurted out.

He realized he shouldn't have said this, and that Everstein probably wasn't neutral in the matter. "Not really, I just suggested she come and stay with me..."

"They're like Castro and his fighters, who won't shave their beards until there is world revolution. They'll only go back to their Russia when it starts."

"When what starts?"

"The Final Battle," Everstein grinned. "Now they're just waiting."

"If it's a story, it's a good one," Volokhov said after another pause.

"Maybe it is," Everstein sighed, as if all the air had suddenly gone out of him. "But when you go back to your Russia, you'll remember how you could call the police here and they wouldn't beat you in the kidneys so you pissed blood for three days. And you could visit the doctor and not feel it would be better if you died than waste a minute of this important man's time, who already has fifty old women at the police station gazing at him like God Almighty. And when you join your army – I know you've done the training – you'll defend this country that isn't yours, and your soldiers will eat barley and fart. Go home and see it all with our eyes, and remember how our women love, and how if you're lucky you'll earn their love. See how they don't want to give birth to a new generation in your country, and think what we could do with it."

"Yes, but there's almost none of you left in..." For some reason he didn't want to say Russia, as if he already felt like an occupier. It had probably been called something else once, and Everstein would be as offended by its new name as Petersburgers were by the name Leningrad. "So why does the killing go on? It's not only the Khazars. If it's a competition in suffering the Russians have suffered just as much – all our old women at the doctors, the beatings at the police stations, the arrests of the oligarchs..."

"You mean our Jewish businessmen, like Khodorkovsky."

"But Russians are being rounded up too. And it's them who have to fight in the army, and none of them want to—"

"Exactly, you prove my point!" Everstein nodded happily. He lit the table lamp, and Volokhov was struck by the gentle, almost fatherly expression on his face. Or perhaps it was just the shadows, and it was a magic lying Khazar lamp. "An occupied people can't defend their borders – how can you die for somewhere that's not yours? In the last war they had special death squads to shoot anyone who wouldn't fight. Don't deny it, it's true. I'm not saying there wasn't heroism, but why was it so suicidal? People threw themselves at the enemy out of despair, because they hated life so much, because the government had turned their lives into a nightmare, and they were cold and hungry and longed to sleep in the earth. They had no other reason to die for a foreign land. Life had been so devalued they saw death as a deliverance. I suppose they don't tell you at your Institute about the girls who volunteered to avenge their fathers. They were heroines, but they weren't dying for their country, they were dying for their fathers who they loved. Everyone had more reason to die the longer they lived. I don't deny there were a few idealists who sincerely loved Russia and its forests and birch trees, but they were mostly intellectuals."

"But the intellectuals are practically Khazar themselves, or at least half-Khazar, especially the Alternatives."

"Because you Alternatives know deep down who the true people of Russia are, unlike the other crazy meshuggeners. The ones who volunteer out of idealism are bullied the worst, and it's even harder for the peasants, because they think the land is theirs and they're reminded every second that it isn't. Your country's as big as Canada, why don't things grow there like they do in Canada?"

"Because it's waiting for you to return?"

"Because you don't farm it properly. How can you, it's not yours. I was in Moscow last summer, and I saw the countryside and the overgrown fields and rubbish tips and half-built houses. Why do you need so much land? You've grabbed more than you can manage and now you're paying for it, which is why there's no movement, no history. Just let us back, and you'll see how things grow!"

"And you'll discover Phlogiston?"

"Why not? Do you ever wonder where Phlogiston is found? It's where the breath of history is alive. Your history's dead, so there's no Phlogiston. Let us back, and there'll be Phlogiston and anything else you want."

"So why didn't you come back and work the land?" said Volokhov sharply. "According to Solzhenitsyn you had plenty of opportunities for your beloved farming if you'd just got on with it and got organized!" He paused to draw breath, and felt something terrible and unexpected happen – a moment later and he would have punched this man who seemed to be taking such pleasure in his discomfort.

"See how easy it is?" Everstein nodded with a triumphant smile. "You've convinced yourself, a good intelligent person, that the genetic memory of aggression is alive in you! I warn you Volenka, don't mess with me, I've learnt a few things..."

He spoke with such anger they were only a second away from a fight.

"Enough!" Volokhov cried at last to him and to himself. "I won't fight you, however much you want me to," he said more quietly. "I've learnt a few things too in our bad army. There aren't enough atrocities here in your museum..."

"I know, and I can answer your questions politely and tell you some of our legends," Everstein nodded peaceably. "Have you heard of Sorochin, where your Ilya of Murom routed the Khazars?"

"I read it was somewhere on the steppe – no one knows exactly where."

"You probably don't know that Ilya was one of ours, our Elijah of Emurom, a Zhidovin, a hero Jew, who went over to your side and betrayed his people?"

Volokhov burst out laughing. "You're not telling me Ilya was a Yd!"

Everstein looked calmly at him. "You think it's a coincidence that the artist Vasnetsov in his painting *The Three Knights* gave him such a Semitic appearance? Vasnetsov knew history, there are masses of allusions there, nineteenth-century Russian art is full of them – look at the horse's harness and headgear, the Khazar cudgel. I suppose you read that Ilya started fighting when he was thirty-three, and before that he lay dreaming on the stove – it's pure fantasy. The Russian word for stove, *pech*, is our old Khazar word for steppe, dear friend, meaning a hot flat place. The Rus took the word from us, hence the myth about Elijah's adventures 'on' the stove, whereas the Khazar texts speak of the hero's adventures 'across' the *pech*, the steppe, and it also explains the name of the nomadic steppe tribe the Pechenegs. So until he was thirty-three Elijah was a Khazar steppe warrior, the commander of the Khan's guards, until three pilgrims passed by, as your Russian schoolchildren write in their essays. These rogues, Russian spies, appealed to his vanity and promised to make him commander of their army. In fact they made him a sort of constable, but he adopted the Christian faith forced on him, even though before that he had knocked quite a few crosses off churches. And as the goblet was passed round at the Khazar's banquet, their Khan said, 'Hand me the goblet. Step up my Cossacks, deliver me from Elijah...' Ours caught him later, after the massacre at Sorochin, when our capital Tsetzar was burnt to the ground. Yours called it Atil, we called it Tsetzar, an old Khazar word the Romans took from us to name their kings, which doesn't mean 'chief' so much as 'god-given'. The scum always steal the best words..."

"Wait, you don't mean the Romans..."

"Well, Judea was a province of Rome. The Khazar civilization preceded the Romans, and our culture was legendary. No one can deny it, we're good at preserving our history – we have our beautifully written Old Testament. But anyone could conquer us, because we couldn't fight like animals even if we wanted to, it would have meant stepping back in evolution and reverting to savagery. You can't destroy people who've achieved this level of culture though, because it's based not on ethnic but ethical ties and inner solidarity. You're my brother not because we're both born in the same place, as your crude countrymen would have it, but because we share the same moral outlook, and that's stronger than blood. The Romans tried to root us out and punished us with the wandering preacher who was crucified, and a whole religion grew from it. Wait and all will be given to you, so don't complain. All the conquerors adopted it, the Romans, the Huns, your beloved Russians. You know how your wise King Vladimir converted Russia? It was in Tsetzar, two hundred kilometres along the river Dnieper, above what's now Kiev. He drove everyone into the river – women, children, old men – and they weren't allowed out until they adopted the new faith. It was called baptism. Hundreds drowned."

Volokhov didn't know whether to laugh or cry at Everstein's version of history. He knew evidence could always be made to fit any theory required, and as an Alternative he was paid to do just that, but the man was solemn as a preacher.

"So in that same year, after the Khazars were defeated at Tzetsar, the survivors vowed never to work the land again until it was theirs, to find other ways to survive and preserve their faith, and end their resistance only if it meant wasting our own and others' lives – there were so few of us left. You can see in the kibbutzes what sort of farmers we are, but we wouldn't work on a foreign land, or plough or sow it or harvest the crops while you managed it."

He produced a green folder with a magician's flourish from a drawer, as if he had already had many enlightening discussions on the subject. "Then in 1929, after our communes were burnt down, there was a memorandum from the Central Committee of the Communist Party stating that the Jewish Question no longer existed – so that was that! Here it is, Pravda, 20th December: 'The RSFSR is the country of the Jewish workers who defended it, guns in hand, and they need no other country. The right to Palestine belongs solely to the working masses of the Arabs and Bedouins.'"

He pushed his heavy spectacles up his nose and rummaged through more papers. "Until the mid-Thirties we sincerely believed we could revive our state. They were scared of us, you see. Rabbi Maze even said the Trotskys made the Revolution and the Jews were paying for it. But we still had some fight left in us, and for fifteen years we held on. They weren't bad years either, there was industrialization, collectivization—"

"In which half the peasantry died," Volokhov put in.

"Perestroika clichés, my friend! There weren't that many of us, we just helped to make the Revolution, and played our part, quite successfully too. But in 1936 they said enough was enough and we should move to the Far East. For some reason they were surprised we weren't keen – it was a lesson to us not to negotiate with the aggressor! And then in '53 we gave thanks when the Devil took your Coco—"

"The Devil, or did Stalin's doctors kill him?" Volokhov screwed up his eyes.

"The Jewish doctors' plot you mean, I thought better of you. It was your anti-Semites who invented that." Everstein waved an arm helplessly.

"I was joking. But tell me, Everstein, didn't the Russians suffer too, under you?"

"Yes, they did!" said Everstein challengingly, without much joy. "A lot! Because they resisted. They wouldn't accept the land was ours. When we asked them to give it to us voluntarily they refused, with mass sabotage and anti-Semitic attacks, and well, it was war. Even the worst of the Red Terror never matched Stalin's purges in the Thirties of the Jews who made the Revolution."

"But surely you did all right after perestroika?"

"Yes," grinned Everstein. "And we opened the borders and gave you the chance to make as much money as you liked, and we didn't stop you getting an education as you had with us..."

"And all the physics and maths departments in our universities filled with our future bankers and tycoons."

"Where else was there for us to go? Government was closed to us, and half of us had to change our names. It's not surprising we wanted power, and we were successful because the country's ours. And when Abramovich and co. had a free hand to run things we were the envy of the world. But you couldn't wait to get us, and now you've succeeded. Only our mountain people are holding out, and you're still killing them."

"What mountain people?"

"The Chechens, Volenka, the last detachment of the true Khazars who were driven back to the mountains. Didn't you guess? Look at their noses and beards, listen to their language. They're nothing like the Adygs or the Armenians, they're a completely separate tribe, the last heirs of the guards betrayed by Elijah. One of ours caught Elijah later though – the Zhidovin Solovei, the Nightingale Bandit, known for his special whistle. We call him Saul Oivai, and he wasn't a bandit of course, that was just one of your stories. For five years he hid out with his men near the ruins of Tsetzar watching Elijah's movements. He'd once been his right-hand man, and he escaped from yours brilliantly several times and was often saved by a freak miracle, which was why you called him—"

"I know, Chudo-Yudo, the Freak, there are stories about him," Volokhov nodded. "So Yudo means Jude! Of course, the heroic Jew, it all makes sense!"

"And you know what Saul did when he caught Elijah? He rode up very close to him on his horse, as close as I am to you." Everstein rose from his chair and leant towards Volokhov, who for some reason wanted to stand up and honour the solemnity of the moment, but he stopped him with a commanding gesture. "He said just one sentence to him, but it was enough. They're serious words Volenka, not everyone knows them, and it shows how seriously I take you that I'm telling you."

Volokhov sat rooted to the spot.

"It was very quiet," he went on in a low, powerful voice. "Just the two former comrades-in-arms in the forest under the stars, with Saul's men watching in silence in a semicircle around them. And Saul said something the Khazars almost never say, even to their worst enemies. He looked into Elijah's eyes and said very clearly, 'Woe to you, to Zhadrunovo you shall go!' Then he turned and rode off from the clearing where he had ambushed him, and Elijah fell to his knees and cried out: 'Release me! Lift the curse!' But he was a Khazar, even if he had been baptized, and he knew the curse couldn't be lifted."

"So what did he do, did he go to Zhadrunovo?" Volokhov asked in a dazed voice.

"Probably. At any rate he was never seen again." He sat down and grinned. "Powerful, isn't it? A beautiful legend."

"So where's Zhadrunovo?"

"I've no idea, I've never been there. It sounds real, doesn't it? Find out when you get back to Russia."

"I wonder if anyone saw Solovei after the curse, and knows what happened to him?"

"He became a storyteller after blinding himself in mourning for his best friend's death, and roamed the villages singing the ballads of the Zhidovins. Later the Russians edited them of course, killing their inner music so they're unrecognizable. We tried to reconstruct the originals and published them. I think there's even one set to Khazar music, but it's rather unofficial. Ask Zhenka, she'll tell you."

He stood up and shuffled through some brochures on his desk, opening and closing files and giving Volokhov to understand their time was up. "Ask Zhenka, she's the expert," he repeated distractedly. "I can share my ideas with you, but I know people migrate and we can't replay history. As far as I'm concerned, we should make the best of what we have and defend it to the best of our ability. But no, Zhenka's hard-liners want to go back. Why? Russia's not the same any more. God knows the Russians have done with it, they've plundered its heart. The only forests left are in Siberia, and Siberia will soon be Chinese. There weren't even any mushrooms when I was there this summer, I used to love picking mushrooms as a child…"

He finished his shuffling and looked at Volokhov.

"No, Misha," Volokhov said calmly, without moving. "It's dangerous basing theories on national feeling, and confusing nationality with ideology, like our bloodthirsty patriots. What's patriotism got to do with it?"

"The fact that your Russian patriotism has always been more about destroying than creating anything," Everstein said, standing before him with his briefcase. "You always need war. The defence of your borders, the need for victory, the praying and beating of breasts – without the beating of breasts, it's not prayer. But unfortunately for you, all Russia's periods of greatness have been when we briefly had power. When industry was constructed in the early Thirties, when we ran things in the Nineties…"

"When the earth was plundered as never before."

"When the greatest oil company in the world was Russian," Everstein corrected him. "When the deposits were mined properly and the profits went to fund educational projects. When there was a free press, which incidentally didn't suit you too badly, with your pleasant sketches and speculations – all published with oil money, which your patriotic government is now pumping into war. Of course the peasants suffered, and the middle class had to sell things in the markets, but now that yours have forbidden us to do business the families of conscripted Alternatives are having their dachas confiscated, *n'est-ce pas?*"

"I know," Volokhov said gloomily. "But you can't not see it partly as a reaction to what yours did."

"Which were a reaction to yours… It's a vicious circle, Volenka, and it all started in 862, when the Khazars' land was seized by the stupid Northerners, stumbling across Central Russia making war. Others beat them off, but not the Khazars. And now these people are calling themselves the true patriots of Russia and want another war, because it'll write everything off. And even the cleverest of you see any opponent as an insult to your national pride and have to punch him."

"What I don't get, Misha, is whether you believe all this. Do you really see me as a Rus who has grabbed your land?"

"I'm not sure." He gave him an honest look. "I just work with sources, and I know the Russians won't achieve anything in their so-called native land, and something's always left behind after each revolution." He looked Volokhov in the eye, then walked to the door.

Volokhov followed him, and stopped. "Wait, what's left? You mean the final solution of the Russian Question?"

"Or the Jewish one," Everstein smiled a painful smile.

"So what about 'This earth's big enough for both of us'?"

"Of course it is, there's a place for you too, but you must go back to it, somewhere in the North you love so much. Just stay out of ours. Find somewhere of your own, go to Greenland and plant apple trees. It's a tragedy you Russians don't have your Israel, but when we return to Russia, you can settle in the Kaganate if you like."

"We'll consider it," Volokhov said, catching his tone.

2

He came to on the street and headed automatically for Zhenka's. All around him, people were eating, shouting, meeting friends, bright, strident and noisy in everything. You couldn't imagine these dark faces and loud guttural voices on the streets of a Russian town. And now Russians were the enemy – it was crazy! Yet it was hard to see what the Khazars had in common with the hated Rus, with their fair skin and pale clear eyes and lilting musical speech. A magical speech, with its irregular stresses, like the dips and bends of a dusty Russian road. The eternal longing and melancholy of a Russian song, sharp as the jagged tips of the pine trees in the sunset...

He stopped and shook himself. All these trite images, like the patriotic clichés of the tabloids. What was this melancholy and longing, this Russian mystery everyone broke their heads on?

"To hell with it," he said out loud. According to the Alternative Guidebook, any idea could take hold, however far-fetched, and would soon become the only one possible. Point One: no one knew what had happened. Point Two: all sources were to some extent falsified. Point Three: there was no truth, only a series of asymptomatic approximations. Point Four: if something appeared to be true, it meant it wasn't. Point Five: forget everything you've read and march onwards.

In the end everyone believed what they wanted to, because it was simpler that way. But then what? The Kaganate existed, no one could deny it, but it wouldn't do to overestimate it. The poet Gumilyov had made that mistake in the last century, reinventing it as a sort of mystical state. Any schoolboy could find dozens of garbled theories on the subject. And would Russians really have sacrificed themselves in the last war to defend a foreign land? Yes they would, said his inner Everstein, whom he instantly tried to suppress; treating their own people as alien had entered the Russian blood. All this he must think deeply about and argue with, as with any idea of racial superiority.

Yet the Khazars weren't claiming Germany, he quickly reasoned, they didn't want Italy or Poland, Russia would be more than enough for them. Perhaps because they had already settled everywhere else and Russia was the only place left, as the Khazarophobe press claimed. It was easy to imagine them getting on with the Germans, the Italians, the Czechs, even the Poles. This eternal bitterness existed only with the Russians, and he had come close to punching Everstein, poor little Everstein with his birdlike chest. What insanity!

For an hour the street had been flooded with the dusty pink heat of evening, and he was reminded of the stories of Isaac Babel. No writer described Russia better than the Jewish Babel or the Jewish Zoshchenko – and who could doubt that the poet Anna Akhmatova was one, with her beaky nose and dark skin?

And what of Zhenka? He would leave her soon and go back to the enemy. Maybe he should give her a present, something cheap to remember him by – would she miss him, did she need him?

He caught himself thinking of her with a sudden jealous hatred. He had felt this jealousy before, but not this hostility, and it was all because of Everstein! Of course, Everstein was jealous, and was trying to drive a wedge between them, the crudest nationalist wedge, and he had only just realized this!

Behind him a car hooted deafeningly, and he jumped back and saw her old Mazda parked by the kerb.

"I've been driving round looking for you. What's wrong with you, where were you?" she shouted.

"What about you?" he countered, feeling all his hostility vanish at the sound of her voice. This was Zhenka, what other truth did he need?

"I was at work, where were you?"

"I was with Everstein," he admitted guiltily, squeezing his six-foot frame into the front seat of her car. "Are you tired?"

"Not really, just cross. Did Everstein enlighten you?"

"Yes, he did. Tell me honestly, Zhenka, is he in love with you?"

"Ever?" She burst out laughing and jerked the car forwards, throwing him back in his seat. He could never get used to the way she drove; everyone here drove like maniacs, and it was strangely at odds with their relaxed Levantine approach to life. "Ever's not interested in anyone, he's in love with Russia. To hell with him. Are you hungry? I'm famished."

"Yes, I am," he said, and he felt hungry and happy and in love, and didn't want to discuss thousand-year-old territorial disputes with her. Peace and love, make love not war. How could he have forgotten that? He had been under a spell, a pure spell. Woe to you Misha, to Zhadrunovo you shall go…

* * *

There had never been a time when Volokhov could honestly, without lying to himself, have lived under the same roof with a woman, talked about everything with her and still wanted her all the time. And now something was telling him this was wrong. He had never seen her before as the enemy, and these new feelings were strange and not entirely unpleasant.

They were in bed later with a night light burning. He lay on his stomach with his left arm dangling over the side.

"You were different tonight," she said suspiciously. "I could have screamed any minute, and that wouldn't have been good, would it?"

"It was like screwing the enemy," he said.

"Where did that come from?" She peered at him, instantly alert.

"I read an article in the Nineties once by someone who picked up a rich girl in a club, and he felt he was screwing the enemy."

"What made you think of it?"

"It's complicated. I thought if we're all occupying each other's countries, what's the guarantee we won't?"

"Well, it's true with us."

"Listen, Zhenka," he said as gently as he could. "If you believe that it's your business, but it's catching, like a woman I knew who was a Tolkien fan and began thinking of herself as a hobbit. You don't seriously think Russia belongs to you, do you?"

"I know it does," she shrugged. "And so do you, you just won't admit it."

"I see, and soon all educated Russians will know this?"

"They already do, books have been written about it."

"Really? I haven't read them."

"I love you, darling, what you don't know doesn't exist. You Russians are all the same, forgive the generalization."

He was afraid she would say something haughty and patronizing to him, as Everstein had. He had held back with Everstein – what was he to him? – but with Zhenka he would definitely have lost his temper and said things he regretted.

"Don't be cross, sweetheart, I didn't realize you were so innocent. I'll introduce you to people, good people, and you'll see we're no threat to you. We're just a sort of movement in exile for the return to our country, that's all."

"It's not that." He reached for a bottle of iced tea. The room was unbearably stuffy; it was odd he hadn't noticed this before. "I feel, God knows..."

"Don't you like me any more?"

"It's not that, and you know it. I just don't understand how it feels to be with the enemy. And in my case we see the enslaver enslaved, and his country going to the dogs without you..." He spoke more bitterly than he intended to.

"What's got into you, Volodya?" she said, with such sadness he immediately felt ashamed. "Neither of us chose this. What's the point of arguing when we've so little time left, almost none at all..."

"So it's all over when I go, if I understand correctly? We'll thank each other for a brief moment of happiness and not spoil it with long goodbyes?"

She sat up abruptly. "Listen, I've given you no reason... You meet Everstein and twist everything I say... I don't want to talk of you leaving. What does it matter how often we visit each other? I could live my whole life with you and never get bored with you, we could have a huge life together. The moment I met you and you were showing off about your stupid Institute, I knew you were someone I could leave everything for, and it's terrible! I just never thought I'd have to say it." She spoke angrily, because confessions weren't her style. "All these days and nights I keep trying to get it into your head that there's no one but you, not in my fucking past or my fucking future."

"Fucking's right," he said, and received a clip on the head.

"Bloody Russian, you'll never understand. I'll spare you when we get there, though."

"Zhenka!" He stared at her. "You mean you're coming?"

She looked back cheerfully at him. "Well, there's nowhere else for us, the Kaganate won't last another ten years. Not that it's any better with you."

"So will you let me in the cafés when you get there?"

"We let you in here, don't we?"

"Yes, but not everyone's like you and Ever."

"Well, firstly, we won't all return, some of us will stay here. And there aren't only our people in the Kaganate, you know, there are even some English ones, and the odd black one, believe it or not."

"So what will you do with me if you win, if it comes to that?"

"I don't think it'll be a final victory, even if you go off and build yourself a Russian Israel." She thoughtfully put her hands behind her head. "But let's just say it would be better if you all got out."

"What, all of us? Old people, children?"

"Well, our old people and children had to get out, didn't they? They'd no choice. And then Stalin finally did for us. None of this would have happened without him. He wanted to keep us in our Pales and ghettos, and somehow they flourished, but however well we cultivate them they'll never replace our own land—"

"*This* is your land! *This* is where your history was made!" Without meaning to, he had raised his voice.

"It's our birthplace, where hundreds of separate histories started. We won the right to it, and things grow best with us, but you think this is our only land?"

"I'm well aware how things grow with you."

"Well at least I don't shut you up and remind you of all the starving old people in Russia forced to sell cucumbers in the markets. To save our country we've always had to do extreme things – revolution, privatization. They're shock measures, but otherwise the patient would rot alive. Remember how in the Nineties there was nothing but dried milk in the shops?"

"No, I was just a child."

"I wasn't born then, but I've read the newspapers. We came and did what you couldn't do because you couldn't take the responsibility! Don't get me started on your wonderful history. You say the Khazars destroyed everything, but we industrialized and modernized the place, and when you returned with that leader of yours you destroyed it again with your bureaucracy and drunkenness, and yet again the Khazars were blamed, although thanks to us you could at least be let out into polite society—"

"And I suppose you won the last war, too," he said, and instantly regretted it.

"And what nationality had the largest proportion of heroes of the Soviet Union? And who did the Germans slaughter first?" She beat her fist on the pillow and turned to the wall. "Let's not discuss the war, it's too painful. You were probably taught that it was the Yds who set Germany and Russia against each other, and before that they were the best of friends? Two regimes, similar in every way. You can't tell me there was any real difference between them—"

"There's a huge difference," he said doggedly. "Fascism's medieval satanism, communism's a biblical utopia minus the mysticism. In practice there were similarities, of course. The difference is that under your hated Stalinism at least you had a chance…"

"For a while," she said, still facing the wall. "And only because the revolution that made your Stalin was mainly a Khazar revolution, and until '48 we still had some power—"

"Forgive me, I'm sorry," he broke in, staring at her shoulder blades. "I'll be leaving soon, surely in bed with the woman I love there are better things to discuss than Russian history."

She turned to face him. "It hurts though. Sometimes I see how much you have in common with your Varangian Huns, and you seem foreign to me. Even though I know—"

"But I'm not foreign, I'm not!" He embraced her and felt her stiffen. "What's wrong, Zhenka?"

"I'm afraid I'll have to fight you."

"There there, it won't come to that. Are you planning to massacre us and rip open our mattresses?"

"Don't joke about it, of course not. But I can't be half a person, and you're so Russian I'm afraid for you. And I had to fall for you, as if there weren't enough good Khazars around…"

* * *

She introduced him very soon to these good Khazars. It was a strange crowd. They were partly familiar to him from Moscow, and only seemed strange to him now that he was seeing them as Russia's native people. Most were under forty, which wasn't surprising, since they weren't allowed to settle abroad yet at their age, and the more he saw of them the more he disliked them, and the more he disliked himself for it.

It turned out Everstein had initiated him. (The very word "initiation" made his head ache, with its connotations of ritual dances around the campfire, *à la* Riefenstahl.) Until now he never imagined the Khazars could have irritated him so much, but at these get-togethers with Zhenka he found himself feeling increasingly ill-disposed towards them. He couldn't understand why, and limited himself to superficial criticisms, like the schizophrenic Pisarev criticizing Pushkin for the clumsiness of his poetry, when what enraged him was his success with women. He said nothing when Zhenka questioned him, knowing she was upset, but unable to formulate what he had against these good, happy, too good, happy people.

It wasn't that he saw them as his future conquerors and persecutors: he saw their desire for revenge as a sort of convenient convention that put the nation's life on hold, like waiting for the Messiah. What annoyed him was their sociability and their playfulness, like spoilt children. There was the feeling they had all grown up together, with a private language of shared quotes and allusions. They all came from the old Soviet elite and got on wonderfully with their parents, and even in Russia they would have prospered. Some lived in the Kaganate, others were visiting friends or travelling around, and one had spent a year globe-trotting. They all seemed to speak in nods and winks, dropping names and words unfamiliar to an outsider, and they would tactfully put him in his place. He was more or less up on things, and had read the classics and knew history, and he was familiar with some of the subjects discussed. It was that they were all on such suspiciously matey terms with Russian culture, particularly the Khazar aspects of it, that made him feel an outsider. This was their milieu, and they were as at home in it as if they owned it, and he was wildly resentful of them without admitting it to himself. It was their sense of superiority that galled him, although he couldn't have said how this showed itself. Perhaps it was just that they didn't take him seriously. He would make some comment, and there would be knowing glances and an ironic silence, then someone would say "Fine" and casually change the subject. He was the enemy, and wasn't allowed to forget it.

They were never rude to him, they just didn't bother to argue with him, although they argued fiercely amongst themselves, often forgetting he was there. The first time Zhenka introduced him to her friends, there was an argument about the Kaganate. Thirty-year-old Lena, who had emigrated from Russia five years ago, flew at quiet spectacled Ilya, a computer programmer from Moscow, who was staying here with friends. They had belonged to the same circle in Russia, and began arguing the moment they met.

"It's only here I can be a person!" Lena cried. "You can lie all you like about how you're not afraid there, but don't you see how they hate you? You do everything to make them like you, and every step you take there demeans you! You want to be like them, talk like them, drink like them, you beseech them to let you live with them, and they treat you like an animal!"

She fired this off with a terrible flamboyant self-regard, gesticulating and gasping at a cigarette, speaking in a low passionate voice ideally suited to weeping and cursing – and seeing all this abstract passion, Volokhov didn't trust a word she said.

Ilya replied phlegmatically that his family had lived in Russia for centuries, and he was damned if he would leave it to crooks and third-raters, and there would be nothing left of it if no one stayed.

"Let them have it! It should have happened long ago!"

He smiled wanly and said nothing, and she went on shrieking and smoking and waving her arms. Even the quiet words of a gloomy, handsome youth in the corner with languid oriental eyes didn't stop her: "Yes, but remember it's not theirs, sweetie." (These people always called each other "sweetheart" and "sweetie".)

"What do I care whose it is!" She turned her fury on him. "It's my life, and I'll live it where I don't have to prove I have the right to exist!"

"Live your life. Just don't tell everyone that escape's the only true path," Ilya replied calmly.

"What do you mean, escape? I chose to be with my people! I came here and purified my soul, which had almost disappeared after years of living in fear. What could I do there, where nobody recognized me for who I was?"

"You need to be recognized? You want people to love you, Lena?" asked a small vicious-looking man with a shaven head and two earrings in his left ear.

"Yes, I do!" She burst out laughing, switching so effortlessly from tragic rage to good-natured fun that Volokhov realized it was all a game for her. She was that female type he had always disliked for its vampishness and vulgarity. He found it all inexpressibly false – the cigarette, the gestures, the passionate defence of her own dignity, which had flourished only here with her people – and he realized to his horror that this type he disliked so much was in fact Khazar.

He shook his head, trying to shake off this unpleasant thought, and the aggressor suddenly awoke in him and he longed to tell them what he thought of them. Zhenka gazed anxiously at him and whispered in his ear, "Is she giving you a headache?"

After Lena and her babble he was sick of the lot of them, and mainly himself, because there was no place for him here. He couldn't join in the discussion. The Kaganate, alas, wasn't the land of his forefathers, he hadn't suffered the problems of assimilating in Russia, and he didn't want to argue seriously with those who considered it to be theirs, so as not to give their insane hypothesis the status of reality and let this little bubble of earth expand and absorb the surrounding air. He could barely restrain himself from saying something sharp and cutting though, after which they would again put him in his place. They were chivalrous young people, and always came to the rescue of their girls. The girls could be as rude as they liked, but anyone who dared argue with them would have to apologize to them. This was how they operated, with the girls at the Front, like freedom at the barricades; the strongest arguments came from the weakest of them, from women and children who couldn't fight. And somehow all this was linked to the cult of the mother – or rather the Khazar mother. Everything the Khazar mother said was sacred.

Apart from all this, though, they were a jolly crowd. They loved dancing, to the bright catchy local music that sounded slightly monotonous to Volokhov's ear, like the brightness of an oriental bazaar. And when they said "Let's dance!" it was as if they knew secretly that the worse things were the better for them, and every misfortune was just more money in the pot. It was during these passionate, almost ritualistic dances of theirs that he could see this mixture of ecstasy and despair. This is who we are, they seemed to be saying, remember us like this! He saw it on Zhenka's face, her head thrown back and her eyes half-closed with pleasure as it was when they made love, and he couldn't look at her and would long for revenge, and catching his look she would wink at him.

Once she had taken him to a concert given by Psish Korobyansky, a multi-instrumentalist who sang in Yiddish and ancient Slavonic, and played synthesizer, flute and guitar. He was fairly well known in Moscow, where he was considered rather fun, and he appeared in all the avant-garde clubs where dance nights alternated with philological and political discussions. He lived both there and in the Kaganate and toured the provinces, and his concert that evening was in the flat of his ardent and evidently non-platonic admirer, Masha Golytsina. Masha was the scion of two noble clans. The Golytsins were an old aristocratic family, and her father had worked in a government department headed by a beautiful Jewish woman named Liza Kagan, whom he fell in love with and married, and the genes of the Russian aristocracy mixed with those of the Khazar to produce brilliant offspring. For this brilliance Liza was forgiven her marriage to the enemy: the Khazars were generally tolerant of mixed marriages, and didn't condemn Zhenka for Volokhov – probably because he was another weapon in the approaching war, he thought.

Masha's elder sister taught in the States, and her younger brother specialized in the art of the Twenties. He had curated an anti-religious exhibition in Moscow, at which one of the paintings was of Christ soaked in Coca-Cola, titled *This Is My Blood*. He was almost arrested for it, immediately receiving invitations to lecture at three major European universities, and was currently giving a cycle of seminars in Heidelberg on 'Style and Ritual'.

Masha herself was large and loud, with dark almond eyes and a bitter almond-scented perfume – she even drank Amaretto. She and Zhenka greeted each other warmly and twittered about various friends of theirs he didn't know. In the corner of the large room, hung with Venetian masks (Masha was keen on the theatre and made them out of papier mâché), Psish was strumming his guitar and smiling at his guests. He too was large and rather stout, with a neat bald patch on top of his head fringed with long dark curls, and some little bells hanging from the wrist of his right hand which reminded Volokhov of the *tefillin*, the little boxes in which the Khazars kept their scriptural texts. Psish referred to his songs as psalms, hymns and even prayers, most of which took the form of a friendly chat with an omnipotent but indulgent father, with whom one could argue and haggle without offending in the least, and Volokhov was disturbed by a sense in them that always bothered him about the Khazars, that only they were eternal, and all others were merely temporary and transient.

People had various explanations for Psish's stage name. It was a sort of masculine variant of the feminine word for the soul, Masha had explained rather patronizingly to him the first time they met; Korober was the shtetl where his family had come from. He preached – apparently playfully, but with a deep conviction in his soul – the return to these places and to the special culture of the shtetl. He had a network of friends who collected Yiddish stories and folklore, and he insisted that Yiddish was more organic and accessible than Hebrew. It was the language of the Khazars who were driven out to Europe, Masha explained, and according to Koestler the living evidence of their exile. Some even claimed Yiddish was the oldest language on earth, the true ur-language of Judea and the everyday language of its people, unlike Hebrew, whose sacred texts could only be read by the few. Accordingly, when the Romans conquered Judea they had appropriated Yiddish, so convenient and practical, and it was the origin of all the Romance and Germanic languages. Psish didn't go this far. He thought the Khazars had probably brought Yiddish from Germany when they were driven out of Russia by the pogroms, and he wanted to preserve this wonderful jargon in which all the best Khazar texts were written. He even sang a few songs in ancient Slavonic, which Masha put down to his special tolerance. Sure they were the oppressors' songs, but there was something fiery and vital about their primitive pagan folklore about Veles and the rest.

All this Masha had told him before the concert. Now he was hearing the psalmist in person. He sang songs from his new album, *Little Soul*, which he addressed to his own soul, his psyche. His soul evoked warm feelings in him, and he praised it in Yiddish, before turning to his "little father", begging him "to be patient a while". Other songs from his album were in a mixture of languages, including French, Old Slavonic and English. (He liked to say he broke down barriers.) Finally, at the enthusiastic request of all present, he sang 'Cunt Mother

Russia' – "my favourite song about my country". "How wide you are, how deep..." he sang in a low peasant bass to howls of laughter, and went on to describe everything contained in her, including Rus, the Kaganate and the performer himself.

The concert ended, and he listened with a sweet smile to the applause. Volokhov kept quiet, feeling out of place at this gathering. A fat man named Osya then toasted Psish with an ecstatic reading of a three-page essay he had written about him, in a high chirpy voice and a style peppered with "metatextuality" and semiotics and a large number of obscenities.

"Do you like it?" Masha asked him.

"No, I don't." He felt the words had been forced from him, and he spoke quietly, but at that moment Osya paused to draw breath and everyone stared at him.

"Well at least someone here is honest," Psish said, genially brushing it aside, and people laughed. But Masha was seriously annoyed.

"What, really?" she said.

Volokhov knew he had nothing to lose. "Yes, really, I think it's rubbish."

"So do I, but nobody listens to me," Psish said happily.

"No, you don't, Psish," he said. "You like it very much, it suits you fine."

"What does?" Psish didn't understand.

"Everything, all this you're doing to literature."

"I'm not doing anything to literature, I swear!" he said, clutching his heart with a jingle of his little bells.

"Yes you are, you want it all to be like this, at least most of it. I'm sure you write real psalms, weighty serious things for yourself and a dozen of your chosen ones, but for the rest of us it's this nonsense, as if anything serious would be bad form."

"Sorry, where did you say you're from?" Osya enquired.

"Sorry, I'm from Moscow," he replied.

"Ah, I see, I'm from Moscow too." Osya smiled, as if he meant nothing by it. It was the way someone from the city spoke to some lummox who dared to butt in, taking him down a peg without him noticing, and he became even angrier with himself for allowing himself to be trapped in this ridiculous situation.

"It was great, Psish, really, very interesting," he said.

"I'm most grateful," Psish nodded.

"No, wait!" Masha was in earnest now. "If you allow yourself to say such things—"

"But you made me say them. You asked me and I told you," he replied sadly.

"So what's your appraisal based on, may I ask?"

"It's an opinion," he frowned. "Can't I have an opinion?"

"Come on, Masha," said the languid youth in the corner, whose name was Valya. There was always a languid youth in the corner – or maybe it was always the same one. By now Volokhov had learnt to recognize the Khazar tactic at these events: the girl kicked off, the languid youth defended her, then someone decisive would step in and clinch the argument. "The man doesn't understand, the man's chakras are blocked. Why don't we sit here and open his chakras?"

Volokhov had a sudden brief urge to open someone's chakras, even though he had always despised people who settled arguments with their fists.

"Oh no you don't," said Zhenka. "Don't talk to our guest like that, Valya!"

"Why not, sweetie?" he drawled. "The man spoke rudely and knew we wouldn't agree with him. He should have thought before he spoke—"

"So what if he was right? Sorry, Psish, I didn't like it either. You were sweet and funny in your blues period, but this wasn't sweet or funny at all."

"Fine, I asked for it," Psish looked at her seriously. "Come on, girls and boys, let's hear what you think. I'd like to know. No offence, honestly."

"Then let's discuss it like intelligent people," Osya said in his high voice. "Korobyansky shared his finished work with us, and to understand it we must know the context."

"Tell me why, Osya?" Volokhov said with a Psish-like silkiness, trying to arm himself with an unbreakable self-confidence and beat him at his own game.

"Oh dear, no one told me there would be children here," Osya shrugged, raising his eyes.

"Fine, we're all children and you're grown-up," Volokhov said even more softly. "You want to know what we think of your semiotics and structuralism in the History faculty, my friend? We think it's a cheap way to crush your interlocutor, a system of renaming things, a banal cabalism, like your love of ritual and magic games, and your books about secret societies and brotherhoods..."

Everyone pointedly looked away and said nothing, but it didn't stop him. "It's just a synthesis of vulgarity and cheap ritual, with no place for anything good in between. And the whole point of your cabal is to keep outsiders out, like a cult, and you despise anyone who's not in your cult. Maybe you want all literature to die, like the old Soviet Writers' Union destroying a writer from his first sentence. And the outsider says nothing, silenced by all the foreign words and names, until he finally gets sick of the word 'cunt' and the incestuousness and metatextuality, and says sorry, your literature and the theories supporting it are crap, excuse my French."

"Lord, why would I argue with you?" Osya raised his eyes again. "A savage has boarded our ship and pissed on our compass. To argue you should at least know the language…"

Psish hooted with laughter.

"Why did you bring this savage on board who pissed on our compass, Zhenka?" said Valya.

"Let's have some tea, Masha, my tongue's hanging out," said a florid heavy-browed man sitting next to her.

"OK, you sit there anointing your compass with the victim's blood, the savage and I are leaving," Zhenka said.

"I don't understand!" shrieked Masha, suddenly regaining the power of speech. "How dare you come here and…" She stopped and burst into sobs.

"Masha, darling, sweetheart, ignore him, he's not worth your little finger!" A plump girl in glasses, who had been looking at Volokhov with an expression of hatred that seemed to banish all rational arguments, jumped up to comfort her.

"Come on, savage." Zhenka pulled him away.

"If that's the case, forgive me," he said from the door.

"God will forgive you," she said, as they made their way down the stairs. "The Kaganate's a strange place. People argued when they were in Russia, but Russia's bigger. Here we fall out all the time over politics, but we have to make up because we all know each other and we have to live together. Ten times I've been with them on that ship and the same thing happened. You know what it was like during the boundary disputes? You'd break off with someone for ever, and next morning when you met on the street it was as if nothing had happened."

"Thanks, Zhenka," he said when they were in the car. "You stood up for me and you suffered for it."

"If only they deserved it," she shrugged. "That Valya and his chakras, the arrogance. He should get out and see what I've seen…"

"But isn't that arrogant too, in a way?"

"I've a right to be, and he'd better not hurt the people I love."

"He's probably in love with you. Is he one of your friends?"

"Lord no, he's one of Masha's, people from the Kaganate are much nicer. You would be too if you lived here."

"But would they take me?"

"No, you wouldn't pass, you're not devious enough."

She turned the corner and parked and winked at him, and he had become so used to her street and her building he was suddenly furious with himself.

* * *

All those nods and winks. It was the same when he read Nietzsche's *Zarathustra*, and had been disturbed by its occult language and didn't understand it. It wasn't their Kharzarness that bothered him so much as this secret confidence of the conqueror, knowing which way things were going and being on the winning side. But the winning side was entropy and disintegration. They guarded their secret brotherhood and threw wood on others' fires to save their invisible city, which was on no map and was therefore invulnerable to attack, and any death of its citizens became another brick in the wall of this city and helped their cause. They were the invisible enemy, who wanted the destruction of all states so they could stake their claim to the ruins. Impeccable tactics, because they had eternity on their side and there was no hurrying it.

The Protocols of the Elders of Zion had spoken of this. They were pure fantasy of course, popular with Tsar Nicholas and Hitler, and republished in Russia before the Revolution in a handsome edition by Sergei Nilus, along with the works of Father John of Kronstadt and the Tsar's other anti-Semitic fans. Nilus could think of nothing better to do than rewrite this French pamphlet, implicating the Jews in a plot to overthrow tsarism. But leaving aside Nilus's moral and intellectual qualities, Volokhov began to wonder if parts of it might be true. The style was weak, the author stupid, but what he was clumsily struggling with would be hard to deny. His methods evoked nothing but contempt, but the pogroms seemed a small thing compared to the mighty power of Khazars, whose ultimate goal was to take over the world. He felt all of this, but he couldn't explain why, as a heathen can't explain the wind. He felt nothing good could be asserted so aggressively, no freedom would produce the slavery that ruled in the camp of its defenders. John of Kronstadt and the others were a drunk witless crowd, fighting a tumorous growth with dirty instruments, but from the dirt and stupidity the growth had become cancerous and was in no way symbolic of truth and freedom. Truth and freedom must wait until the final victory. Afterwards the Kaganate could discard the humane discourse which was their main weapon, with old men, women and children at the front so the enemy wouldn't shoot. But as soon as the tumour consumed the enemy and spread, they would set up a regime that made the pogroms look like a picnic.

Everything would collapse into itself and they would ascend to the ruins, because the rust hadn't corroded their noble metal, and Volokhov was sickened by his attraction to the conquerors and his desire to make common cause with them. He thought of Nilus's writings about Prince Oleg, the medieval Varangian ruler of Kiev, who was avenged not by the Khazars themselves but by the snake in the skull. It would be hard to imagine a better symbol of the ancient Varangian wisdom than the dead skull, but why should he identify with the snake?

As a teenager growing up at the end of the last century, he had hated the constant sniping about Russia's imminent end. If his country was perishing from the enemy it would be worthier, but it was dying from decay, wheezing and demanding pity from the contemptuous onlookers as they winked and nodded and waited. And it made it no easier for him knowing the country mightn't be his. For a while he was afraid he would return from the Kaganate a confirmed Khazarophobe. Khazarophobia was an unforgivable sin in his eyes, like any national phobia but worse, since the Jews had done nothing to deserve it and their history had been exclusively one of persecution. Each nation had things to atone for. With the Germans it was their Teutonic spirit and *Bürgerlichkeit*, two world wars; with the Russians, their bloody history of torture and self-destruction. The English, the Italians, the Greeks, all had things to answer for; only the Khazars, robbed of their own state, hadn't gone in for mass purges or bloody adventures abroad. That was the horror of it, they had done nothing but be doctors and lawyers, lend money with interest and bless humanity with their skills. Hence their fantasies of world domination, to grab something for themselves. They had simply lived in poverty, meekly enduring the persecution and retaliating only against the Arabs, when they at last had a tiny state of their own.

Everyone had destroyed the Khazars, although the powerless couldn't be destroyed, only weakened. They winked and wailed, and their wailing seemed about to turn at any moment into a song of victory, which was why the most triumphant of their songs were so doleful, and the most doleful so unconsciously joyful – there was nothing so victorious as their vaunted defencelessness, he thought. Shame on him, what had he come to, how could he hate them so much? Could there really be something genetic in it?

Then he pulled himself together. Any man who loved a woman from another tribe would hate this tribe because he wanted her all to himself. If the Montagues and Capulets hadn't been enemies, it would have started with Romeo hating Juliet's family for daring to claim her. It wasn't Khazarophobia, it was banal sexual jealousy, he realized, and he stopped tormenting himself. One thing bothered him though: if she could drive him so crazy here, what would happen when he got back?

3

"It's probably best we don't write," he said at the glass doors of the airport, where she had driven him in silence. As usual she had some meeting or press conference later that she couldn't get out of, and they were both wonderfully restrained. It was like some film from the Seventies: a Siberian town, he's a visiting commander, she's a native, three days of happiness, then they part for ever, with the usual Soviet setting of lads in peasant shirts and women holding babies, and a Komsomol work group or spaceship in the background.

"What would we write about?" Unlike him, calmness came naturally to her. "People only write when things aren't clear. Everything's clear, even if it hurts. You love me and I'll love you for ever. I knew the moment we met – terrible, isn't it?"

He forgave her everything then, all her past and future sins, and at their last meeting many years later he would remember that moment at the airport, when his old love for her flooded his heart and almost choked him with tenderness.

"Yes, it's terrible. Writing would ruin it. Maybe I'll come and visit you?"

"Absolutely," she nodded. "Not for long, but I'm sure you will."

"Or you'll visit me?"

"I don't think so," she said evenly. "We'll have to wait."

"Will you warn me when it starts?"

"It won't be soon, let's see what happens."

"I'll come back, of course," he repeated. "I don't know when. Listen, Zhenka, I know I shouldn't say this, jealousy's a weakness, but don't sleep with too many people, will you?"

"Of course I will. You want me to go crazy without you?"

"You know," he couldn't help laughing, "I remember Alec Baldwin screwed five women all at the same time when Naomi Campbell left him, and he said even five couldn't replace her. I hope you won't replace me with five Khazars..."

"Of course I will, and it hurts," she said seriously. "Don't worry, I'll send them all packing when you come back, all two-and-a-half of them."

"Perhaps I should emigrate here."

"It wouldn't work. I can't tell you what to do, but you know how hard it would be. You're such a patriot – leaving your country for a woman..."

"Would you stop respecting me?"

"No, I'd respect you for it."

"You see, Zhenka, the thing is—"

"Yes, I know, I love you too, very much and for ever," she said, and ran off.

He tried to call her, but she had switched off her phone as he knew she would. Good for her, he thought. He felt sorry for his country if it had her to contend with.

He drank himself into a stupor on the plane to Moscow, and left Sheremetevo airport with a throbbing head, barely able to take anything in.

* * *

He returned at the beginning of October, and sometimes he glanced at her blogs on the Internet, dipping voluptuously into her writings without finding much of interest there. She obviously had a personal life but she didn't discuss it, writing in detail about the terror, politics, new people and places and her endless trips, and attaching photographs – her life went on without him exactly as it had before they met and while he was around, and this both hurt and comforted him; he couldn't lose his mind over a woman who managed so well on her own.

A week later though he phoned her.

"Hi, beast!" she said.

"Hello," he said curtly. "How are you?"

"Same as usual. I'm not bored."

"Don't do me any favours," he growled.

"OK, I won't. Be cross if it helps."

"And don't give me advice!" he yelped, then calmed down. "I know, I phoned you. Listen Zhenka, let's drop all this, why don't you come and stay with me?"

"I can't Vol, I keep telling you and you think I'm joking. You should come here, I'd be terribly glad to see you."

"Yes, I can do that," he said. Dammit, why play games, he had always been honest with her. "I miss you, that's all, and what's more I'm jealous."

"But why? You love me, don't you?"

"And you me?"

"Don't ask me that, you know I do."

He sensed from her voice that she was in a hurry.

"You're off somewhere?"

"No, I'm in the office. We can talk."

"And who's kissing your hand there?"

"No one at the moment."

"So you won't come here and you'll sleep with whoever you like?"

"You've got it, whoever I like," she said tenderly. "But my single professional life doesn't concern you, we agreed not to talk about it."

"I never agreed that."

"Well, tell me about your successes then."

"There've been a few," he said shortly. "I can probably get away next spring."

"Fine."

He hung up.

There were a couple of letters from her too, rather bland and impersonal, with a few comforting words dropped in as if out of kindness. But something else was happening to him. Usually he would experience a sort of melancholy joy on his return home. Whenever he was away he would think of his friends there with whom he had spent so many pleasant hours discussing Alternative history, and he would thank the Lord he was back in the rank, muddy waters of his birthplace. It was a matter of national pride for him to catch the bus from the airport rather than squeeze himself into one of the shared taxis, and he hated it when people complained about the way the Motherland welcomed its children back with squalor and chaos, from the first surly customs official to the stink of the lavatories. He liked to think all this misery would produce good people who could dream of great abstractions (it would be hard to think concretely in these conditions), and he always felt awkward in the States, where an honoured guest was greeted almost like family. He preferred this honest discomfort, living in unheated rooms and snacking on takeaways, and saw it all as a necessary precondition for an honest life, and it seemed to him that in exchange for comfort and security Russia's citizens were being offered a model for something incalculably greater. But over the next five years in Moscow, cracks began to appear in this self-preserving system of his, and however much he had mocked Everstein's rambling theories, his life here merely confirmed them, and he began unconsciously, then consciously, to find more evidence for them.

How else to explain Russians' attitude to their country, whose vastness seemed merely a burden to them? It was hard to know what to do with so much of it. Whenever there was a successful harvest the farms would let things rot, annoyed by all these surplus tons per acre, like a poor family with an unwanted child who has no right to exist but must be fed. No one on the street felt at home here, everyone was tainted by the same proud, almost sensual pleasure he used to feel when he jammed himself into the underground at rush hour, as if to prove to himself he could survive in this can of sardines, where everyone looked at each other with loathing, trying to read a book or grope the girl next to him. How dare we enjoy ourselves, we must suffer! Even the vandals trampling on the flower beds and tipping over the litter bins seemed to be doing it in the name of some invisible god, as if to say "Look at this, see what we're doing!" And he had never wondered before what "this" was.

It was only now that he was aware of having to prove his right to exist to people who in no way earned it. During his army training, the sergeant gave orders like a sergeant, and the major like a major, and above all of them stood the colonel, who in every way, intellectually and morally, was worse than the sergeant. It was the sacred principle of negative selection in all its glory. When he ran up the stairs and had to catch his breath, or chopped wood in the country and didn't always split the damp log at the first attempt, he would feel some invisible sergeant behind his shoulder, watching him with a true commander's contempt. These were rules of the game. No officer ever encouraged his men; only fear could force them to sweat for this buffoon in these conditions. Fear was the only incentive, and every achievement was devalued by the endless indignities and humiliations.

The problem was that no one wanted to work any more, and the few who did were regarded as idiots, and were pitied, if not hated. All work was for the Man, no one worked for themselves, and he knew from his studies that this was the first thing that happened in an occupied country. And maybe he had known it all along, and was simply angry with Everstein for expressing it.

No one in Russia felt their land or their home or their woman to be theirs; they could be taken from them at any moment, and they wouldn't be surprised if they were. As a long opponent of revolutions, who knew how they turned out, seeing the blade under the velvet and in any free spirit a mass murderer, he began to ask himself why people put up with the situation. And the answer was that they knew no better. You could put a Russian in chains and steal all he owned, and he would grumble for a while, but deep down he was resigned to it, because slavery had entered the blood of all who lived under the iron heel.

Everstein was right about another thing too. You could find sources to contradict the Khazars' right to Russia, but no one could deny that the main purpose of every Russian government, whatever its character or duration, had been to crush its citizens. Revolutions were made in the name of the people, starting with reforms that turned into hecatombs, all with the people's direct participation and a masochistic eagerness to throw themselves into the next adventure, anything to break the intolerable existence forced on them.

This hatred for life was seen mainly in those meant to educate, heal and comfort us – the teachers, doctors and priests. He remembered his first teacher at school, shouting at her terrified pupils until the windows rattled. He had been spared many trips to the doctor, but on his visits to the clinic for his travel documents he would see the wretched queues of old people waiting hours for their five-minute appointment with the irritable local medic. Everstein was right there too. The priests were the worst, christening infants with disgust and burying the dead in a rush, so they could get back to the sacred business from which they had been rudely distracted. There was no enlightenment, no comfort from the tormenting teacher, the tyrant doctor, the trickster priest, and looming over them all was the Russian god, like a sergeant. Unlike other merciful, even sentimental gods, the Russian god could only punish and was never satisfied. No sacrifice was enough, all prayers were onerous. This god could only have been invented to enslave people. No grass-roots religion, no heartfelt desire for a better life could have created this monster with his piercing gaze.

No one could pray to a black canvas, the smutty prototype of this Russian god, no restorers could scrape off the layers of grime to reveal the godlike beauty beneath, since each layer exposed another, even blacker. And this enslaved life was followed by an enslaved death, and the only difference beyond the grave between the righteous and the sinners was that the righteous had bawled drill psalms on the parade ground, while the sinners took care of everyday life, working in the filthy catering detachment and cleaning the latrines.

Everyone in Russia had to push themselves to the front of the line, and essentially did nothing else – on the roads, at the shops, parking the car – as if exorcizing the memory of some ancient trauma or historic defeat, hating those ahead of them and despising those at the back. It was there in Russian business, and in the long queues winding outside the poor people's supermarkets. And this frenzy of self-assertion went on because all those queuing, handing out credit or pumping oil were united by nothing but a sense of personal injustice, which merely sharpened the pushes in the line. Everyone suffered from this sense of injustice. No one had the right to their own oil, or even a bag of apples from the cheap supermarket. It was everyone for himself, with God the Commander against all of them.

The Russian terror had been kicked off from below. The government only had to kill a dozen or so people before they started destroying each other in their thousands. The first arrested conspirator produced an avalanche of denunciations, and soon everyone was a conspirator. The Bolshevik Revolution, which started in such a wonderfully bloodless fashion, soon turned into an orgy of slaughter, and instead of emerging from this bloody font vowing not to repeat the mistake, the paroxysm of self-destruction continued.

Russia couldn't be a single nation by definition: subjugator and subjugated had nothing in common, nothing to agree on, and no wish to do so. And since there were almost no Khazars left in Russia, the conquerors set about massacring anyone they described as the native people, after which they would start massacring each other.

They already had a niche for some of the occupied people. The first law of the new rulers was always to appoint a temporary administration of the natives, to promote the colonizers' culture and customs. To enforce this law, it wasn't necessary to read Roman history, just the memoirs of survivors of the ghettos and the concentration camps, and the rare occasions when these administrators appealed for indulgence invariably ended badly for all sides. The number of survivors reduced over time and became the occupiers' trained slaves – they didn't need too many of them. The occupiers themselves had some laws they followed, possibly even some principles, but their subjects had no right to them, and in order to stop them discovering any for themselves, a new faith had to be instilled in them every ten years or so. This had happened throughout Russian history, with its freakish twists and zigzags. People would be told first that they were gods, then that they were trash, until they finally lost all notion of what gods and trash were, and could never unite once and for all to be free.

This was the cruellest result of the colonizers' law: that the colonized people would soon conform to their negative stereotypes, because they had forgotten their history and had learnt to live in a state of passive irresponsibility. The new conquerors would begin by wiping out the few cultural institutions that somehow survived the preceding ones, and under the new generation of local administrators, who proudly called themselves not jailors now but managers, only cheap popular books were published and hundreds of comics, because the colonized people could no longer read, and their only goal was to drive out the colonizers.

But although an entire population could be destroyed by fire and the sword, and their literature buried and their monuments destroyed, these unhappy people's posthumous revenge would be that the colonizers would ultimately turn on themselves, crushing all who could work and promoting only those who could kill. He had seen how in colonized Khazaria a Khazar was anyone who could call themselves a human being, and the proud right to call themselves Russian belonged to those who exceeded them in cruelty and stupidity, and it amazed him that he had only just realized this.

He pictured it all with the sudden clarity with which we see the patterns of our future in the random unpredictability of chaos. No transformation in Russia, revolutionary or reformist, could be carried through to the end, for its logical outcome would be the Russians' expulsion from this country that they hung on to for dear life. Approximately once a century there would be a revolution that triggered a Deep Freeze of terror, then a few freedoms to let off steam, a so-called "Thaw", before the regime collapsed into dementia, and the only way to transform it would be with another revolution, for its people no longer reacted to anything but the axe. Each new axe revolution would set the country back fifty years, destroying its achievements and those in whose name it was made, producing a new enslavement, and new rulers and protesters. The protesters would grow up and grow clever, the rulers would grow old and stupid, the government would fall, the protesters would die in chaos and hunger, and a new tyrant would reset the clock on the ruins.

Revolutions always ended in a military putsch, sometimes delayed, but inevitable as Ivan the Terrible's guards. Stalin's Deep Freeze preceded the Second Great War, and if the war hadn't happened he would have had to make one. During the Thaw of the Fifties and Sixties the arts had come back to life, because the Freeze had wiped out all talent and now it could flourish again. Then after the Thaw all those who had passionately believed in it and gained from it were imprisoned and sent to Siberia.

He enjoyed tracing the specific features of these four stages in Russian history. Ivan the Terrible, whose canonization he had noted with disgust on his return to Moscow, had started as a revolutionary and ended as a strangler, and was apparently planning a thaw, which was later carried out by Boris Godunov. Only Peter the Great's death saved his former comrades from exile and disgrace, and they were later exiled by his heirs. The blessed Alexander II, who in his early years had made a revolution by emancipating the serfs, then presided over Russia's push into Asia.

Anyone could reach the highest level of state power as long as they didn't try to pick mushrooms in winter or throw snowballs in summer. The paradox was that to achieve power meant to achieve complete powerlessness. Anyone who fought for it and achieved it with their own hands would die of shock from its illusiveness, like Boris Godunov and Lenin.

Obviously, if the country belonged to people who claimed it as theirs, the cycle would have been broken long ago. Russia had already passed through five of Dante's circles: the circle of Ivan the Terrible and his Boyar insanity; the first Romanov; the circle of Peter the Great and his Freeze, and the twenty-year thaw of Catherine; the golden circle of the nineteenth century, and the reforms of Speransky and Stolypin; the Lenin circle, ending in Perestroika; and now the start of the sixth, which crushed anyone who knew long words or foreign languages. According to Dante, there were only three more circles left until the ninth, which was eternal darkness and damnation, and no one knew if they would reach the ninth. More and more now it seemed to Volokhov that this one would be the last – or rather he wanted to believe it was, for it would only be followed by something new, and he was terribly tired of this sad merry-go-round he had ridden on for almost thirty years without realizing.

Yet instead of hating Russia, he felt an overwhelming pity for it. The natural conclusion would be to help the Khazars return to their land and find Phlogiston, and work with them for a better life. But he felt Russian, and there was nothing he could do about it. Despite all the arguments and his sense of justice, his conscience stopped him catching the train to the bright future of personal freedom. He had seen precious little freedom in the Kaganate in fact, where liberalism was preached for export but wasn't practised. Essentially they attacked the evil of all vertical hierarchies, with the aim of replacing the rusting Russian machine with their own, and he might even have yielded Russia to those who honoured and protected what was good in it, but not to those who would dismantle and smash it.

After his stay in the Kaganate, he had no doubt what sort of Russia they would make in place of the old one, which had become intolerable to him. Willingly or not, they would become the new enslavers, and it would be business as usual. But it wasn't the Dark Ages, they wouldn't go in for mass annihilation – or would they? He wasn't so sure now. Perhaps he would agree with an aching heart to surrender Russia if they limited themselves to its culture – not that they had asked him of course – and as he walked down the street he found himself having a conversation with an imaginary Yd in his head. Yes, you can have it, he told him. Perhaps Russia would be better off without it, and something new would be created from nothing. All our Tolstoys, Dostoevskys and Chekhovs were writing out of the guilt of the oppressor, which was why our best writers were so depressing; none of them could breathe the damp air after rain or gaze at the sunset or eat a ripe strawberry warmed by the sun without this crippling sense of guilt. Let it all go, let the liberated people write a new poetry in the liberated land, and finish the work Khazar writers like Pasternak and Mandelstam had started. "With the furnaces of Bacchus everywhere, as if on earth were only guards and dogs..." God, how he loved that poem of Mandelstam's. Nothing better had been written in the language, even by Pushkin, even Lermontov's "The Terek slips along the stones, splashing the muddy shores..."

They could have had it all, even that, if he thought there was a chance Russia would be better without it. But it wouldn't, and he knew what they would replace it with. The Khazar state already went far beyond the Kaganate now, and they would become the colonizers.

Colonization could take many forms of course; it could be benign and enlightened, but it could be something quite different. "Don't make me say it out loud!" he said to his imaginary Yd, and a passer-by stopped to stare at him. "You won't be happy with throwing out the Russians, you want to break us and break the circle, because you're sick of being pushed around. It's quite understandable. You want to be rid of us once and for all, so you can start a new life in a new place. You don't want to enslave us when you arrive, you simply don't want us here." And his inner voice replied, in Everstein's tenor, then in Psish Korobyansky's reedy mocking baritone, "But isn't that what you did to us?"

"No, it isn't," he replied, stunned.

"Really? When you burnt our towns and drove us into exile, and set up our Pales of Settlement? You want your own ghetto? For God's sake, we'll give you one. Otherwise we'll open the borders and you can go wherever you like, to your Hyperborean North if you know where it is. We've no idea where you came from when you invaded Khazaria, somewhere it snows all year round and no crops grow. Go back there – welcome to Greenland! If you don't want to you can stay, just keep out of our way."

He shook himself, trying to shake off these wild visions. Where had they come from? There was obviously no question of mass annihilation, the country would simply be left to second-raters. Oh my vile Russian head, you don't want to give your country to those who are obviously right, who could build something humane here. *Could*, he agreed, but he knew they wouldn't. He didn't want to submit to yet another mindless power, another absolute truth, and he knew that they wouldn't behave like the masters of the country when they got here, but the masters of life, which wasn't the same thing at all.

4

At first, when he still regarded the theory of occupied Khazaria as an insane fantasy, he observed closely the few Khazars still living in Moscow, some from his own circle, including a few mixed-race ones (although the Varangians insisted there was no such thing as a half-Khazar). They all seemed to know their origins and destiny and to share the same secret language, but discussions of race were either silenced or went nowhere. For a long time the Khazars hadn't concealed their hatred for all things Russian. The cleverer ones said they liked living in Russia, but only a scoundrel could take pride in having been born here. Some repeated the platitudes of the late Eighties, that the true Russians were those who knew the language, and the Khazars knew it best, and wrote the best literature and were the best scientists and politicians. "Enough, you've made a mess of things, let us have it!" None of them seemed to know much about the Kaganate, and they would refer to it with affectionate irony, and he recognized their habit of self-mockery as a sort of defence mechanism they had developed so as not to give others the chance to mock them, like a mother slapping her child so its father won't thrash it.

He had only one serious argument with a Khazar in Moscow, and that was because he was drunk, which was a dreadful mistake, since vodka always brought out the very worst in him, making him boorish and abusive, turning despair to madness.

Ten months after his return, he had visited the friends of a history graduate and liberal activist he had met, a girl from a good circle who lived in a large flat and owned two dachas, one of which she rented out, and boasted of her noble antecedents and that she was of the intellectual elite. This new short-term girlfriend of his had taken him to a large bohemian flat where a crowd had gathered to say goodbye to someone leaving on their long-awaited emigration. The hostess, Sonya, was a typical Khazar, loud and flashy, and he disliked Khazar women even more.

"How come they have these mansions?" he asked his girlfriend rudely.

"Her grandfather was an academic and a famous Marxist – he published ten books on the subject," she told him.

"Ah, memories of past glory."

"But Sonya's different – she hasn't read Marx at all!"

"How ungrateful of her, she should know him by heart," he said, which made her laugh.

After a few drinks everyone started arguing about which song to sing. For a long time there had been a shortage of songs that everyone liked. The Russians would sing one, the Khazars would drawl another, and the sad Khazar ones sung by a Russian sounded as offensive as a Varangian in a crowd of factory workers. But all these people here loved the singer-songwriter Bulat Okudzhava. They couldn't stand Okudzhava in so-called Russian circles, but they didn't really sing much at all there, and didn't like the *style russe*. They preferred service jackets to peasant shirts, and the hatred and despair of rock was more to these kind military souls' taste than folk.

But all the Khazars loved Okudzhava. They sang his thoughtful bohemian Georgian songs with a strange passion not specially suited to the material, the way they did everything, and while Okudzhava would smile at himself, they would perform them with the solemnity of a preacher, full of tragic emotion and emphasis – *this* is what they mean, *this* is what he's saying.

Volokhov had distanced himself from a row that had broken out after someone hummed an old hymn for a joke, and Sonya snapped, "How plebeian!"

The joker was covered in confusion, then everyone discussed what plebeian meant, and whether one should sometimes "go outside one's own circle to meet the common people". They spoke with a frankness which would have been shocking even ten years ago, when one was expected at least to pay ritual respect to the masses. Sonya imitated them, twitching and pulling faces, and seemed to think they deserved to live in slums and should aspire no higher. The man sitting next to her grinned – a short, fit, cocky-looking bald fellow of about Volokhov's age, with round glasses and a small ginger beard, probably her latest conquest; she changed them more often than he changed his socks, Volokhov's girlfriend had gleefully informed him.

After a few drinks they began discussing their charity work and the battle against evil. At first he didn't understand why they talked this way, but soon realized that their so-called human values were just a mask, allowing them to insinuate themselves into an environment weakened by humanism and assert their authority, and anyone who didn't acknowledge it would be thrown to the satraps of the mad mullahs.

They loved Okudzhava's exhortations to cry out against injustice and take care of each other, and they would refuse to shake hands with anyone who disagreed with them. Poor Okudzhava didn't know what they'd done to his songs, and he didn't survive a year when he did! How he grew to hate his calls to people to cry out against injustice and take care of each other! And although he renounced it all at the end, they didn't listen. Then there was their way of arguing too, calling someone a shit, then swooning over them. ("How's your little head, darling? Does it hurt, sweetheart? Here? Here?") But all this was just a sort of intonation, and Volokhov was more interested in ideas. He guessed their philanthropy was mainly about undermining the state and exposing its cruelty and inefficiency, since they needed it to be weak to break its backbone, and when Sonya discussed her charity work he realized with a smile that he was right. She ran a shelter for stray dogs, and was revered by them all as a saint, and when she opened her eyes wide and said "I simply don't understand how you can argue about politics when dogs are dying every day in the city!", they cut short the discussion in which Volokhov was just beginning to get the upper hand. Fine, you can have the last word, they seemed to be saying, what does it matter when sick dogs are dying?

But there were more serious arguments too, about sick children. A young curly-haired artist named Ida described with a breaking voice how children with cancer were left to die, and how this was the first, the first sign of a country in decay, and if such things happened it had no right to survive. She spoke passionately about them and mentioned the show she was putting on to raise money for them, listing by name all the children she was supporting, and Volokhov, who was fairly drunk by now, began to wonder what inhuman crimes she must have committed and had to atone for. But she really was painting her little roses and animals for charity, and had been commissioned to paint a mural in a children's hospital near Lyons, and she had persuaded the French aristocrat with whom she was having an affair to donate five thousand euros to some Moscow hospitals.

"Parents mortgage their flats, and when the children... I can't... When they pass away, they still have to pay the money!" She covered her face and broke into sobs, and a sad silence fell over the table. Then the inevitable quiet girl jumped up to comfort her. "Ida my darling, my sweetheart..."

"What you say is fine, Ida." Volokhov could keep quiet no longer. "But don't you think your charity just makes things worse?"

Ida dried her eyes. "You don't think I should help dying children?"

"Well, if they're dying no one can help them, let's call them sick instead." It was important to define terms with them at the outset, since they tended to change the meaning of words as they went along. "You're collecting money, essentially for bribes—"

"Because that's how it works!" she went on the attack. "You have to pay seven, ten thousand roubles just for an X-ray, and it's a matter of days, minutes—"

"Well, firstly there's more than one X-ray machine in Moscow, and in some hospitals you don't even have to wait a week. And secondly, by collecting money for bribes you simply keep the system going."

"So what do you propose?" sneered the inevitable effete good-looking young man in the corner, in an aristocratic, slightly French accent, and he recognized the usual Khazar tactic: like the Teutonic knights who could make their bloodbaths on the ice, they could make a triangle in any geographical conditions, with the woman at the top.

"I propose keeping quiet about it," he shrugged. "It's nothing special, I was taught as a child it's wrong to brag. You help sick children, great. Virtue is its own reward."

"But my example encourages dozens of others!" Ida said, horrified. "If we do nothing, we all..." She threw out her arms at those present, including many who would never in their wildest dreams have considered giving money to charity. "People like you will never understand!"

It was impossible to argue with her: charity with them was like flowers on a tank. But he had seen the tank and he knew it. He knew things were wrong in Russia, but that this pure-white truth, merciless with its enemies and indiscriminate in its methods, was worse than life here, dying and dirty as the February snow.

"You're wrong if you think we don't understand," he said softly. "I help several invalids' families, our Institute makes regular payments to our local hospital, but that's our private business. You may encourage others, but you'd do better to expose corruption. It's more useful, even if it doesn't make you feel so good—"

"Sack one and there'd be ten others!" she cut in.

"Yes, but it's mostly about you, isn't it? The children don't care if Ida Turkovskaya or the government's helping them, but Ida Turkovskaya feels holy and the holiness spreads to her little watercolours... Sorry if I've offended you."

"You can't offend anyone here, to offend someone you have to be at their level," the good-looking youth spoke up for the shocked Ida. "You should know what an honour it is for you to sit at the same table with her. But how can you, the idea of honour doesn't exist in your society."

"It does, as it happens, and I'll shove it down your throat!" Volokhov said, raising his voice. "Stand up, you hear me? Come outside, you little shit, I'll show you who honours who!"

He lunged at him and tried to drag him from the table, but several strong pairs of hands pulled them apart.

He raved on drunkenly, and people kept holding him back, but their charity stopped them throwing him on the floor. "Heirs of a great culture, Soviet informers… Sonya's grandfather was a Marxist – you know who her grandfather was? Wasn't it Comrade Kogan, specialist in the early Marx, who denounced Comrade Helfand, specialist in the late Marx, for the crime of mechanistic metaphysical mysticism? You chose the right road comrade, with your plush flat—"

"Get him out!" Sonya screamed.

"Don't worry, I'm going. Honour, what honour? What right have you to honour, culture or anything else? But you can do whatever you like because you'll win in the end!" The room swam before his eyes, and their faces blurred in a mist of alcohol and fury. "We don't need your elite! You hate our elite, and you're right, we're dead, finished, but at least ours were born of fighters, not petty whingers biting each other under the blankets! You've created nothing! Your Mandelstam was a genius only because he wrote in Russian! What sort of elite are you? You're the snake in the skull! You'll get the upper hand, but don't claim to be a higher life form!"

No one had any idea what he was talking about, and at that moment a strong hand grasped his shoulder and dragged him away.

"Don't hurry me, I'm going," he mumbled. "Stay and celebrate your victory, just don't pretend to be aristocrats. Are you an aristocrat?" He turned to the man who was pushing him firmly to the door, and he recognized Sonya's bald boyfriend.

"Of course I am," he murmured. "Come on, let's talk."

"All right, we'll talk." The triangle was now complete and, although shaken, he was confident of his strength. He threw on his mac and followed the fellow out to the landing.

"Shall we fight?" he challenged him.

"Why fight?" he said. "Rub-a-dub-dub, a pudding and a tub."

This was what the fuddled Volokhov thought he said, anyway.

"Come again? I must have had a few…" he mumbled stupidly.

"OK, I'll make it simple," the man said calmly. "A cat sits in a tree, with a hook to the left and a fork to the right. What's above?"

"A circling falcon!" Volokhov said confidently. Only in his drunken state could he have peeled through the layers of memory to this riddle. He didn't know where he remembered it from, he might have read it as a child in a fairy story or heard it from his nanny, an old woman from the Tambov region. It was nonsense of course, but something about the words was inexpressibly dear to him. He remembered a toy he used to play with when he was about three, of some wooden peasant dolls looking for mushrooms under a pine tree, and that the riddle was about a magic forest and a wood goblin who lived with a cat, only the cat was a wild cat, more like a lynx; he might even have seen one somewhere.

"So you do remember!" the bald man beamed.

"And how do you know it?"

"Why wouldn't I know my own language? Have you seen a circling falcon hereabouts, my friend?"

"Of course not, it's just make-believe," Volokhov said didactically.

"It's nothing of the sort," he replied with a broad smile. "The falcon, well, that's a falcon, and the cat and the wood goblin in the tree together go up and down, up and down. Surely you've seen them?"

"You mean like a see-saw?" he asked, baffled.

"Yes, but better, you probably went on one yourself as a child."

"Never."

"It's all ahead of you then. Try this: 'One, two, out of the blue. Three, four, smack the floor…'"

"'Five, six, dig up sticks,'" Volokhov laughed. "It's a counting game, we used to play it at school!"

The man slapped him on the shoulder. "It sounds like a good school you went to."

Volokhov's girlfriend peered anxiously round the door. "Is everything all right, boys?" she said.

"It's more than all right," the strange guest said. "Tell Sonya we're leaving."

"I'll fetch my coat."

"Stay here," he said masterfully, as though he had the right to order Volokhov's girlfriend around. "We've things to discuss that aren't for women's ears."

"We're fine, Katya, I'll call you tomorrow," Volokhov reassured her.

* * *

"So that's how it is," Gurov finished, puffing with gusto at a cigarette in Volokhov's kitchen, where they had ended up. He did everything with gusto, and behaved as if he owned the place, his bald head shining cosily under the lamp.

"What an idiot I've been. It's all so simple," Volokhov said dully.

"You're not an idiot at all. You've got half of it, not many get that far."

"So when did you say they came?"

"The Khazars? Around the sixth century."

"And the Varangians in 862?"

"Yes, when they burnt their capital down. Incidentally there's some lovely stuff in Koestler about the Rus. He quotes from a traveller who noticed they always went to the lavatory in threes, with two to stand guard in case of foreign attack. Hilarious isn't it, the way the Rus always do things in threes, like the Khazars!"

Volokhov liked Gurov very much at that moment. He was the first person who had finally lifted the curse of the love-hate he felt for his country. He could calmly hate Russia now and not feel part of it, and just as calmly hate the Khazars, who had no more right to it than they did. He didn't know why he had instantly trusted this stranger, but he said things he had suspected all along, and was just adding the finishing touches to the picture.

"The Khazar Kaganate is the Thirteenth Tribe," Gurov went on. "It was the time of the great migrations, the world was breaking up, people stumbled around not knowing what they were looking for, grabbing what they could. And here was this land of milk and honey, and our people were gentle and peace-loving. The Khazars settled in quickly, but soon the music stopped and another landless tribe arrived, only these ones meant business. I don't know why they were driven out of their land in the first place, maybe they'd committed some crime or they were just travellers, like gypsies. You know, I've a theory each race is guilty of some crime for which they're driven out, which is why no one can live in their own land, but they've forgotten where it is, so they have to wander around looking for it. It happened in the sixth and seventh centuries when the world broke its chains – Gaul got the Romans, the Mongols got Chukotka, and we got these two. I don't mean original sin obviously, that's rubbish."

"I like that, the idea of everyone looking for their land. You should come to our Institute."

"My General Staff's not bad either. So the Varangians arrive and claim we invited them, and who knows, maybe we did, maybe we were sick of living under the Khazars. They stayed and burned the Khazars' towns and the Khazars fought back, and we sat back waiting for them to finish each other off. But they didn't. It seemed the Khazars had won in 1845, then a century later with the Great War it was the Varangians. It's a circle, as I say. When no one believes in anything it's always a circle. And both the Varangians and the Khazars trampled on us."

"And who is 'us'?"

"I'll come to that in a while. It's... well, painful, there are so few of us left. I was thirteen when my father told me and it almost broke me. Although it's easier for a child, of course."

"So why do we put up with them?"

"It's complicated," Gurov said. "Just don't wave your sword around or you'll set them off. We keep them apart you see, like ants keeping off the lice."

"Yes, but what do we get out of it?"

"Well, if they weren't going for each other they'd go for us, wouldn't they? This way we're above it all, without annexations, revolutions or terror. It's a higher form of life – you could almost say we've reached the state of the angels."

"Really? Angels?" Volokhov frowned.

"At any rate we're better than they are, and they're too busy grabbing and killing each other to notice us. Some of the grabbing and killing comes our way, but not much."

"Like hiring gangsters to protect you?"

"Exactly," Gurov grinned. "Only it's two sets of gangsters pissing on each other and there's no end to the pissing. Most convenient for us, don't you agree?"

"I just don't understand how this culture that doesn't believe in anything with its circles and oppression is so unaggressive," Volokhov objected.

"We are sometimes. We know almost nothing of our true culture though, there's not much of it in books. I'm a sort of guard, you see," he confided happily to his new compatriot. "You know what fascinates me? That Russia's so-called golden age is virtually defined by two types, the repentant Varangian and the repentant Khazar. If they'd come together at some point they would have been a force to reckon with, but thankfully they didn't. Consider Pushkin, an atheist and Khazar who aspired all his life to be a Varangian, and died for it because someone ordered to twitter mustn't sing – and he wasn't killed by his own people of course, but by those who didn't want him to be one of them. Then Lermontov, who started as a patriot and Varangian, with the cult of death and the North, anti-Christianity and Borodino and so on – and at the end of his life, 'Farewell, unwashed Russia'. They try to claim he didn't write it, but it seems he became converted in the Caucasus, where he had a Chechen bondsman and friend."

"For God's sake keep the Chechens out of it. It's good though, the repentant Varangian and Khazar, I suppose you see it with Tolstoy and Dostoevsky too," Volokhov said thoughtfully. "Tolstoy started as an officer who strutted with the nobility, then turned against the government and loved the Khazars to the point of learning their language. Whereas Dostoevsky started as a rebel and ended as the friend of the Tsar's family. Didn't Tolstoy say there was something of the Khazar in him?"

"That's right, to Gorky. Gorky was a textbook repentant Varangian, all Nietzsche and sentimentality and so on, he only wised up at the end. It's all so obvious, the whole of Russia's so-called culture rests on these two types, and as soon as they begin to think a little they fight each other."

He smiled, and Volokhov found himself smiling too, and felt as if he had fallen into the warm bath of his own people after being trapped outside in the freezing snow.

"It's terrible, terrible," he nodded happily. "I see it all now. But you know I'd hate to think everything's determined by nationality, or history, even though I'm a historian — that you're born a Khazar or a Varangian and you just carry out their programme. Surely personality comes into it?"

"Of course it does, with us," Gurov nodded. "I'll tell you our name for ourselves later. Forget the name Slav, we're not slaves, we just know who we are."

"Meaning?"

"Well, to put it simply, if you don't care for either of them and they're not for you, it means you're one of us. I've figured you out, brother, I've an instinct for these things!"

"But you say there are almost none of us left, the third ones. Or rather the first ones?"

"There are quite a few in Moscow in fact," Gurov shrugged. "You see them every day on the underground, travelling around on the Circle Line. Do you know who I'm talking about?"

"No, who?" Volokhov said, baffled, and he told him.

* * *

By the first millennium of our era, Gurov explained, a multitude of tribes had settled along the Central Asian transport system known as Rus, but information about them was unreliable and often deliberately muddled. The early history of Western Europe and the Near East was scrupulously documented, but that of Southern and Eastern Europe was a patchwork of theories that their various proponents couldn't agree to share.

According to him, there were four main versions of the origins of the Russian state – the Khazar, the Russian, the Norse (or Varangian) versions, and the true native one.

The Khazar one held that the medieval Kaganate, with its white castles and numerous trades, was part of a vast state covering most of Southern Europe to the shores of the river Dnieper. The Slavs paid a tax to the Kaganate, but the Rus resisted it, and this tax was mentioned in the ancient *Book of Days*. Various sources referred to these two tribes, the Slavs and the Rus, including an anonymous tenth-century Arabic tract, *The Limits of the World from the East to the West*, which stated that the river Ruta, a tributary of the Rus, "flows from the Rus to the Slavs". *The Limits of the World* wasn't translated into Russian in its entirety, and until recently was considered a forgery. The Rus were described there as:

> ...of a bad disposition, insolent and indecent and inclined to quarrels and war. Living among them are a number of Slavs who serve them. Kyaba is a town of the Rus that is close to the Muslims and is the residence of the Tsar. Slaba is a pleasant town that trades with the land of the Bulgars. In Urtab all foreigners are killed.

Also living in the land of the Rus were a separate tribe, "who had come from the uninhabited North and conquered it and settled there".

To the east of them was the land of the Khazars, "a flourishing place of great wealth, trading in cows, sheep and numerous slaves". Their capital, Tsetzar, and the residence of their Tsar, Khan Tarkan, was divided by the river Atil (later the Volga). Tula and Lugkh were two regions of the Khazars, where people were military and possessed a large number of weapons. The other main source of information about Khazaria was the so-called Jewish-Khazar correspondence, consisting of just two letters, dating from the middle of the tenth century, from the Minister of Finance of the Spanish Caliphate, Abdurahman Khasdai Ibn Shafrut the Second, to the Khazar Khan, and his reply.

By then the Khazars had migrated through the Caucasus from the Caspian to Derbent, and had settled in Crimea and along the Volga, where their Khan Joseph converted to Judaism. Information about Joseph relates to this late last period of Khazar history before 862, when the Kievan Prince Svyatoslav sacked Tsetzar and the Kaganate ceased to exist.

The Russian version maintained that the Kaganate was a small state in the Eastern Caucasus on the delta of the Volga, which by the ninth century covered the lower Don. The central Russian plain between the Don and the Dnieper was ruled by the Rus and the tribe of the As, who had been driven from the North by the Great Freeze, and had migrated through South-East Europe between the third and fifth centuries and settled there.

The As had a European appearance and were devotees of the cult of weapons, and passed on through the generations the legends of their magic skills and their "bright, royal" antecedents. According to the Arabic tract, "Constantly in their hundreds they marched on the Slavs and seized their goods with violence".

The Varangian, "Hyperborean" theory held that these As were descendants of the vanished race of the Aryans, and there was a widespread view that the Rus too were heirs of these wise men and warriors. Some historians even believed that it was the geopolitical catastrophe of the Freeze that inspired the legend of Atlantis, and a small number of independent scholars claimed As was the Atlanteans' name for themselves.

The native version, the true one according to Gurov, was that the territory of the Eastern Slavs was divided by two mighty states, the Varangians in the North-West, with their strict military code, and the Khazars in the South-East, with their hedonistic culture and success as traders, and that the Slavs and Rus lived with both of them. Unlike the Rus, the Slavs knew many crafts, and their culture was defined by the circle, with their circular dwellings and ceramics and round headdresses. Little had survived of this circular, cyclical culture of the Slavs, as it was systematically destroyed and driven underground, and virtually nothing remained now of their language, since the invaders used words without understanding them and changed their meanings.

Sources refer to the clashes between the Varangians and the Khazars for territory, and the natives suffered under both of them. From these sources though it was clear that the battles weren't merely for territory, but what might be called values, as the vertical military hierarchy of the North imposed itself on the horizontal one of the South. (This hierarchy was only for the conquered people in fact; they themselves were ruled by mutual understanding and equality.)

The followers of Odin weren't known for their restraint, and unlike the Khazars' indolent, hedonistic reputation, their society was strictly regulated and their energy as traders was legendary. But their will was broken and freedom and dissipation was their lot, and the meek natives served each of them in turn.

Now, at the beginning of the second millennium, almost none of Russia's native people were left, which was why no one knew how to work, and the main quarrel was between those who wanted to fight and those who wanted to trade. A few natives still survived however, to preach the cult of the circle and stop the world destroying itself.

"You've guessed who we are?" Gurov asked.

"No, who?"

"As I said, you see us travelling in a circle on the Moscow underground all the time."

"No, I don't believe it – you mean the Joes who go round on the Circle Line?" Volokhov said in a horrified whisper.

5

All this had happened four years earlier, and Volokhov was now Major Volokhov, commander of a small crack detachment called – Heaven knows why – the Flying Guards, pulling wet spiderwebs from his face as he stumbled with them through the forests north of Degunino, feeling indecently happy because that evening he would finally be seeing Zhenka again.

The Flying Guards had been launched in the third year of the war with all the high-flown lunacy of the late Varangian spirit. The government had recently lost all shame and had introduced a huge number of new holidays, mainly military ones. The black days in the calendar were increasingly crowded out by the red, and they all merged together for Volokhov in the image of the black-winged dragon Stratilat, reptile and martyr in one, eating its tail in indescribable agony.

The holidays were celebrated in great style, and each year the new Day of National Unity triggered more violence. There had been street battles before; demonstrators against illegal immigration would march through the cities bearing swastikas, and scanty crowds of disgraced democrats would protest against them, at first with flowers, then with condoms filled with water. "Peace and love!" they would cry. "We're waiting for everyone who's not afraid at the building of the so-called Friendship of the Peoples!" And the demonstrators would smash everyone who wasn't afraid to a pulp.

Volokhov found the condoms and the swastikas equally revolting, but action produced reaction, and the following year would see twice as many swastikas and twice as many people out against them. The Jews were still attacked on the streets, but not so often now, as almost none of them had stayed, and those who had would retaliate with their fists. At first the proud Aryans were shocked by their audacity, but the Jews soon got the hang of things, and suddenly it was no joke for the white race.

That was how it started, with punch-ups and skirmishes in the capitals that spread to the surrounding towns, until the unrest reached the Caucasus, and a month later, hardly knowing how it happened, the country was at war.

This one differed radically from the national revival in the dark days of the seventeenth century, when Citizen Minin and Comrade Prince Pozharsky rallied the people against the Poles. As an Alternative, Volokhov should have known what was going on, but no one knew anything any more. Varangianism picked up its heroes wherever it could, moulding them in the sugary image of Minin and Pozharsky, and the demonstrators would hold aloft portraits of their old enemy, cunning King Sigismund of Poland, with his suspiciously non-Aryan features, with howling music and garlands of Russian wood betonies. The word "Antichrist" flooded the press, and a new wave of self-destruction started all by itself, without a signal from above. The government caught on to what was happening, and soon even telling people to grow tomatoes would end in a massacre, and potatoes meant food riots. And just as any physical matter, even a stool, can be distilled into moonshine, any spiritual matter can be distilled into a pogrom. It was no surprise then that one of these new holidays of peace and unity was the start of it all.

To begin with, the government spoke of local disturbances, and claimed things were under control. But before long they were coming up with reasons for war and preparing for one to be on the safe side; and a month later it was total mobilization.

Volokhov had long been expecting it, especially since meeting Gurov, and they had met again a year later, the day it was declared, soon after his thirtieth birthday. It was just before the New Year, and they had chosen a crowded spot at Poklonnaya Hill where a patriotic meeting was taking place, so they could chat unnoticed. Gurov could pass unnoticed anywhere though: Volokhov was sure he wouldn't have noticed him that night at Sonya's if he hadn't introduced himself. He had no idea what he did, only that he worked for the General Staff and was constantly travelling around the country checking schools and inspecting the troops, and that he was phenomenally well-informed about the most unexpected subjects, such as the steel industry and fishing. He had friends in both intellectual and work circles (although the circles were so mixed up now that they were virtually indistinguishable), but since their first meeting they had met infrequently. This was mainly because their initial friendship had quickly turned to mutual distrust. Volokhov realized Gurov had designs on him for some secret mission he might not want to be part of, and Gurov thought because Volokhov was now one of the chosen people he should be ready for anything. Volokhov had no desire to listen to the voice of the blood; he found this voice equally repellent in Varangians and Khazars alike, and didn't see why an exception had to be made for this secret population he was now supposedly part of. He suspected Gurov of assigning him a special role in his plans, and Gurov suspected him of no longer wanting to be part of his plans, and being angry that he had none of his own.

"So it's started?" Volokhov asked him, straight out.

Gurov nodded, calm as ever, but his glasses sparkled gleefully.

"Just like that? All by itself?"

"That's right, exactly as I said."

"You think they'll kill each other?"

"It's inevitable, they've had it, their number's up."

"And how will it end?"

"In nothing, absolutely nothing," he said rubbing his hands. "I told you there'd be no victory, they'll just devour each other. A worthy end for two worthless tribes."

"Surely they're not ready to finish each other off yet, it's much more likely ours will win."

Gurov frowned. "Who's this 'ours'? When will you stop being a Varangian?"

"When I feel like it."

"Will you join the army?"

"Why not? I'll have to when I'm called up, they just haven't got to my age group yet."

"Go ahead – they'll kill you, you fool, then how will we raise our people?"

"When exactly are you planning to do that?"

"When the others have gorged themselves!" he beamed.

"So you really think you can find enough of them to do something with?"

"Definitely," Gurov nodded. "All over the place."

"Surely you won't get much out of them after a thousand years of suffering?"

"Not suffering, waiting," he corrected him in the same calm tone.

"You're waiting, the others are waiting..."

"But my people have waited long enough," he said, nodding, and Volokhov noticed he wasn't saying "they" any more.

"Don't you think they'd be pretty useless though without us around?" he goaded him.

"You're a numbskull, Your Highness," the representative of the native population said patiently.

"Fine, have it your way." He didn't want to argue with him. He had decided long ago what he would do if war started, but he had seen it all as a distant hypothesis. It often happens in history that just as things are going in one direction something else comes along, and it was history's holy irrationality that made him love it. But Russia's history was subject to a hopeless melancholy. It was as if this war had been spun out of thin air. Everyone needed it, and all the evidence said it would be to the death – the final solution of the Russian Question.

That was what he thought in the first year anyway, when there were real battles, with large-scale operations and lists of the dead. There were food riots too; even in the second year it was clear that these would have happened anyway, and the war was just the pretext for them. And the irony was that, in a country where everything was scarce and rotting, the war soon became a mocking imitation of itself, like the Varangian holidays in honour of Stratilat. By the third year, when he was called up, there was no longer anything left to fight for. The Varangians had forgotten how to die for their country and were sending their own men to the firing squads in their thousands, and the Khazars didn't know what to do with all the land they had grabbed and were no longer sure if it was worth it. Neither side could be bothered to kill the other, and both tried desperately to avoid fighting, unable to live together but ashamed to pack up and go home. Things couldn't go on like this. It must be ended once and for all, so a new person could start on a new land, and this new person would be Volokhov.

He knew what he had to do. He had learnt the Khazar way of operating, and was just waiting for the right moment to apply it. As soon as he was called up and was made an officer, he worked out a plan for a diversionary detachment in the rear of the enemy, to carry out sudden silent attacks. He researched his proposal carefully and presented it to Zdrok and the other commanders. Paperwork was always obsessively checked at HQ, and beautiful long words were appreciated, and after he had persuaded them of his complete and utter inactivity, his plan was approved. The rest was just a matter of logistics and equipment. His main purpose was to avoid battles and make sure people ran away from him, but he couldn't reveal any of this to his detachment as he dragged them pointlessly through the forests and abandoned villages of central Russia. Only Zhenka knew, because Zhenka knew everything, and he couldn't hide anything from her.

Gurov was lying when he said the new life would start all by itself; there would be no new life if things went on as they were. Volokhov realized this shortly before leaving for the Front, when he went to say goodbye to his old girlfriend, whom he had split up with after meeting Zhenka. The memory of it still haunted him.

She had stayed on in their one-room flat he had left her, and she still went to work and even watered the plants. But the plants seemed the only thing she could cope with; the rest of her life had become overgrown like an abandoned meadow. It was a helpless, hopeless fading. She spoke even more quietly, and dressed all in black like a nun, and she lived so wretchedly he felt overwhelmed with guilt. There was nothing to eat in the flat, nothing to sit on, and she would spend hours pasting collages with her neighbour's daughter, telling her the folk tales she used to tell him, bleak and cheerless as the wind whistling through a tumbledown log cabin. She greeted him with the same meek tenderness he had once found so endearing, which merely irritated him now after Zhenka's joyful exuberance. She wasn't angry with him, she didn't blame him or make demands, and the simplest things seemed beyond her; when she offered to darn his old shirt, she managed to sew the sleeves together without noticing.

She was stuck in her dreamy madness, untouched by life, and even the outbreak of war had passed her by. The television hadn't worked for a long time, and the screen was thick with dust, like everything else in the place; the sink was piled with unwashed dishes, and when he tried to mend the dripping tap, the water gushed out and there was no washer, and he only avoided a flood by cutting a new one from the sole of his shoe. Only the plants thrived, as if this was their territory now. Ashes are the best environment for them, and the place was slowly turning to ashes, full of dust and rubbish and overflowing ashtrays and piles of old clothes. Sometimes she whispered to the plants, and they seemed to listen and reach out to her, and he sighed with relief when she saw him off. She cried a little, but appeared not to understand where he was going, and when he left her some money she pushed it distractedly on a shelf, evidently hoping to forget it. There was no core to her existence, and he told himself she would have been like this even if he had stayed with her. He had sometimes seen her before in a stupor, sitting with some sewing or a book in her hands, but now she was constantly in this state, and it frightened him to think how she would be when he got back, with the plants slowly filling the rooms like a jungle and blocking out the light.

He had considered introducing her to Gurov to show him what he was up against with people, but he was ashamed to let others see her. So he kept his knowledge to himself and pinned all his hopes on his Khazar campaign, which wouldn't only help the Khazars of course, and would be best for everyone.

He was struck by how smart and resourceful his detachment had become lately, as if they had to be torn from where they lived to discover themselves. There was Yakov the Carthorse, whose real name everyone had forgotten, a tall fat lad invaluable in any campaign, who had got the better of his easygoing nature and was finally thinking straight. Nurse Anyuta, who hadn't bandaged the wounded for a long time, which made her very happy. Saboteur Fedka the gypsy, who was in love with her and played the guitar rather well; his tribe understood the nomadic life and he followed Volokhov unquestioningly. Sniper Mikhail Motorin, whom all the girls from the villages fell in love with. Krymov, a former schoolteacher, who would discuss the masterpieces of world literature with them in the evenings. Drovnenkov the cook, who improvised tasty meals from local ingredients, including sometimes tree bark and grass.

There were many of them, these slowly awakening souls. Why should they go home and wait five years to be enslaved again? Hadn't those advancing on Berlin, sometimes covering forty kilometres a day, entered as new people? This was the simple secret panacea for the Russian people, to leave home: nomads, escaping serfs, those who went North to cultivate the Virgin Lands, furrowing the earth in all directions and digging in – all had been uprooted from their homes, knowing their work and freedom could be taken from them at any moment. Serfdom in Russia had been defined as an attachment to the land, but the land was foreign to them and only the road was theirs. The road was the natural home of the escaped serf, and the road was what freedom meant to him. Stupid Gurov didn't understand this, racing round the country looking for the natives and testing them with his nursery rhymes and riddles. The only way to make people from nothing was to be like Moses, leading them through the desert for forty years, although Volokhov's detachment knew nothing of this yet.

They consisted mainly of natives with a sprinkling of Varangians, and he had chosen them himself for their gentleness and good nature. He saved them from battles and gave false reports on his mobile, and such was the confusion at the Front that neither side ever tracked them down. Sometimes, as they journeyed on, he vowed to forget Zhenka and lead them to Siberia, where people had food and freedom and were barely aware of the war. He could quarter them tonight in the nearby village of Degunino, which the Federals had just left, and move decisively east with them in the morning. But he couldn't be away from Zhenka, and he despised himself for it. The Khazars had been in Grachevo for two days and she was their commissar there, and he was going to Grachevo. Despite all his evasive tactics, he knew his first night with her would mean his complete and final treachery, but there was no way out. Perhaps this was the reason for the war, so that they could be together again. And now he was tramping through the wet forest, kicking anthills and mushrooms and tearing off bunches of white and scarlet berries to eat, with his Flying Guards, down to fifty now, following behind.

His mobile rang.

"Seven here," he said expressionlessly.

"Fuck you, where are you?" shrieked Zdrok. "You were meant to liaise with Captain Gromov two days ago and carry out a joint operation at the appointed location, arsehole!"

"I'm on my way to Grachevo, comrade Colonel," he replied calmly. "I've a unique opportunity to capture the commissar of the Khazars' Third Army. According to my intelligence, her HQ is in the cottage of the peasant Pakharev. I plan to take her in a sudden night attack." He smiled, imagining how he would take the commissar that night, if she let him, of course.

"Ah," Zdrok said, disappointed. "Take her, do as you wish, the Flying Guards are the pride of the army. Mind your Eagles don't get up to any tricks." This was a favourite phrase of his, like a father warning his officer children against too much reckless daring.

"I'll report back in the morning," Volokhov said.

He hung up, and it immediately rang again.

"Are you coming?" Zhenka laughed.

"You've broken off negotiations?" he asked her.

"Ages ago!"

"And you know where I am?"

"Of course I do. But you won't want me, I'm just an ordinary army lay. I've no make-up and I haven't washed for a thousand years!"

"Oh lord, as if it mattered," he said in a stupid happy voice. "I'll be there in an hour."

"Alone?"

"Yes. You'll warn the patrols, won't you?"

"I already have," she laughed again, making his head spin, and rang off.

The rain dripped from the branches and the forest smelt of wet pine needles, and the long grass whipped their boots.

He looked back at his Flying Guards. "Quick march! Keep tight!" he shouted. "Si-ing!"

"'Not alone in the field, little road...'" began Private Chudikov in a wavering voice.

The others picked up the tune in a ragged chorus. He could never teach them marching songs, it seemed they only liked 'Little Road', which you couldn't march to at all.

> "Not alone in the field, little road,
> Not alone burning, not alone turning,
> Not alone in the field, little road..."

Chapter Three
Maugham's Way

1

The Governor sat down to breakfast in his best pale-cream trousers. It was filthy weather; all week the rain had battered the arched green windows of the dining room and the misty green depths of the garden. His faithful Nikita, who was both his butler and valet, brought in a steaming tureen of buckwheat porridge with mushrooms; the Governor preferred Russian buckwheat to European oats, and considered it more nutritious. Two neat round chicken cutlets garnished with parsley followed, with a gravy boat of mushroom sauce. Waiting on a tray was a loaf of his favourite black bread, baked with thyme according to his special instructions. He didn't drink coffee, just tea, strong and sweet, and today it was mint tea, which he had ordered the night before.

He always breakfasted early, no later than seven-thirty, to give him time to check his mail before receiving the natives at nine. He would see them before the officials and hear their complaints first: many governors in the surrounding provinces had followed this democratic practice, and the locals appreciated it. Their disputes could be settled in a few minutes, and their complaints were always the same. Sometimes he felt like a village doctor whose patients only ever had two ailments, either their "guts ached", or their "sides hurt". But he would listen patiently, without hurrying or interrupting them. He was amused by their naive tricks, but instead of exposing them immediately he would allow all sides to display their meagre acting talents; sometimes he even suspected they were merely pretending to be stupid, putting on their shows to make him feel like a white man.

Asha was different. Pale and slim, she looked nothing like the dark, squat Chinese-looking peasants and proletariat of the Russian East. She was intelligent too – not the coarse animal cunning of the natives, but the deep thoughtful delicacy of a truly refined nature. The Governor had known her for over a year now, and he doted on her. Two years ago he had been sorry to uproot from Moscow to Siberia, and now he couldn't imagine his life without this girl, who seemed the justification of all his sacrifices and responsibilities far from the capital. She was unusually robust too, and unlike the lazy natives she was capable of any sort of domestic work.

The Governor had read Somerset Maugham, and Maugham was his guide here in Siberia. He was a cultured man, and boasted a library of three thousand books in Moscow, of which he had brought five hundred with him so he would have a literary reference for every occasion. Books always made life easier, coming to dark places and showing the light, and his reading had served him well. He had worked first in the Ministry of Culture, before moving smoothly into geopolitics and being promoted to Governor.

He was nothing like the immortal self-replicating official of the Soviet era. By the end of that era everyone had grown sick of these types, and it seemed they would all die out – the fat aunties in big hats, with legs like table legs; the secretaries drinking endless cups of tea, rushing off to take turns queuing at the Yadran and Balaton shoe shops to buy boots that fell apart the moment they put them on; the old ladies on benches spying on the buildings to see who went in and who came out, chewing it all over with their toothless mouths as they chewed their bread to pap (as recommended on television to make it more digestible). And there were the senior officials like him, whom he would meet at political get-togethers, who evoked the same mixture of fear and disgust and embodied something sad and hopeful too, which in Russia was called state pride. He knew this existed everywhere, and had even written his postgraduate thesis on the subject, and he knew the form it took was specific to each country – for some the flag and coat-of-arms, for others a pure abstraction – but that the natives had no concept of it. Living here it sometimes seemed to him they had become a completely separate nation, incapable of self-government or self-discipline, and allowing the old self-replicating type of official to thrive, obtuse and obsequious and at the same time his own man, which made him especially dangerous. The severe, polite but benign style the Governor aspired to wasn't fashionable now, which was why he knew he had reached the end of his career.

The post of governor was no longer very prestigious: everything happened in Moscow, and appointments to the remote provinces were seen virtually as exile. It was a comfortable niche, and reasonably secure, but not nearly as secure as it used to be in the old raw-material days, when three years' administrative work in Siberia would guarantee secure jobs for one's sons and grandsons. The raw-material days were probably over for good now, and he couldn't count on a job in Moscow any more. He didn't slap his subordinates on the back, or wear his hair in a quiff; he didn't like banquets and saunas or make his secretaries sleep with him, and instead of shouting at the locals he kept a polite distance from them, showing them that he belonged to a different civilization. Perhaps all in all he was in the right place. He was called here to be a civilizing influence, and apart from Asha he had no vices. And was it really a vice to take the girl as his mistress? Which of his colleagues here didn't sleep with the native girls?

But he knew his affair with Asha wasn't just another fling with a local beauty. He was divorced for one thing, which partly explained the slight awkwardness he felt with his superiors, and somehow however much he demonstrated his loyalty he could never be one of them. Perhaps in spite of his administrative career and his years of experience, it really was a sort of exile.

He simply had a better grasp of events and a quicker mind than was proper for an official, he reasoned, picking a more flattering explanation for his appointment. He often thought of his role here as like the British in India. How much better to be the son of a mighty empire, wearing his helmet in the sun and dressing for breakfast, even when he was alone. He was shocked by the way some of his colleagues had let themselves go. Klimov, for example, and that dreadful woman he was living with. But Asha! For the last three nights he had slept alone, and he found himself thinking constantly of her. She had gone off to visit her "folks", as she called them, and she had something to discuss with them. All these secrets! But he had let her go; the girl had the right to her life at her own social level.

Talk of marriage naturally hadn't come up, but although there was a risk she might start taking her role as his mistress for granted, she seemed to be more burdened than proud of it. He could see her as clearly as if she was sitting there before him, tall and pale, with a few imperfections – but what delightful imperfections they were, with her unnaturally long fingers, her tiny breasts and her thin body! There would have been something almost unhealthy about her thinness if it wasn't for the natural grace of her movements, and while living with him she had become more womanly and put on three kilos – there was some flesh on her ribs now from all the good food he was giving her. She was only nineteen, and at the age of forty-three he could have been her father, and sometimes he caught himself thinking of her as his daughter. He thought of her huge brown eyes that kept filling with tears recently, and the way she would weep silently over silly things like a bird or the sunset. Something was definitely wrong with her. He could never be bothered with women before, he was curt and cold with them and had no idea what they were thinking; she was the first one who had taught him the meaning of tenderness. It was time to open his mail.

There was a lot of it that morning – two Moscow newspapers, a fortnight old, and five letters. He put these aside and read the papers. Like all officials, he had learnt to read between the lines, and when meeting colleagues he would subtly manoeuvre the conversation to topics that made him appear well informed. But alone with himself he realized he knew absolutely nothing, and had simply buried his nose in the papers like a puppy in the corner. The war was a series of meaningless manoeuvres, as if both sides were waiting to lash each other in the Final Battle but lacked the will for it, knowing its outcome would be their mutual annihilation. They scrapped over trifles, cutting off roads and surrounding small groups of men, and every day three or four would die, or sometimes twenty-six (for some reason this was the commonest number). The Caucasus was smouldering, and he learnt of daily bombings there from the Western radio stations when he could pick them up. It was still quiet in Siberia, thank God, but things were slowly deteriorating. The Chinese were mining the remaining oil, and all industry had stopped, apart from a few Chinese factories in the towns turning the forests into hideous flimsy furniture. The natives lived an animal underground existence, and it amused him to think he had expected an attack from abroad to push the country into war. What was there to fight for? The dwindling oil, which the rest of the world had already learnt to live without? The gold, all sold off and exported? The earth? Who needed this vast fetid swamp with its unpredictable population? The world had given up on it, and he wasn't afraid to speak out sharply about this – not too sharply of course, as he might be reported, but he had his reputation as a Westerner to maintain.

There was little to be learnt from the war reports in the press and on television, since all news was embargoed by intelligence. The West had declared its neutrality, despite talk of the Khazars receiving American rifles and jam, and it seemed both sides enjoyed Chinese jam too. The Russians (alone with himself he never called them "our people") moved towards their designated positions with jars of jam and saunas for the commanders, and the Khazars advanced in two or three directions, but slowly, and had become bogged down. He had read too of battles in the South, close to Ukraine, around the large village of Degunino, known as the magic Degunino cauldron. All the armies were drawn there, since as soon as it was sucked dry of food it would fill again. He had read the communiqués and studied maps, and he still couldn't make head or tail of it. There, in the middle of nowhere, the earth bore unheard-of quantities of fruit and grain with a farewell passion, as if in a hurry to feed people while there was still something left. The apple trees groaned under the weight of the apples, and the grain trickled from the stalks, and nature was drained by its overflowing surplus, knowing people could do nothing with it, spilling over the fields into the abandoned factories, the empty settlements and the suburbs of the towns, where here and there rusty train tracks poked through the long grass. Perhaps soon the old engines abandoned on the lines would sprout iron flowers from their tangled wires, and this fruitful earth would grow things from metal, machine oil and coal.

The press described these fantastic harvests and the problem of supplies, and advised the government to put the entire economy on a war footing. Fortunately however the only positive result of the general disintegration was that there had been no government for a long time, and ration cards were issued only in the large towns.

He read about the manoeuvres around Degunino, and the troops being sent to Zhadrunovo, about a new cinema in Moscow showing *Russian People*, an earthquake in Greece and power cuts in Detroit (it would soon be the same for them in the States!) Then he turned to his mail.

There was a mass-vaccination order, and a call for more patriotic propaganda in advance of the autumn mobilization, which was no different from the spring mobilization. Of course he never fulfilled his quota here, but who did? The natives would arrive obediently at the call-up centres and be home in six months, claiming they were on leave; he knew quite well it was desertion – and it wasn't for him to judge them – and merely reinforced the cordon around the forests where they might be hiding.

The Directive of the Day concerned partisan warfare. He and his deputies were warned of raids by bands of partisans on the new railway line, cutting communications and demoralizing the neighbouring villages, and they were ordered to hunt them down "up to and including felling the forests". He smiled wrily to himself, since this would mean removing every last man from work on the line. He had no idea why this line was being built. Moscow kept hurrying the work along, and it was the only job the natives did willingly, because of the rations. Special Services were in charge of the operation, rather than the Ministry of Transport, which was understandable, since it was a border area close to China. What he couldn't understand was where the line was going. There was already one transport network connecting the town to Moscow – why did they need this new branch cutting through the unpopulated forests along the border? It made less sense the more he thought about it. Of course there was a certain brainlessness to all government decisions, but a line running from nowhere to nowhere through the Taiga? And who were these partisans attacking it? If they were Khazar bands he would have understood, but there was no whiff of the Khazars here. He read the Directive again and shrugged, then phoned the mobile of Khryunichev, regional head of the Ministry of Internal Affairs.

"Mikhail Nikolaevich," he said in a dry formal tone, "I've received the Directive about the partisans, I'll announce it at our next meeting. Tell me, have you any partisans in your area?"

"Absolutely not," replied Khryunichev, a fat man whose great love was fishing, which was fortunate, since otherwise he would have flogged the entire population to death by now. "We've plenty of deserters. We cordoned off Zakharovka and caught two of them yesterday, but I don't know of any partisans. Who are they?"

"I've no idea either," the Governor said cautiously. "Should we tighten up security on the line?"

"No need, there are no trains on it yet," replied the head of the Ministry of Internal Affairs. "I'll ask around and find out who these partisans are. Don't worry, Alexei Petrovich, all these letters are written by machines. I suppose the thieves stealing the wires are partisans. We'll just have to catch them."

The Governor politely said goodbye, and read the rest of his letters. The Kremlin wished him a happy birthday and many happy returns, two months late. He had put off opening the last one, assuming from the messily scrawled envelope that it was another local complaint, as stupid and vicious as the rest. But it turned out to contain such an unpleasant surprise that he had to jump from his chair and pace the room smoking a cigarette, which he hadn't done for a long time, before reading it twice more.

According to this revolting letter, the reason for Asha's increasingly frequent absences was that she was being unfaithful to him – yes, unfaithful, not the word used here of course – and the writer gave the address of the flat she had rented in town for her trysts (so this was how she spent the money he gave her; she swore she gave it to her family!): "Go to 8 Tchaikovsky Street and see where she sleaps nights shes not with you," his anonymous well-wisher wrote with disgusting familiarity.

Naturally there could be no thought of sending someone there, or of going himself. He couldn't act on the word of an anonymous letter, it might be a plot to kill him, and he caught himself thinking this would be preferable to her betrayal. What if it was true? Could this be the reason for her recent sadness and tears, the way she kept refusing him recently, saying she wasn't well? Yet on those nights she had been so touchingly childlike and loving with him. She was incapable of lying! He didn't believe a word of it! She wasn't here with him though, and the writer had lodged these suspicions in his mind, and he had no one to share them with and dispel them.

Pulling himself together, he threw the letter aside and briskly went through his files. Since his email had gone down he had been inundated with these spidery documents, and there was no stopping them. And now he had to receive the natives, and he felt such a loathing for them he longed to send them all to hell. Damn the girl, damn the lot of them! He choked with rage. Unless of course it was just jealousy, and people were envious of their closeness... He called Nikita and ordered a glass of iced water.

The complaints today were the same as usual, and he listened with half an ear. To maintain discipline he had recently introduced flogging. Moscow thought he wouldn't have the stomach for it, but far better flog a few scroungers and alcoholics twice a month than have some other governor thrashing them to death, as he had heard of happening. People howled, of course, but he knew Nikita and his assistant Artem didn't carry out the punishments too harshly.

Today it was the Ryakins and the Streshins again, and their interminable squabble over a house. He had long despaired of making sense of this case, tortuous and squalid, like all these people and their tricks. Young Ryakin had married a Streshin, and had made over half the house to her, then vanished without trace. She had three children and wanted more than half the house, and the Ryakins wanted more than half too, claiming young Ryakin had signed the papers when he was of unsound mind. "Look, sir, here's the receipt for his coat from the pawnshop, why would a normal person pawn his coat in autumn?"

Before the Governor appeared a silver tray piled with grubby documents. The Ryakins claimed Streshina had been having affairs on the side, and more evidence was produced to prove the children weren't Ryakin's, something to do with them having an unusual curvature of the nose. The whole village knew about it, and both sides had left for town with their paperwork and queued up to see him.

He listened to their saga all over again, trying to remember where he had cut them off last time, dribbling snot and venom…

"Who knows who the father is!" said the spokesman for the Ryakins, a squat womanly-looking man with his fat arms folded over his chest. "She won't tell us, the bitch, she has no shame!"

"You? What are you?" croaked the spokesman for the Streshins, who was also small and round, with narrow Buryat eyes. "She was never with another man, she never thought of it! They said 'Who are you making the house to?' and he said 'It's not your half, it's hers!'"

"What's half to you? Half a house, live like a mouse!"

"Shut the door, eat straw!"

"Sing, sing, what shall we sing!"

By now the Governor had no idea what was going on. Their dispute seemed to be turning into a sort of song-and-dance routine. One beat his chest, the other his thigh, one hopped, the other squatted. They whirled round in a circle, then Ryakin whipped out a handkerchief and Streshin quickly put on a pair of embroidered boots, and they advanced on each other shrieking and squawking. They whirled round again, bowing deeply to the Governor, until finally exhausted by all the hopping and squatting, they bowed to him again and panted and fell silent.

"The folk-dance 'Dispute'!" announced the Governor's secretary, appearing from behind a curtain. "It says everything."

"I don't understand," the Governor smiled uneasily. For months he had put off settling things, fearing any decision he made would be unpopular, but he never imagined it ending this way. "Thanks for the dance, but what is it exactly you want?"

"It's not me wants it, it's him!" shouted Streshin (or Ryakin), pushing Ryakin's (or Streshin's) fat shoulder.

"It's not me, it's him!"

"What do we want? We don't want nothing!"

"That's right, we've everything, thanks to God!"

"The 'Thanking God' dance," the Governor's secretary said in a cold high voice.

"Enough," he said loudly. "I thank both of you. You take him (he pointed at Streshin), and you take him (he nodded at Ryakin) and leave, immediately, this minute."

"Thanks, Governor," one said and bowed.

"Thankee Gublinator…" said the other.

"Bovernor, Brovernor…"

Babbling and bowing and slapping each other's shoulders and thighs, the petitioners withdrew.

"What on earth was that?" the Governor demanded.

"The 'Friendship' dance," explained his secretary. "Disputes are their favourite pastime, Alexei Petrovich, they're a national ritual, sometimes they go on for years. As soon as they get a hearing with you, they celebrate."

It was his second year here, and he still hadn't got the hang of the native customs. Their quarrels always seemed to end in reconciliation, and now it turned out the only reason they quarrelled was to see him, as if merely being in his presence allowed them to blossom.

Next to see him was a woman called Semyonovna, who confessed in a state of great agitation that the local doctor had molested her. Semyonovna was eighty-five, and he was in no mood for her nonsense. Another time he might have been amused, but today he was racked by jealousy and suspicion about Asha. She still hadn't returned. He must put an end to these absences of hers once and for all.

The rain was falling more heavily now. From midday until dinner time he normally worked on his correspondence. He got up, went back to his living quarters and rang her mobile, but got no reply. Then he rang her parents (he had had a phone installed in the hovel where they lived), and her flustered father gabbled that she had left yesterday evening. It was a mystery how such parents could have produced her; her father was a big brute of a man, and her mother was tiny and downtrodden with mousy hair. He had forced himself to eat dinner with them once, and everything was filthy and the food was disgusting, and Asha was too ashamed to swallow a mouthful. Where was she?

He wrote half a page of a report and played two games of Handkerchief patience, the hardest version, with three cards, but didn't throw an ace. He stared out at the garden. It was the only tended place in town. He had personally supervised the laying of the gravel paths, ordering expensive seedlings and making sure the pond didn't dry up and was kept free of leaves. If only the locals cared for their homes and gardens as he cared for his residence, life might be tolerable in this godforsaken place; apart from Asha there was absolutely nothing of interest here. He checked himself in the mirror. Surely, despite his thinning hair and a few wrinkles, there was no one else she could prefer? Of course he wasn't her first; one of her uncles or brothers-in-law had abused her in the bath when she was fourteen, but that meant nothing, it didn't count. He already knew he would go to Tchaikovsky Street, cursing himself for believing this anonymous swine and for distrusting her.

2

"8 Tchaikovsky Street," he told Vasilich, his driver.

Vasilich looked puzzled. "Why, what's there?"

"It's a hazardous building," he explained reluctantly.

Vasilich grumbled with the familiarity of a trusted member of staff: it was late, they should have turned in long ago – did he have to inspect every dangerous building God knows where?

The Governor looked out at the town. There were still a lot of Soviet features to it, with its House of Culture and cinema. The cinema had turned into an amusement arcade, then back to a cinema, and was now a night shelter for Joes, as if it had a small part in a film about the life of the lower depths, with the latest technology including the smell, and the posters in the foyer stained yellow by endless cheap cigarettes. He had set it up himself, but the Joes weren't keen on it for some reason, preferring to sleep rough and staying there only in the coldest weather. He had them rounded up periodically and thrown into jail, but it seemed to have no effect; their place would instantly be filled by others, as if the town needed a certain number to keep going.

At the top of Tchaikovsky Street he ordered Vasilich to stop. Number 8 was no different from the other houses, a crumbling, semi-derelict, two-storey mansion from the century before last, of which there were a great many in Siberia. Vasilich offered to follow him in, but he wouldn't hear of it. If it turned out to be true, he didn't want a witness to his humiliation. What he would do with her if... Never mind, he had thought of that. He would have her arrested for anti-government activity, nothing less than jail would do; there was nothing to be done with her parents, there was nowhere further to exile people here in Siberia. But let a spell in prison teach her a lesson after her life of luxury with him. He should never have become involved with a native; being kind to them had never done anyone any good, in Siberia or Algeria...

Judging from the broken windows the house was empty, and the front door was unlocked. He pushed it open to complete darkness. He

149

went back to the car for a torch, and entered the building, which smelt of mildew and decay. There had been flats here once, and people had evidently been moved out because of the condition of the place (he had guessed right with Vasilich, but half the buildings in town were in an even worse state). He stopped and listened. There seemed to be no one downstairs. What had induced him to come to this doss house to meet some filthy native? He thought of Maupassant's story about Marroca, who leaves her handsome Frenchman for a dirty Arab from the desert, and returns exhausted and emaciated, and it cheered him up a little. But by now his eyes had finally adjusted to the darkness. He looked round and saw the place was completely bare. The natives rarely left anything or threw things away; it was terrible what hoarders they were, hanging on to old rags and newspapers and children's toys. He had asked Asha about it once, and she was hurt and said, "They'd miss them!" And when he suggested it might be easier to buy new ones, she said, "Silly, of course they can't." She herself kept the little notes he wrote her to amuse her, and it wasn't hoarding of course, just a strange sort of sentimentality, which you couldn't take from people whose will and intellect had been so crushed, as if they were plunged in perpetual darkness.

He walked all round the ground floor, through empty rooms with lighter squares on the walls where pictures had been removed. There was no one there. It must be a practical joke. He walked up the stairs to the first floor and shone his torch at the walls of an empty flat, and something felt different; it wasn't the emptiness of downstairs, where every scrap had been removed, and he sensed the remains of some dark wretched life, as if someone was staying there. He pointed his torch at the corner, and saw a jar of jam and some bits of food on the floor. He felt a strange leadenness in his legs, and wondered if he was afraid. No, he couldn't be.

"Who's there!" he called softly. Nothing. The floorboards creaked as he went into the next room, and something behind him stirred, not so much a sound as a whisper of air. He turned back sharply, and there in the corridor, holding an axe over his head, stood a tall pale peasant with bulging eyes.

He dropped the torch and the peasant howled, a thin shrill howl like an old wolf, and at that instant the Governor fired his gun at him. He seldom went out unarmed: the rules now were to carry a revolver at all times. Putting it away, he stooped to pick up his torch and shone it at the peasant. He had missed, and he was squatting with his back to the wall still holding the axe over his head, with an expression of dull terror on his face.

"Who are you?" the Governor asked him hoarsely.

Vasilich had heard the shot and was pounding up the stairs. "Who's here?" he yelled, throwing open the door.

"I'm fine, Vasilich, I'm sorting it out," he said, regaining his composure a little. "Who are you? What are you playing at?"

The peasant mumbled something inaudible.

Vasilich kicked him and he dropped his axe. He looked almost comical, squatting by the wall with his bulging eyes, but the Governor knew that if it wasn't for his prompt action he would be lying dead on the floor of the hazardous building with a split skull. There was something strange about the peasant though. He moved silently, like a real Joe, and he smelt of one too, and he had spared the Governor's life not because he wanted to; he could have killed him and had wanted to kill him, but for some reason he couldn't, although he was clearly in no state to explain, sitting there looking beseechingly at him and howling.

"Cut it out!" said Vasilich. "We'll hand you to the police and they'll knock some sense into you."

"Go away," the peasant said at last. "Leave her, we'll deal with her without you. You're not a bad man, you've not sinned, just go away and no harm will come to you. Leave her – she doesn't need you."

"Leave who?" the Governor asked him in a harsh voice.

"You know who I mean. Leave her, I'm begging you, you shouldn't be with her."

"Where is she?" he roared.

"I don't know, we're looking for her. She doesn't need you, you must leave. I was going to put you away, but I couldn't, see, I didn't hurt you. Be a man and leave, or it'll be the end of us all. Hurry, scurry, rumble, tumble—"

"Call the police," the Governor interrupted him, turning calmly to Vasilich. "Order a search party for Asha."

Vasilich got out his heavy mobile, and at that moment the Governor's phone rang in his pocket. Apart from the Kremlin and his secretary, only Asha knew his number.

"Yes?" he barked.

"Quick, come home," she said. "Come to the residence. Are you all right?"

"I'm fine. Where were you?"

"Come back and I'll tell you. Come quick, please."

"I'm coming." He caught Vasilich looking at him and heard sirens on the street; the police were always instantly on the spot if it was the Governor.

"Go easy on him for now," he told the fat sergeant. "Check the crime scene and the axe, and there's a jar of jam..." He had to explain everything to the local police.

"Go away!" the peasant wailed. "If I don't get you, someone else will!"

The sergeant punched him in the stomach and he fell to the floor.

"I said go easy on him," the Governor told him. "Come on Vasilich, let's go."

Vasilich raced downstairs, and he tried to control the trembling in his legs, telling himself the coward was afraid before danger, the hero afterwards.

In the car Vasilich grumbled that good people couldn't go out now without a bodyguard, but he wasn't listening. The whole nightmare and his miraculous escape paled into insignificance beside the fact that Asha was alive, and apparently unharmed. He dialled her number again, wondering if he might have imagined her call; such things happened sometimes in moments of stress.

"Quick," she repeated. "Please, come quick."

3

On their first night together she had told him about the local beliefs, and she knew them well, for she was descended from an ancient race of native prophets and Wolves.

"I see, you do spells and magic, do you?" he chuckled.

"Call it what you like. You only joke because you're scared of us."

"Scared of you? What would I be scared of?"

"You'll see. You're with me, and that's our magic. I wanted you to be with me and you are."

"What, right from the start?"

"The moment I saw you. You're from the government and you're the most important man here, and now I'm in your court and your bed. We have our Wolves' spells against the enemy, but I can't tell you them yet."

"Why not? Can't you teach me?"

"Have you enemies?"

"In the government, Asha, in the government, it might come in handy."

"You can sort out the government yourself, Governor, I don't need your government."

She was probably from one of those tribes who had migrated to Siberia and were conquered by Ivan the Terrible, and memories of those times had been passed down through the generations. He didn't know how to knock out of her head her absurd notions about the occupiers. People always needed external enemies – the familiar psychological process of projection – and he was obviously as different from the natives as the Elois were from the Morlocks in Wells's *Time Machine*. But it wasn't because he was an occupier, it was simply two separate paths of evolution. There was nothing to stop the natives becoming Elois. They had education at their service, he had personally opened two village schools – and closed a dozen more, but what was to be done if the teachers in some villages were ignorant crones? Let them find teachers who could teach. Drunkenness, dirt and degeneration, you could teach them anything and they would never learn...

"What's this nonsense about the occupiers, is it just pride?" he asked her once.

"You've no brains, Governor!" she said angrily, and he grew angry too; even a Wolf should remember her place. "You were taught by stupid people and you repeat their stupid words. You can't make us forget our faith, even though you tried to and now only the Wolves remember it."

"What faith? You mean paganism? Veles and the rest?"

"Veles is our god," she said with a vehemence he would never have expected in someone so frail and pale. "You turned him into your hairy Northern god with his goat's beard, then you took Christ and made him Veles too. You can make your terrible Veles out of anyone. But you can't stop us celebrating our holidays."

"Which holidays?"

"We have two, and two gods," she explained seriously. "The year goes round in a circle, and the wheel turns and is stopped twice in its path, and those are our holidays. The day of Smoke is in November. We celebrate it in my granny's village, it's a lovely day, we smoke geese and pigs. The day of Heat is your Easter, when April turns to May..."

"And what happens? Let me guess, all the boys run after the girls!"

"Of course not, we don't need that," she said scornfully. "It's beautiful, we go round in a ring and sing, and the girls wear rings and the boys wear rings – you know, flowers round their necks..."

"You mean garlands."

"We say rings. Anything round is a ring, they're the most important thing for us."

"And this?" He touched the ring on her third finger.

"That's a ring too, all the girls wear one on this finger. That cap I knitted is a ring. Have you noticed how many people who come to see you wear rings?"

The locals often appeared in these white knitted caps like Georgian ones, and would remove them respectfully and bow; for some reason they called this "breaking the hat".

"That's right, breaking," she said. "Taking off with us means being with someone – I take you off. You break a hat, or someone who annoys you. You can just take them off, like taking off your hat."

The Governor's head was spinning. He didn't know if she was simply making up these words, derived like all occult languages from silly superstitions and slips of the tongue. He detested paganism and ancient cults, and regarded all these secrets of the ages as mere fairy tales, including – if he was honest – the Bible.

"You don't get a single word right," she continued. "Wheel, that's another word you get wrong, but you go on saying it. The proper word for wheel is ring."

He laughed. "Asha – did I say that right?"

"Yes, you did."

"So you have two gods?" This was a new idea to him: he had read a bit about paganism, in which each stream or bench had its own little god and everything became so complicated no one knew what was what, and they all muddled up at the feet of Zeus demanding immortality. The system was eventually simplified and replaced with monotheism, which was clearer and more unambiguous. The problem was that whereas human contradictions had before been explained in terms of the jealousy of Athena and Artemis, or the quarrel between Mars and Apollo, a single god required people to look for no logic and had no such let-out. He had never heard of two gods, though. There were rudimentary signs of it in monotheism, where God was mocked by Satan, the fallen angel, or by the holy Trotsky, who was brought down by his pride; it was as if people had deliberately encouraged him, exalting him higher and heaping all their sins on him so his downfall would be more spectacular. There was something of this too in the oil tycoon Khodorkovsky, who was allowed to puff up for a while before being thrown in jail. (Where was he now? There were rumours he was with the Yds. Whether he had escaped or was captured even the Governor with his connections didn't know, and you clearly didn't get much information from a man in shackles.)

This was why he disliked all religions, because they were so human, too human; every official of a certain rank must trip up his rival by fanning the spark of vanity in him and watching him crash. But the fallen angel could never be the equal of the supreme deity, otherwise all progress would be impossible: the enemies would hold each other back, and the world would hang in a precarious balance. And now it turned out that the natives' world hung in precisely this balance, in which the two gods flew up and down like a see-saw, each ruling in turn.

"Two gods, Give and Take, because there's two of everything," she told him. "From the day of Heat to the day of Smoke it's Give, then it's Take and it's winter."

"Ah, of course," he said. "You know what I think?" When he lay in bed with her and they talked, he would feel surprisingly clear-headed, and he could forget about work and a thousand tedious details. "One god suits places with temperate climates, more than one god suits extreme climates, where the weather's always changing. In the Mediterranean the weather changes five times a day – I'll take you there one day and show you. So I suppose half the year's life for you, and the other's death?"

"You've got it backwards," she said without rancour, and he appreciated the way she didn't fall into angry fanaticism when she discussed her faith with him. "You say we have two gods because of the weather, we say it's the two who make the weather."

"OK, that's one point of view. And what does Give do?"

"He gives you everything, whatever you ask for. He makes things grow and there's no stopping it. Take puts frost on the harvest and takes everything back."

He noticed how her rich, flexible, correct Russian would often slip into peasant sayings, and imitate the speech of the locals, even pronouncing her "o"s the same way. There was a laconic quality to these sayings, but they weren't sharp and aphoristic, they were heavy and lifeless, as if people were afraid to express themselves clearly or finish their thoughts. The only ones that made any sense to him were about work – get the sledge ready in summer and the plough in winter; you won't catch fish without bait. These little thoughts, often rhyming, reminded him of slogans on a building site, or the board of shame and honour in town – and surely it couldn't have been the natives who invented them (which of them ever wanted to work?), but the civilizers and new arrivals.

"I see. And after death the good go to Give and the bad to Take?"

"After death?" She looked at him, puzzled. "After death there's nothing, where would we go?"

The natives had no concept of mortality. Their world had no beginning or end, it went round in a circle with these two alternating deities in the dynamic equilibrium of the world's scales, and death had no meaning, because individuality didn't exist for them. They thought collectively, like a single unit, not remembering their birth, not knowing death, living eternally under these two gods and wanting nothing to change.

"Everything's two with us," she said. "Two lights in the sky, two invaders."

"Which invaders?"

"As if you didn't know. You and the others."

"Asha, stop this nonsense. No one's invaded or hurt you, you just hurt yourselves."

"Why would we do that?"

"Because you won't work!" He grew angry again.

She didn't understand. "Who else works but us? We do everything for you, and whatever we do is just an excuse for you, and it's bang-bang, you're dead!"

"OK, we invaded you and conquered Siberia. And who are the others?"

"The steppe people, from the hot places. You take it in turns, like Smoke and Heat."

He didn't try to argue with her, thinking at some point he could write an interesting article about her pagan beliefs. He thought what an interesting opportunity he had to study them with her, far more interesting than meeting the goths at Arkaim, and how lucky he was to have met a Wolf. The other governors lived with the local girls without noticing them, like trees, and now for the first time he was peering into the mysterious undergrowth of her branches. She spoke the native language too, which he was vaguely familiar with, since most of the words were Russian, but with completely different meanings.

"You did it, you took our words and you don't say half of them right. What's that?"

"A chair," he said fondly, indulging her. Of course she was making it all up. She was a smart girl, her talk of the invaders was obviously just the fruit of her imagination and she was merely wearing the mask of an ignorant peasant, like many other folk poets and native talents.

"There, you see, a chair's not that, it's where two paths meet in the forest. The word for chair is ceiling, we sit on the ceiling, and a table is oat-flour."

"And what's that?" He pointed to the ceiling.

"The sky, of course." She looked surprised. "It's easy, everything above is the sky – the ceiling, the roof of the mouth. It's where you can't go higher and have to stop."

"And a man?"

"A man's half and a woman's half, two halves. And the floor's not-sky. What's below is not-sky. But you'll never learn our words, and we've almost forgotten them ourselves."

She told him the invaders had banned the most sacred ones and called them bad, although a certain four-letter one scrawled on all the fences in town was apparently magic for them; it was the rattle of the wind, the bark of the Wolves when they celebrated a success or took away an enemy. Killing was forbidden to them and they were incapable of it, but when they called the magic word the wind would blow and would do everything for them. Although she confessed sadly that in recent years, now that the invaders were replacing each other more frequently, the old spell was losing its power.

He laughed at the idea that the word on the fences was an ancient spell. "I see. So what's your name for it?"

"Name for it?" There was an almost contemptuous note in her voice. "We've no name for it."

If she was to be believed, there were only a few people left now who knew the language, and all that saved them was that the invaders were too busy killing each other to bother with them.

"Asha, what are you saying!" he said, seriously angry now. "This is disgraceful nonsense, when have I ever hurt you?"

"You haven't, but it's true, isn't it?"

"I should have a harem so all the women here could be so lucky!"

"You're always making jokes," she said sadly.

"What jokes? You say we oppress you, but you oppress yourselves with your laziness and drunkenness. You should look honestly at yourselves—"

"It's you who make us lazy and drunk!" she shot back. "We have to live like this! Your work is about killing, you kill everything you

157

touch! We're forbidden to work like that, our work's different, you can't see it."

"Aha, so one god gives and it's fuck the rest," he said, and as he spoke a sudden fierce wind sprang up outside the window.

She jumped up and ran to it and flung it open, whispering something.

"Shut the window immediately!" he roared.

She turned round angrily.

"Never say that word to me! You're an ordinary man, not a Wolf, and now look what you've done!"

"I've said it a million times before in different situations," he grinned. He could never stay angry with her for long, and she looked so lovely by the window, pale and slender in the glow of the street lights.

"Not to me, never say it to a Wolf."

Sudden gusts of wind frightened her, she would read the Morse code of the branches scratching the windows and see omens in the rain, and perhaps it was true she could cast spells. The moment he met her, he had been free of the colds that had plagued him for a fortnight, and he almost never got headaches. He had the blood pressure of an astronaut thanks to all the sport he was doing – cycling and rowing – and because he was never unwell he couldn't test her magic powers. Once, though, he had rowed her across Kamysh lake to show how a real master did it, and a wind sprang up and the boat tossed in the waves, and she whispered for a long time to them. He laughed. He wasn't used to rowing in choppy water, but he was confident he could handle it. True, at one point he worried the wind was so strong the boat might capsize, but his survival instinct was slightly diminished, according to his trainer, and as soon as he calmed down the wind calmed down too, and they drifted across the glassy surface to the shore of the island famous for its wild raspberries.

"Your work has no meaning," she told him once. "I see you sit at your desk and tire your eyes reading papers, so many papers. But why?"

He knew there was no particular meaning to his work, but that being able to do meaningless work was the main requirement of a Russian government official. The words "meaningless" and "government" were practically synonymous; they were the ABC for any official at a certain level, and had even become a special discipline studied in some of the military academies. The very idea of meaning derived from positivism and the French Enlightenment, and was seen as a dangerous Khazar heresy. It wasn't for the Russian official to look for sense or purpose in his work, and the more senseless and purposeless it was, the more gladly he did it. The Governor received regular directives to raise standards in the village music schools (of which there were none in his jurisdiction), organize lectures for the peasants about the health benefits of sunflower oil (as if they ever used anything else), and to measure the winds with anemometers. All these measures might be appropriate in a country that was thriving, but not now in these days of utter poverty and war. True greatness, however, bordering on heroism, was to worry about things that made no sense when everything was falling to ruin. The greatest military valour wasn't to anticipate the next attack and save the most lives, but to march on to glory and put the best face on things. Not that he always agreed with the Varangian military strategy: he had even called the Military Commissariat a few times to suggest they didn't mobilize the cripples and one-legged victims of tram accidents, who had already been called up last autumn.

But only the natives ever asked the question "Why?" – to get out of working of course. The basis of any true Northern state was a severe monastic devotion to work for its own sake. Forget the liberal illusion that the state served its people like a housing office or bakery. The state served no one and was accountable to no one. Man differed from the beasts because he was concerned with things that had no immediate benefit, and it was probably best if they had no benefit at all, for this was another petty Khazar concept, the endless haggling with the Almighty. Monks in monasteries didn't ask why. If they were told to plant radishes with their roots in the air, they did so, for it wasn't their common sense being tested but their obedience, and Asha's "Why?" infuriated him. She had gained access to his residence and had seen how he worked, and it wasn't for a silly nineteen-year-old to pass judgement on government business.

"You're not to discuss my work with me," he told her curtly.

"Go ahead, tire yourself out," she said tenderly. "They tell you to work and you run round like a squirrel in a wheel, and I don't understand why."

Of course, he thought, she was jealous. In two days he was flying to Moscow with a delegation of twenty other governors, and would be attending the opening night of Swan Lake with them – a fine Russian ballet and emblem of the Russian state.

"I won't be gone long," he said.

"Fine, go." She waved an arm at him. "I won't get in your way."

"You know very well I can't take you with me."

"It's not that, it's just I know you're the Governor but why do you need so many assistants and secretaries and deputies? Who gains from their work? What are they doing here? Wait..." She interrupted him, and the love in her eyes instantly extinguished all his irritation. "I know it's not my business, but you don't need a deputy for me to love you and obey you, do you?"

"Asha," he grinned, "I can't sleep with the whole province!"

"I don't want you to. But if you're not invading us, why do you have so many soldiers and officials? You don't know the important things. You don't know spells, you can't float."

"Can't what?" he said.

"Float. You can't work. You invented the word work, it's what slaves do, with a stick for a conscience. You work like slaves because nothing here is yours. You're fighters, you can't float on the earth, it doesn't listen to you. You should talk to it, like this." She went to the window and whispered to the withered violet on the sill, the eternal symbol of Russian power, found in every office in the land. Nothing happened.

"Now what?" he said sharply.

"Wait until spring. I can't take you to Granny's, like you can't take me to Moscow, but we'll go to the country and I'll show you how we float."

4

This conversation took place in the autumn, and in the spring she reminded him of her promise.

It was a mild early April close to the Day of Heat, which was calculated according to certain signs known only to the Wolves. The Governor took her to his summer residence and ordered everything to be prepared for their arrival. The house was small and badly heated, and he never stayed there in winter.

"Send everyone away," she said. "No one must see."

He told the servants to leave for town, with just the guard at the gates whom he was obliged to keep, and at midnight she put on a robe and told him to get dressed. They went out to the cold transparent garden, where the first shoots of green were already showing, and it seemed she really did belong to an ancient race of shamans who knew dark hypnotic practices. Waving her arms in big flowing movements, she circled and squatted, murmuring to the earth, the trees and the bushes, as if begging their indulgence:

"Open earth, break the cold, peel the mist, the frog, the bird, the gale and the fire, baskets of grain, ripen the fruit, soar water, the singing of things, a chair in a tunnel, gather straw, open the door..."

That was how it sounded to him anyway, like some mad futurist poem. There was more too, but he couldn't make sense of it, even though she stood only two steps away from him, rocking and swaying and chanting. She threw out her arms to all four corners of the garden, as if throwing something away, then she reached up to the sky with her wide sleeves falling to her wrists, calling and whispering and beseeching, and he was amazed to see the birches and apple trees sway in rhythm with her. The night was two colours, black and green, and the air seemed to be dreaming of green, with green blades of grass cutting through the black earth, and the green water in the pond and the green stars in the black heavens.

Bowing low to the ground, she wriggled like a snake, throwing herself right and left, and seemed to be bargaining with her invisible interlocutor, tossing her head and stamping her foot. Then she bowed again, and soon her murmurs became loving as a lullaby, and he felt himself being soothed to sleep. She continued her light swimming dance, driving away the cold and bringing back the warmth. The air floated, and the moon floated in the sky from west to east, dancing and pulling faces. He had often seen the moon like this as a child, especially at full moon, and he would lie in bed by the window not knowing if he was asleep or awake, seeing it dive, hop and wink at him, and now it was the same moon of his childhood, changing colour from red to blue and from yellow to green, turning somersaults in the April sky.

After an hour she staggered and was unable to go on, and he caught her in his arms and carried her inside.

Next morning she woke him with a delighted laugh: "See, I told you!"

They returned to the garden, and all around the house everything that could flower was in flower, the six huge cherry trees planted long ago in Soviet days, the apple trees and lilacs, and no miracle of the weather could explain it.

"It's the day of Heat! Look, the earth's floating, the water's floating!"

It was true. Steam rose from the earth, swarming with blue phantom-like shapes, and the grass was thick and green and the water in the pond shone gold in the sun. She wandered around clapping her hands, and he had never seen her so happy. "It worked, it worked! There'll be a harvest!"

He still didn't really believe in her powers. The earth couldn't listen to a native, even if she was a Wolf, and she was terribly hurt when he reminded her of Foma and Erem and all the other local peasant types who knew nothing of working on the land.

"We don't need to slave on it, it listens to us. You only know slavery because the earth's not yours!" She narrowed her eyes at him. "Where does it listen to people? In America? The natives didn't know the wheel or the plough, and it gave them everything! In France? There are only fifty left there who can talk to it! You can't get on with it, because it's first you then the others, and you don't talk to it. To talk to it you mustn't grab, you must listen."

He was struck yet again by the harmonious duality of her mythology. Everything led from one thing to the other – two gods, each obliterating the achievements of the last one, putting nature to sleep then waking it up, and always returning to the same point of departure, like the two aggressors, turning the natives' history into an endless circle and absolving them of all responsibility.

From what she said, a picture emerged of her race. Not knowing literacy and not wanting to ("everything's there and always will be, why write it?"), they had lived for centuries spread over a vast area, and had made the South their free enchanted land, with its magic stoves and apple trees. The boughs broke from the weight of the fruit and the earth there didn't need tending, it fed everyone without being forced, as a mother feeds her baby or a cow her calf. This golden age lasted until the arrival of the steppe people who knew no trades, only how to trade in the labour of others, and the Governor learnt to his surprise that these steppe people were the Khazars; he had no idea the Russians' dislike of them had such ancient roots.

He saw all of Russia's history in her stories. The natives groaned under the Khazar cabal, and appealed to the Northern warrior tribe to drive them out. So they came and they burned their capital, Tsetzar, and the natives begged for mercy and wept for the Khazars, and the Varangians dealt with them not with cunning and persuasion but with crude military force, and instead of letting them float peacefully on their land they enlisted them in their hairy cohorts. They fought badly, but you don't need a brain to die, and they were thrown into battle like wood into the fire. They fought and died, and those who could escape hid in the forests, occupying the grey wastelands where there was no life, trying to heat the snowy landscape with their wretched warmth. They went to the mountains, to the stony earth where nothing but thorns and thistles grew, they went to the mossy forested land of the North from which the Varangians had escaped because they couldn't talk to it, and they prayed to it for months and years, and soon the forests produced berries and the wild onion began to grow in Siberia, and blades of sorrel poked through the mud.

"But why didn't you fight them?" he couldn't resist asking her.

"We can't," she replied, surprised. "We float, we make spells, we don't fight."

"So it was easier for you to crawl off to the forests and talk to the mud than drive them out?"

"How can you say that? I couldn't kill a loaf of bread," she said, shocked.

"A loaf of bread?" he asked. Sometimes in bed with her on moonlit nights he would feel afraid of this creature from another world lying beside him.

"You say chicken," she sighed. "With us chicken is something that smokes, like a fire. You'll never learn, you're not one of ours, and it's a sin that I love you."

He tried in vain to reassure her that every race had its special flaws, and every love for a foreigner could be seen as a betrayal.

"Look at yourself, are you one of ours?" she said. "Your hands are different and so are your eyes, that's why I love you."

* * *

As he listened to her stories, he realized no one person could have invented them. The Varangians and Khazars succeeded each other with mathematical regularity, and every hundred years or so they would slaughter each other. There had been attempts throughout history to divide Russia in two, first by Ivan the Red (so named because of his bloody hands; apparently it was the Varangians who had called him Terrible). He gave his Guards the best lands and the rest to his Boyars, but the Khazars still longed for freedom, and the Northerners defended their right to make others die for them, and during their clashes the natives would have a brief breathing space. Some of these clashes had happened despite the two of them, such as the Bolshevik Revolution, but it had soon turned into the usual battle between North and South, and the natives were again driven from their homes.

She spoke of all these things as if homelessness was in her genes and she had been there herself, roaming the frozen fields looking for somewhere to stay, which was what made her stories so sad.

"I suppose you'll say Peter the Great was a Khazar next!" he said to her once.

"Of course he was, he was from the steppes. Look at him, with his red hair and blue eyes, he's not a Northerner, he's not one of yours."

"So why did he bring Germans to work in Russia?"

"Not ordinary Germans," she explained. "They were the steppe people who escaped to the West and travelled round Europe. He didn't like Russians, he wanted to get rid of them."

He hadn't the strength to listen to any more, yet the worm of curiosity still gnawed at him. "Surely your circle can't continue endlessly though?" he said one dry, brittle autumn morning just before the day of Smoke, when she was saying goodbye to the summer house and comforting the plants, whispering spells and helping them sink into their winter sleep. "Surely things must dry up some time, and the earth will have had enough?"

"We don't think about it," she said evenly, but he sensed she was anxious.

"That's childish, only children don't think about death. Do you want to be children all your life?"

"Why children? We don't know about death, we're not afraid of it. Nothing changes after us, things just go on."

"But nothing's eternal, and look at your people, they're all Joes. That's what happens when you don't work – sorry, float. You become like animals."

"That's how you see it, but for us they're the best ones. They're not what you think, they're like Wolves, but better."

"I see, the local buffoons, stinking saints."

"You can think what you like," she said mildly.

"OK, leave the Joes out of it. But every religion has its vision of the end. Things break down, you can see it with your own eyes."

"But it's you who break everything," she replied, raising her large brown eyes to him. "Well not you, you don't flog the natives to death, you even let some off prison for stealing bread. And you're always good to me, I can't complain about you. But you're not a true Northerner. Though I'd love you even if—"

"Yes, yes, of course," he interrupted her, and wondered for the first time if his liaison with a native girl was proper. Perhaps this too was a sign of social breakdown. According to Maugham, all the governors had native girls, but that was in the dying days of the British Empire.

"What if I left you?" he teased her once. "I read a story about an official who met a native girl and swore to love her for ever, then he sailed to England to marry a rich woman, and as soon as the ship left shore he started hiccuping. He hiccuped in agony for three days without stopping, and after a week he died because he couldn't eat or drink. What would you do to me? Would you put your Wolf's curse on me?"

"Never!" she wept. "We don't have curses like that, even if you left to marry a rich woman!"

He imagined her alone, silently enduring everything, weeping and defenceless, and he knew then that he would never leave her. She had bound herself to him with her pitifulness, and there was no woman he would abandon her for; he would as soon abandon his duty to his work. She was also his duty, his work.

"So will you ever leave me?" he asked her.

"No, I won't."

"Even if your granny tells you to?"

She jumped back and stared at him.

"Why, what would she say?"

"I don't know, grannies sometimes don't like their grandsons-in-law. Why are you so upset?"

"You don't understand," she sighed. "If I'm not allowed to be with you, that's it, even the Wolf's spell won't save us."

"And you'll leave?"

"It doesn't matter if I leave or not, it's the end," she said, and he didn't get another word from her after that.

5

"I must leave," she said, when he returned from Tchaikovsky Street. She had been standing by the window in his office waiting for him.

"Please, no more shocks, someone's just tried to kill me."

"Who?" She clutched her hands to her heart and looked distraught.

"Some Joe, a strange peasant I'd never seen before. He kept mumbling that I should go away. Can you please tell me what it's all about?"

"Did he talk about me?"

"He said a few things. Wait, sit down, why don't you put on the light?"

"No, don't, leave it off!"

"Nonsense, who are you hiding from? It's my house!"

"I'll tell you everything! Leave the light off. Come here. What did he say?"

"God knows, Asha. I've tried to understand this native business, your beliefs—"

"What do you know?" she moaned. "Did he say you must leave?"

"Yes, he said they'd deal with you themselves. What is it, what have you done?"

She trembled and he embraced her. "There there, it's all over now," he whispered in her ear. "A drunk peasant waved an axe at me, but he didn't kill me. You're right, he said they can't do it."

"No, we can't," she nodded. "I never tried it, I couldn't. I have to go away."

"But why, where? Tell me, I don't understand!" He strode to the light, and the instant he switched it on a large cobblestone crashed through the window almost hitting her, shattering glass on the floor. There were curses and whistles below, and his bodyguard rushed in.

"What happened, Alexei Petrovich, are you all right?"

"Asha, are you hurt?"

She cowered and covered with her face with her hands.

"We'll catch the bastard, the boys have run after him," his bodyguard said, going to the black window with its jagged teeth of broken glass. "He was standing right opposite, the swine. He won't get away, Alexei Petrovich, you can be sure of it, I'll question him myself."

"Bring him to me when you catch him," said the Governor. "Tell Vasilich we're going to the dacha."

"No!" Asha whimpered. "You must stay here!"

"Hell," he said wearily, rubbing his temple. "OK, put more guards at the front, they can sleep on the ground floor, and tell the boys to mend the glass. You can go now and we'll drink tea."

"It's all covered," said his bodyguard. "Don't worry, Alexei Petrovich, I'll put guards around the perimeter. Your driver told me you went out without me, who knows what could have—"

"Nothing happened," he said. "Don't spread it around, it's my business where I go. I'll sort it out."

* * *

"Well, I'll be damned," he repeated a little later in the dining room, completely reassured. Only one thing worried him now, or not so much worry as the worm of something squalid and disturbing. A thriller is frightening not when someone is murdered, but when it's done clumsily. It was less frightening to get a letter written in blood than one written in a childish scrawl filled with spelling mistakes, and it was the clumsiness of the attempt that frightened him in this story. He had been convinced with no proof that Asha was being unfaithful to him, the peasant had waited for him with an axe, but couldn't kill him, a stone was thrown through the window when the light was switched on and had missed them... He realized that the natives, who had never done anything in their lives but dull farming, didn't merely hate him, they wanted to kill him, and she had now explained to him the reason. He had no idea why this foolish myth about him was so vivid in these unhappy people's imagination, but if in Moscow they believed in the White Brotherhood, why shouldn't people here believe that the baby she was carrying was the Antichrist? She had told him the legend from the time of Rurik, of a man from the North who would sleep with a Wolf-girl, and their child would destroy the equilibrium of the two gods, and history would no longer run in a circle. The natives couldn't let the child be born. The few who had known about them had tolerated their relationship, but as soon Asha went to her grandmother to tell her she was pregnant (their word for it was "heavy"), the natives' bush telegraph began buzzing with rumours of the Governor's lineage.

"Why didn't you tell me you were a son of Rurik?" she asked him reproachfully, with a sadness he found irresistible, and he immediately felt guilty for all her past and future woes.

"Lord, Asha, I'd no idea it was important! I'm a Kononov on my father's side, but I never used the name. My mother remarried a year after I was born and I was always Borozdin. Kononov never even lived with us, I've no idea who he is—"

"What are you saying, Governor? Kononov, Conan, it's a Varangian name, you're the son of a Rurik. If you'd told me I'd never have entered your shell."

"My what?"

"Your door," she said with a guilty smile.

"Wait, where did I read about this?" he frowned. "A man loved a witch, and the villagers cursed them and threw stones at them. I know, it's Olesya! You've been going to my library, haven't you? What a fool I was not to guess!" He smiled at her, and she smiled back, a sad crooked smile he took as assent. "Poor little thing, was it so I'd take you seriously? There was a granny too in that story saying silly things, there are hundreds of such stories. That's enough now. We'll find out who threw the stone. You'll see, it's probably a petitioner with a grudge against me."

He seemed to have sudden powers of premonition, for at that moment the internal phone rang on his desk and his bodyguard told him the criminal had been caught, or rather two of them, and they were ready to appear before him for preliminary questioning.

"Fine, bring them in," he said. "I've an idea who they are…"

Once again his premonition was correct, and his bodyguard pushed Ryakin and Streshin into the room – or was it Stryashin and Rekin? – the same sweet pair who had exhausted him for six months with their dispute and had entertained him that morning (it felt like a year ago) with their dance of friendship and thanks.

"Good day to you, Governor!" said Streshin.

"Ay, good day, good day!" quacked Ryakin.

"Don't be cross, Governor!"

"Sorry, Gublinator!"

"It just happened."

"It shouldn't have!"

"We shouldn't, we shouldn't!"

"Six months we been watching you."

"We think and we think…"

"And today we know."

"It's Him!"

"The very one."

"Be quiet!" roared the Governor. Ryakin and Streshin looked frightened and fell silent. His bodyguard had been told not to touch them until he got the go-ahead, but they had both been knocked around, one with a big bruise under his left eye, the other with a swollen ear.

"They won't stop babbling," he said. "Never mind, they'll come to their senses in prison."

"Yes, we will!" Ryakin started up again.

"We will, we will, we'll do everything!"

"We've told everyone everything—"

"What have you told everyone?" the Governor said, at the end of his tether. "Speak clearly, one at a time!"

"She'll tell you," Streshin nodded at Asha.

"She'll tell, she'll tell," echoed Ryakin.

"She knows."

"Now she knows."

The Governor turned to Asha, sitting motionless with lowered eyes.
"Are they friends of yours?"

"We are, we are…" mumbled Streshin, and the bodyguard pushed
his fist to his face to shut him up.

Asha raised her eyes, and they were full of tears. "They're from
Granny's village," she nodded.

"Have they been following you?"

"I suppose so," she said.

"Is it about your ridiculous dispute?" he demanded.

"It's not that, not that," Streshin said in a scared voice.

"Our dispute is good," said Ryakhin.

"We've come on business, Governor."

"Yes, business, Gublinator."

"We didn't follow her, we didn't, we're little people, Governor."

"Little people, Gublinator."

The bodyguard banged their heads together and the conference
went quiet for a while.

"Which of them threw the stone?" the Governor asked.

"This one," said the bodyguard, shoving forward the one on the
left.

"It wasn't to hurt you, Governor."

"Or her, Gublinator."

"Just so you'd know…"

"To go away."

"Otherwise it'll be bad."

"The earth will rise!"

"It mustn't, it mustn't, Gublinator!"

"Really, what earth?" the Governor said coldly. "You mean the
world?"

"It's true what they're saying," Asha said suddenly. "Even the old
people don't remember the last time the earth rose. If we don't leave,
the town will die."

"And the villages, the villages," said Streshin.

"And the forests!" added Ryakin.

"And fields!"

"Ditches!"

"Rivers!"

"Mountains!"

"Quiet!" said Asha in a loud commanding tone the Governor hadn't heard before.

"They know I'm heavy, and now you know too Governor," she stated firmly. "I said nothing for four months, and I've five left."

It was only then that he realized he had said nothing to her yet about their future child, so shocked was he by the prophecy. Not that he believed a word of it, of course, but she was clearly in no state for him to talk of the joys of motherhood and his willingness, if not to marry her, then at least to take responsibility for the baby. First he must calm her and comfort her, then... Suddenly he grasped the most important thing – she was four months pregnant, and he hadn't noticed! This explained her tears at the sunset and her fears and sensitivity. Lots of women became confused and deluded when pregnant: this was why she believed this nonsense. She needed a doctor, quick! If he found a good specialist who made her see the absurdity of it all, he would get her better in no time.

"I must leave," she said after a short pause. "I won't let them kill the baby. I know my fate. Whoever he is he's mine, and I won't let him grow up to be a criminal. I can't be with you Governor, we can't be together."

"You're not going anywhere," he told her.

"Be quiet and listen! It has nothing to do with you, it's my business. I'll go on my own and you mustn't come with me."

"No one's going anywhere without my permission," he said calmly. "I'll tell the guard." He picked up his internal phone and his bodyguard barked, "First! Seven!"

"You don't know anything," she said softly.

"I know what I need to know." He waved his hand. "You're not leaving without me. We'll find somewhere for you, I'm ready to..."

"How kind of him, he'll marry a native!" she drawled. "It's my fault, I wasn't careful. It's true what you say, everything's broken. The Wolves didn't see it, but these good brothers did." She nodded at Streshin and Ryakin.

"Fine," he snapped. "Question them and hold them separately from the Tchaikovsky Street peasant, or they'll talk to him and we'll never get to the bottom of it. And fix the window. Nikita, more tea!"

Nikita glided in with his glass in its silver holder with the official Russian crest.

"Come on, Asha, you're staying here tonight."

He took her hand and she followed him listlessly with her eyes down, dragging her feet. But at the door she turned back to the bodyguard.

"You think I can't get away? I'm staying with him so he's not alone, but I can escape if I want to, and you can't stop me. Eh, Uncles?"

"Yes, she can," nodded Streshin.

"She can, she can," agreed Ryakin.

"Don't question them, I'll tell you about them myself," she told the bodyguard imperiously, and the Governor saw to his amazement that he was nodding respectfully at her. "Feed them and let them sleep. And you, Governor, hop."

"Hop where?" he asked stupidly.

"There, on the spot. Can you do it?"

"You know what, Asha," he said quietly. "Don't forget yourself or I'll say the Wolf's word, even if you are pregnant."

"Oh yes," she said calmly. "I've always known what you were like. I can't tell you what to do, I can only love you."

"It's late," he said. "Let's go to bed."

"Just remember, Governor," she said, "If the earth rises, I'll go. You don't have so much power over me either."

"I have some," he said, and led her to the bedroom, hoping that morning would restore logic to this shaky picture of the world, and let him work out a way to be with her and the baby. The rain turned to a sudden downpour, and the residence shuddered slightly in the storm.

6

She became a little calmer in his bedroom, and was his quiet submissive Asha again.

"So what are you saying? How am I to understand this nonsense?" he asked her gently.

"What's to understand? It's too late now, I'm not giving him to the Wolves, I'm going to Degunino."

"Degunino?" he said, surprised; just this morning there had been something about it in the papers again.

"My aunt's in Degunino, it's where our old people live. I'm not afraid."

"Stop, tell me the whole thing again from the beginning."

She sighed and sat up in bed. "Don't you understand yet? I don't know what will happen, we never know who'll be born, only if it's a Wolf or not, and this one will be the Wolf of Wolves and he'll be

171

the end of us all. Can't you see the signs? We're barely alive. I used to think it would all pass, so many times it turned out that way—"

"The end of what? Everything, the world?"

"No, we're not the world, you know that, Governor. I sit here all my life praying to the wheel, and you've travelled, you've seen places. You can see things aren't right here. If we break the circle there'll be nothing left. The world's stopped and started so many times and we're still here. The only thing we can't do is love one of yours."

"And what about the Khazars?" He couldn't dismiss this strange myth of hers until he fully understood it, possibly the vestige of some ancient taboo against sleeping with the enemy. "Could you have a baby with a Khazar?"

"I don't know about them, I just know I can't be with someone from the North."

"How strange," he smiled. "I wonder if it's because they're a more feminine race? I read somewhere—"

"What's that got to do with it? What do you want from me?" She raised her eyes to him with a look of such anguish he felt powerless in the face of her madness. "Maybe a Wolf man's with a Khazar woman now. Everything's in pairs with us, misfortunes never walk alone. You're in the government, you've seen the signs, you should know."

He couldn't deny he had seen the signs, but as a government official he valued instinct above reason. His reason told him the end was near, but his instinct said Russia had always lived this way. His worldview had been formed in the era of the first stabilization and high oil prices, before the world sniffed Phlogiston. Which of his fellow rationalists could have foretold this fabulous Russian upsurge that seemed to come from nowhere, simply from expensive oil? The rest of the world had stopped hoping for stability, but for Russia it was wages, credits, a planned life ten years ahead, and no disasters expected. Who could have known that soon no one would need oil any more, and fountains of the damn green gas would gush from the earth throughout Europe and the States, even in Greenland, leaving Russia with nothing but its oil? The voice of reason said there was no stability under the green slime, yet people had thought it would grow hard as marble and the Russian miracle would last for ever.

"Forget signs, Asha, there are no signs, I don't want to hear about them," he said.

"Don't listen then. You Northerners are all the same, what you don't know doesn't exist for you."

"What do you plan to do?"

"I can't stay here," she said quietly, looking away from him. "I'll go to Degunino, and if they say I can't stay with them I'll go south to the mountains. When the Wolves are driven out they always go to the mountains. I'll bring up the baby there and make sure he doesn't see anything wicked. I'll raise him so there'll be no wickedness in him."

"But they say it's me who must leave."

"Because they think they can kill him if you do. Kill, kill, they keep saying. They can't do it themselves, but they can get someone else to do it if they need to. They can find me anywhere."

"And what if I don't leave?"

"They'll just do it with you here, you won't be in their way."

"So we can't be together?"

"Only if you go to the mountains with me." She looked at him with an angry smile he hadn't seen before. "Will you go to the mountains with me, Gublinator? Will you bring up the baby with me?"

Even if he was prepared to say he would go to the ends of the earth with her, even if this cliché was possible, his habitual self-control would have made it impossible for him to say so. But of course he wouldn't go with her. There was no question he loved her, perhaps even wanted her to have his child, but run off with a native? Believe their idiotic legend and become a pawn in their game? Naturally he wouldn't let her go anywhere, but the idea of her dragging him with her... She had definitely got above herself.

"I know you won't, Governor," she said wearily. "Why would you? You'll stay here and read your papers and work."

"You'd like me to go?"

"Why not? It's frightening alone in the mountains and I've got used to you. I've lived behind a wall and you've fed me. But it's a long way to Degunino, what would you do there?"

"Tell me kindly what Degunino is. The papers keep writing about the Degunino cauldron, and now you believe this lunacy?"

"You wouldn't say that if you'd been there. It's a magic place, people come and they take them in, but not everyone can stay, there's no room for them all. We say it's where Give lives. Well, he doesn't really live there, but our main church to him is there. It's beautiful, Governor. We haven't many churches, but this one's worth the lot of them. Do you know why we've built so few?"

"I can guess." He knew what sort of builders the natives were. He was appalled by their squalid village architecture and their huts and hovels, and it maddened him that they never used nails so everything fell down; according to Asha they liked it that way, and cracks allowed a place to breathe.

"No, you can't," she laughed, without hostility now, and to his relief she seemed slightly calmer. "It's because churches just bother him, they're like a sort of drawing room for him. You'd go crazy if you had a drawing room in every village, but as soon as the Northerners arrive anywhere they always build churches. You saw how we put onions on ours and you copied us and built your domes. We have the most onions in Russia, they're ours, we made them first. The whole world's like an onion, do you know why?"

"I can guess that too. So when you peel them you cry and the governors feel sorry for you!"

She didn't get the joke. "Do a lot of people cry when they come to you?"

"A few, sometimes."

"Well, they should cry about the life you've made for them, Governor."

"You're right." He couldn't argue with her. He knew the locals had nothing to thank him for, and no reason to count their blessings.

"Everything's like an onion. The earth's an onion, a person's an onion. Peel one layer and another and you end up with nothing. Up there..." She pointed to the ceiling, to her low peasant sky. "That's where it wants to be. Dig it in the earth and it grows, and a turnip's the same. Everything that grows has a soul, do you understand now?"

"Why do you say there's no immortality then?"

"There isn't – what immortality? When you die you go into the ground and a tree grows from you. You can chop it and saw it and it'll go on growing, and that's the soul. Some of us become a pine tree, others become an oak or an apple tree. And you'll be a spindle, Governor, because you don't understand simple things."

She said this so lovingly and looked nothing like the witch who had ordered him to hop on the spot, and it seemed her madness had passed.

"You thought that up yourself, about the trees?"

"How would I do that? It's how it is. They burn us but they never bury us, because they don't want trees to grow from us. Burn us and the ashes fly in the wind, but they don't need trees."

How logical, he thought. Christianity exalted people's humanity as their most precious quality, and everything natural in them turned to dust.

According to her people, the most precious thing was the soul, because it was a living growing thing. Nothing human mattered to them – culture, duty, history – just this blind vegetable force they called the soul, with their druid tree-worship, their wooden architecture and their observance of the vegetable cycle of life, sleeping in winter, procreating and bearing fruit in summer. Some souls made houses, others were burnt in the stove, and all was as it should be; a person had served their purpose.

She explained to him that they didn't build churches to Take, because there was nothing to pray to him for, and he was struck yet again by how well-crafted the myth was. Goodness needed people to pray to it and beg for favours. Evil acted by itself and needed none of this. Take was harsher and probably older than Give, although she hadn't told him yet about their creation myth. He had never heard of tree-souls, and he was probably going to learn a lot more, like a child hearing things for the first time from his mother. She seemed to have become more open with him since the night in the garden he had watched her float...

"So does Take live somewhere?" he asked her.

"Yes, he does," she replied seriously. "Our two main villages are Degunino and another one, but we don't say its name."

"I know, it's Moscow!" he said triumphantly. "Am I right?"

She didn't get this joke either.

"Outsiders won't find it, it's deep in the forests, you don't need to know about it."

"Please won't you tell me where it is?" Telling him her stories seemed to calm her.

"I can't, Governor. If we say its name you go there and never come back."

"It's not on my patch, is it?"

"No, don't worry. We just say the word and you go there, do you understand?"

"I think so," he nodded. "Is it the word on the fences that calls up the wind?"

"You're joking, you're always joking."

"So what's so wonderful about Degunino?"

She cheered up again. "I only went once, my granny took me to see the church. You can't imagine what it's like, it's the most beautiful place. I saw our magic stove there, have you heard of it?"

"What stove?"

"The one that bakes pies all by itself. It baked me a rhubarb pie. It doesn't do that for every child, even a Wolf, but it baked one for me. If someone has a bean in their pie it means they're a special Wolf, but no one's had a bean for a long time."

Poor girl, he thought. The old woman had taken her to stay with her relatives, and they had glamorized their wretched life by pretending the village was an island of plenty and the pies were a miracle. There couldn't have been many miracles in her life if a rhubarb pie was a miracle for her.

"I saw their apple tree in the forest," she went on. "Its branches were down to the ground with fruit and it grew all by itself – no one watered it, nothing! They gave me an apple and it was the size of your head!" She clutched his head to her breast and embraced him.

"So why didn't you visit it every year?"

"I couldn't," she replied, surprised by his ignorance. "People must live on their own land or it'll get scabby. And now all the soldiers in your war want to go there. There are plenty of other villages, but they don't fight for them. It's in all the papers."

He must read more, he thought. But even if she was making it all up, it still intrigued him. What was this Degunino cauldron, in this senseless location of no strategic importance to anyone, which was captured and abandoned so many times? By a strange coincidence her granny had taken her there as a child, and from reading the papers she must have concocted this fantasy of it as some sort of heaven for all the invading armies. It was the only possible rational explanation for this bizarre myth.

"You'll go there then? You won't stay with me?"

"If the earth doesn't rise I'll go tomorrow. I don't think it will, though." She seemed to be reassuring herself rather than him. "We don't know when it will be, but it can't happen until Degunino says so."

"Yes, yes." He stroked her back and felt how tight her muscles were, although they had been lying in bed for an hour while he talked to her and tried to calm her. "You should sleep, you need plenty of rest now. If I'd known, I wouldn't…"

He wanted to say he wouldn't have touched her if he had known she was pregnant; he knew it was already dangerous in the fourth month. She knew what he meant, but it didn't worry her.

"I won't come to any harm with you Governor, it's others who'll harm me."

* * *

176

It seemed to him they had slept for only an hour, but it was already light when he was woken by the deafening ring of the telephone. He had slept fitfully and dreamlessly, waking every so often to make sure she was still there. He jumped up to answer it and checked his watch, and saw it was six-thirty. Moscow was on the line.

"Yes?" he mumbled, not bothering to pretend he was awake and on top of things. On the contrary, he wanted Moscow to know he had nothing to be ashamed of and wasn't putting on a show for their benefit.

"Instructions for Alexei Petrovich Borozdin on the fifteenth of July," an official said. "The Quote of the Day is from Chapter Six of the Holy Evstakhy of Distant Battles: 'Whosoever dishonours the pure-white memory of his forefathers who spilt their blood in the far corners of the Fatherland, may he be spewed from their mouths as a sticky fluid.' The slogan of the day is 'Conservative Modernization'. The Sun is in Aries with its house in Venus. In the Druid calendar the Day of the Tradescantias is auspicious. Accordingly at twelve hundred hours you are to fly to Moscow for a meeting at the government palace in Arkhangelskoe. A plane is being sent at their urgent request – urgent, is that clear?"

"I understand," he said in a toneless voice.

This summons to Moscow after the blitz of horoscopes which now preceded all official pronouncements was like a blow to the head. He was prepared for idiotic orders to install anemometers and improve music schools, but this was serious, and he knew instinctively that it was to do with Asha. He remembered her saying people could find her anywhere, but what he couldn't accept was that the authorities cared about the natives and their silly superstitions. If they were in league with Ryakin and Streshin, it meant it really was the end.

She woke and sat up.

"They've called you to Moscow?" she asked in a strained voice.

"Yes." There was no point lying to her.

"I told you. It means they know."

"Asha, what are you saying!" he shouted, unable to control himself. "You're no fool, you're not a savage. Do you seriously think I'm being called to Moscow because you'll give birth to the Antichrist?"

"I don't think it, I know," she whispered.

"Then fly there with me."

"Never. They'll catch me as soon as I arrive."

Lord, how deep was the fear in them of being caught. "Fine. What do you suggest?"

"Send me straight to Degunino. Put me on a train or give me a car."

"But I don't know where it is."

"It's two hundred kilometres from Kursk. You have to dodge through the back roads, but I know the way."

"And what if there are battles there?"

"I'll get there, so long as no one harms me on the way," she said, looking at the floor.

"I'll take you myself."

"It's too far, Governor, you can't leave your work. And what will you do if they send me to the mountains? Will you come with me?"

"Nonsense, of course they won't."

"Forget it then, how will you get me there?"

"I must fly to Moscow now, they've sent a plane for me. Stay here with my bodyguards, and I'll send you away this evening when I get back."

"No!" she shouted. "I can't stay here, they can do anything to me! You must hide me somewhere in town!"

"Can't you go to your parents?"

"No, they don't want anything to do with me."

"Oh hell!"

He dressed, trying feverishly to think where he could hide her. Damn them and their nonsense. Then he remembered Grigory, a harmless alcoholic from Moscow who sold local handicrafts and had told him a few things about the history of the place. Grigory's knowledge was sketchy and superficial. He had only heard of the Wolves and couldn't boast a personal relationship with one, but he knew the town and its outskirts like the back of his hand. No one knew exactly what had brought him here. He hinted vaguely that he used to work for one of the Khazar oligarchs who had subsequently been "de-Khazarized". Shortly before the oligarch was arrested with his whole family, this PR man had run off to the woods, deciding his only chance of survival was to escape to some dark corner of Siberia and go native, and he was right. They might have been looking for him in Moscow, but he lived well here and had married a simple illiterate woman, swarthy as a monkey but not without charm. He lived in a crumbling fleapit with her in the suburbs and earned a few copecks writing for the local paper – in other words he lived the normal life of a provincial intellectual, apart from the dark secrets he carried with him from his PR past. The Governor was amazed by how modest Grigory's needs were. According to his stories he was used to a life of luxury, but either it was part of his professional code of conduct to adapt to changed circumstances, or he was just glad to be alive, even in a Siberian fleapit.

No one would look for Asha at Grigory's. He had vanished so successfully that people had simply forgotten his existence, and he had recommended the same strategy to the Governor. "Everything will change soon, mark my words, and they'll be after you too. Just slip out of sight for a year and they won't notice you. Keep Nikita with you, he knows the form. No one needs to know anything now but how to jail people. The government will gradually devour itself and they'll definitely devour you. They need to take out a few like you so people won't grumble."

The Governor had listened to all this with a wry smile, and realized that if these charming cowards and time-servers had once run the major corporations the government line must have been correct. It wasn't necessary to kill them of course, just to break their spirit. And now this unprincipled opportunist was the only person he could trust here, ex-people being generally more trustworthy since they had nothing to lose.

He went up to the computer in his office, where the window had already been replaced, and printed out some information for Moscow from last month to be on the safe side, then he put it in his briefcase and called in his driver.

"Vasilich, we're going to the airport in a quarter of an hour. We'll take Asha with us and you'll drop me off and drive her round for a while in case anyone's following, then take her to Grigory Emelyanovich's. I'll tell him you're coming. Go in with her and check it's all clear, don't stay and chat. I'll phone you from Moscow and you can pick me up later."

Vasilich nodded. He was probably the most reliable of all his staff; he was so used to dealing with machines he had practically become one himself.

He then phoned Grigory, apologizing for the earliness of the hour, and got straight to the point. "Grigory, I've a favour to ask, could you put up a girl in your flat today? She needs to hide, the natives think she's a witch and are threatening to kill her."

"Why me?" Grigory said, frightened. "Couldn't you put her in the cells for the day?"

"I can't leave her alone, if the locals find her they'll kill her. I've only my staff at the residence, she can't stay here. God knows what people would do to her."

"And where will she go afterwards?"

"I'll send her to another district, she'll be fine. They'll believe any rubbish these days, witches and wolves and so on. Don't worry, she'll be driven discreetly to your flat, no one will see her. I'll give you a bodyguard."

For a moment the fear of getting involved in a scandal battled in Grigory with the fear of falling out with the Governor.

"You'll give me a bodyguard?" he said at last.

"Absolutely, one of mine. You understand my chief concern is to avoid disturbances in town. There aren't many civilized people here I can count on."

"To hell with it, I'll do it. I'll send my wife to her parents', I don't want her seeing the witch."

"Very wise," the Governor said.

Asha sat pale and silent in the car.

"Vasilich will take you to a friend of mine, you'll be safe with him," he said. "I'll fly back this evening and collect you."

"You won't come back," she said calmly.

"Why on earth not?"

"Because they won't let you."

"You think they'll arrest me?" he mocked her.

"They'll arrest you or send you to the war, they'll find a place for you. They're luring you away, and without you I'll—"

"But you know I can't take you to Moscow. They'll meet me straight off the plane, what would I do with you? Just wait till I get back and I'll take you to your Degunino."

"I'll go on my own," she repeated stubbornly.

"Please wait, it's only for a day!"

He felt sure he could persuade her to stay when he returned, or at least work out the best route for this ridiculous journey to her aunt's. It couldn't be that he was being called to Moscow because of her. How could they know about her? Which of the natives would have written to them? "This is to inform you the gublinator is sleaping with a girl as his wife…" Moscow no longer bothered to read people's denunciations; everyone denounced each other now, and the writer was more likely to be arrested than the person accused.

The plane was waiting for him on the landing strip. Most internal flights had been cancelled long ago due to lack of planes, and they were only for emergencies now. Small planes were sent from the Kremlin fleet to fly the governors to their conferences in Moscow, but these conferences were only once a year and were just for form's sake.

There was no sign he was in any trouble when the steward met him with a short report which didn't mention the purpose of his trip: he obviously knew nothing. He left Asha in the car without kissing her goodbye; he would be back that evening, and long goodbyes only led to tears. Vasilich started the car and it shot off, and at 8 a.m. local time, 5 a.m. Moscow time, the Governor was in the air.

7

At Terminal 2 of Vnukovo airport he was met off the plane as arranged, and here too there was nothing to suggest that he was in disgrace. He was led as usual through the VIP area and picked up some newspapers. He read only the government ones in Siberia, and saw no point in ordering any others: there was always some information to be gleaned between the lines of the official ones.

A car was waiting for him. Moscow was a half-hour drive from Vnukovo, and it was another hour to Arkhangelskoe. He settled himself in the back seat and called Grigory; trunk calls ate up money, but he had to make sure Asha was safe.

"Is the girl with you?" he asked.

"She's here, she's here," Grigory muttered. "I need to talk to you when you get back."

"Why? Has something happened?"

"Nothing specific. Say hello to Moscow for me. Are you in town?"

"Not yet, I'm on my way to a meeting."

"Well, give Tverskoy Boulevard my best if you see it."

Feeling slightly better, he opened his newspaper, the non-government *Izvestiya*, which was battling in its own way against the state monopoly of written Russian. This had been introduced two years ago, and a tax on the language had been imposed the year before. (Attempts to extort money from the West by copyrighting the words "Russia", "Russian" and "Conservative Modernization" had come to nothing, which meant Russia was hardly mentioned there at all now.)

As a member of the government, he understood his country needed something to live on, but the monopoly was the reason he refused to read anything but *Russia*, the *Russian Newspaper* and endless copies of the *Parliamentary Digest*. The tax had first covered all official words, such as "President", "Parliament" and "Fatherland", but papers simply avoided them or used euphemisms, so it was finally brought in for the whole language. Exemptions were made for books, and all textbooks were published by the state, but magazines and newspapers had to pay in full, which severely restricted their numbers. There were no more than six papers in Moscow now, plus the two government ones which were practically identical, and each tried in their different way to avoid the tax. *Izvestiya*, which he was reading, would change one letter in a word, and each time it would be different, so the law couldn't keep up with them. The reader would understand everything, but the words weren't taxable since they weren't to be found in Ushakov's definitive dictionary of the language. Thus: "The advence of liberol forces in the Sooth..." Or "The glittering crows at the premiere of the blackbuster *The Farest* at the Okhtober cinamo..." The newspaper *Power* was even more inventive, creating dozens of new words each week to keep the government busy compiling an alternative dictionary. Almost all their new Esperanto consisted of strange Russified Western borrowings, such as "Changy and transaktsii, bringushchi and bankovki". The patriotic press, whose patriotism didn't extend to paying for every word, took another route with its own anti-Esperanto, a new language with unquestionably Russian roots but only a vaguely discernible meaning: "The vehicle of the government's integrated Russification objectives as indicated by the projections of its collateral multi-national targets..." Naturally it took a lot of time to write like this, but with nothing much happening in the country it wasn't hard to put such papers out. The few weeklies would occasionally contain some pages of actual news, but the dailies limited these pages to just one. The rest were mainly taken up with advertisements for Rusoil. Rusoil advertisements flooded the airports, the press and TV, and its billboards lined the route from the airport to Arkhangelskoe.

Today's *Izvestiya* announced three new Rusoil deposits, and there was no tax on the name, or it would have incurred a fine larger than the entire monopoly economy. More oil was springing up than people knew what to do with, and sausages, butter and tinned foods were made from it, all quite nutritious despite the smell. The construction workers on the Governor's railway line were fed nothing else, and he himself at the start of his journey that morning had sampled an oil breakfast: it wasn't bad, he had swallowed a few spoonfuls. The whole of the Komsomolka area he was now passing through was full of advertisements for oil coffee ("Black Gold"), oil bread ("Tyumen bread") and oil milk ("Gift of the Earth"), and the slogans were correctly spelt: even if every word had to be paid for, the advertising people could afford it. The press was read only out of habit now, and because the Internet worked reliably only in Moscow and Petersburg, this *Finnegans Wake* of newspapers was one of the few entertainments left to people.

* * *

They reached Arkhangelskoe, the governors' palace where meetings were held and the governors delivered their reports. Because of the large number of regions to be governed now, they no longer met at the Soviet of Federations, and their contact with it was through a special government representative. For the past few years this had been Tarabarov, a squat, red-faced man practically indistinguishable from a district Party Secretary from fifty years ago. In Tsarist Russia he would have been a coachman, since his whole demeanour suggested his main occupation was flogging exhausted nags. The Governor despised such officials, but he knew Tarabarov had the power to make trouble for him.

He climbed out of the car. The weather in Moscow was delightful. The pine forests lining the road smelt sweet after yesterday's rain, and he could hear the twitter of the local birds he had missed for so long in Siberia. Nodding at the driver, he ran up the steps to the entrance of the new three-storey building.

It had been built in the second era of stabilization, a typical pseudo-aristocratic mansion in the classic style, and like all these reproductions of grand buildings it spoke of power rather than of comfort and convenience. It was large and wide, with two low narrow wings on either side, presumably to symbolize the triumph of centrism. Centrism in general dominated the visual arts these days: even the butterflies in children's picture books were drawn with tiny wings and inordinately large muscular bodies. The conference hall inside was also disproportionately large; there were no more than eighty governors in all, and they gathered together only on the Day of the Fatherland (the new main national holiday that had replaced Independence Day, and was mentioned in the Book of Veles). The hall was always empty, and Tarabarov held his countless federal meetings huddled in little rooms on the first floor. There were only a few guards around, two students and a porter, as the main filter was at the heavily fortified entrance to the grounds.

He had to wait a long time in the waiting area on the first floor, although he had arrived promptly at midday as requested. There were no other visitors there. The softly-spoken male secretary (at a certain level of power all secretaries were male) suggested he watch television, and he unenthusiastically agreed. He detested male secretaries: there was something unbearably two-faced about these elderly men whose main job clearly wasn't to bring in glasses of tea and switch on the television but to guard their masters and taste their food, and possibly torture people if necessary. They weren't secretaries at all of course, but bodyguards, and behind their soft movements, slipping about like chambermaids, he sensed a secret malevolence. He was reminded of the revolting hands of the killer barber, powerful yet tender, and there was something pederast-like about these men. How unlike his Nikita, who wasn't his secretary but his valet and practically his friend, who treated him without servility and was even allowed to grumble at him occasionally. The Governor hadn't brought him from Moscow, but had picked him from the natives, training him for a year until he beat the obsequiousness out of him and taught him an independent but respectful attitude. Now, as the secretary mouthed the words "You must wait. Savely Ivanovich is busy", like a loyal old servant, he heard such voluptuousness in his voice he felt almost embarrassed, as if he was witnessing an act of love, or worse, masturbation.

He switched on the television to a talk show, and a crowd of people at the Ostankino studios discussed whether dummies were bad for babies or not. They shouted and jousted, and he flicked channels to another show, in which the advocates of daily sex shouted down those who recommended it once a week. He watched an interminable weather forecast on Channel Three, mainly positive, and an economic review on Channel Four, which explained that the reason petrol prices were so high in Russia was the lack of hard currency needed to process it. The picture flashed to an anti-Phlogiston meeting in Crimea. It was a lifeless gathering, and he spotted the usual strolling players in the crowd. One had asked the President last year live on TV why he was looking so ill, and another had just been on the show about dummies, a beefy beetroot-faced woman with high blood pressure who insisted they were just for lazy mothers, and why couldn't they rock their babies to sleep for Heaven's sake! The gall of the woman quite charmed him.

He caught himself wondering why, during the first stabilization before Phlogiston, when people still needed oil, he and many other loyal patriots who genuinely loved their country had been simultaneously overwhelmed by a feeling that could only be described as nausea. In those days, when oil cost seventy dollars a barrel, there appeared a sort of boorish Russian version of freedom. The first signs of it were stability and contentment, although stability and contentment were the first signs that the heart of a country had stopped beating. Healthy societies weren't stable, they developed noisily and tumultuously, and the worst thing was the way this stability appealed to the lowest common denominator. Everyone – the government, the army, the Governor himself – smothered their intellect and worked at half strength, all helped along by television, because strong government or even a clever book would be destabilizing. Post-Phlogiston Russia couldn't tolerate even people's simple feelings of self-respect, and this first stabilization had given birth to a new class of mediocrities who lived wonderfully. He didn't envy this new class, he knew only that before long the country would be run by a cook, because a literate leader might change things, and change was fraught with danger.

He felt he was ten years behind on everything, and remembered he hadn't checked his mail that morning. He went to the landing to call Nikita on his mobile.

"What's happened, has anyone called?" he said.

"Don't trouble yourself sir, everything's fine."

"Good."

Perhaps he was better off in Siberia, where the wretchedness of life wasn't so apparent. He glanced at the decorated ceilings of the waiting room and the huge samovar, with its pattern of birch trees and berries. The whole place was done up like a cheap painted peasant box, and jarred oddly with the heavy Nordic scene depicted in the calendar on the wall – some heavy, big-bosomed Brunhildes waiting for their men (from battle of course, what else would proper men be doing?), with gothic forests in the background and knights with hawks and what looked like albatrosses on their shoulders. These Varangian images didn't fit with the Russian folklore theme. To connect them would need taste, and to have taste meant being someone other than Tarabarov. He examined the calendar at length, drank two glasses of tea and ate a "Ladybird" chocolate.

"Savely Ivanovich will see you now," rustled the secretary, striding with great peacock steps in his felt slippers to the door.

Tarabarov sat behind a desk of varnished Karelian birch, beneath an intricate wood carving of a girl by a river. His study was all wood, like Tarabarov himself. There seemed to be two winds blowing in the carving; the birch trees were blowing one way, and the handkerchief the girl was waving for some reason in another. There were often these girls on the walls of senior officials' offices, ripe, plump and heavy, with a calf-like, almost sadomasochistic sadness about them. In explaining the Nordic theory of the birth of the Russian state, the school history books described in loving detail how Russian virgins would ask to be interred under the watchtowers of their towns, because towns built on virgin bodies couldn't be captured. The towns would be captured again and again, yet somehow the myth survived. One of these patriotic virgins, all in white, was depicted on the opposite wall, sacrificing herself to a tower. Her face expressed a brave acceptance of her fate and her love for her town, which had collectively dealt with her in this blameless barbaric way. All the women working at the top levels of power seemed to have something of the virgin volunteers about them, these ideals of Russian womanhood.

Tarabarov scribbled away, dipping his pen in an inkwell of violet ink. It was a familiar ritual. The Governor stood at the door waiting for the plenipotentiary to finish; he was fairly sure he was just writing his name.

He finally raised his pale eyes, the colour of sour milk. In fact he had just drunk some, and there were two empty bottles beside him on the desk.

"Take a seat, Alexei Petrov," he said, without greeting him.

He drew up a chair.

"You want tea?"

"No thanks, I've had some."

"What is your business?"

"You called me," he replied in a neutral tone.

"I know I called you," Tarabarov said sharply. Like all officials of his type and rank, he smelt of milky coffee and a recently eaten sandwich. "I thought you'd like to tell me what's going on in your region."

"Things couldn't be better, Savely Ivanovich. I send you regular reports, don't you read them?"

"I do indeed," Tarabarov said even more sharply. "But reports are just dead paper, aren't they?" He coughed, and his throat gurgled. "I want to hear it from you, Alexei Petrov Borozdin, from your own mouth." ("Petrov", or even "Petrovson", rather than the Russian "Petrovich", was now the standard form of address in the top echelons.)

"Couldn't be better," he repeated. "Roads are built, national projects are fulfilled, we've installed anemometers. People are happy—"

"Anenom what?"

"Anemometers," he enunciated clearly.

"Ah." Tarabarov paused for a moment. "And what's your opinion of their morals?"

The Governor froze. What he had dreaded and refused to believe appeared to be happening.

"There's no problem with their morals. I've no complaints about them," he said.

"Really? Well, I've had complaints about yours." Tarabarov fixed him with his sour-milk eyes. "They write that your morals leave a lot to be desired, Alexei Petrov. We read the workers' letters too, you know, not just your reports. The true voice of the country delivered to our desk, so to speak. I suppose you know what I'm getting at?"

"I'm afraid I don't," he replied.

"Yes you do, Governor Borozdin, you know quite well what I'm getting at. This is a young man's game. When you were appointed, your age and your divorce were born in mind. I had my doubts when they asked me." He pointed significantly to the ceiling. "I said I respected your abilities, but couldn't vouch for what might be called your personal qualities. They said it would work out – and now, with respect, they're saying it hasn't. I've received more than one letter about you, Borozdin. They say you live with a native girl flagrantly, without attempting to conceal it—"

"Why should I conceal it?" he enquired haughtily.

"What company are you keeping?" spluttered Tarabarov. "How dare you disgrace the name of the state! Anemometers, you say! You may know long words, Alexei Petrov, but look at Governor Batyushkin! You don't see him shacking up with the local girls, he still wears the trousers! This man likes proper Russian baths, not saunas. It's a fine Russian tradition, a good rub-down, then out in the snow and beat yourself with sticks. Batyushkin doesn't have anemo-ometers." He drawled the word mockingly. "His region manages without anemometers. He fulfils his quota for the spring call-up, he catches partisans, his harvests are better than his neighbours', and he doesn't allow himself liberties! People don't write about him! They're not dumb cattle, you know, they'll write if they need to. If a governor doesn't treat the natives correctly, they don't respect him, do you understand?"

"My personal life is my business, Savely Ivanovich," the Governor said, without raising his voice. "We work for the state, it's not for us to pry into each others' secrets." He knew he mustn't give in to weakness at this point, or the man would soon be telling him what to eat and when to go to the lavatory.

"You have no personal life, Governor Borozdin!" Tarabarov raised his voice. "You'll have one when you've lost your job, which will be very soon, I promise! Fly back now and send the girl home where she belongs! Clear things up with her, then we'll review the situation, and if we find your behaviour immoral in the future, you'll be replaced. If I hear again that you're sleeping with a local girl, this one or another, I shall take immediate." (He omitted the word "measures", as recommended at meetings, and the governors always laughed at this.) "You may go now."

"You called me from Siberia for this?" asked the Governor.

"Me?" Tarabarov blustered. "I just wanted a friendly chat with you." His official tone softened and he became almost avuncular. "We're friends, I don't want to whip you like a puppy, but you must see how bad it looks. How can people respect you if you let this girl twist you round her little finger? I've ascertained that she's of a dubious race, a mutinous race." The Governor couldn't think where the authorities picked up these archaisms. "They claim to be special, but they're trash. Couldn't you have found someone better?"

"Don't forget your place, Savely Ivanovich," the Governor said quietly.

"What?" Tarabarov roared. "Do you know where you are?"

"Yes, I do," he nodded. "Whether you know how far you've exceeded your authority is another matter."

"Don't tell me what my authority is! My authority covers every dog and Joe in the province! What have you come to that peasants wave axes at you!"

So they did know, he thought.

"I won't bandy words with you, Borozdin. You will arrive home at twenty-one hundred hours local time and inform me that you've dealt with the girl. I want a full report from you on my desk, or she'll be in serious trouble. We can do it these days, you know, we can send people from Siberia to Siberia and leave no trace. You think you're at the end of the earth there, but there's plenty more beyond it, I assure you! I won't tell you again, Governor, I've had plenty like you standing before me." (He wasn't lying; he had previously been a prosecutor in Moscow liquidating the oligarchs.) "You can go now. I shall await your report."

"I would remind you, Savely Ivanovich, that it's not you who appoints or dismisses us, and who we sleep with is none of your business. Government prestige should be enforced on other fronts. In my region schools are open, children don't starve, there are X-ray machines in the clinics – show me anywhere else in Siberia that can boast all this. Who spends the night with me is a matter for my own conscience. Reading anonymous letters isn't proper for someone of your rank, and forgive me, but I've never allowed anyone to rummage through my private life. Don't try to pass off your sordid interest in other people's beds as state interest."

To his surprise Tarabarov didn't become hysterical after this outburst, sharp but essential. He merely stared for a moment at the dull yellow surface of his Karelian birch desk, then stood up, giving him to understand the interview was over.

"I shall await your arrival in the place of your duties at eighteen hundred hours Moscow time, Governor Borozdin," he said in his official voice. "And by twenty hundred I shall expect a fax from you" – he nodded at the machine on a side table – "informing me that everything's been cleared up. Those are my orders." He glanced at his watch, which was enormous, in the style of the second stabilization. "Given at thirteen hundred hours seven minutes. I advise you not to waste time. A car is waiting for you."

The Governor bowed curtly and left, shaking with rage, and only just managed to control his trembling fingers in the car and switch on his phone. There were three texts from Grigory asking him to call immediately, but when he tried his number there was no reply. Asha's phone was still off; he had told her to keep it off all day so no one could trace her. What if it wasn't a joke, he thought, and they really were looking for her? Why all this fuss about one girl in remote Siberia in wartime? He thought he must be losing his mind. He certainly wasn't prepared to abandon his post. He was valued, he had contacts in the cabinet, and if he wanted to he could fight Tarabarov, who was widely regarded as a turkey. He just didn't know what the whole sordid business was about.

What was even stranger was that when he called his residence no one answered. He rang his office, and a rough male voice he didn't recognize replied. "Office of the regional administration here."

"This is Borozdin. To whom am I speaking?"

"The courier," the voice replied after a pause.

"What, could none of my staff come to the phone?"

"Dinner," the voice said unconvincingly.

"What's going on?" the Governor shouted.

"Government business," said the strange courier and hung up.

8

Vasilich met him grimly at the landing strip.

"Go straight to Grigory's," the Governor said.

"Perhaps you should stop at the residence first."

"Why, what's happened?"

"You'll see."

"What? Tell me."

"Khryunichev came with his men and searched the place."

"Khryunichev? On whose authority?"

"How would I know, Alexei Petrovich, they didn't tell me."

"So they were authorized to search it in my absence?"

"Seems they planned it that way, it's obvious what they were looking for. Or rather who," he added significantly.

He called Khryunichev on his mobile. "Mikhail Nikolaevich," he said in a harsh voice. "I'm informed that you searched the residence in my absence."

The sky was a sinister violet colour, and as the car sped through the forests smelling of pine and damp undergrowth, he had never felt such a foreigner in his country.

"Who told you?" Khryunichev asked, sounding far from pleased.

"What's the difference? Is it true?"

"Are you there yet?" he asked without replying.

"I'm driving back now. I was called to Moscow for a meeting with Tarabarov."

"I know you were," he snapped. "It wasn't a search, it was a standard operational procedure."

It was the usual tactic of renaming things – counter-terrorist measures, collateral damage, temporary price adjustments and so on.

"On what grounds – that I'm hiding partisans?"

"Nothing of the sort, we've nothing against you personally," the fat man wheezed.

"What the hell were you doing then?" he shouted. The whole thing had so knocked him off course he couldn't think of Asha or Grigory, whom he had again tried unsuccessfully to phone from the plane.

"Don't ask me, ask Tarabarov," Khryunichev said severely. "You were with him, you can ask him yourself."

"So he cleared it?"

"I've no idea. We have our duties, he has his. Go home and phone him from there. Nothing of yours was taken, I give you my word. If anything's missing, it's probably your staff taking advantage of the situation, and you can fill out the forms. Go back and let us know."

The Governor cursed under his breath. He didn't even know if he was Governor any more, and whom he was responsible for – just the lazy natives? It seemed none of the departments were answerable to him now, and perhaps never had been. Tarabarov clearly hadn't ordered the search. Tarabarov had told him to send Asha away, and they had come looking for her while he was with him in Moscow – someone must have tipped off Tarabarov to call him there and free their hands, which meant Tarabarov took his orders from people above him in Siberia. It turned out the Governor had no one above him he could rely on, which was why he texted his colleague Kalyadin: "I need help. Write if you can." Kalyadin was head of the Ministry press corps, and they would generally have dinner together when he was in the capital with his fellow governors. But this time he hadn't even called him, and had flown in for his reprimand and flown back with his tail between his legs. And what could Kalyadin do if he was one of them?

He assumed they were after Asha. But what if it was something else? He racked his brains to think what it might be. What if all the authorities had joined forces with their horoscopes and quotes from Confucius, and believed this barbaric myth about the pregnant Wolf girl? What if everyone had finally lost their minds?

After talking to Khryunichev anything seemed possible, but he wasn't prepared for what met him at the residence. The residence no longer existed. From the outside it was the same cosy comfortable mansion, but inside everything had been ransacked, with the clear purpose of creating as much havoc as possible. They couldn't have done this to a senior official, only to someone who no longer counted for anything. It had been done insolently, and clearly had nothing to do with Asha – they wouldn't find her in his wardrobe or the drawers of his desk. Of course there was no Khazar literature lying around, and he never kept anything incriminating, but his personal things, his immaculate shirts and ties... As Governor he could have had people arrested for this, he would have just phoned Khryunichev. But he could hardly tell Khryunichev to arrest himself. Nonetheless he couldn't help phoning him again.

"What's the meaning of this, Khryunichev? What were you looking for?"

"I've already told you. I've nothing more to say."

"Who ordered it?"

"The Ministry of Internal Affairs."

"Which minister?"

"My minister, our Russian minister. No one else gives me orders, thank God."

"He ordered you to vandalize the place?"

"I've got it in writing here." He rustled some papers. "'Search Procedure Category Five, Level One.' That means a full search, including personal effects. I assure you those were my orders, it was authorized at the highest level, I'm not playing games." (He stressed his words on the first syllable – PROcedure, INstructions – Varangian-style.)

"Why wasn't I informed in advance? I'm entitled to be present while you go through my things!"

"Not at all, it's not written that you must be there. There were witnesses – ask your valet and your cook."

Lord, they'd done it in front of Nikita, how could he ever give him orders again?

"Well, you can at least send someone to clear up the mess."

"I'm afraid not," said the head of the Ministry of Internal Affairs. "They didn't take anything of yours, I can vouch for it, and to send them all round to put things back… Well, forgive me Governor, but you must do that yourself with the help of your staff."

"As from tomorrow you won't have a job here, Khryunichev," he said in a brittle, toneless voice. "I'll report you to Moscow and have you fired."

"No, you won't," huffed Khryunichev. "You can't fire me, your authority doesn't even cover interrogations. I'm talking to you as a friend, but we can talk very differently if you like. Carry out your duties, but don't interfere in mine. A Category Five search means you're a suspect and you can be arrested. I can demonstrate personally if I have to. Go to the top with your complaints, but you can't touch me outside the working day because you're subordinate to me!"

He hung up. It was unheard-of rudeness, an unprecedented breach of official etiquette. The Governor accepted that Khryunichev's Ministry might have a different management style, but it was a slap in the face to hang up in the middle of a conversation with the Regional Governor, who was presented with his credentials once a year by the President. And his tone of voice! Something had broken irrevocably, and he longed to sleep.

He called his deputy, Mstislavsky, who ran his office and was responsible for his correspondence and his reports to Moscow, and asked him a few general questions. "Oh, and by the way, Victor Andreyevich, make sure the residence is cleared up, won't you?"

"Of course, right away," his deputy replied in a friendly tone; at least this man hadn't betrayed him. "They're just finishing up here."

"What, you mean they've searched the office too?"

"Oh yes, but they didn't make much mess; the boys are just putting things straight. They wanted your computer passwords, but I told them they'd no right to them. They said they'd be back in the morning to talk to you."

"They won't want my passwords when I've finished with them," he promised. "From Siberia to Siberia, uh?" he added, mainly to himself. "I know who's going to be seeing Siberia."

It was already dark now. He stood alone in his ransacked bedroom, where he had said goodbye that morning to Asha. Asha, of course – he must collect her immediately and take her away. He knew now that things were desperately serious for him, and if Moscow didn't act on his complaint against Khryunichev and sack him tomorrow, he would be sacked himself. How would he survive this? Where could he go?

"Nikita!"

"Coming, sir." Nikita was there instantly.

"Mstislavsky will send people round to tidy up and check that nothing's missing. I'll collect Asha and be back with her shortly. Make sure dinner's ready."

"Very well, sir."

He hurried from the bedroom and told Vasilich to drive him to Grigory's, taking his bodyguard with him.

"You swine, letting them get away with it," he said bitterly to him in the car.

"What could we do, Alexei Petrovich? They'd have shot us. Mishka went for them and they threw him face down on the floor." (They would answer for that, the Governor thought.) "They showed us their papers. We're officials too, you know."

"Officials" was the local excuse for anyone who refused to take responsibility for anything. He himself had been an official once. If he had to flog, he flogged. If he had to catch deserters, he caught deserters. But for a long time he hadn't fitted into the government pyramid, where not one of his pluses was needed, just his minuses, and the only basis for a successful career was lack of talent. And what would happen now that the official had forgotten his duties?

"You could at least have stopped them making a pigsty of the place," he said.

"We didn't see anything, they locked us in a cupboard until it was all over. Khryunichev said he could explain everything and you shouldn't be cross."

"I've had quite enough of Khryunichev's explanations," he said.

* * *

At Grigory's there was no light in the windows. He ran up to his flat on the second floor, with his bodyguard close behind, prepared for another scene of devastation – a smashed door perhaps, or worse, a dead body – but the door was locked.

He rang, and Grigory's frightened voice whispered, "Yes?"

"It's me, open up!"

"Are you alone?"

"I'm with my bodyguard. Where's Asha?"

"She's here, in the kitchen."

"Why are you sitting in the dark?"

"I wanted to put the light on, but I was afraid they'd come for her. The local papers keep talking about signs…"

"Signs? What signs?"

"They say there'll be an attempt on the Governor's life."

"You mean me?"

"You're still Governor, aren't you, or did they give you the boot?"

"Let them try," he said, without much conviction.

They went to the kitchen. Asha was sitting on a stool with her hands in her lap, her whole body radiating a strange dull meekness. "They've sacked you?" she said quietly.

"Of course not, they just asked me some routine questions."

"Don't lie, they called you there so I'd… Never mind, tell me where you're sending me. I must leave, they keep talking about signs."

"Stop." He sat on the floor with his back against the ancient fridge. "Tell me in plain Russian what's going on and why they're after you."

"It's not me, it's the baby," she said wearily.

"And what will this baby do?"

"No one knows, we only know he'll be the beginning. You say the end, we say the beginning. We live our lives so there's no beginning, and now we've let it happen. I didn't know what race you were, I never thought about it, I loved you very much and I still do." She spoke very softly, and he felt a shiver of goose bumps up his spine.

"Asha, when have governments run on prophecies?"

"Plenty of times," Grigory put in quickly. "The Romans divined from the entrails, and who could be better than the Romans? If the masters love them, it breaks the cycle and starts something new, and they don't want that, don't you understand? You're a good chap, Governor, but I always said you shouldn't be working for the government. You should assert yourself more, this baby of yours might give us a proper life, if you survive of course, which I very much doubt. You can't stay with me. If they find you it's the beginning for me."

"That's enough," the Governor snapped. "I'm still in charge here."

"Nonsense, the Ministry's in charge, you're just Moscow window dressing. You thought you worked for the state, and now it turns out the state wants to murder your wife and your child because it had a bad dream on Friday. And you helped make it happen, didn't you? So you could open schools and spread enlightenment? I wouldn't want to be in your shoes, Governor, and thank God I'm not."

The Governor's mobile rang, but no number came up.

"Alexei Petrovich, you must leave at once," said the cautious voice of his deputy Mstislavsky. "The boys have heard how your valet informed on you. I assume you know Nikita's one of Khryunichev's. If you weren't followed, it'll take them a while to find you, but you should leave now. At least find somewhere safe for her."

"Where are you speaking from, Vitya?" he interrupted, wondering if Mstislavsky too had been bribed and was out to trap him.

"From a payphone. They haven't traced me yet, but they soon will, it's a small town. You'd better not tell me where you are. I'd suggest you go to Zakharovka, but it seems you cordoned it off against deserters. Best get Vasilich to drive her somewhere safe, he's unquestionably yours. Unfortunately I've nowhere to hide her myself, and of course she can't stay with her parents—"

"How the hell do you know all this?" the Governor said in a loud whisper.

"It's my job to know things and tell you. The natives have been trying to find her all day – it seems they're better organized than we realized. Oh, and there's a fax from Tarabarov, about some sort of confirmation—"

"To hell with Tarabarov," he said. "Thanks, Vitya, I won't forget this."

"They're closing in?" asked Grigory, trying to piece together the conversation.

"Yes, damn them." He looked out of the window; his car was still parked by the kerb. Everyone in town knew it, it wouldn't be hard for them to find him. He called Vasilich.

"Drive back to the residence," he told him. "If they ask where we are, say we're inspecting the railway line. I'll be back tomorrow."

"Smart move," Vasilich replied knowingly. "Good luck."

The car roared off. It was a noisy one, a BMW.

"What will you do now?" Grigory asked.

"I'll call a taxi to take us to the next province, then catch a train and take Asha to Degunino. It'll take three days. Mstislavsky can run things while I'm away."

At that moment he wasn't thinking like a statesman, or of Asha, he was thinking of himself, and his wounded state pride. He had sacrificed everything good in him on the altar of his work, he had been ready to serve anywhere he was sent, in any post. And now twenty years of irreproachable service in various jobs and capacities had been wiped out in one day, because he refused to believe this insane superstition. But what right had he to complain, asked a hateful inner voice. Hadn't he been intoxicated by these superstitions and thought they were beautiful nonsense? And hadn't he argued with those liberals who regarded the state as a big housing office or laundry, and told them it was the earthly embodiment of the heavenly motherland? Take, eat from the trough! It made no difference if it was the absurd Khryunichev giving him orders or some handsome Westernizer like himself, well turned-out and smartly dressed, with more elevated interests than fishing. He knew his qualities no longer counted for anything, and that the individual's role in the state was insignificant. Its victims would yield yet more to the torturers, and so it went on, it was pointless to ask why: the state didn't have to explain its motives, and nor did those punished.

But all this was just self-pity, he told himself. People wronged always babbled about freedom, and freedom was the enemy. He couldn't drop his self-discipline for a minute, or accept that anything should be changed, any ritual simplified, because freedom destroyed order and led to anarchy. He was a government servant and would die one. His government flogged its enemies and created more, but he would never give in to this. He would give them time to recover from their insanity, and soon everything would go back to normal. He was still Governor.

His phone rang. Moscow was calling.

"I'm waiting, Alexei Petrov," came Tarabarov's rough voice.

"Me too, Savely Ivanovich."

"I'm waiting to hear you've carried out your orders. I'm sure you remember."

"I've already carried them out," he said levelly.

"Really, Alexei Petrov? How?"

"I took the girl to her parents and won't be seeing her again."

"You take me for a fool, Alexei Petrov?" Tarabarov screamed in his ear. "You think I don't know they've put guards at her parents' house? I'm telling you, at twenty-four hours—"

"And I'm telling you to get fucked, you red-faced clown!" he said and hung up, and at that moment a gust of damp wind flung open the window and whistled through the room.

"I told you never to say that word in front of me," Asha said sharply, and he imagined the wind bursting into Tarabarov's office and blowing him off his chair – it cheered him up.

"OK. Thanks Grigory, we're off."

"Where to?" Grigory asked.

"I know the way," she said suddenly. "I've got some money, I saved everything you gave me. We'll catch a bus outside town where they're not looking for us yet, then take the train to Degunino. I know the villages where the Wolves and the good people are. Come on, Governor, before something happens."

He followed her down the dark stairs. The rain had stopped, and big shaggy stars slipped through the clouds like tears through closed eyelashes.

"Look at you, running like a rabbit from your government," she said.

"Not for long though," he reminded her.

She led him through dark courtyards, and they walked for a long time past scrapyards and dimly lit shacks and heaps of old rags and barbed wire. The Governor had never been in the outskirts of town before, and was pierced by a sudden vision of sleeping in this wasteland where the Joes lived, and where perhaps corpses were buried. Everything rotted and bubbled and fermented, and the smell of wet earth mingled with the stench of sewage, and he was no longer governor of anything.

"Is it far?" he asked her.

"Yes, it's the roundabout route, don't be afraid," she said. "I'll take you to Degunino and it'll work out, you'll see. This baby gives me strength. Remember how weak I used to be? The wind's blown the weakness out of me. I'll get there and take you wherever you want to go, then you can come back. Our people will love you and your people will forgive you. There aren't many like you."

"We'll see," he said.

* * *

In the next town he found a cash machine and withdrew all his money. He was just in time: when he checked again two hours later his account had been blocked. Asha carefully hid the notes in their pockets. After a sleepless night and five hours in a jolting local bus, he thought she would be half dead, but she seemed to grow stronger every minute, as if travelling was in her blood. Say what you like, it hadn't made her happy when he moved her into his residence, because it wasn't hers, even though hers was no better than this.

"We're used to it," she told him, guessing his thoughts. "All of us wander, perhaps the Joes save the world with their wandering."

"How do they do that?" he asked dully.

"By going in a circle so nothing begins. Joes are your word for them, we call them circling falcons. It's all a circle, you know that now," she said patronizingly. "And when you've got no home and no job you can be one too."

"I don't think so. So the Joes are holy for you?"

"Yes, they are. And the holiest ones make the roads. In the old days we used to stamp a path where we wanted to go, now we're building the railways. It's the holiest work for us."

They arrived at the station in the middle of a police round-up of Joes, so in a way they were lucky. He had authorized several round-ups himself as governor, but he hadn't come down too hard on them. Ultimately they didn't do much harm, and he knew what awaited them. He had visited a model hostel in Moscow once with his fellow governors on an excursion organized by Tarabarov himself. But before being packed off to these places, they would be caged like monkeys and told their rights, then someone would try to beat information out of them, but half the Joes couldn't remember anything at all, so they were beaten again for that.

A final purge was promised every year, but somehow there were never enough hands for it, and since new Joes had almost stopped coming to his town, there seemed little point. What was happening now at the station resembled in its savagery the Final Solution to the homeless question. They were being dragged from the corners where they had been sheltering and kicked into open trucks, and the station stank of homelessness. Most people looked on with evident approval, although a few turned away in disgust, and a woman tried to remonstrate with a policeman to no effect. One by one the Joes went off quietly to the trucks, with that expression of perpetual suffering with which they wandered their dark roads. Their faces were yellow and swollen, with matted tufts of hair like the wool of an old jacket. Although it was summer, most wore shabby padded jackets, and almost all of them wore something red, or what used to be red, for all their clothing now was the same dull brown colour. A few resisted silently and were dragged off, but one Mashka, of whom the only thing left of her as a woman was her shrill piercing voice, clung to a lamp-post and howled beseechingly to a cop, "Let me go sir, let me go!" The cop tried to pull her away, then got sick of her helpless resistance and hurled her into a truck. She seemed to fly three metres through the air, and as she landed on the flaccid bodies her howling stopped.

In the chaos of the round-up, the Governor and Asha, both smartly and respectably dressed, calmly made their way to the train for Barnaul.

"And you call them holy!" he blurted out.

"Be quiet," she said, and he saw she had bitten her lips until they bled.

"What is it?"

"One word, one word from me, and they'd have left them alone," she said. "I'd have said it to the cops and that would be it. I've said it a hundred times to your people, and they've let them go."

"I never knew you'd spoken to them," he frowned.

"It's not for you to know everything."

"So what's the word?"

"I can't tell you, you must find out for yourself."

She looked back, and as the Joes were driven off, some of them stood at the sides of the trucks and stared at them with a strange intensity.

"They recognized me, of course they did," she said. "Don't worry, they won't tell anyone."

"Where are they going?" he said, as if it was she who should know this, not him.

"Don't ask me, that's your business. Didn't you hear they were planning something big when you were in Moscow?"

"No, I didn't," he confessed, remembering his official welcome at the airport yesterday. To be honest, if the final purge had started he was glad to be out of it.

They walked to the train and boarded the shabby green carriage without buying tickets, just pushing some money at the guard. Buying tickets was dangerous, the cashiers always asked for ID, although the search for them didn't seem to have reached the town yet; either that or it was being organized badly, like everything else these days. Thank

God, he sighed, it had never occurred to him that in this deteriorating country even the repression was deteriorating.

He had switched off his phone after texting Kalyadin. It was a long shot, and Kalyadin's reply had come back: "I can't do anything". Fair enough, he would have said the same in his place. When everything was untangled and Tarabarov was sacked and Khryunichev sent off to Siberia, he would phone him and perhaps he would understand.

At that moment a policeman appeared at the end of the platform and walked slowly down the train, peering in at the windows. The Governor's seat faced backwards and he couldn't see him, but he saw Asha blench and her face told him everything. He looked round: the cop was just five carriages away.

"Give-Give-Give..." she murmured in a barely audible voice, moving her lips. "Give-Give-Give-Give..."

The train clanked and seemed about to move. "He won't make it, we're safe," he said.

But the train didn't move. The cop had a piece of paper and a photograph in his hands, and was almost at their carriage now. Perhaps they could run back to the one he had just passed...

"*Not alone in the field, little road!*" she shrieked suddenly.

He stared at her in amazement.

The cop looked round.

"*Not alone in the field, little road!*"

The cop stopped thoughtfully, dropped his piece of paper and walked back down the platform, and at that moment the wheels juddered and they moved off.

Asha smiled proudly. It was a long time since he had seen her smile like that.

"I suppose if I live with Wolves I'll have to learn to howl with them," he said.

"That's right," she laughed. "Just wait, you'll learn to howl with us!"

He smiled at her uncertainly. Beyond the window flashed wastelands buried in weeds and fences, and garages scrawled with the familiar four-letter word.

"Not alone in the field, little road," she sang.

"Not alone grassless, not alone pathless.

Not alone in the field, little road,

Not alone with the train..."

Chapter Four
The Joe

1

Since she was eleven, Anka had dreamt of having a Joe.

"Over my dead body!" her father would say.

His dead body was often thrown in the way of any innovations at home. If Anka's mother wanted to buy her a hamster, or replace the furniture or the curtains, it would only be through his death and his stern disapproval from the grave, which was why after moving into their new flat they were still sitting on the landlord's uncomfortable sofa and watching their ancient television with its faded picture and sound, as if it had grown blind and deaf from all the rubbish that was on.

Anka tried telling him she didn't want a Joe to play with, but because it broke her heart to see them on the streets every day on her way to school. She had already seen one she liked, a big healthy-looking bearded one; her charity didn't go as far as taking a sick one, and there were special places for them.

She had almost talked her mother round. "Just not off the street," she said. Fine, they would get one from a shelter, which sent them out washed and house-trained, some even with professions. In their Moscow Knowledge class at school they were told that the new liberal Mayor had laid on classes for them in the shelters, and her friend Sasha Khudyakov's parents had got one who was a joiner and did a bit of carpentry for them at their dacha. He had spent the summer there and made Sasha a see-saw, and two fat bearded friends of his would appear sometimes and take turns on it. Sasha was very upset when he was sent back in the autumn, and said their Joe had grown attached to them – although Sasha's mother told Anka's mother a different story. "There's something emotionally not right about them, they're hopelessly limited," she said. "He didn't even say goodbye."

"Must have been the shock," said her father sourly. "They take a human being in for the summer and make him part of the family, then in the autumn it's thanks for the work, you can buzz off."

"Nonsense, they made it clear from the start in the agreement he signed. If he could write, of course—"

"And if he couldn't? I know what it's like, a chap at work had one and the same thing happened. They need to know they're staying. If you tell them it's only for the summer, they don't bother to work."

Anka didn't like what Sasha's parents had done, although surely spending three months in the fresh country air picking strawberries was better than hanging round the shelter all summer. But she didn't want one just for the summer, she wanted one for life, or at least a year – longer, if it worked out. Even having a hamster was a big responsibility, and she had cried through three lessons when hers died. Fortunately the Joes were toughened by their hard life and hardly ever died, although in the third year Lena Firsova had had a child one who died, and she mourned him terribly and had to take a week off school. He was almost talking by then, and had grown fond of her, and her essay 'My Pet' won a prize at the Moscow Olympiad. Afterwards the Department for the Homeless stepped in and said it was fine to have pets, but they shouldn't be spoilt, and there was a special lesson on the subject at school. Lena's had spent his first nine years not knowing what a room was, or sweets, and the shock was too great for him. Even the grown-up ones often overdid things, and it was important to watch their diet and not overfeed them: their teacher had read with tears in her eyes from Saint-Exupéry's *Little Prince*, about being answerable to those you lead and so on.

Anka didn't want a child one, she wanted a trained, experienced one. In the fifth year she had shot up and become much taller than her friends (and cleverer too), and she was suddenly bored of children her age. And the young Joes frightened her, to be honest. They played strange games and bit each other, and were hard to manage. Sveta Babash had had a young one with shining black eyes who was clever and could talk, but things had turned nasty, and he persuaded her to run off with him. Her mother had called the police, who picked them up at the station and sent him back to the shelter, and as he was being led away he laughed and pulled faces and shouted horrible things about Sveta, although before that he had lived with them as a normal Joe. Sveta's mother had asked him to be sterilized early, terrified of what he had got up to, but they assured her at the shelter that he was still immature and couldn't have done Sveta any harm. They even showed her the poor little Joe afterwards, covered in knife wounds and very quiet, although of course there was no question of them taking him back.

Anka knew she could wear her father down, it was just a matter of time. Some children forget their requests after the first refusal, but not Anka: she was on a mission, and wouldn't sleep until she got her way.

At the age of twelve, she got to work on him in earnest, dripping away like Chinese water torture.

"It's a nightmare," he complained to his journalist friend Uncle Shura when he came round for a glass of brandy accompanied by his Joe, a smartly dressed young man who talked, with a good haircut.

"The child wants one, what can you do?" Shura said indulgently, gazing at his Joe as he rolled on the floor and let Anka scratch him. His name was Petka – the talking ones were often given names.

"It's all wrong!" fumed her father. "Sorry Shura, I'm from the old regime, I don't get it!"

"You're saying it was better when they cluttered up the streets and subways?" Shura said lazily. "It was you who kept writing 'Something must be done!'. And now something's been done and still you aren't happy!"

Petka screwed up his eyes and smiled fondly at him. He had put on weight, and like most Joes had quickly come to resemble his master, although sometimes he would sniff the air and rush to the door, and at these times Shura too seemed to prick up his ears and change. Anka didn't want to think about it.

"But doesn't it bother you, this new Salvation Plan?" her father demanded.

"What's the alternative, Slava? Remember what it was like when Luzhkov was Mayor? What do you suggest, turn them into sausage meat?"

"Please, boys!" pleaded Anka's mother, covering her mouth with her hand as she tucked into her Macedonian salad.

"Don't blame me, Nadya, blame your husband," Shura flared up. "No matter what we do, it's never right. Wasn't it you who wrote an article in the last issue attacking the circuses?"

"So you read it!" Anka's father said, happy to change the subject.

"Only for work, of course. I can't think what you've got against the circuses, it's not as if anyone gets killed. Although frankly, if they agreed—"

"And would they have a choice?" he flared up again.

"But you and I aren't on the streets, are we?" Shura stared out of the window at the rows of lit apartment blocks in the sleepy Mityaevo district.

"It's a fine line," said her father morosely.

The two of them often had these arguments, and Petka would listen attentively. Anka felt him tense, although he didn't stop her scratching him. She didn't know where Uncle Shura had found him. According to her mother, he had appeared one day during a police raid and shown him a crumpled diploma from the Mining Institute. There was no way to turn him into a man of course, but he was ideal for Shura, a confirmed bachelor, who had taken him in to do small domestic tasks such as peeling potatoes, washing dishes and minding the house while he was away on business.

Anka didn't like the circuses either. For the past three years the Day of the City had been celebrated with fights at the Vernadsky stadium, and she hated it when the boys in her class noisily laid bets. Her friend Sasha Khudyakov was a Spartak fan. All the Spartaks were enormous, like Sumo wrestlers, and it was impossible to train them properly as all food turned to fat with them. They suffered the blows remarkably well, because they were used to them, and it was an ugly spectacle. She had seen a fight on television once and had to switch off. They fought wildly, poking each other in the eyes with tridents, or sometimes below the waist (for which they were sent off), or biting each other (which was allowed). The President was in the audience once and had given the thumbs up, and the organizers misinterpreted the gesture and announced that the wrong one had won. They were never killed of course, Anka's teacher explained this would be barbaric. The losers were merely thrown off the team and sent back to the shelters, where the food was much worse because the gladiators were given all the meat; she had read an article about it in *Moscow Pravda*, with a picture of two big joints of ham.

"I don't see what's so interesting about the fights," she said to Sasha as he walked her home one afternoon after their Moscow Knowledge class.

"What about boxing?" he asked. He was slightly shorter than she was, but there was already something solid about him, and he spoke in a deep bass voice.

"Boxing has rules, it's a sport. This isn't a sport, it's just cruelty."

"Really, Anka, don't you know biology?" he said patronizingly, a bit like Uncle Shura. "They're not like us, they enjoy it, can't you see? Some of us are born with brains, some aren't, it's why they drink and why they can't stay in one place. It's better this way."

Anka still didn't understand. Sometimes at the dacha she would look through old magazines – children's ones no longer interested her

– and would come across the mysterious word "*bomzh*", the old name for them, meaning "of no fixed abode". *Bomzh*! Like the strike of a deep bass gong, ending in a long buzzing echo. It was only under the new humane programme for them that they were called Joes, and were sent treated and sterilized from the shelters to stay in people's homes. There weren't only Joes in the shelters, of course. Sometimes an old granny with nothing to eat would apply to live there, or a runaway with nowhere to live. They would have to pay for a doctor's certificate saying they were Joes (the proper medical term was "Vasilenko Syndrome"), and without one they wouldn't get in. Several illegal deals had been exposed, and the scandal was discussed at length on television; her father said it was only the tip of the iceberg.

When her mother first told her about the Syndrome she wondered if it was catching, but her mother explained that it was genetic, and if no signs of it had appeared at her age she was definitely in the clear. Professor Vasilenko himself said in his talks on television that if it was infectious everyone would have it by now, and after they were sterilized they were perfectly safe to take home. He had seven of his own, two living at his dacha and five in his flat in Moscow, or rather four Joes and three Mashkas, all very friendly and well trained, and he showed them doing amazing tricks, jumping over chairs and catching bits of liver sausage in their mouths.

Anka had already decided how she would train hers. Perhaps she could even cure him of Vasilenko Syndrome, which was said to be incurable. It would be the first case of its kind and she would be famous, although that wasn't the point of course, the point was to help humanity.

* * *

She finished the sixth year with top marks and her certificate of merit, and her mother offered her the choice of a week in Crimea or a trip to Beijing Disneyland, where you got a load of free plastic toys that broke on the first day so you didn't have to take them home. But she refused both holidays: she wanted a Joe.

"What can you do, the child wants a living person!" her father moaned like a woman.

"Not as a toy though, she wants one to look after," her mother said seriously. "You know, when I was her age, I dreamt of looking after a little homeless girl from a fairy tale and making her my friend."

"It's not right," said her father, frowning. "When someone feels they don't deserve a proper friend, they find someone less fortunate than themselves who'll love them out of gratitude. It worries me that she's not interested in her classmates. I don't know, maybe she's too bright for them and wants to buy herself someone who'll listen to her fantasies. People just need them to compensate for what's missing in their lives. Shura needs his silly dependable Watson, the Khudyakovs needed a carpenter, that idiot Kaloshin in our office needs an enraptured audience, and half the editorial board sometimes take a Joe or a Mashka for the usual thing. Galina took hers on holiday with her, and he didn't just carry her suitcases!"

"But that's—" her mother gasped.

"What, cruelty to animals? They're fed, aren't they?"

"Well, they've been brainwashed then."

"Maybe some aren't, anything's possible. That's why I don't want one – it's unnatural. If you can't find a friend or a lover or hang your own wallpaper, you get a Joe. Rabbit would do better to go to summer camp. I can get her into Oakwoods. It's a lovely place, all the children from the President's office go there…"

Anka didn't understand what they were talking about, but guessed from the way her father called her Rabbit that he was in a bad mood and was already resigned to having a Joe.

It was amazing how quickly they had become part of everyday life. The TV show *My Joe*, in which they competed to pull weights and do tricks, was weekly now instead of monthly, and there were financial incentives for those who took their Joes with them on cheap breaks to Thailand or Egypt. Special seats were reserved for them at the back of the buses and the underground, and a party of visiting American Greens had observed that until a cure could be found for the Syndrome, Russia's approach was the most humane. The only question was why there were so many of them here, although plenty of other places had them too, notably Africa. Meanwhile scientists still tried to explain the Syndrome: two famous physicists had recently disproved the idea that it was caused by some genetic mutation, with one blaming history and the other the climate.

By August Anka had worn her father down and, cursing and laughing, he wrote himself a glowing reference which his boss signed without reading. They got a letter from the housing office confirming that their accommodation was satisfactory, and her mother dug up the certificate for a medical course she had done years ago after leaving school. Then the three of them went off to the clinic to give samples, an unpleasant procedure involving a glass tube being poked up their backsides. But Anka was ready for anything. She even copied a page from her diary referring to her good school marks, and they set off for the nearest shelter in the south of the city, near the Yugo-Zapadnaya underground station, next to the abandoned half-built glass pencil of the Aganbegyan Academy.

* * *

Anka fell asleep happy, but when she woke in the morning she felt suddenly apprehensive. They set off in the car, and as they approached the grey concrete shelter a sick bitter taste filled her mouth and, worse, her soul. It was a horrible building. She remembered choking on the same taste in her mouth on her first day at school and wanting to be sick; everyone around her was laughing and happy, and she knew nothing good awaited her there.

They walked in, and it felt like a prison. She clutched her mother's hand, and it was drenched with sweat. But a friendly woman in a white coat had already hurried out to meet them. She took them to the Director's office at the end of the corridor, which had a soothing medical smell, like a children's clinic, and she felt slightly less anxious. The happy pictures on the walls were like those in a children's clinic too, with Snow White and the Seven Dwarfs, and a rabbit and a giraffe, which for some reason had five legs.

"The inmates painted them, they're all their own work," said the woman in the white coat.

"You don't say, they did it themselves?" said Anka's mother.

"Oh yes, we have an art group here, they'll show you their work. We run lots of classes, everyone has to attend and they all manage to do something."

The Director was a strict, fat, jolly woman, who looked like the canteen manager at the boarding house where Anka and her mother had stayed last summer. She carefully checked their documents and spent a long time reading the copy of Anka's diary, then gave her a broad smile.

"So we're good at our schoolwork!" she said.

"We try," Anka's father replied for her.

"Splendid. We've got just the one for her if she needs help with her maths."

"My maths is OK," Anka said, hoarse with nervousness.

"Good for you," she smiled again. "We can always arrange some coaching if you need it. Now, Maria Stepanovna, take our friends to see the inmates while I sort out the release forms."

They went up the stairs to the large inspection area on the first floor. Screwed to the door was a list of rules, splashed with white paint. It had evidently been there before the door was painted and the painting had been done carelessly, like everything else here, like the five-legged giraffe. The Joes probably hadn't learnt to paint properly yet. Apparently they used to work only for drink, but they weren't allowed alcohol now because it would ruin their educational achievements. According to her Biology teacher, you could teach any of them, you just needed an individual approach and to know how to stimulate them.

"Here they are, they're all waiting for you," Maria Stepanovna said, throwing open the door.

The Joes and Mashkas stood up from the little children's chairs they had been sitting on, which must have come from a kindergarten. Anka had never seen so many of them in one place. They were all different, poorly dressed but clean. There were some young ones and a few children, with black eyes and rotting teeth, but most looked about forty, and were respectful and reserved.

"Good morning," they said in a ragged chorus.

"That wasn't very friendly," Maria Stepanovna rebuked them. "Our guests will be taking one of you home with them. Try again, you want them to like you, don't you?"

"Good morning!" they said more loudly and smiled, showing their toothless gums, then they all jumped up and there was a sudden commotion in the hall. Two elderly Mashkas skipped over a skipping rope, and another played with some elastic. A Joe of about forty lay on his back, jerking his legs round in circles as if riding a bicycle. A child raced round with another on his back, whooping and whistling like a bandit, while a young black-eyed Joe with a broken nose and furtive wide-set eyes climbed on a chair and began declaiming: "When wise Holeg rose to havenge the foolish bazaars…"

He was doing his best, but clearly had no idea what he was saying, and his eyes kept darting around as if looking for something to pinch.

They must have been told the little girl wanted a pet to do tricks, and if they wanted a carpenter they would have shown off their woodwork. Anka had known she would choose the unhappiest of them, not so he would be dependent on her, but to make the best use of her charity. Yet each of them here was so unhappy and so frightening that she longed to bury herself in her mother and not have to see them. But she couldn't lose face with them, and they were trying so hard, looking out of the corners of their eyes at their visitors, desperate to be chosen. One tried to juggle with two balls, another struggled to do a handstand, putting his legs against the wall and tumbling down again and again. Two more Mashkas of about sixty clapped hands and sang a Russian folk song with a sad rakish tune, although she couldn't make out the words. She noticed a couple of young ones sitting thoughtfully over a game of chess, moving the pieces at random: the Syndrome clearly made it impossible for them to learn the rules.

She had discounted the idea of a child Joe from the start. She liked one of about thirty-five, with a long face and big teeth and glasses, but at that moment he did a somersault and gazed up at her with such doglike devotion that she wanted nothing more to do with him. Her eye fell at last on an elderly Joe with thin straw-coloured hair, who had been sitting quietly in the corner gluing a little box and not trying to impress anyone.

"Have you seen one you like yet?" asked Maria Stepanovna. "They do all sorts of handicrafts and make soft toys. It's lovely work, almost Chinese-quality. We had some workers here from a toy factory, and they were amazed. You can buy some if you like, and we'll introduce you to the ones who made them."

"I've already chosen," Anka said. "I want the one in the corner."

Maria Stepanovna screwed up her eyes at him. "That one?" she said. "An excellent choice. Come here, Vasily Ivanovich!"

The others instantly stopped what they were doing and stared at him.

"He's a very good patient, he's been with us for two years," Maria Stepanovna said, unembarrassed by his presence and by the sudden silence. "He'd forgotten most things when he came here, but now he knows everything. He can read the newspaper!" she added proudly, as though reading the newspaper was a gift bestowed only on the lucky few. "Vasily Ivanovich, when did the first man go into space?"

"The 12th of April!" he replied in a pleasant muffled voice.

"And what's five times eight?"

"Forty," he smiled.

"And do you like our guests?"

"We always like our guests," he nodded.

209

"You know the rules, you can send him back in a month if he doesn't suit you. It's no problem, we'll find you another one and return the money for his food. But the little girl's made a good choice, he's kind and sensible and will look after her on his walks…"

"Vasily Ivanovich, what were you making there in the corner?" Anka asked him boldly.

"A little box," he replied bashfully.

"What's it for?" her mother encouraged him.

"Just, you know…" he shrugged.

"He's always making them," Maria Stepanovna cut in. "We teach them to glue envelopes and boxes, and the less mentally advanced ones do envelopes. He'll make as many boxes as you like for your bits and pieces, and clay money boxes too. We have an excellent pottery teacher—"

"Vasily Ivanovich," Anka said firmly. "I'd like to invite you home with us." (She avoided the word "take".) "Will you come?"

"I don't mind, it's up to you," he said.

"Please come with us if you can, I'll try to make it nice for you," she said.

"Go and pack, Vasily Ivanovich, while I take our friends to the Director and fill out the forms. I'll collect you later," said Maria Stepanovna.

* * *

"So you've picked one?" asked the Director with a smile.

"They want Vasily Ivanovich," reported Maria Stepanovna.

"That's good, he's waited long enough, people usually want the younger ones. Fetch his personal file, will you, Maria Stepanovna, and I'll take them through the rules."

Maria Stepanovna left the room.

"No tobacco or vodka of course, and feed him strictly as prescribed. No fats, most of our inmates have bad livers." (Anka giggled nervously.) "You can send him alone to the shops so long as they don't sell alcohol, but he's quite reliable, he'll only drink if it's given to him. Plenty of black bread and iron and outdoor exercise and daily walks. It'll do the child good too, she looks a little pale." Anka wondered with horror if all these things that were supposed to be good for her meant she too had Vasilenko Syndrome. But fortunately this was the end of the Director's briefing, as Maria Stepanovna had returned.

"Here, you can see his notes." She opened a large file and placed it before Anka's father as head of the family, but when he tried to go through it, the pages had all been glued together.

"Sorry, it's office information, it's just for the staff," she smiled.

Her mother looked nervous. "Is it something serious?"

"Don't worry, it's all in the past now," the Director said gently. "Thanks to our therapy he hardly remembers his old life before he was picked up. We've erased it and we don't mention it. We guarantee to supply healthy inmates who are safe to stay in families, he won't hurt the little girl. Just don't ask him about the past, it wasn't a very happy time for him, as you can imagine. We probably don't like to remember our twos, do we?"

"I don't get twos," Anka said, frightened by this comparison with him.

"That's good," she smiled at her. "Bring him down, Maria Stepanovna. Did you come by car? Phone in a week and let us know how you're getting on. If there's an emergency you can call our twenty-four-hour helpline."

By now Anka was regretting the whole thing. But Vasily Ivanovich was standing by the entrance with his blue rucksack, and there was no going back. In the car her father was flustered and her mother kept biting her lip, as she did when she wanted to say something but couldn't find the right words.

"You must let us know if there's anything you're not happy with, Vasily Ivanovich," her father said. "We've no experience of this, you see. We don't even have the family around much, we're a small family. So if something doesn't suit you—"

"Why wouldn't it suit me?" Vasily Ivanovich said quietly. "I'm grateful to you, I'll do my best to please you."

"I'll try too," Anka said, trying to brush off the awkwardness. "I'm not easy to live with, I get frightened at night."

"What of?" he asked her with interest.

"All sorts of things. I'm afraid of bats, and once I was frightened by a snake."

"What nonsense, what snake?" said her mother.

"An ordinary one," she babbled. "I measured the crack under the door and it was big enough for one."

"Well, someone might have had one and it escaped," Vasily Ivanovich put in.

"Yes, I read of that happening, or perhaps it was a parrot," her father laughed. "We're quite easygoing here, don't let her upset you with her nonsense, she worries about everything. Until she was seven she used to howl at night and have to get into bed with her mother."

"Dad!" Anka said indignantly.

"Honestly, she was sorry for a dead crab once. I brought one back for her from the beach after a work trip, and she said it was so small, and its mother was probably crying for it and missing it. That's Anka, she's sorry for everything!"

"It's a very good thing," Vasily Ivanovich said quietly.

"No it's not. I don't like people crying, do you hear me, Anka?"

"Yes," she muttered.

"I'm out a lot and her mother works too, we're both busy, I think you're just the person to keep an eye on her, Vasily Ivanovich. Her schoolwork's fine, you don't need to push her on that, although personally I'd watch her algebra. The main thing is to make sure she gets to bed on time. She reads until two in the morning sometimes, then we can't wake her. Don't be too tough with her, just don't let her run wild."

The fact that he had called Vasily Ivanovich a person clearly meant he was pleased with his acquisition.

* * *

Vasily Ivanovich was very shy in the flat to begin with, and felt in the way. They had moved Anka's old bed into the kitchen, which was too small for him of course, but it was better than his metal cot at the shelter. Anka showed him where everything was and took him to the lavatory, with its picture of a little boy on the door, and the bathroom, with one of a little girl washing. He followed her in and looked round, and she almost had to force him to leave his red toothbrush there. They were all given them at the shelter, and he refused to put it in the glass with the others and hid it in the cupboard. Her mother had bought him some new underwear and children's pyjamas with a dinosaur pattern ("They were all they had!"), and he thanked her. Then Anka showed him where the balcony was.

"I know," he nodded.

"What do you mean?"

"I know where it is, and the view."

"Why?"

She wondered with a shiver of fear if he had once lived here. All day she had been dreading something like this would happen. They had brought him here and it turned out this was his flat, and they must have driven him out in some terrible way. It happened sometimes. She had seen a TV programme about a gang of gypsies who lured some alcoholics out of town to steal their flats, then gave them vodka and klofelin to drink until they died.

"I lived somewhere like this," he said.

"Like this, or in this flat?" she asked him in a frightened whisper.

"Not this one," he said quickly. "Don't worry little girl, why do you worry so much? It's good you do of course, but it didn't happen, it wasn't like that."

"What did happen then, won't you tell me?" she asked, and realized she had tactlessly reminded him of the glued-together pages of his notes that he was supposed to forget.

"I'll tell you everything Anka, I'll tell you as soon as I remember."

But as he stepped confidently onto the balcony and looked out at the landscape, she felt sure he must have lived here, perhaps even in this flat, built in the Seventies of the last century in what was then the edge of town. She was determined to get it out of him and discover where he had lived and why he left. She needed to know how someone could just leave like that. Some were kidnapped, of course. Not far from here were the flats where the General Staff lived, and there was a rumour (it wasn't in the papers of course) that a general had been kidnapped by the Khazars for his secrets. Some said he had in fact run off to America to sell his secrets and that the Americans didn't want them. But Anka couldn't get the story out of her mind, and for months she was afraid to leave the flat on her own. Yet there was something thrilling about running out at night, with the sharp smell of the autumn leaves and the glow of the street lamps, and gusts of cold wind that seemed to blow straight from the sea. She would stand there, then rush back inside before someone grabbed her. Not that anyone would want to kidnap her – she didn't know any secrets. But what if it wasn't about secrets, and she knew something else, something she herself didn't know about? She imagined being thrown into a car, unable to scream or escape, passing all the places she knew and seeing them for the last time (unless they put her in a sack, then she would just sense them), and the people they drove past wouldn't see her, and she would die alone. It seemed wrong that people died alone; such a hard thing should be done with others. They did other things together, they celebrated New Year and birthdays together, but they died alone. She liked the idea of the end of the world, because everyone would die together and it would be less frightening, like a holiday, when you didn't have to rush anywhere or do anything.

She had always been ashamed to let anyone know these thoughts, but Vasily Ivanovich was different, and she could talk to him as she talked to herself and did her best to explain it all to him. She had trusted him from the start, because he was completely dependent on her, and was the only person she had ever met who was completely without selfishness or vanity. Her parents too trusted him utterly, knowing he was far too incompetent to steal anything. He couldn't do anything properly. He tried to help around the flat, but would raise dust when he swept the floor and put things in the wrong cupboards so the doors didn't close, and when he washed his clothes he did even that clumsily. The only thing he was good at was gluing his little boxes, which he did constantly. They were all different sizes, and he made them in the most fantastic shapes. Some opened like flowers, others had masses of little compartments, others were octagonal. He said he was taught some shapes at the shelter, but had thought up most of them himself, and he felt he had a talent for it. He said nothing of his old life or his old job, and Anka didn't press him, but you couldn't live with someone and not know the most important thing about them; she had to know why someone would leave home and go off, not because they were forced to, but because they wanted to. She was terrified of the idea of leaving home. She imagined shutting the door behind her one night and creeping off, trying not to wake her parents, and it would be for ever. She already sensed in the depths of her soul that this would happen, you couldn't be so afraid of something unless it was in you already, and she imagined Vasily Ivanovich forcing her out of the flat one day, out of her cosy world into another she couldn't imagine. It seemed to her if she left – for a long time, for ever – she would be like a snail without a shell, its ripped skin flaring in pain from even a light breeze. And the more time went by, the more convinced she became that it would happen, and that this was the reason she wanted a Joe, not simply to bring another living soul into the flat.

* * *

Vasily Ivanovich settled in quickly. After a month they had to take him back to the shelter for his check-up, then another month passed and another, and their guests soon grew used to him. Yet he still felt awkward sitting at the family table, and unlike Petka he didn't put on weight. He was as fastidious as ever and ate almost nothing, and was always offering to do little jobs, and when he went to the shop to buy bread he would return with exactly the right change, to the last copeck, as if they didn't trust him; there was nothing they could do about it, it was as though he felt guilty all the time.

He reminded Anka of Akaky Akakyevich in Gogol's story 'The Overcoat', and after six months she had become attached to him and loved him. She had never met such a delicate, helpless creature. He would thank her touchingly when she gave him an apple, and would walk her to school every day and collect her, and although other children had their Joes, none was ever as happy to see their owner. He took her to the cinema too, and explained things she didn't understand. His knowledge was disorganized but wide-ranging. The subject he knew most about was engineering, but exclusively the theoretical side of it; using a screwdriver was beyond him. Her father tried to teach him to hammer nails, but it was hopeless, they would bend and he would hit his fingers, and eventually he gave up; this wasn't why they had a Joe.

He told her very little about himself. She knew only that he had been just over thirty and had a wife and two children when he developed the Syndrome and took off.

"I had a boy, yes, a boy called Mishenka," he said thoughtfully. "I made him a boat."

"You made a boat, Vasily Ivanovich?"

"I could then, Anka. I couldn't now, of course."

"Why did you leave?" she asked him once. She expected anything – prison, some terrible crime, that his flat had been stolen or he'd been punished for not having a residence permit, all the things they said about the Joes on TV. But it was nothing like that, he said, he had just gone off one day, out of the blue.

"I don't know why we do it," he said in answer to her question. "If they say it's because of prison or our flat, don't believe them. We just have to go and that's that."

"Is it an illness?"

"I suppose so, if the doctors say it is," he said. "In the shelter they kept asking why I'd left, and what could I tell them? Some remember, but most don't. It seems they found me in Irkutsk – what was I doing in Siberia when I'd lived in Moscow all my life? They sent me to a shelter in Moscow so I'd remember, and I can't even remember my address. But the flat was like this one, on the edge of town, and the view was the same. Sometimes I dream I've almost remembered it, and my wife Olga's calling me. I dreamt of Lilac Boulevard once. I'd like to go to Lilac Boulevard, maybe I'd remember something there, but it's probably too far."

"Why? Let's go!" she said, bursting with curiosity.

Lilac Boulevard was a short walk from the Izmailovo underground station, and they set off on a soft grey day in May. It had just rained, and bright drops ran off the lilacs. They walked the length of the avenue but he didn't recognize anything. She took him to the courtyard of some flats, an ordinary Moscow yard with a creaking see-saw, and he stood by the see-saw and the flower beds, where blue spears of irises poked through the earth, and he closed his eyes with pleasure and breathed in the smells, but he still didn't remember anything.

"I probably just dreamt it," he said. "It's a nice name."

A boy came out from the flats with a young hunched Joe and tried to teach him to play football, and the two Joes nodded at each other and exchanged barely audible greetings.

"What did you say to him, Vasily Ivanovich?" she asked him afterwards on the train.

"Who?"

"You know, the other... When the two boys came out and you said something?"

"Well, we said hello," he said, embarrassed.

"But it sounded like 'a little bit, a little bit'..."

"I don't remember, maybe it was 'little friend'?"

Vasily Ivanovich had the most terrible memory, and couldn't remember the simplest things.

* * *

Every morning Vasily Ivanovich had to be taken for a walk. He wasn't a dog, but walks were good for him, and they were even better for Anka. Her parents could never tear her from her books or her computer games for some fresh air, and they had made her promise if she got a Joe that she would take him for walks every day, and she kept her word.

A lot of people in Moscow were on the streets shopping with their Joes these days. It was convenient to load them up with the bags – or get them to wash the car or babysit while they gossiped in the square next to Anka's building. They were hopeless babysitters of course, but they did their best, desperate not to be sent back to the shelter.

As the fashion for Joes caught on, people were paid an allowance for them, and Rusoil, as part of its charity work, paid a monthly bursary to families with more than one (they paid more for Mashkas, who were harder to train). At least five Joes would be in the square every morning. Sometimes they quarrelled and fought, but this was very rare; mostly they greeted each other with a little bow and chatted quietly.

Sometimes outsiders would come and talk to them, and Anka kept seeing a short, fit bald man with a ginger beard and round glasses, who would have long murmured discussions with Vasily Ivanovich and listen respectfully to him.

"Do you know him?" she had asked him.

"Not really, he just had a friend in the shelter and wants to know what's going on there," he replied hurriedly.

"Did you know his friend?"

"I don't remember him, I knew a lot of people. He's all right, don't be afraid of him."

She wasn't afraid of him, she simply couldn't understand why he kept coming and talking to her Joe so respectfully. He would appear roughly once a fortnight and question everyone, but he seemed to like Vasily Ivanovich best. She had gone over once and tried to hear what they were saying, and he stopped and said loudly, "What about butter, Vasily Ivanovich, did you get butter there?"

And Vasily Ivanovich had replied, in an unnaturally deep voice, "Yes, every morning, and mornings and evenings at weekends."

"Excellent. I'll be back soon."

"What if he's trying to trap you, Vasily Ivanovich?" she asked him afterwards.

"Who needs me?" he smiled, looking at her with his honest brown eyes.

"So what's his job?"

"You see, when I was travelling I learnt a lot of riddles and stories, and he's a specialist, a collector. He asks everyone about them, I just know more than other people."

It was true, Vasily Ivanovich knew a huge number of stories, and they made her love him even more; it was almost as if she couldn't live without them.

They were well constructed, as if they had been composed long ago, and they were strange and sad, sadder than anything she had ever heard before. He would come into her room in the evenings, and in a quiet shy voice he would tell her an endless saga about some toys in an abandoned cottage. It was a peasant cottage, and when the owners moved to the city the children forgot to take them, because they had outgrown them, and left them in an old trunk. The velvet dog managed to push it open and let the others out, and soon the cottage was knocked down to make way for new flats, and the toys were thrown out in the rain. At first they lived in a cardboard box, then winter came and they were cold, so they set off for the city to look for their owners.

Anka wept and tried to hide her red eyes from her parents in the mornings so they wouldn't notice anything. If they had, they would definitely have told him to stop telling his stories. It annoyed them that she cried over her books and even pitied the criminals on TV, and they thought it showed weakness and lack of moral fibre. Her father would angrily use all sorts of clever words and forget he was shouting at a twelve-year-old. But she understood everything, and had read much more than anyone else at school. She knew her parents didn't like her compassion for the underdog and, to be honest, she didn't much like it herself.

The saga of the toys went on for six months. They all had their own voices and personalities, and Vasily Ivanovich never forgot where he had stopped in the last episode; his memory for this was excellent for some reason. What struck her most was that nothing good ever happened to the toys as they kept running away from people; the police would try to arrest them, greedy children would steal them, and a vicious little girl grabbed the prettiest doll once and threw it away when it refused to play her cruel games. There was a beaver too, the good spirit of the cottage that had been knocked down. It was hardest for the beaver on their travels, because his job was to guard the hearth, and he was frightened outside. He longed to be taken into a house and he would have brought it happiness, but no one wanted him because he was old and shabby. A boy took him, but his parents threw him out. He returned, wanting to thank the boy, but the house burnt down. He survived and managed to escape, and was homeless again. No one ever found anyone, everyone kept crossing paths, and even the toys' old owners didn't recognize them when they finally reached their new flat in the city.

Anka laughed. She had expected this, and when something's too sad it's funny. "You've gone too far this time!" she told him. "I'll tell you a story about a poor little ball who kept being kicked around by footballs, and he loved everyone but couldn't tell them!"

"You've grown up. You're a good girl, Anka," he smiled, but deep down he was hurt.

After the toys there were more sad stories, whose heroes were always helpless in the face of evil. Evil always got its way, and no one could stop it. It wasn't defeated, as happens in most stories, it swelled like yeast, brazen and triumphant. Sometimes there was no evil, just an eternal sadness. He told her one about a boy who ran after a beautiful butterfly, and the butterfly took him far, far away over a stone wall, and his mother waited at the gate for him and wept and mourned him: "You ran off to play and forgot me!" The boy walked and walked along the wall and grew tall, and returned to his mother an old tired man, and she put him to bed and sang to him. This story was sadder than all the others and finally finished her off.

"Did you make it up yourself?" she said through her tears.

"How would I do that? It's an old story, it was written by one of ours."

"You mean a... traveller?"

"No, he didn't travel, we're all different. But no one knew our language like he did."

"You have a different language?" She stopped sniffing.

"It's a bit different. It sounds the same, but the words have other meanings."

"Like what?"

"Well, how about: 'There are so many people in the world they don't need to live for good to exist.'"

"So? It's Russian isn't it?"

"It sounds like it, doesn't it? Go to bed, I'll tell you more in the morning," he said and, ignoring her entreaties, he returned to the kitchen, where he grunted and wheezed for a long time on her old bed.

*　*　*

After that he began to recite poems to her in his own language. The lines flowed naturally, but were twisted somehow; almost all the words were familiar but with a different intonation and melody, as if they didn't quite fit together. Some were about war, but these were always lamentations about defeat, or funeral poems for the fallen: "When the forest lay on the road they had no power of speech and burnt their bodies." "The last warrior still fleeing fled the arrows of the rain."

219

There was nothing about actual fighting, though. "That's not our business," he told her gently.

"How do you remember all these poems?"

"Why wouldn't I, it's my language."

"Say something in your language! Say 'Anka'!"

"It's the same, 'Anka'. The words are the same, but the meanings are different."

She thought his travels might have made him a bit cuckoo, as they said at school. But she loved his old verses, and she liked his stories even better. Most of all she liked the one about the old couple who lived with a rooster and its little magic mill.

"What kind of mill, Vasily Ivanovich?" she asked.

"Let's see. Maybe tomorrow I'll show you one," he said, and sure enough, the following day a Joe called Tolya from the next building made her at his request a little wooden mill, with sails that went round and turned the millstones to produce invisible flour. In the story though the mill was golden, and the millstones were blue, and they didn't need wind or grain, the sails turned by themselves and the flour poured out.

Vasily Ivanovich told her how a wicked nobleman passed the old couple's cottage one day, and saw the mill and stole it from them. The rooster flew at him and sat on his collar, crying, "Gentleman, gentleman, give me my mill, my darling golden mill!" The nobleman ordered it to be thrown in the well, and it drank all the water and again flew to his collar, crying, "Gentleman, gentleman, give me my mill, my darling golden mill!" The nobleman threw it in the stove, but it poured water on it and put it out, and the nobleman was afraid of the clever rooster and gave back its mill.

The rooster had won not through strength but through cunning, and perhaps afterwards it returned to the cottage. But according to the logic of Vasily Ivanovich's stories the nobleman's servants had probably burnt the cottage down, and the couple wandered round looking for the rooster and it couldn't find them and give back their mill.

She told him her version of the ending as she walked with him in the square next evening with her mill. Tolya, who had been listening, grinned. "You've taught the child well, Vasily Ivanovich. Soon she'll—"

"That's enough, Tolya," said a cheerful bass voice behind them, and she turned to see the bald man with the beard.

"Who made it?" he enquired, looking at her toy.

"It was Tolya," she said quietly. "I keep seeing you, who are you?"

"He's a friend, a friend," Vasily Ivanovich mumbled, narrowing his eyes almost as if he was afraid of him, although she couldn't think why he would be afraid of the bald man; he seemed cheerful and pleasant, and spoke politely to the Joes, unlike some of the old ladies in the building.

"I've noticed you too, Anka," he said. "Next time I'll bring you a circling falcon. Do you know what that is?"

"I can make one," nodded Tolya.

"No, I don't," she said.

"You should, it's a fascinating toy, there's an apple on a plate – not an ordinary apple, of course. It goes round and round like a gyroscope and does amazing tricks. You hardly ever see them now, there are no proper craftsmen left."

Tolya hung his head, and realized he wasn't a proper craftsman after all.

"What's your name?" she asked him.

"It's Gurov, but you can call me Petya," he said. "Here, take this, you might need it." He reached in his pocket for a business card with his name and phone number, but no job title or address.

"You're a folklorist?" she said, proud of knowing this difficult word.

"Among other things. I'll bring you a falcon tomorrow."

He didn't come the next day, or the next week, but in the autumn, when she was about to go up to the eighth class at school.

He appeared suddenly, out of nowhere, as he always did, and pulled a wooden plate and ball from his battered briefcase, and put them on a bench. "Shall we set it off?" he said to Vasily Ivanovich, who was observing respectfully.

They were walking that afternoon with two of Anka's classmates, and Vasily Ivanovich gave them sidelong glances, but Gurov wasn't bothered. "Hello, little girls. I'm Anka's friend, aren't I, Anka?"

Anka nodded. For some reason she trusted him.

"The ball runs round the plate, so," he said, releasing it with a flourish, and Vasily Ivanovich straightened up and stared at it, although Anka saw nothing special, just one wooden thing going round another.

The ball stopped, and Gurov threw Vasily Ivanovich a challenging look, as if expecting a critical comment from him. "And what do we see?" he asked him with a forced cheerfulness.

"Almost nothing at all," Vasily Ivanovich said through clenched teeth.

Anka's friends burst out laughing and she joined in, and couldn't forgive herself afterwards for this brief betrayal of him.

"And?" Gurov persisted.

"It's time to leave," he muttered.

"That's right, straight away."

"No, not straight away," Vasily Ivanovich said. "Don't ask me again."

2

Soon after Gurov showed Anka the falcon, there were clashes in Moscow, and the country was gradually drawn into war. In the avalanche of events in those months, she grew up quickly and stopped feeling sorry for everyone, because feeling sorry was no longer enough. No one spoke of war. The stabilization they used to discuss on TV ended suddenly, almost overnight, when Phlogiston was discovered in the rest of the world. Before that, when Russia was still living on oil money, almost all the émigrés had returned. There were thousands of them, and they all repented and were allowed back to enjoy happy times. Most of them returned from the Kaganate and apologized on TV looking suspiciously happy, and they didn't seem sorry at all; she was never so cheerful when she had to apologize to her parents.

These repentant returners must have known something no one else did, coming back to a country that hated them and even held demonstrations against them on National Unity Day, and these demonstrations were the trigger for military action. A few ultra-liberals wanted to hang on and wait for Phlogiston to be discovered, but most thought Phlogiston was just a Khazar lie; Anka's Chemistry teacher explained that the formula for it contained many errors, and nothing could replace oil.

But somehow thanks to this mythical gas Russia could no longer sell its oil, and it had nothing else to sell. Businesses closed and dark clouds loomed, and the newspaper where Anka's father worked was about to fold. Fortunately though he managed to jump ship at the last minute and get a job writing advertising copy for Rusoil sausage and butter. He was given plenty of oil foodstuffs to take home and they practically lived on them, although they gave them terrible stomach aches.

Vasily Ivanovich stopped telling his stories and became very quiet, trying constantly to show how grateful he was that they had kept him. As people lost their jobs, the Joes were sent back to the shelters in their hundreds, and soon the government had no food for the shelters and they were thrown back on the streets. Old Nelly Alexandrovna's Tolya, who had made the mill, came back ragged and stinking after his shelter closed, not asking her to take him back – she had a sick mother and nothing to eat either – but simply to say goodbye and give her a wooden knick-knack he had made, of two bearded men on a see-saw: for some reason a lot of Joes liked to make these, and would give them to their owners, saying they brought luck.

In October, three months before the war started, when everything was falling apart, Gurov unexpectedly reappeared. Anka was out on her own without Vasily Ivanovich, because his sad silent presence oppressed her and he didn't want to be a burden. She was walking through rustling piles of dead leaves, thinking it wouldn't be long before the first snow, when he suddenly stepped out from behind a tree, looking unusually sober and severe.

"I want to thank you, Anka," he greeted her.

"What for?" she asked, feeling awkward with this man she was supposed to call Petya.

"You treat Vasily Ivanovich very well. If it wasn't for you, your parents would have sent him back long ago."

"No they wouldn't, they won't send him anywhere!" she said, springing to their defence.

"I know, and that's because of you. Ever since you took him I've been keeping an eye on you. It's important for me to know he's in good hands."

"Why? I know – you're his son!" It was quite possible. Vasily Ivanovich was in his mid-fifties, and Gurov was probably no more than thirty, even though he was bald.

"Good guess, Anka!" he said. "No, I'm not his son, we're not related. But I'm sure you know he's no ordinary person, he's a remarkable storyteller and he's of interest to me."

"Then why didn't you—"

"Take him myself?" he asked serenely. "I'm hardly ever at home, you see, I'm always working and travelling, and I couldn't drag him round with me. And it would kill him if I left him alone in the flat. He's completely useless when it comes to practical matters, as you know."

"Is it a bad case of the Syndrome?" she asked, frightened.

"Yes, or rather the highest form of it, I'd say. But forget the Syndrome, what he has isn't an illness, it's part of his nature, and I'm happy you're friends with him. Now listen carefully. This man could be the salvation of you and your family."

Anka was afraid then, with good reason, alone with Gurov in the square, where a cold sunset had quickly turned from a morbid red to total darkness.

"Bad times are coming, Anka, very bad, I don't want you to have any illusions. Under the present government the country can't survive the crisis, and there'll be war. It will be no ordinary war, and people won't call it that, but I assure you it will be very real. Anything can happen. They'll kill their enemies and look for us everywhere, and it will be hard for you to keep Vasily Ivanovich safe. I'm not always in Moscow, a lot depends on you. If anything happens, you must call me at once, or here…" He handed her a piece of paper with a phone number and an address. The address was 78 Lilac Boulevard.

"But we went to Lilac Boulevard!" she barely managed to say.

"I know. They're good people, they'll look after you if you need anything. Take care of him, Anka, he's important. He knows everything, even if he doesn't talk about it."

"And how will the war end?"

"In absolutely nothing as usual!" he beamed suddenly. "When times are hard there's always a big war, or a little one, it makes no difference. I won't fill your head with rubbish, my job's simply to make sure we lose as few of ours as possible, and Vasily Ivanovich is one of our best. Don't be surprised, Joes are never what they seem."

"I know," she nodded.

"I know you know. Where were your parents born, by the way?"

"My father's from Moscow and my mother's from Saratov. Why?"

"Nothing, don't worry, you're of good stock. Pudding and pie, away you fly."

"What?" she gasped.

"Don't worry, it's just a saying. I'm a folklorist, remember? Promise to take good care of him, won't you?"

"I promise," she nodded.

"I believe you," he said, and slipped behind the tree and vanished.

After that there were demonstrations and skirmishes in the cities, and before long it was all-out war. The day before it broke out, all the Khazars fled the capital, which unlike the rest of the country still had a police force and an army. According to voices on the radio, gangs of Khazars were occupying towns and villages and seizing vast areas of the South, where it was hot, and the North, where there was oil, although there were many black holes in Moscow where the voices couldn't reach. Information from the other territories was muddled and contradictory. Anka's granny in Saratov wrote that the Khazars had entered the town twice but had been driven out. There were partisans too who blew up the trains, probably trying to stop them getting to Moscow, although no one knew whose side they were on; they probably just liked blowing up trains.

* * *

After a cold hungry winter when Anka's school didn't always open and the teachers weren't paid, her parents finally discussed sending Vasily Ivanovich back. She overheard their conversation and burst into the room in tears, and they dropped the subject, although there was no knowing when they would return to it.

By the end of the eighth year, Anka had turned into a pretty, graceful girl, although her face was still terribly strained and anxious. She almost never cried now, but she was afraid all the time. She tried not to watch television; there was nothing especially bad on the news, but it was clear terrible things were happening. The country no longer belonged to itself. Neither the Khazars nor the Federals knew which parts of it were theirs. There was still food in Moscow, but almost nothing in Saratov, and the television was showing reports of last year's harvest instead, which she remembered thanks to her photographic memory.

At the beginning of June Gurov materialized again, looking thin and unsmiling. He had shaved off his beard, and wasn't waiting for her in the square this time but came to the flat; she had no idea how he knew the address.

"Hello, Vyacheslav Viktorovich, Nadezhda Andreevna," he greeted her parents. "Will you call Vasily Ivanovich please? This concerns him."

"With whom do I have the pleasure?" her father asked stiffly.

"Inspector Gurov of the General Staff," he said, showing them his little red book with the eagle insignia – so he wasn't a folklorist after all. "It's important you tell no one of my visit, it's a serious breach of my duties, but the situation's critical. Next week will see the start of a mass purge of the so-called Joes, the Anticyclone Plan, and they'll be sent out of the city and..." – he gulped – "if my information is correct, shot."

Everyone looked at Vasily Ivanovich, who came in looking pale but composed.

"I don't think you can hide him, or that you'd want to. I can take him today, and that's why I've come. If you've become fond of him, then I'm sorry."

"I knew it," Vasily Ivanovich said quietly.

"Since when?" he asked.

"Since the falcon," he replied. "There's nothing you can do, Pyotr Antonovich, I'm not going with you."

"Why not?"

"I know where I'm going, I'm going to Alabino."

"But Alabino's dangerous, Vasily Ivanovich."

"No it's not, it's not been dangerous for a long time, a lot of us are there."

"But why? I'm going to Degunino in July, won't you come with me to Degunino?"

"Don't bother about me, save the rest. I have people who care about me and they've no one."

"Please, Vasily Ivanovich." Gurov clasped his hands and seemed oblivious to Anka and her parents. "You must see we can't lose you, there are so few like you."

"Nothing will happen to me, take care of the others," he repeated, with a firmness Anka hadn't heard before. "In a week I can reach three or four towns and warn them."

"But that's what I'm doing, travelling around warning people!"

"You can't tell everyone though, and they won't all listen to you. They'll listen to me, I'm their brother. I wasn't sure if the time had come yet or I was just imagining it. Decisions are hard for me—"

"I know."

"But I've decided now. I give you my blessing to take care of the others. I don't give you my blessing to take care of me. Thanks for the warning, Pyotr Antonovich, I won't forget it."

"You're selfless. I expected nothing less of you," Gurov sighed after a pause.

"I used to be," he said bitterly. "Not any more."

"Forgive me, Vasily Ivanovich, but you're so impractical," he pleaded.

"In some things, but you don't need brains to travel. I travelled for twenty years and can do it again, I can look after myself. Go now, we've a lot to do."

Gurov glanced distractedly at Anka and her parents, as if he had no idea what they were doing there, then vanished.

They sat in stunned silence for a while.

"Thanks for everything, it's time for me to go," Vasily Ivanovich said at last. He was still very pale, but his voice and hands weren't shaking and he seemed to stand taller.

"You're not leaving, Vasily Ivanovich," Anka said. "We'll find somewhere to hide you."

"But if you hide me how will I tell the others?"

"Couldn't you write to them or phone?" she persisted.

"What, on my mobile? As if we Joes have mobiles!" he grinned. "No, Anka, I must do it the old way, with my legs and my voice. When the falcon flies, you can't catch it. I must get ready. In two days I'll leave."

"Wait, Vasily Ivanovich, this is ridiculous!" said Anka's father. "Some character claims he's from the General Staff and spreads rumours... Do you really believe they'll kill you?"

"Why not? The Varangians are merciful people, if they can't feed you, they kill you to put you out of your misery."

"Who are the Varangians?" her mother demanded.

"You say Russians, we say Varangians," he told her and went to the kitchen, where for the past two years his blue rucksack had lain packed under Anka's old bed.

* * *

The next night was cold and rainy, and Anka went to bed early, saying she had a headache. Vasily Ivanovich had mumbled a half-hearted goodbye to her, almost as if he didn't mean it, and told her he would leave at three in the morning, when there were no people on the streets and the police were inside keeping warm.

"It's tragic," her mother moaned. "The poor child's so fond of him, it's much harder than losing a dog."

"Nonsense, he'll be back," her father said. "What purge? I've never heard of it. Personally I didn't trust that Gurov."

"But what about his ID from the General Staff?"

"Most likely a forgery, I could find dozens of them. Did you pack him some food?"

"Of course, I left sandwiches and a thermos."

"Why a thermos? He needs apples and vitamins..."

Anka lay under the blankets with her clothes on so she wouldn't have to crawl out of her warm bed later and get dressed. She had never left the flat in the middle of the night before, although she was already fourteen.

Her parents went to their room and she could hear them talking, but hoped they would be asleep by three. She read a stupid adventure story under the blankets with a torch, and at a quarter past three she heard Vasily Ivanovich get up. There were footsteps in the hall as he went to the front door, then the lock clicked and he closed it behind him. Counting to twenty, she jumped up and grabbed her school bag, in which she had packed some essentials, then crept out after him.

She caught up with him standing at the entrance to the building. The rain had washed away the flower beds in the yard, and he was either waiting for her or had forgotten how to travel after two years, and was unsure which way to go.

"What are you doing, Vasily Ivanovich? Did you think I'd let you go on your own?" she said quietly, touching his shoulder.

"Anka! Go back at once!"

"No, I won't!"

"I planned everything! I waited so I wouldn't wake you!" he whispered.

"You're very clever, Vasily Ivanovich," she said respectfully. "But I'm not stupid either."

"Good, see me off then. It broke my heart that I didn't say goodbye properly to you. Go back now, look at the rain."

"I've got an umbrella," she remembered, realizing suddenly with an aching heart that she was leaving home for the last time. Well, perhaps not for the last time, but for a long time.

She opened her umbrella, and he tried to take it and hold it over them, but it slipped from his hands and blew off in the wind and she had to chase after it.

"Now you see why I can't let you go alone!" she panted. "I'll take you to Alabino, then come back. You won't be caught if I'm with you, we'll say you're taking me to Granny's in Saratov. I've got her address."

His wet face crinkled into a smile. "You're clever Anka, you've thought of everything. But you don't know where Alabino is."

"I know you though," she said simply. "Let's go, Vasily Ivanovich. Where is it?"

"Outside Belgorod, between Degunino and the border with Ukraine," he whispered.

"Fine. We'll take the local trains, they're safer. I have some money."

"Listen to you," he said admiringly, then his face clouded. "Your parents will think I've kidnapped you."

"No, they won't, I left them a note. Let's hurry before they wake up."

* * *

Anka dozed on the train. There were almost no other passengers, but a youth sitting opposite kept scowling at her for some reason. Vasily Ivanovich seemed frightened and tucked his feet under the seat. She didn't understand why he was frightened of the boy; he was probably just irritable because he had been out on the town and hadn't slept. The hoarse voice of the driver announced that the train was going to Tula, stopping at all stations except Silikatnaya and Pokrovsky, and she curled up in a ball and for the first time that night fell asleep.

She was woken by someone falling on top of her, breathing heavily and trying to open her legs. In her half-awake state she couldn't think what the boy wanted from her.

"Help!" she screamed. "Help me!"

Vasily Ivanovich was her only hope, but he stood helplessly raising his arms wailing, "Anka, Anka! Lord, the grief of it, what's to be done, what's to be done!"

"Press the button!" she gasped. "Press the red button!"

She knew the local trains had an emergency button to the driver, but even if it worked, he probably wouldn't want to stop the train and run to their compartment. There were no police on the trains now either, as they were all in Moscow catching Khazars, although the Khazars had left long ago to fight in the war.

She went on screaming as the boy crushed her with the weight of his body, reaching under her sweater and into her trousers, with his dirty lips and his garlic breath. She shuddered with fear, and her hands and legs refused to obey her. She didn't know what would happen next, only that there was no one to help her.

"Anka! Anka!" Vasily Ivanovich sobbed. "Anka, my child, what's to be done!"

He tried to grab the boy's raincoat, but the boy kicked him across the compartment and he crashed against the door.

She was saved only when a large middle-aged man got on at the next stop. Grabbing the boy's collar, he punched him in the jaw, and he fell to the floor. He jumped up, and was met with another blow to the nose, at which he gave up and ran off. The man started after him, then looked back at Anka, realizing she needed him more.

"Are you all right?" he asked her.

"Yes," she replied in a trembling voice, pulling down her torn sweater.

"What are you doing alone at this time of night?" he admonished her.

"I'm not alone, I'm with my grandfather," she said.

"A fat lot of good he is," he said, taking out a flask of coffee. "Here, drink this. Get up, granddad, are you hurt?"

"I'm fine," Vasily Ivanovich whispered.

"Let's go to the corridor, Vasily Ivanovich," she said, still trembling.

He shuffled after her. It was growing light, and grey cabbage fields flashed past the window in a grey rainy dawn.

"What happened, Vasily Ivanovich?" she said sharply. It was the first time she had spoken to her Joe like this.

"I told you I should go on my own, Anka," he said. "I'm not afraid on my own, but who knows what they'll do to you? What can I do?"

"I see, so you can't defend me. I'll have to defend myself now, is that it? Oh, Vasily Ivanovich," she said with an adult sadness in her voice. "It's hard for us, dear friend."

"It is, it is," he nodded. "Go home, Anka."

"It's too late now," she said, and went back to the compartment to thank the man and drink coffee. She looked out at the corridor every so often to make sure Vasily Ivanovich didn't escape, but he stood with his forehead pressed to the cold glass, silently moving his lips and singing. She drank coffee from the metal cup, embarrassed that she couldn't stop trembling, and only realized then how frightened she had been.

"'Not alone in the field,'" Vasily Ivanovich murmured, and sang on, wiping away the tears.

"Not alone in the field, little road.
Not alone endless, not alone friendless.
Not alone in the field, little road…"

Interlude

"What shall I sing about?" asked the old man with a mandolin on his knee, who might or might not have been the village elder, and might or might not have been blind.

"Sing about war," Colonel Lavkin said carelessly. He was sitting opposite him with Cossack Batuga, gnawing Varangian-style at a bone. Lavkin was a scout, and he liked Batuga's fighting spirit – he had ordered a goat to be slaughtered and roasted for him that evening in his hut. There was a lull in the fighting – the lull had gone on for two years in fact. The armies kept running away from each other, capturing people occasionally for the pleasure of stringing them up, and each side was busy with its favourite pastimes. The Varangians continued to shoot their own people, and the Khazars colonized the natives, even though shooting everyone made no sense, and colonizing them was pointless, as the Varangians had discovered from long experience.

"Which war?" asked the elder, who might or might not have been blind, his sharp eyes under their bushy brows darting around the hut. "About Julius Caesar? Or the Babylonians, from the ancient Babylonian texts?"

"Give us the Babylonians!" cried Batuga, picking his teeth with a yellow fingernail.

"It's an old song, I don't remember all the words," said the old man, plucking his mandolin.

"Never mind, get on with it," the Ataman belched.

"'I mounted my chariot and went unto the city of Babylon,'" the man began in a pensive sing-song voice. "'Yea unto Babylon, to drive out the whores of Ashtarot. Twenty dozen chariots there were, and they thundered—'"

"That's a lot!" Batuga smirked.

"'Twenty dozen chariots there were,'" the blind man continued, ignoring him. He found the tune at first strangely similar to 'Moscow Nights', but with every line departing from it into something without rhyme or rhythm but with a strangely uplifting military beat:

"Give me my chariot, yea and my helmet, my golden helmet.
Give me my spear, five metres long, three measures of weight.
Give me my shield, six metres wide – a shield to defend my
people—"

"Yes, yes, get to the fighting part," said Lavkin.

"And the Lord delivered the whores to me,
Children of worms, slimy snakes, bags of giblets,
And their legs were the legs of girls,
And their arms were green as cucumbers,
And their muscles were weakened by drunkenness, yea,
And their veins were like wisps of hair.
And my chariots hunted them to their filthy lair,
And in one chariot sat I, with my sword and my spear—"

"Sounds like us," Batuga said happily.
The old man's eyes stopped darting and fixed first on him, then on
Lavkin.

"And we took their virgins and made them our wives,
And we took their wives, yea, and made them our slaves.
And we took their slaves and turned them into cutlets.
Then we took their dogs and ravished them, yea,
And we ravished their cats and we ravished their sheep,
And we crushed all the cockroaches and their chattels,
Yea, and we crushed the dogs and cats and concubines,
So all may know the glory of Babylon!"

The old man's voice was low and menacing. When he came to shagging
the dogs Lavkin felt goose bumps up his spine, and he cursed his
inactivity, sitting in his stupid peasant hut torturing people who had
already been tortured. The spirit of war spoke to him in the song, and
the live fresh spirit of Varangianism.

"Let none gainsay the glory of Babylon!
Let us spill our blood, yea, and fight!
And I, the fierce spirit of war, am ashamed to look at you,
Ashamed to ravish you…"

The old man stood up and threw aside his mandolin.

> "Cursed be those who eat goat and forsake war!
> Cursed be the corrupted!
> Curses on you! Goodnight!"

He stamped his foot angrily and vanished into thin air.

"What the hell was that? He's a barrel of snakes!" Batuga said after a long pause, trying to calm himself with the sound of his own voice.

"No, he's right, Batuga, he understands the spirit of war. This isn't war," said Lavkin gloomily, throwing his bone on the floor.

"But where did he go?" asked the Ataman, frightened.

"Don't ask me, what does it matter? Nothing's going anywhere now," Lavkin said.

Part Two

Arrival

Chapter One
Bella Ciao

> *Partisan, partisan, carry me away,*
> *Goodbye my darling, goodbye.*
> *And if I die on the mountains,*
> *You can bury me there,*
> *Goodbye my darling, goodbye.*

"It's a big, big village. In the middle of the village is a pillar, and on the pillar is a face, and whoever looks at the face becomes a pillar, and all around are the pillars of the people who looked at the face. The clouds are low over the village and there's no light. Beyond it the land is flat, and there's a field and a forest, but you can't go there. After the forest is a station. It takes ten minutes to walk from the station to the village, but ten years to walk from the village to the station. There's no way out of it and no one ever comes back. People's huts are big and black, and they go naked in all weathers and they're black too. If a living soul arrives and asks them the time, they don't tell them..."

They should put a clock on the pillar instead of a face, Gromov thought, then people wouldn't turn to pillars and they would know the time.

"Why don't they tell them?" the little boy asked his mother.

"Because they don't understand living speech," she sighed, and went on telling him in a depressing monotone about the village of Zhadrunovo, where the conductors on the trains sent children who wouldn't sleep.

What was Zhadrunovo? There were vague reports of battles there in the first months of the war, then the reports stopped – evidently the government had been defeated – and Gurov had threatened to send Gromov there if he didn't get to Koposovo. He imagined the place as a sort of giant lock-up, with the face of Zdrok on the pillar, and any soldier who slept at his post would be sent there and become a pillar, in the same numb, half-awake state as the slow trains on which he and Voronov had been travelling for the past twenty-four hours.

Voronov slept quietly in the ancient compartment they had boarded five hours earlier, after the local train from Degunino. A mad old woman wailed in the next seat. Her fat son, who was taking her home from a funeral, told her to shut up, then slapped her. A baby cried, and young and old wailed together in the pale half-light of the July dusk. The lights hadn't been switched on. "Give it some tit!" the fat son shouted to the baby's mother, and she snapped that she had just fed it. Then just as the baby fell asleep and the old woman fell silent, the little boy sitting opposite Gromov had woken from a bad dream, and his mother could think of nothing better to do than terrify him by describing this village he would go to if he didn't sleep.

Legend had it that Zhadrunovo was somewhere east of here, near Kazan on the Volga, although it was hard to know what to believe, since no one ever came back from it. Perhaps someone had written: "Dear Mother and Father, I've stupidly landed up in the village of Zhadrunovo in the Kazan region, and now I can't get out. Please send me some food, there's nothing to eat. The cows give black milk, and if you ask them the time they strangle you, because there's no time in Zhadrunovo or anything else..."

It was part of Russia's national folklore, Gromov thought, these letters from political prisoners to their peasant parents. If the parents knew about Zhadrunovo they wouldn't send anything, since everything disappeared there. If they were from Degunino, they would send parcels of bacon, butter and cream, but the post wouldn't reach them. Kind white women lived in Degunino. In Zhadrunovo they were strange black people, possibly Negroes. And now everyone had turned to pillars, like the pillars and posts along the railway line, and he hated the pillars and trains and these people, incapable of anything in peacetime or war. The train dawdled along with its pillared people, the three mothers and the ancient relative pillar, mewling with her toothless feline mouth... When would it all end? They should have been there long ago...

The train juddered suddenly and clanked to a halt. It wasn't a station, but Gromov wasn't worried. It had probably stopped in a field to rest and draw breath before moving on. But at that moment someone rapped on the window above his head, and the frightened conductress rushed along the carriage yelling, "It's partisans! Don't kill us, boys, we're on your side!"

She was followed by a young man in a padded jacket with an orange armband, who came into the compartment and announced: "Comrades, ladies and gentlemen! The track has been blown up by the Revolutionary Alternative Fighting Organization! You can stay put, but I warn you it's pointless, the train's going nowhere. Please leave your seats and remember to take your things. We're not greedy, we don't want your clutter." It seemed the young partisan liked to talk. "Our purpose is to cut communications and stop the senseless killing. If anyone asks who did it, give them personal greetings from fighter Pyotr Kalanchev, known as Kalancha..."

"Kalancha!" Voronov shouted unexpectedly from his seat.

"Who's that?" the partisan replied stupidly.

"It's me, Voronov!"

"God, Voron, I thought you were at the Front!"

"I'm going to Koposovo on... an assignment," he said.

Gromov realized that their roles had been reversed, and he was now in Voronov's hands. The Private could betray him to the partisans, who wouldn't look kindly at this Federal officer, and it would be goodbye to his leave. But it seemed Voronov wouldn't betray him.

"Permission to speak, comrade Captain!" he whispered, and Gromov was struck by the way army etiquette had been so drummed into him he couldn't speak simply even in a crisis.

"Go on then."

"I used to be with the Alternatives, you see, they're my comrades," he said, still in a whisper. "They didn't... well, they didn't join the army, and it was only later they started blowing up trains. They weren't doing it when I was with them. They're OK, comrade Captain, they won't hurt us. Perhaps if I talk to him they'll let us through to Koposovo. We have to get there, don't we?"

"Fine, go ahead," he shrugged.

The baby woke and started squalling again. Fighter Kalanchev, who was small and puny, jostled past it to Voronov. "Who's this you're with?" he asked, grabbing his friend in a clumsy hug.

"This is Captain Gromov, he's on his way to Moscow on leave," Voronov said. "He's our best officer, he looks after his men."

"I don't need a reference from you, Voronov, remember your rank," Gromov said curtly. "Hello Kalanchev, I'd like to talk to your commander."

"Oh would you!" Kalanchev laughed. "You're not in charge here!"

"Kalancha!" Voronov squeaked reproachfully. "He's a good person. Really, you shouldn't—"

"You think everyone's a good person. So you're on leave, Captain?" Kalanchev said, still looking at Gromov, and Gromov saw a lurking fear in his eyes, and realized the boy was a greenhorn and would be easy to break.

"I don't answer to you, but I've something to say to your commander," he told him.

"What if I'm commander?" asked Kalanchev cockily.

"OK, Kalanchev, why did you blow up the line?"

It was pointless trying to have a sensible conversation with these characters. He was a fanatic, one of those intellectuals and ex-students who read a lot of pamphlets and had no luck with girls, and tried to impress them by issuing proclamations and throwing tomatoes. Normally such people did no particular harm, but in wartime they became saboteurs and blew up trains. Until now he had thought the partisans were a government myth – whenever a train was raided or derailed for the hell of it they were always blamed. And now it turned out they actually existed. This was where the snivellers from the anti-war demonstrations went, the wealthy idlers and golden youth from Moscow's garden suburbs, perpetually reliving the Sixties. Fuck the partisans, would this war ever end?

"You want our commander?" Kalanchev said in a menacing tone. "You can see our commander. Hey, Voron, has he insulted you?"

"Cut it out, Kalancha," Voronov said earnestly, dropping his voice. "I told you, he's all right…"

"Come and see our commander then, quick march," Kalanchev said. "He's giving the driver the forms to say he isn't responsible."

They stepped out of the train. It was dark, and the air smelt of dynamite and burning and fresh dew. A bird twittered. Ahead of them the embankment had been churned up by the blast, and beside the engine the driver was being harangued by a large man, also in a padded jacket but without the ridiculous armband. The other partisans were smoking some way off, and the passengers were being told to walk down the tracks. "Off you go then!" ordered silly Kalanchev, pointing the way. "Cunt!" one of them spat.

* * *

The sparks of the campfire flew into the dark sky in fiery zigzags, and around it sat the members of the Revolutionary Alternative Fighting Organization. Voronov and Gromov had drunk two measures of rum with them as their honoured guests. It was three in the morning. A tall dark-haired Asiatic girl with long fingers strummed a battered guitar that had probably accompanied many bards on their travels.

"I recall the stuff you used to write, Gromov," said Commander Cherepanov, a bulky, big-nosed, intransigent man of about fifty, known as "Che". Gromov knew the type. He was probably one of those underground sectarians and gurus who infected children with their hatred of the adult world and led them off to the forests; things started in a theatre studio or shelter for stray animals, and invariably ended in abuse and mass suicide.

"Something about first love," he said. "'Tum-ti-tum, first love'. Very musical, but emotionally empty. I thought at the time the writer would soon give up. When did you stop?"

"I don't remember," Gromov said. "It was all stupid."

"Why stupid? We have our poets too. Come on Vanya, let's hear one of yours."

Partisan Vanya declaimed some angry verses about everything he was against, and there was something false about his anger, as if he were slashing a doll with a razor.

"What do you think?" the Commander asked Gromov proudly.

"I don't know," he said. "I'm out of touch with these things. I expect it's good."

Che looked disappointed, but Vanya winked at him.

"What I want to know is why you blow up trains," Gromov said. "If it was the top brass travelling in ours I'd have understood, but they were ordinary people. One was on her way back from a funeral, one was visiting his father—"

"But we blew up the track, not the train, don't you see the difference?"

"You've brainwashed them, Che, it's ridiculous what you're doing," Voronov put in.

"They've spoilt you in your army," the Commander said, frowning and turning back to Gromov. "I suppose you know the new Plan for the Railways?"

"No, where?"

"All over the place. I've made a special study of it, you see. Before this I was a railway engineer. I studied at the Moscow Institute of Transport Engineering. Do you know it?"

"I worked not far from there... before," Gromov nodded.

"They didn't tell us anything there of course. How the new branch of the Baikal-Amur Line in the Far East was built by slaves from the camps, or why they're working flat out now on the new branch to the Arctic. There are just the Chinese and a few of our administrators there, why don't they build a road instead for the oil?"

"Because the earth's frozen and it has to be sleepers and rails?" Voronov suggested tentatively.

"Yes? What about the crash on the China-Eastern Line?" Che said, with no apparent connection. "Why were so many trains derailed in the last war, and why did it happen in villages where there were no Germans? And why do you think so many peasants now are hiding in the forests?"

"To escape the army," Gromov explained.

"Have you seen what they're doing there though? I have, they're building more railways! It's virtually all they do! All our industry works for the railways. You should see how many railway engineers our Institute turns out. You don't need so many in one country!"

"So what's this new line for?" Gromov asked, humouring him.

"It's all part of the Circle," he explained in a stage whisper. "They want a circle of tracks around the country!"

The only sound was the crackle of the fire, and in the glow of the sparks the Asiatic girl laid down her guitar and listened.

"I don't understand," Gromov said.

"Of course not, you're not an engineer. The Plan goes back to our first railways during the reign of Nicholas the First. No other country has so many railways now, everywhere else people use cars. In Russia you only use the car to go fishing. Have you ever driven on the Moscow-Kazan Highway? It's a cart track! No, the railways are our destiny and we can't escape them, because they're made of iron!"

He paused to let this sink in.

"I'm sure you're aware that the Khazars call themselves the Iron Units," he added tersely. "As do the Federal SWAT Teams."

"Really?" Gromov said, suppressing a smile.

"You're clearly not from the Academy, all the top officers know this," Che said, as though disappointed in him.

"They must be very secret units if I haven't heard of them as an officer."

"Or you don't want to," he said equably. "It's a cat-and-mouse game, everyone knows."

"I see. And why are they both called Iron Units?"

"Because they're both part of the Plan!" he said in a ringing voice. "There's no difference between them! The Khazars and Russians are fighting for the same thing: the railways! They both need them so nothing will change under either of them, and the natives want them too, to cut us off from the rest of the world so nothing touches us and nothing will change. The world will perish but we'll survive – it's our Great Wall of China!"

"So the Plan is to build a circle around the country?" Gromov said, trying to get to grips with this lunacy.

"Exactly, it wasn't so hard, was it!" the Commander laughed, and the other partisans smiled good-humouredly. "Endless trains will run round without stopping, and they'll set off Maxwell's Currents in the towns along the lines. Do you know what Maxwell's Currents are? They fog up people's brains so anyone can do anything with them, and things continue in an endless circle. I haven't been in the Circle myself, but a friend in Moscow told me about it, a historian named Volokhov. He's a Major now in some secret flying detachment – have you met him?"

Gromov shook his head. "I've heard of him, but never met him. He was supposed to liaise with me near Degunino, but was nowhere to be found. It seems his detachment's so secret no one's ever met him, like your Iron Units."

"Sooner or later he'll join us," Che said. "He knows it's all a circle, he just doesn't know why. I do though. They want to throw an iron ring round Russia. Do you know why each town has its ring-road, and how much they spent on the Moscow Circular? And it wasn't because the Mayor stole the money or had to pay double for the trucks. Every village starts with a fence around the edge, and it's the same in the cities. And now people wander around in a daze of Maxwell Currents thinking they can protect themselves with a circle of trains. Everything's a circle in Russia, like our peasant circle dances! In Switzerland and Germany the boys run after the girls. Here it's 'Round and round the birch tree, choose who you want!' But how can you choose if everything's a circle and it's made of iron!"

Gromov had suspected some time ago that the partisans were insane; normal people didn't run around in orange armbands blowing up the tracks under the noses of the drivers. But it was only now he realized the full extent of Cherepanov's insanity, and it alarmed him.

"I'm sick of being trapped in an everlasting circle with no choice!" he went on. "I won't raise my sons to believe it's all destiny!" He pointed to two little boys of about eight and twelve, looking timidly at their guests with wide black eyes. "I don't care who wins in the end, it's a war to build more railways and enslave people who want to be enslaved – and they both think when they finish there'll be eternity! I don't want their eternity! We're blowing up the trains now, but it'll soon be the Moscow ring roads and we'll finish with this pagan circle for good! And you'll join us, it's inevitable, all intelligent people will join us, because it can't go on like this." He tossed his head in ecstasy. "It started with the Cherepanovs and it will end with us. We'll close the Circle and break it!"

"That's enough, Che," said Voronov. "You've told us all this before."

"Yes, and you wouldn't have joined the army if you'd listened to me, you nitwit."

"And I'd have lived with you in the forests instead?"

"Why not? It's a good life, people are free."

"Don't listen to him, Captain," Voronov said, as if Che was an old friend. "I like him a lot of course, I've been on journeys with him and he's taught me brilliant things, like how to make a campfire. Kalancha introduced me to him. Well, you know what it was like, everyone was asleep, nothing was happening, and he woke people up. Before I met him my brains were like porridge."

"They still are, chum!" Cherepanov spat in the fire.

"I thought all this about the railways was a sort of boys' adventure," Voronov went on. "That was how he described it, wasn't it, Che? We were just twelve. A branch of the line ran past our school, and he used to take us there and tell us it was part of a big ring that would keep us safe. He was like a normal teacher then, and later when some of us went off with him to the forests I would definitely have joined them, but I had bad knees."

"Weakling!" Cherepanov grinned, evidently unoffended that his ex-protegé had exposed him.

"He toughens you up," Voronov explained. "After you've blown up a train, you're not afraid of authority. The summer before the war we raided a munitions dump, so if the guns didn't kill anyone it was thanks to us. It was a good education."

"I'm sure it was," said Gromov.

"And what sort of education does your army give you?" Cherepanov turned on him. "You're just playing at soldiers! As far as I'm concerned, children should join the partisans in their thousands, not your damned army where they kick everything human out of you!"

"Maybe," said Gromov. "And will you still be in the forest in the winter?"

"Che will stay with his loyal cohorts, the rest will run home to keep warm," Voronov replied for him.

"That's the difference between us then: ours is fighting for real," Gromov said. "I was born in Russia and it's my duty to defend it. I joined up without looking back or asking why. The reason for the circle you hate is that everyone avoids their responsibilities and there's no sense of duty. I understand romantic gestures, but not blowing up trains. The tracks can be repaired, but it wastes people's time. It's not freedom, it's anarchy!"

"So freedom means fighting in your army?" smiled the Asiatic girl with the guitar.

"Freedom means despising death, because duty is more important than life or death. For you freedom means despising others and thinking you're better than they are. You have to grow up a bit to be better than others, and I don't doubt that you will."

"Listen to him," drawled Cherepanov. "Lies are truth, slavery is freedom. You'd be useful to any regime, think of Auschwitz—"

"People only talk of Auschwitz when they've nothing else to say," Gromov said wearily. "I know partisans and your 'I'm against everything'. Your self-importance is fine for teenagers, but adults are bored by it."

"You're not an adult, Gromov, you're a dead man," Cherepanov said loftily. "You mask your cowardice in duty. Your government doesn't give a damn about you."

"So fighting at the Front makes me a coward?"

"Fighting at the Front isn't bravery, killing people is cowardice. I refuse to fight on behalf of anyone."

"I see – make love, not war. Che Repanov in the Bolivian jungle near Blatsk, demanding the impossible. It's you who make this circle, blowing things up so that nothing's ever finished and there's no progress."

"We won't convince each other, it's best we don't argue," sighed Cherepanov, who had evidently had many such discussions.

"Why argue? You have your assignment, I have mine," Gromov agreed.

The night was dark before the dawn. The fire flickered, and the Asiatic girl strummed her guitar and sang in a low voice the old partisan song 'Bella Ciao'. It had been sung by Italian partisans in the last war, in conditions far more dramatic than these, yet it managed to encompass the damp forest and the collapsing country and the fake partisans, and make something heroic of them. Partisans were good, partisans everywhere always had the loveliest songs. What could the regular army sing about? At worst the Motherland, at best banging the girls in the next village. The regular army was dull, like everything else regular. Partisans offered the delight of the illicit and the forbidden. Their songs were about their tormented country they couldn't return to, and camps in the mountains, and hurried tearful partings under big stars, and love with dark desperate little partisan girls who hadn't long to live. None of them had long to live, which made their songs so proud and sorrowful, and so full of compassion.

And it would all end the minute their country was briefly returned to them, Gromov thought. The colonizers' palaces and tennis courts would fall into ruin, and nineteen-year-old generals would strut in and butcher the staff, and elderly writers who had been journalists would write short novels with long words. And as American helicopters bombed the surrounding areas, the survivors of the toppled regime would escape to the mountains, to become the next generation of partisans...

The Asiatic girl went on playing and the partisans stood up, stamping out the fire and singing:

"To arms my friend, our hour has come!
Miners, metallurgists, students, peasants!"

Then they all lined up in threes and marched off singing into the forest, leaving Gromov and the distractedly smiling Voronov alone together by the dying fire.

"So much for the partisans," Gromov said. "According to Cherepanov, Koposovo is ten kilometres east of here. Come on, Voronov, onwards and upwards."

246

Chapter Two
The Bath Hut

1

"How long will you string them along?" Zhenka said.

"Four years. Your Moshe strung them along for forty," Volokhov said carelessly.

They were lying on the bench in the village bath hut behind the allotments, where they had been meeting secretly for the past two months. The green light of a July night glimmered through the little window, and it smelt of birch twigs and damp. Soon it would be August – there would be showers of falling stars, and nature would burst into a final flourish before dying into autumn.

"I could stay here for ever," he said, "I read a Ray Bradbury story once about how we're all time-travellers. Time passes and we don't have to do anything, like travelling along a long country road. I haven't seen you for five years, and it's as if nothing's changed. Perhaps life just confirms things we know already, and we're sent here to solve five or six problems, and if we don't solve them we have to repeat a year, which is why history keeps repeating itself. But you and I solved everything the first time, which means we'll die soon."

"Not me, I'm not done with it yet."

"Nor me, but it's not us who'll decide."

"I'd love some tea," she said, rolling on her stomach. "But I can't call the orderly and I'm too lazy to get dressed, and they'd get a shock at HQ if they saw a Varangian put on the kettle."

"I'll bring one next time," he promised.

"When will that be?"

"Tomorrow, I hope."

"So you can come and go just like that, when you feel like it?"

"Pretty much, I'm the boss of my invisible diversionary detachment. The more invisible the better."

"So how long do you think our happiness will last?"

"I don't know, maybe for ever. Maybe nothing will change. We've fought all the way, and now almost nothing's happening. It's not war any more, both sides are knackered—"

"We're not!"

"You used to fight, but not any longer. It seems something terrible's happened, you're not even biting each other."

"And you still believe your insane fantasies about the native people?" she said, with a sudden flash of anger.

He could never get used to the way she would switch from tenderness to rage. She kept everything personal strictly separate from the Khazars' programme and beliefs, and any discussion of who the native people were was strictly forbidden. The land belonged to the Khazars, and they had come to reclaim it. The natives had ruined it with their laziness and bad farming – they had only themselves to blame for their hard lives. She refused to listen when he reminded her that the Khazars too had once had hard lives, and for the natives things had stayed exactly the same. But unlike Misha Everstein, now adviser to the Khazar Chief of Staff, who had accepted the situation long ago, she couldn't admit that after waiting a hundred years in the wilderness, and before that another hundred and several more, and after seizing so much territory and meeting almost no resistance, there was now nothing for them here. Power could never be an end in itself, and neither side had any idea what to do with it, but for her to admit this would be more suicidal than telling HQ she was sleeping with a native. The guard at the camp, a non-Khazar, the Shtabes-goy, was giving her suspicious looks as it was, although as Commissar she had the right to go wherever she liked.

"Yes," he said, "I not only believe in this insane fantasy, I actually am one of them, although there's absolutely no proof of it, of course. You can be one too, but I don't think you'd like it."

"No, darling, sorry, I wouldn't. I know who belongs here."

"Bless you, goldfish. Well, it's your problem now. Close the farms, open banks, install your market economy, destroy culture, preach your cabalism, but your wonderful ideology has to go underground to survive, and you'll gradually try to exterminate all others, but no one's allowed to say so. Sorry, but it was already obvious in the Kaganate."

"I tell you what's obvious, that we produce the best physicists and the best doctors!"

"Not in the Kaganate you didn't, all your best ones are abroad. At home you were floundering, everyone could see that. You're geniuses at surviving in the wilderness, and geniuses when your time comes and you can seize what's yours. But you're useless when it comes to telling people their new life programme. Only the Varangians are more useless than you, inventing plots and throwing people into the army. The natives only manage to live a little when by a miracle the two of you are fighting each other, otherwise we'd all be your victims. And it'll go on, and the Varangians will go on killing themselves—"

"And us? What have we done?"

"Absolutely nothing. Or rather you've done everything in your power to stop the Varangians, who cripple ninety-five per cent of the natives. But what have you achieved? Zero. You're wonderful at PR, and as middlemen and managers. You tame the natives and repackage them. You even translate our language into other languages with the help of some black magic. But there's nothing else for you here, forgive me a thousand times, my chosen one."

"You sound like Hitler! That's exactly how he spoke!"

"Not only Hitler but thousands of others, they just drew different conclusions. Hitler was a madman. Others didn't like you and said the same things, but they didn't want to exterminate you. The 'Protocols' were a forgery and written by fools, but if someone had written intelligently about your acquisitiveness and double standards, the way you divide the world into Yours and not Yours, your absolute solidarity, beyond all criteria—"

"I tell you what—" she howled.

"And if you say 'I tell you what' one more time... Sorry Zhen, but I'm taking a risk too coming here."

"No one forced you to."

"Maybe we can stop then, when we're together, and be neither of them but a third one, or a fifth or a tenth one, and stop arguing idiotically about which of us is the superior race."

"You want me to forget who I am, and it won't happen," she scowled.

"Not who you are!" he shouted in a whisper. "Forget the microchip, forget the great Mission, forget the Chosen people and everything else! When we're together you're mine and I'm yours, and nothing else matters!"

The bath hut was in a secluded spot behind the allotments, next to the burnt ruins of a house that had been shelled last year, but they still had to keep their voices down in case someone heard them, and found the Commissar's negligee on the floor, and the Commissar locked in battle with the commander of the Flying Guards.

"For you," she said. "Nothing else matters for you. You're called up and you join the army, you get your leave and go home, like a dog, to be honest. I'm not like that, I don't get leave, we couldn't survive without what you call this chip. We'd all scatter!"

"No, you wouldn't," he said, moving closer to her and caressing her, and she didn't push him away.

"It's terrible," she said helplessly. "I've two programmes in my head, one's us and the other's you, and they're both stronger than I am and I can't bring them together."

"We just need time. It's obvious, people will fight a bit longer and stop, and everything will go back to normal. You'll live here, in the Khazar territories, and I'll move somewhere close to the border—"

"And how does my being pregnant solve anything?" she said.

He clutched her, stunned for a long time.

"Forgive me, Zhen," he said at last.

"No, I want it. I've always wanted it."

"Not that, it's wonderful. Forgive me for lecturing you."

"You didn't too much," she said, and he heard the Khazar in her, her lightness and her lack of grudges, the easy way she changed tack, despite her intransigence. "We're bound together even more now, you'll feel everything I'm going through, and when I'm sick you'll be sick too, not just of your Varangian friends but of your natives who you believe in."

"Well I'm sick of them already, if it's any consolation, with their idiotic passivity. You can't believe a word they say, not because they lie, but because they don't understand themselves what they're saying. I hate them, if you want to know the truth, and I hate myself for being weak. I was overjoyed when I met one of them and he opened my eyes to them, I'd found a brother! But when I saw these brothers happily living in a cabal with you or anyone else so they needn't be responsible for anything... What sort of people's elite go round on the Circle Line? What are their achievements, apart from fairy stories and mad Futurist poets? And now apparently they're all being herded up and arrested."

"Yes, but what about this little half-breed of ours?" she patted her stomach.

"What do you want to do? Will you stay here?"

"I can't go back, almost all of us are here."

"And I suppose you thought your time had come and you could live here as citizens with full rights... Well there's my flat in Moscow, we could go there together."

"And what about your brilliant plan to lead your people through the forests for four years?"

"Well, I'd visit you... It's just an experiment really, to see if you can't shape them up so they can achieve something. After two years' travelling you can see the difference, there's the germ of responsibility there... I'll come back often to Moscow though, and perhaps I'll throw the whole thing up. Let it all start with us – you, me and him—"

"Or her."

"Whatever, I don't care."

"It means I'll have to desert, of course."

"What, doesn't your army give you leave when you're pregnant?"

"Not in wartime, it's considered desertion. And how would I explain going to Moscow? It would be seen as defecting to the enemy."

"I'll hide you and no one will find you. I'm one of the natives now, everything comes my way including success. We'll meet tomorrow and come up with something."

"I'll try to make it, but I don't need to come up with anything. We're here now and I'm staying."

"Don't get rid of it, will you?" he said in a barely audible whisper.

"I wouldn't think of it, it's not allowed with us. But don't imagine I want a quiet family life with you in Moscow. I'm a Yd and always will be."

"Fine, whatever you say."

He suddenly felt unbearably sorry for her. He knew what she was returning to: she was returning to the same hierarchy that knew no compassion, where the voice of the blood ruled, the same implanted chip. The Varangians had their criteria, and valued a bewitched iciness. For the Khazars the criteria were simply Ours or Not Ours.

"Won't you come with me Zhen? Please?"

"It would be better if you came with me. I'd take you to HQ and say, 'Here comrades, I caught the Commander of the Flying Guards stealing carrots in the allotments. Take a look at a live Varangian!'"

"I'm not one and you know it."

"It's just a cheap psychological trick, a way of dodging who you are so you're not the aggressor."

"I'm serious. No one will find you in Moscow."

"It's all right, I'll think of somewhere."

"Where, in Europe, like your colleagues?"

"No, I'm not leaving here. I'll wait till it's ours."

"I see. Wait for victory, then take me to your family as your prisoner or perhaps your butler."

She tried to box his ears, but he grabbed her hands.

"Don't fight me, it's only because I'm sad."

"If we win, and we will, I'll bring up the baby on my own of course," she said seriously. "I don't need you as a prisoner. You'll run around Russia with what's left of your Guards keeping out of the way, and sometimes you'll visit me and we'll meet up in bath huts. If it's a boy, I'll tell him you're on a dangerous mission. If it's a girl, I'll say you're a bastard and all men are bastards. You'll run with your gang for another two years and find out who you are, then you'll have to kill me. It's the only thing you can do. And you'll take the child to the forests and raise it as Tarzan or Tarzaness, the universal avenger—"

"I love you, Zhenka."

"And I love you too, Volodya." She rarely called him that, and he felt afraid for a moment, and remembered her saying goodbye to him at the airport all those years ago in the Kaganate.

"We have no one to ask, have we? No one to tell us how to live?" she said.

"Thousands of us have lived and survived."

"That was before. This war's different from the one with Germany. It was two Varangians then, just of different origins. But we're two completely different races and it's civil war, and the terrible thing is that you've got your programme too, you just don't know what it is. I know what mine is, but yours is probably something too terrible for you to face, even more terrible than what's happening with you and me."

"I don't have a programme," said Volokhov. "My programme is to be with you, that's all."

"No, that's not a programme. Fine, I must go."

"Don't go, it's not time yet."

"Yes it is. This is going to be huge, so get up."

"I'll leave first."

"No, you won't. What will our people think if they catch you and I'm here? Stay and I'll call you when it's safe."

"Zhenka!"

"Don't, Vol. Tomorrow, same time."

Grabbing her ugly map bag, she quickly hugged his head, winked and clicked her teeth at him and left, and he sat on the bench quietly hating himself. After ten minutes his phone rang.

"Yes?"

"It's all clear, you can come out. See you tomorrow."

"Zhenka!" he groaned, but she had hung up.

He left the bath hut and cut across the allotments to Degunino, a mile from Grachevo, where he had quartered his Flying Guards, the future bastion of his people's consciousness.

2

Yes, it would be August soon, Zhenka thought as she headed back, and she was afraid. She had arrived in a foreign country with its foreign smells, like a colonizer on an island full of scorpions and hostile natives. She remembered growing up in Russia as a child and thinking of Russia as her home, and this was why she had joined the army – her sacred belief that it was hers. Even in these last shudders of the Varangian empire she had still felt it to be hers. People had damaged it, but it was still dear to her with its birch trees, and as if to spite her, the ones here were all weeping birches, casting their sinister black shadows on all sides. She smelt the wet grass squelching under her feet, and everything was driving her away from this landscape she had loved as a child, with its secret joys and consolations.

It would be suicide to admit they had no right to be here, and it was time to call it a day. But it turned out that all the waiting and preparing had been for nothing, all the years spent studying local history, all the dreams of luxury buildings and kibbutz-style orange groves, the utopian projects to promote freedom and enlightenment. She had always argued with those in the Kaganate who said freedom and enlightenment were wasted on the Russians. She knew this was simply demagogy, and that it was easier to condemn the colonizers than spread civilization; the Khazars never planned to exterminate them, despite what their enemies claimed. The soldiers were another matter. But she couldn't imagine taking revenge on civilians, the soldiers' relatives, starving them and throwing them out of work and mocking their beliefs. And now it turned out the Khazars were behaving not as the true natives returning to their land, but as normal aggressors. Nothing wanted to grow here in the damp climate of Russia: even in the rich black earth around Degunino the crops had rotted in the rain and turned to mud. The soldiers' ammunition broke, the machine guns didn't work, and she herself was never sure – it was a source of shame to her as Commissar – which parts of the country belonged to them. It seemed Voronezh had been theirs, but now wasn't. There were optimistic communiqués from Vologda, then Vologda was abandoned, and there was no logic to any of it. Generally towns were left alone after battles, but now both sides replaced each other chaotically, and none of the commanders could say why this or that town was abandoned. They would enter villages that put up no resistance, and leave without meeting either the Federals or the partisans, like an impotent man creeping from a woman's bed. And so they marched on, trying to achieve something, unnecessary to everyone, enduring these crushing, totally peaceful defeats. She had imagined it would be a welcoming landscape, but it swallowed them up, alien and insatiable. Like itinerant actors they travelled to the depths of Russia, trotting out their tired clichés about free enterprise and a free press, closing unprofitable enterprises and opening new ones, and the peasants meekly did what they were told, and nothing worked. They listened and obeyed, like jelly taking the shape of the mould into which it was poured, and she no longer knew what she was meant to be doing here.

She stumbled on, frightened by the damp Russian night and the dark sky and the distant rumble of the rain, and imagined falling in the mud with no one to help her. Perhaps Vol was right, and the Khazars were good only at being against things, not at proposing anything new, and their values were just for the Chosen ones and didn't suit others.

The light was on at HQ, and the stove blazed with the cosy smell of birch smoke. She went in and sat down at the table, tormented by premonitions, and was greeted by the spectacled colonel sitting opposite. He was a former illegal who had helped prepare the invasion, and was known only by his underground name of Gurion. He was now something big in intelligence. He attended their meetings, providing valuable statistics about the neighbouring villages, and generally acting as if he ran things, rudely interrupting Everstein when he got carried away. She didn't know what his actual powers were, or who was behind him. Sometimes he seemed open and friendly, but more often he seemed crafty and treacherous. His little pale eyes behind his round spectacles looked at her without love, or even lust, and he evidently didn't take her seriously. She automatically checked the top button of her tunic; under his scrutiny she always felt obliged to smarten up, and she hated herself for it. Gurion wasn't one of them, she knew that, there was nothing Khazar about him, with his bald head and his pale face. He seemed made for underground illegal work, and she suspected him of being a Varangian spy. This was probably what real spies were like, alien to everyone including their own side.

"You've been out for a walk?" he asked her with a veiled malevolence.

"Yes, I couldn't sleep." There was none of the so-called military etiquette in the Khazar army, and a captain like her could address a colonel as an equal.

"Work, work. I couldn't sleep either, I've been reading." He pointed at a book of folk tales. "There's nothing more revealing than these native stories, I expect you read them as a child?"

"I read them, but I preferred Tolkien."

"A poisoned generation. I'd advise you as Commissar to acquaint yourself with them: they'll help you understand what we're dealing with. They're a wretched people, I'm afraid."

"It's their life that makes them wretched. The initiative's been crushed out of them, but we'll wake them up."

"Yes? You've woken a lot of them?"

"A few," she said drily. "They want to work, now they know the results of it won't be stolen from them. But you know better than I do that those stories in your book are fake."

"Really? How so?" He looked interested.

"They were authorized by the Tsar, weren't they? All our true Khazar folklore was banned. The main thing about the heroes in those genuine stories of ours, if you've read them, is their hatred of the oppressors, the priests and commanders—"

"Yes, yes, of course I've read them." Gurion took off his glasses and wiped them carefully, without looking at her. "Tell me, Zhenya, do you sincerely believe you and I are the true population of the country?"

"I've never doubted it, I was born here." She didn't know what he was getting at, and resorted to the usual stock phrases.

"Work, work," he repeated meaninglessly. "Don't think I'm testing you, there's simply this heresy going round that the Khazars are no better than the Varangians, and that there's a wonderful race of people who are oppressed by both of us. Have you heard this?"

"Yes, I have."

"From whom?" he said quickly.

"Well, these ideas aren't new. Plenty of people discussed them in the Kaganate."

"Yes, of course," he nodded. "I've been away for a while, but I still get their literature. There's far too much loose talk in the Kaganate nowadays, wouldn't you agree?"

"I think you suspect me of something, Colonel, and I'd rather you came out with it," she said, lighting a cigarette. "I feel I'm being interrogated about the Torah and my views on Christianity. If you've got something against me, let Intelligence question me properly instead of fumbling around."

"Lord, Zhenya, why would I fumble with you!" He giggled nastily, but she knew he was deadly serious, although what about she had no idea. "I must understand your worldview, you see, an exceptionally important assignment depends on it. Exceptionally important. I can't take any risks. I need to know clearly, for instance, how you regard the view that our Kaganate's being damaged by too much tolerance? Or that we ourselves don't always follow the principles we impose on others? We're often attacked for this, as you know."

"Yes, I do. Propagandists are always attacked for not practising what they preach."

"That's interesting. And don't you think it weakens our fighting spirit when people say the invasion of Russia was a mistake?"

"Talk never hurt anyone," she said. "In the Trojan War the Greeks won because they didn't forbid their soldiers to weep for their fallen comrades. The Trojans thought mourning them would weaken their fighting spirit and forbade it, and they lost. The forbidders do more harm to the fighting spirit than a thousand discussions. It's the ABC of democracy."

"Ah, I'm happy to hear that," Gurion nodded. "It seems to me, Zhenya, that you're the best commissar I've met since the invasion began. Or perhaps you prefer the word Mission?"

"Yes, I do," she replied uneasily.

"Waiting for the Mission, very lovely. Yes, Zhenya, I too prefer to put my cards on the table. Unfortunately what we're dealing with is treason."

She shivered.

"Don't worry, it's not about you," he shrugged. "Your case has nothing to do with treason."

"My case?"

"Let's be frank," he said. "If you love a man, that's your personal problem, and has no bearing on your military duties. We don't forbid soldiers to be people, as you yourself said. No, this is mutiny. Our reserve units in the village of Zhadrunovo are saying they're sick of the war and didn't sign up to be occupiers. I'm sure it's not the Varangians stirring them up – they're not that smart. It's our people,

Zhenya, our people, those scum who were capitulators even in the Kaganate. We've never had to deal with heresy before, or fight on two fronts, which is why we won't shoot the Zhadrunovo garrison, although we could. They just need someone to talk to them, and I think you're the right person for it. A woman is what's needed in this situation."

She was so shaken by what he had said about loving a man and her personal problems that she was only half-listening.

"Did you hear me, Zhenya?"

"Yes, Colonel, of course."

"You must go to Zhadrunovo immediately, or we'll lose our garrison. They can't be put down by force: you must go and explain things to them. No one but you can do it, Zhenya, I heard your speech the other day to the soldiers, it's just what's needed."

"Immediately?" she said.

"Yes, at once. It's only seven hundred kilometres away, I'll give you some men of course – sending a woman there unprotected would be suicide." He spoke quietly, but she could sense almost physically the force of his will, and she knew she had no escape. "It's not an order, it's a request. But as you know, a request from a colonel in Intelligence in our army is the same as an order."

"I understand, Colonel," she said.

"You mustn't tell Volokhov of your journey, this is a deadly serious mission, Zhenya.

She realized her last hope had collapsed, and he knew it was Vol, not Everstein or one of the others. He must have followed her, the bastard, and now the game was up. He was luring her away so he could wait for Vol to arrive like an idiot at the bath hut tomorrow, and he would take him alive. He couldn't kill him with her there, they still needed her for some reason, and now they had been caught, and it was all so stupid and it was all her fault.

"No one's planning to kill your Volokhov," Gurion said dismissively, reading her mind. "You think a detachment of forty armed Varangians could be quartered a mile away and I wouldn't notice? You think it doesn't suit us to have them there? You *shlub.*" He spoke the Khazar word with a slight accent.

"But why—"

"Because he's fallen under the influence of corrupt forces, the so-called pacifists who hate war. They tell the Varangians and the Khazars the aggressors deserve each other, and it's not us or the others who are the native people, but some third ones. I expect he's told you this twaddle?"

She nodded silently. It was pointless lying to him.

"I can't be sure he's not mixed up with the Zhadrunovo business and they're not all part of the same network. You see what this heresy has brought a normal officer to, dragging his men through the forests for two years instead of fighting us properly? And now the whole garrison is infected with it. Our garrison, Zhenya, our Khazar guards. Something must be done, I'm sure you agree."

"I agree," she whispered, with a dry mouth.

"You've half an hour to pack. My car will take you to the station. I'll send five men with you – I picked them myself, they're utterly reliable. I'm sure nothing will happen to you in Zhadrunovo, my man there keeps me informed. The village is near Kazan, have you heard of it?"

"I don't know, maybe I've heard the name."

"Well, never mind. It's just an ordinary village near the Volga, and the sooner you get there the better. I give my word as an officer that no one will know anything, and Volokhov won't suffer. In Intelligence we don't lie to our own side."

She knew something terrible was happening, and she was being sent off on some obviously impossible mission, possibly to her death, to get her away from Vol, whom she might never see again. And there was nothing she could do about it.

"I won't blackmail you by threatening him, but if anything happened to him – well, it wouldn't be difficult. He thinks the country's in chaos, but I assure you there are still people capable of wiping him out, and his detachment."

"And if I carry out your assignment and put down the rebellion?"

"In that case you'll be offered more comfortable accommodation than your bath hut when you return," he smirked. "You can meet him in Baskakovo. I gather he and Everstein have already met in the Kaganate, but I'll sort Everstein out."

"Can I write him a letter?"

"No."

"I'll be ready in half an hour then." She stood up and adjusted her tunic.

"Excellent. Hand over your mobile, please. Not to me, to the Shtabes-goy, I already have one!"

"Gurion," she said. "I know about subordination, but I swear on my life, and you know we consider false promises a sin, that if something happens to Volokhov while I'm away I'll bury you alive with my bare hands. Do you understand, Colonel?"

"You're wasting time," he said coldly. "The train for Zhadrunovo leaves at six-thirty, changing at Koposovo. About turn!"

3

That evening, while Volokhov was with Zhenka for the last time before another long parting, Misha Everstein was in his hut in Grachevo, putting the Khazars' policies into practice.

Everstein had no time for most of the naive youngsters he worked with, who were utterly incapable of running things. Serious, knowledgeable people were needed now, who had no illusions about their inherited right to the place. The right to it belonged to those who could manage it.

In the schools of every town and village they captured he would hang up a collection of photographs from the Kaganate, a comprehensive history of the Khazars' sufferings under the Varangians (and the natives too, who had never defended them), and in Grachevo he had opened a local cell of the Civic Society. This was a non-government educational organization established in the early days of the war to lay the groundwork for the Mission. There were cells everywhere, headed by reliable locals sympathetic to the Khazars, whose first task had been to encourage people not to send their sons into the Varangian army. This soon fostered a critical attitude to all orders from the criminal state, which used their taxes to pay the police to kill them, and local government to rob them. People realized that a government that hadn't the money to treat sick children had no right to hang out flags on holidays, and that every flag meant another ruined life, and although tearing them down didn't make money for the children, it made the point. The Civic Society had recently defended an arrested embezzler, who had donated large sums to hospitals, and they called the prosecutor a child-killer, and it must be said he looked like one. But the Civic Society had served its purpose now in the Khazar territories, and there was no further need for it.

Everstein's first visitor that evening was Vova Sirotin from the Society, a scruffy unshaven young man, who had been inspired by the Khazar way of thinking to join them.

"Thanks for all your good work, Vova," Everstein said in a ringing tone to his protégé, who was gazing respectfully at him. "I'm very satisfied with you, your mission is complete, you can do something else now. Perhaps farming to start with – find yourself a bit of land and cultivate it, I'll give you people to help you. Later, when we get to Moscow, a job as adviser will await you. Ideological work, or perhaps something else interests you. Historical research, car mechanics? Have you a car?"

"No, I haven't," replied Vova fervently.

"I'll give you one. Just work out how best you can realize yourself. We won't forget the Society, we'll definitely put up a plaque in Moscow to the memory of those who prepared and carried out…"

Lord, what an idiot the man was, nodding and smiling at him.

"Surely though there's still the need for some sort of social control, now that you're mobilizing people into the army?" Vova smiled, looking him in the eye.

"What are you saying, Vova?" Everstein sighed. "Don't you know our army? There's no bullying in our army, our officers aren't just interested in square-bashing, we're psychologists too, and poets…"

God, why was he so talkative these days, he thought. Vova was still gazing spaniel-like at him.

"Can I ask what's happening to our papers *Tocsin* and *Voice of the Society*?" he said, still smiling.

"You see, *Tocsin* was for the bad times," explained Everstein kindly. "In times of misfortune we ring the tocsin, don't we? But what misfortunes do we have now? We have decent political management, a proper government, not an occupiers' government. Why sound the alarm when we have people who know how to govern?"

"Well, you know, freedom of the press…"

"What press, Vova!" Everstein admonished him. "What was the circulation of your *Tocsin*?"

"Fifty!" Vova replied defiantly.

"Right, and you printed them on my printer."

"Remember Fuflygin!" Vova cried, raising a finger. He couldn't mention the name of Fuflygin without emotion. Fuflygin had for a while been the symbol of a free press in Russia.

"Vova!" Everstein couldn't restrain himself. "You know quite well Fuflygin was a hopeless alcoholic. Yes, we needed brave people to write about what they saw and expose it, but who did he expose? He wasn't even one of your correspondents! You wrote it all for him yourself and he just put his name to it!"

"But, but…" Vova stammered. "You mean the occupying power makes no mistakes the Society should expose?"

"I've told you not to call us the occupying power," Everstein said sharply. "Do you think you can teach the Khazars about human rights? It's absurd, my friend, it's arrogant, and frankly offensive. You have a free press, and that's that. There'll be a new organization tomorrow in the Society's office, do you understand? Now I've a mass of work to do."

"But what about human rights?" Vova said quietly.

"Human rights are our business!" Everstein raised his voice. "We guarantee human rights! What rights does someone like you have! Where would you be without the Kaganate? You'd be worse than Fuflygin! Three times I've seen you on CNN, jabbering and wringing your hands! Get out of here before I tell you your rights!"

"I was discussing an article I'm writing for a conference in the States…" he mumbled.

"Write it, Vova, write it, your conference awaits you, just don't bother me, I've a headache."

Vova flushed and muttered something and left.

His next appointment was with the village schoolmaster who taught all the classes himself, and had to be told tactfully that his school was no longer needed. An emaciated village intellectual came in, a Varangian reject and obvious failure. What could he possibly teach? He didn't trust the man.

"Good evening, Ivan Andreyevich," he said gently, standing up to greet him. "I want to thank you in the name of the army for your many years of excellent work in education."

The teacher's handshake was limp and consumptive. "I understand you're closing my school because there aren't enough children," he said. "But you know we have a very talented little boy called Andryusha Dyldin – his name may not be pretty, but he's an exceptionally gifted accordionist."

"That's marvellous," Everstein said. "It's nice when a boy plays the bagpipes too, we always respect that. Please sit down, Ivan Andreyevich, I need to talk to you."

Everstein enjoyed mimicking the manners of the Varangian intelligentsia – that deformed growth on the body of the brontosaurus, the walking wounded, good for nothing but penning their wordy columns. The Varangians called these hypochondriacal babblers intellectuals, and they were the weakest of the fighters, yet they still expected mercy. How unlike Khazar intellectuals, who were jovial and expansive and loved women!

"How can I help you?" Ivan Andreyevich said, cautiously sitting down.

"You've been teaching for thirty-two years, if I'm not mistaken, and spent most of your career under Varangian occupation?"

"I've worked under yours too, such as it is," he said distractedly.

"Very well, we'll call it that. But the old government, such as it was, imposed its ideology, did it not?"

"I taught children to read and write." He said it almost as a challenge, which amused Everstein from someone who looked as if a light breeze might blow him away.

"Ah yes, reading and writing," he said. "You teach them to write and they learn nothing. What about history? And the fundamentals of law? I suppose you brainwash your children to believe it's their country?"

"It's their country," the teacher echoed.

"You know quite well it's not," he said calmly. "We were persecuted and driven out, and the occupiers didn't have the basic skills to work the land. And now the persecuted and oppressed have returned and are in charge. That's it, that's our history, end of story."

"Then perhaps you could explain it to the children, if you don't mind?" the man said after a pause.

"I won't be explaining it to anyone, Ivan Andreyevich. As you yourself said, you haven't enough of them to keep your school open, and it's time to terminate your teaching career. Thirty-two years is long enough. You've taught them the Varangian version of history and about Prince Vladimir, the great grabber of lands, who drove us out. Thanks a lot, enjoy your pension. I hope you're not expecting much. Your Andryusha Dyldin means your reputation will speak for itself, won't it?"

"I expected as much," Ivan Andreyevich murmured.

"You're right, it's time for some sober self-assessment. Look at the photographs of atrocities on your way out and see what the occupiers did to us, whose politics you represent. The occupiers whose children you abused – yes, abused, I'm not afraid to say it!"

Everstein's voice had become shrill and plaintive. Children were the Khazars' trump card. It would be hard to find another race who loved them so much, and people were often alarmed by his shrieking. But the teacher wasn't alarmed, and sat on his flimsy chair staring at the corner.

"We obviously deserved it," he said quietly. "I just don't understand what you're doing. Do you really think you'll succeed and that this will last for ever?"

"We always succeed," Everstein said, changing to a brisk businesslike tone. "Why wouldn't we, it's our land. We didn't die in the camps to come here and worry about the rain."

"I don't mean the rain," he waved an arm. "I mean don't you know you'll never make any progress, with ours or with yours? How will it end? You'll close the school, what next?"

Everstein was in no mood for discussions about history and philosophy and the question "what next?"

"It will end with you going back right now to your cottage and staying there, you old fool, and thanking me for not kicking you like a dog," said Everstein, and the teacher scuttled from the room with his eyes down.

He smoked in silence for a while, trying to regain his composure. It was ridiculous that this puny representative of his race tried to give him advice. They thought the land would submit only to the boot and the fist, yet he was tolerated, he wasn't punched in the mouth or killed.

He put out his cigarette and smiled, adopting a more convivial manner for his regular chat with Pasha Zvonarev, the local hooligan.

"Greetings, Pasha!" he said as Pasha glided in, pausing to admire himself in the mirror. He was a true Varangian, with his classic blond good looks, and knew he had little to hope for from the Khazars.

"How's life treating you?" Pasha stretched out his palm to him like a plank, and Everstein was surprised by its hairy hardness. "How did you sleep?" he asked, in a pleasant deep voice. "I like a nice feather pillow myself, it's like your mother rocking you to sleep. Sweet dreams!"

"Mustn't grumble, mustn't grumble," Everstein replied, echoing his tone. "Any complaints about you from the police? They've not collared you again, have they?"

"Not at all, no complaints, they're very pleased with me!"

"Tell me, doesn't it bother you as a Russian to have all these Yds around? What if they wanted to buy you a drink?"

Pasha knew what he was getting at, and how as a Russian he could be used, but he pretended not to.

"Hell no!" he said, bowing and scraping his feet. "It's our joy to drink, we need it to piss!"

"Don't wriggle out of it!" Everstein said in a foolish sing-song voice. "Where would you drink in Russia now if it wasn't for our bars? And if your mates there said the main evil was the Yds, it would be music to your ears, wouldn't it?"

"Yes, but if we thrashed you, you'd smash us!" Pasha said thoughtfully.

"Not at all, we need you brave bandits to fool around and have fun!" said Everstein in the same silly sing-song voice. "You'll have to tone it down a bit, the ballroom days are over, just make a racket to keep us on our toes. As for me, I can offer you this." He handed him a soft leather purse containing some gold coins.

"So you won't blow my legs off?" Pasha said, ogling the money.

"No," Everstein shook his head. "Although we can, as you know."

"Right," the Varangian said, dropping his idiot talk. "Most civilians, as far as I can see, want nothing to do with you fine people, or us either, so if something accidentally happened to me I'd have no one to complain to. I'm a collaborator, I was born greedy, but if we Varangians can pinch a bit from you Khazars the war will suit us all fine, you get me?"

"And you really think everyone feels like this?" Everstein said, egging him on.

"Definitely. The country's gone to the dogs, we might as well become Muslims. The civilians are bored of you to be honest, and there's no Kaganate left now."

"That's right," Everstein agreed evenly. "Who needs it? This is our land. We're back where we belong!"

"We all know what's yours," Pasha said darkly. "Don't take too much or I'll kick your Khazar teeth down your throat."

"I understand," Everstein smiled sweetly, and handed him another purse.

4

"Are you there?" Volokhov whispered.

He had been calling Zhenka's mobile all day and couldn't reach her, but he had gone to the bath hut anyway. She would have switched it off if something had happened, but for hours he had got the engaged tone. He had to go.

"I'm here, darling! I'm all yours!" answered a high mocking tenor.

The voice was vaguely familiar. He switched on his torch – it was too late to worry about his safety now – and sitting on the bench grinning at him, his little glasses glinting, was Inspector Gurov.

"Where's Zhenya?" he squeaked. "His girlfriend's gone, he's got a boyfriend now! Kiss me, darling, make love not war!"

"What are you doing here?" Volokhov dropped his eyes, grimacing with horror.

"I was waiting for you, aren't you happy to see me?" Gurov gloated. "Wait for me, be patient and I'll be back! Wait until the Khazars lead you into the wilderness, isn't that their true manifesto?" he said in his normal voice. "Wait until the snow clears, wait until it's summer, wait until they're waiting for no one else. It's the same old Khazar tune in their ugly Khazar voices, their Old Testament 'Kill him!'. And you pop up all over the place, a Khazar with the Varangians and a Varangian with the Khazars, mixing Varangian ethics with the Khazar aesthetic. It's the first sign our two enemies really are as bad as each other!..."

"You love to scintillate, don't you Gurov?"

"What else is there to do, go through people's bags? Let the Varangians do that."

"Where is she?"

"She's rather a long way away." He lit a cigarette and puffed at it, smacking his lips. "And soon she'll be even further away – what a tragedy. I suspect you won't be seeing her soon, if ever. Put your hands down, I have a gun and I'll use it. And now the time has come to tell our boy something of his native mythology. You must know your land, as you Varangians say, which by the way is a gross distortion of our language. Land for us means border, frontier. Our word for it is 'cut', somewhere you cut across or cut into. You must know your cut."

Volokhov said nothing.

"In a nutshell, you're not my enemy, Volodya, you're my brother," he continued. "I'll never send you anywhere. But we natives shouldn't have affairs with Khazars. Something's about to happen. I don't know what will start it, but Vasily Ivanovich went off without telling me—"

"Who's Vasily Ivanovich?"

"Never mind, dear friend. We've already discussed how we go in a circle, and whatever the others do to us the circle always goes on. But there's an old curse against us if we marry them, because their child might be the beginning of something. Must I tell you what the beginning means?"

"Where is she?"

"She's alive, don't worry. The beginning, dear friend, means the end. If a man from our noble race loves a Khazar woman, or one of our girls loves a Varangian, or the worst happens and both these things happen at the same time, as I fear has happened now, it means the end of our history as we know it. Curtains. It happened in the past, but we always managed to stop it. The last Tsar Nicholas loved one of our native girls who gave birth to Crown Prince Alexei, and he'd have usurped his father if we hadn't stopped him. History's a cruel business – either plot against the Prince or send our country to hell. Well, we've survived, we're still here, although the signs are…"

He put his cigarette out and sighed. "Think of the great civilizations. Rome's kaput, Byzantium's kaput, and soon it'll be America. Europe's already kaput, in my opinion. But here we all live happily together, and our deaths from the tyrants are no more than you'd expect from drink and old age. I'll go into more detail later. Any questions, Major Volokhov?"

"You mean that because of some hideous superstition I can't see her again?" he asked dully.

"It's up to you, you can see her if you like."

"Where is she?!" he asked a third time, banging his fist on the bench.

"She's on her way to one of our villages, I don't remember its name," Gurov said. "We have two main villages. In Degunino there's everything, and in the other one there's nothing, but we don't know its name because no one ever comes back from it. It's a fascinating place, anyone who goes there disappears for good. Perhaps it's so wonderful they don't want to leave. Your Zhenka's on her way there now, so I'm sure she'll find out. It's possible she'll send you a signal since she's so fond of you. It's been known to happen."

Volokhov was silent.

"I'd have told you before, Volodya, but I didn't want to burden you," he said. "You're not one of our simple people, you're one of our Wolves and diviners and the best sort of foresters. You think a forester is just a sort of tree specialist? Nonsense, that's another distortion of our language, it's someone who can lead their men through the forests and fool two armies for two years! Some might wonder why you weren't caught – not everyone could pull it off. But you can't just fall in love with anyone, we can find someone better for you."

"You know what the village is called," Volokhov said.

"Sorry, friend, I don't."

"Well I do, Petya, it's called Zhadrunovo. Do you want to go to Zhadrunovo, Petya?"

Gurov was silent in the darkness. Volokhov switched on his torch again, and instead of fear he saw a look of irritation on his face, as if he was chewing a bitter pill.

"How did you know? Who sent you there?" he asked at last.

"Someone called Misha Everstein, I met him in the Kaganate. Strangely enough he's quartered not far from here."

"I'll kill the bastard," Gurov said angrily. "Does he think he can curse a Seventh-generation Wolf? Never mind, maybe you and I will go there together one day, I'd quite like to see it."

"Wouldn't there be rather a lot of us?" Volokhov smirked.

"There's plenty of room, it's a big place. But not everyone can send me there, you know, I'm not an ordinary man, as I'm sure you're aware."

"Yes, I am," he nodded.

"Well perhaps it won't work on you either. Everstein's clever and he's read a lot, but their cabal hasn't much power over us. You're a fairly important Wolf, I don't expect you'll go to Zhadrunovo."

"Nonsense," Volokhov said firmly. "Their cabal can do what they like, I'm going there, and not because of some idiotic curse. You think as an Alternative I'd believe this nonsense? May God punish you for sending her there – and I'm supposed to believe you'll save the world—"

"Not the world, to hell with the world, I'm saving my people. Don't believe me if you don't want to, it's up to you."

"And how will you save them?" he said, sitting opposite him on the other bench. "Who are you saving? Your natives who can do nothing but go round in a circle? Thanks a lot, I don't need your immortality! No, Gurov, Zhenka and I will build a new world in Zhadrunovo. We'll have the baby there and your circles will be smashed to pieces and leave only the stench!"

"She's pregnant already?" Gurov said with interest.

"As if you don't know. You won't catch her though, you're not man enough to go there."

"Possibly," Gurov agreed. "But why should I? I've things to do here."

"You mean keeping both sides at each other's throats? It's a hard job you have. I can explain your mythology to you in five seconds. You can divide any society in the world into the Varangians and Khazars. You see it all over the place – the Kaganate in Gaza, the States under Bush, the French in Algeria. But people always find something bigger than their differences. It's the same with men and women, so that the human race will survive. Everywhere else in the world people find something more important than what divides them, it's only we who don't, because we're not a proper nation, thanks to Guards like you who want us to have no history! Why do we put up with it? We've made ourselves like this!"

"Like what?" Gurov said in a steady voice.

"We're victims. First it's one lot, then the others, so we might as well lie down and die!"

"I see, blame the victim. See what your Varangian army has done to you," Gurov sneered. "Perhaps you just need the Khazars for some balance. I'm with them now and I assure you there's nothing I can't get away with!"

"It's quite an art, you're obviously a genius. In our village everything's already balanced. Ninety-five per cent of them can't or won't work, and the five per cent who can are us, the elite. I see why you like this life, a Seventh-Level Inspector lording it over the dregs and the Joes. And now history's about to start and you'll be finished!"

"You may be a Wolf, Volodya, but there's still a lot you don't know about the natives," Gurov said levelly. "We're a special race, prehistoric in the true sense, because we don't need history, we understand each other without it. We didn't choose our fate, it's anthropology. All our major singers and diviners and foresters lived a long time ago, and there aren't many of us left, but we've survived, unlike the Mayans and gypsies and the people from Atlantis. And you know why? Because we're lucky, we've had these two fighting each other!"

Volokhov sat on the bench where Zhenka had lain only yesterday, guilty of nothing, and dangled his hands helplessly over his knees, feeling as if his skeleton had been removed.

"I'm going to see her anyway," he said.

"Go on then, you think I'd forbid you?"

"But why her?" he blurted out. "What has she done to you? Do you follow all the Khazar women around so they won't sleep with us and the natives so they won't sleep with a Varangian?"

"Sometimes, if we have to," he shrugged. "It's worked so far, we won't fail."

"But surely it's not possible to go in an everlasting circle. The trains will overload, the wheels will fall off..."

"But they'll take longer to fall off!" he said, enunciating clearly as if explaining it to a child. "Let them live as they like, and let us live the life we love outside history." He stretched like a cat as he spoke, and seemed to purr.

"Live like this, you mean?" Volokhov threw his arms out at the damp walls of the hut, and a frightened woodlouse scuttled out.

"Why not? It's not a bad hut, I've seen worse." He lit another cigarette, and in the glow of his lighter Volokhov saw him smile affectionately at him. "Have you ever been in Latin America, Major? It had a splendid civilization once, like ours, and what's happened to the natives? They've ten occupiers in succession and don't know what's happening from one day to the next. We have just two and it suits us, we're used to it. I won't let this perpetual motion be broken for some redhead – do you hear me, Major?"

"I understand. Nothing must change, the baby likes the womb and doesn't want to come out."

"Why should it? The other two will finally die out and we'll do great things – travel, write poems in our native language, sing songs, preserve our folklore. Our girls are remarkable, our priests are clever, our farmers are like farmers nowhere else. The crops will grow all by themselves, the apple trees will bear fruit, the stove will bake pies. I say, 'Heat, bath hut!' and it heats up. Go on, you say it, you're a native, it'll understand you!"

"Fall down, bath hut," he said.

"You fool," Gurov smiled. "Those are Varangian words, it doesn't understand them. It understands heat though."

A damp heat rose slowly around them. "We're steaming, Major!" he cackled. "A bath's for having a nice steam, not sleeping with the enemy. What shall we put on the coals? Eucalyptus, birch?"

It had become unbearably hot, and Volokhov's head was spinning. "Sulphur," he said, running out from the enveloping clouds of white steam, from which he could hear Gurov laughing.

He raced back to his men as if the Devil was chasing him, and woke them at six.

"We're leaving. You've ten minutes to get ready. Five for a smoke, then we're off," he said.

The damp grey dawn countryside stretched before him, and a thin rain dripped onto the grey roofs and grey fences. The birds seemed to want to live for ever and stared contemptuously at him, and the thought of living the rest of his life without Zhenka – how long had they left? – filled him with such a hopeless sadness that he wanted it all to end. A good woman had honoured this dying landscape with her presence and it had devoured her.

"Where are we going, Commander?" said nurse Anyuta, who was allowed as a woman to question him directly like this.

"To a village called Zhadrunovo," he told her.

Chapter Three
The Town of Blatsk

1

"Blat" is criminal underworld slang for the network of bribes and unofficial contacts in Russia that keep the system going. The word is also suggestive of mud. So it was appropriate that the town of Blatsk, in the muddy northern part of the Central Russian plane, had become the nerve centre of the country's con artists, career criminals and crooks.

It is striking how in societies in decline people tend to cluster together according to age, lifestyle and profession, and in the third year of the war, the pensioners had all settled in the quiet sleepy areas, the beautiful women and redheads and cyclists in the hot spots, and the crooks had all ended up in Blatsk.

In the old days it had been an important Varangian staging post to the Greeks, but after conquering Russia the Varangians had no need of the Greeks and their trade route turned to mud. Before the war it had been a normal provincial town, with a fourth-rate theatre troupe and a museum of local handicrafts. (The locals turned out a rough woollen creature with arms and legs and, by special request, an enormous prick, which was the source of numerous legends: there used to be a secret master craftsman who made them, before turning to drink and becoming moody and unpredictable.) And now the place had filled with mysterious hoards of guests – first the Varangians, then the Khazars, both calling themselves masters of the country. Their success must have been due partly to Blatsk's remoteness and inaccessibility. Although they lived there legally, and even appeared on television saying there was honour only in their society and the others were crooks, they had clearly picked somewhere as far as possible from the busy highways where they could get on with their business, and to this day only the most determined traveller would find it.

Those living in towns near the main roads are energized by passing travellers, and some even dream of travelling themselves; stories are told of happy townspeople who leave for a while, returning with their wings broken, but knowing at least that there was a road beyond the town.

But in other places loose women roam the streets, the houses aren't repaired and the wells dry up, and no one dreams of leaving because there's nowhere to go. Soviet power meant a brief frenzy of tidying up. A few churches were knocked down for form's sake, and bookshops opened selling cut-price gramophone records, which are still sold to this day. But soon everything collapsed into mud and dust again, as if none of it had happened. People didn't care what others thought of them in these places, and they were their own masters there.

They lived like this in Blatsk, and crooks were drawn to it because no one thought of looking for them there. The locals treated all their new guests as brothers, Blatsk-style, with the indifference of the all-engulfing mud, and until recently some of them had worked. Everyone knew that work was no longer profitable, and only Blatsk could survive as a criminals' Mecca, but the locals liked working and inactivity killed them. They needed it not to forget themselves, as some claimed, but as they needed to breathe, as their normal state of being. And now ever since the Khazars arrived there had been no work. The cement works and the shoe factory were closed, and the choir at the Palace of Culture was wound up, and soon there was just one farmer left who virtually supported the whole town. His name was Ivan Zavarzin. Realizing there would soon be no work, Zavarzin expanded his meagre plot of collective land and bought cows and goats and sold milk and pickles, roping in his whole family to help. And since as a native he knew how to talk to the land, he had three harvests a year and his farm flourished, just as the cement works had once flourished. Zavarzin fed the town with his potatoes and apples, and his creamy goats' milk and the tender meat from his cows, and at first he prospered under the new government. But it wasn't long before he fell victim to the racket.

The Khazars at first behaved in Blatsk as guests, but as time went on they became the masters, raking up anyone who got above themselves. Not that they brought nothing but ruin. The number of orphans and widows increased, since the crooks needed somewhere to live and many people resisted handing over their flats. But thanks to their passionate love of widows and orphans they built a children's home with a sauna attached, where they could visit the children and fondle them. The older ones they weren't interested in, but the young ones were sent to the orphanage with the sauna to be fondled.

Eventually the crooks reached Zavarzin, who had lost track of who the bosses were. At first they demanded a comparatively small tax from him, and he didn't complain and his farm flourished. And even when the tax was quadrupled, he paid up, not understanding that the Racket's purpose wasn't to steal cash: cash could be stolen from safes and from people on the street, and from the government, in a thousand subtle ways. The Racket's purpose was to replace happiness with humiliation, and show the toiler who was who; to show him there was no honour in working for pleasure, only in feeding the racketeers. The Racket's purpose was to teach the worker that life wasn't about shovelling dung, it was about partying at the Golden Soch restaurant, with huge feasts that ended in gunshots and magnificent funerals and armed champagne salutes, and the masters would belch and check out the children, the younger the better.

But despite being burdened with ever heavier taxes, Zavarzin still enjoyed working and wasn't about to throw it in. It was only when they finally robbed him of all he owned and burnt his barn down that he hanged himself in the shed. His wife left town to protect his daughters, and at first the crooks rejoiced. Then on the third day there was nothing to eat. They raided the shops, leaving nothing but government soap, and searched everywhere for Zavarzin's grain stores. But it was as if he had taken everything with him, and high in the sky floated a cloud that looked like a cow, and another that looked like Zavarzin, gently milking it. Hallucinating with hunger, one of the crooks tried to dig the earth with Zavarzin's shovel, then gave up, since things would take too long to grow. Some left town, but the masters couldn't leave their residence, and somehow it all worked out, and life became even better. A concrete air strip was built outside town, so that proper imported foodstuffs could be flown in. These didn't reach the shops and went straight to the restaurants, of which there were already almost as many in Blatsk as houses – the Khazars' "Little Odessa", "New Jerusalem" and "Brighton Beach", the Varangians' "Hunting Lodge" and "Fireside", with violins and psalteries and underground strip shows and blowjobs. The leftovers from their feasts were thrown to the town's residents, and the orphans would be woken early to lick the plates, and the crooks boasted that they were providing work, although the citizens didn't see it as proper work at all, merely as consumer services, which under the Khazars had replaced industry; according to the new Khazar doctrine, industry was secondary to consumption, and the consumer was king.

Gradually the crooks settled in, accumulating property and building large houses in the suburbs (they called it "investing in the local economy"), and the town prospered at an unheard-of rate. Occasionally people from Moscow would come to work there as consultants and officials, and try to muscle in and get tip-offs, but they were soon exposed, for Blatsk had its own database with the names of everyone who had made a packet and done time, and they would cut down anyone who tried to outsmart them.

* * *

Gromov and Voronov had arrived in the town on the local bus, which ran just once a week and was now the only public transport left. The locals had gone over to cars long ago, as they had in the States, and even the taxi drivers had vanished, since only drunks needed taxis, and for some time drunks had been boldly taking the wheel, including the police.

They were greeted by a cacophony of music from the stalls lining the bus station. The rock groups Convoy and Shmar vied with the Whores, and a poster for the Whores' next show was displayed outside the Central Casino, so named for its central location. In the middle of the little square sat a row of seven card-sharps, who with no schmucks to swindle were trying to swindle each other. Three pickpockets worked the other side of the square, and another happy trio approached Voronov and Gromov and tried to sell them tickets for a fail-safe lottery run by television's Channel Five. For a thousand roubles the lucky visitors could win a Chinese meat-mincer, some Chinese toothpicks or a Chinese-made Mandavoshka motor car, and by paying another thousand roubles the winner would be eligible for more prizes. Gromov restrained himself from punching them in the face, and instead asked them politely when the next bus to Koposovo was.

"Hey, why Koposovo?" asked a dark-haired one with an earring, and the other two sniggered. "It's sweet here, man, stay here!"

"Because I'm going there," Gromov said.

"Why?" asked a gypsy fellow. New visitors were a rarity in Blatsk, and they couldn't let them go without having some fun with them. "You're pissing with me, brother, are you the law? You're not my brother if you're the law."

Gromov had a gun, but it was two against three, and the card-sharps were gathering round and the pickpockets were watching with interest. And at that moment Voronov surprised him again. "We need to see Ruslan, mate," he said. "We've got a red salmon for him."

"Shit, man, why didn't you say!" said the gypsy fellow. "Why go to Koposovo when you can see Ruslan?"

"We'll see him first, then leave for Koposovo," Voronov said.

"There've been no buses to Koposovo for a long time," the gypsy said. "You need to go back to Konoshi and catch one from there. It leaves at four."

"So tell me where Ruslan is?" Voronov wheedled.

"He's in the sauna," the man said respectfully, and Gromov was relieved to see the card-sharps return to their posts and the pickpockets to their pickpocketing. "Gosha Gomelsky's having a party tonight at the Ostap restaurant and he'll be there. What sort of salmon?"

"It's a whopper," Voronov said solemnly. "It was caught specially for him. Thanks, mate."

He dragged Gromov off from the square.

"Who's Ruslan?" Gromov asked quietly when they were at a safe distance.

"Haven't you heard of Ruslan Blatsky, comrade Captain?" he asked. "Priest-Captain Ploskorylov's always talking about him."

"I don't listen to Ploskorylov," Gromov said, trying to control his irritation. The idea of this fat eunuch who had never been in the trenches lecturing him, a fighting officer, was more than he could bear.

"But all the officers in Baskakovo—"

"They're not officers, they just work for HQ."

"Yes, I know," Voronov said hurriedly. "Anyway, they told the men about this Ruslan Blatsky, who sponsors Orthodox Varangian fighters. Not that there are many in Blatsk, but he's tremendously religious, so he's financing them. Nodary Batumsky doesn't believe in God and sponsors the Khazars, and it's this game they play, like the lottery. I used to hear about them at home. But Ruslan's very respected. He gets his Orthodox fighters foreign jam and biscuits and all sorts of treats."

"I should have listened to what Ploskorylov said. He has interesting backers," Gromov said.

"What's the difference?" Voronov asked naively. "You're doing your duty, what does it matter where the money comes from?"

Gromov was about to tell him to mind his own business, but remembered he had twice saved him. He was embarrassed too: it was his fault they had ended up in Blatsk. To hell with these endless names and buses, they would never reach Koposovo by midnight as Gurov had ordered. It wasn't entirely his fault, though. There was nothing wrong with his map-reading, but all the old maps were wrong and new ones hadn't been printed; some villages had vanished even before the war, some had fallen during the first battles, others had been renamed by the occupiers. Even as they left the forest they had veered too far west – perhaps Cherepanov deliberately misdirected them – and had arrived in a little village called Chumichkino, where they found just one old woman who had lived there for a hundred years in a grey cottage full of greasy rags, who told them to go to the concrete bus stop and catch the bus to Blatsk. And by a miracle it had arrived.

"So what are we doing with Ruslan?"

"Nothing, I've no salmon for him."

"You don't say. You're a clever boy, Voronov, you've good reflexes. Couldn't you have thought of some way to wriggle out of it when you were being questioned?"

"They almost shot me!" Voronov said. "They were going to shoot me for nothing! I can't understand it, comrade Captain. When Major Evdomikov was shouting at me I kept thinking of things to say, but I couldn't get them out. We're different people, you see, Evdokimov and me. Like Private Pakharev who was guarding me, he's completely different too—"

"No, they don't like clever recruits," Gromov said. "Smersh is always suspicious of a soldier who thinks." He knew he shouldn't criticize an officer to a private, and it was a breach of army ethics, but he realized Voronov wasn't an ordinary private, and that Gurov hadn't simply handed him over to him to escort to Moscow. He wasn't a talisman exactly, but he would undoubtedly have been lost without him.

"I'm not clever though," Voronov frowned. "I know some things. I was at university studying Zoology when I was called up, in my second year—"

"Yes, well, we won't be discussing zoology with these people," Gromov said. "Come on, let's get out of here."

"The bus isn't for a while. Shall we look for somewhere to eat, comrade Captain?" Voronov said.

2

Cecile's wasn't far from the bus station. Gromov was appalled by Blatsk prices, but they had to do something with themselves before four, and he wasn't keen on hanging around town.

At Cecile's they unexpectedly found themselves guests at a party being thrown by Marik Kharkovsky, a major sponsor of the Khazar Mission.

In Blatsk practically everyone backed one side or the other, and Marik found it more fun to back the war than some damn charity or the Joes' fights at the circuses. Now though, with the war grinding to a halt, the lottery had again become Blatsk's main entertainment, and the party was to celebrate the fortieth anniversary of his first successes. He and his friends had set up a stall selling tickets, and he had done the dirty on them and repeated the trick three more times, and he was soon able to give up his stalls and move into the property business.

The party was already in full swing when Gromov and Voronov arrived, and they were welcomed by a red-faced Marik. "Soldiers!" he shouted. "Come and join us, boys! Where are you serving, brothers?"

"The 125th Artillery Brigade," Voronov replied. Gromov said nothing and let the Private do the talking; it was he who had wanted to come here after all.

"I respect you!" Marik beamed. "Come and eat! I've nothing against you little Federals! I'm an old Khazar myself, but we're all the same in Blatsk, we've none of that here!" He flapped his little arms in the air, depicting the war. "The businessman and the soldier are brothers! We both risk our lives and we both love women! Klavonka darling, look after our soldiers. What's Ruslan feeding you, barley? I told him, Ruslik you must feed your soldiers, a hungry army can't fight! Old Yd Marik knows that, because we Yds have something to eat! Give them vodka! Let's have music!"

On the stage the balladeer Glum crooned 'A Bouquet of Lilacs'. He had a broken nose which gave an unspeakable vileness to his song, about a young but hardened criminal who steals a bunch of lilacs from a cemetery to give to his sweetheart, but the slut has just given herself to his neighbour, so he kills them both and his first bouquet to her is his last, and the flowers are laid on their dead bodies. Glum wept convincingly and called the sweetheart "little girl", and a corps de ballet of girls in ostrich feathers whirled about behind him.

"Sha, hush! I'm singing for Marik!" Glum cried to the audience as he finished. "I love to sing for you, Marik, you're a man of your word. None of these people here," he swept an arm round his corps de ballet, "will say you're not fair. And now I want to sing about the person who every man needs to come into this dirty world. I want to sing about my mum, Marik, my mum!"

The chandeliers dimmed and the restaurant was flooded with a pale-blue light, and his mother was carried up to the stage in a chair. Every restaurant had its old woman: they were picked from Blatsk's old people's home and they were happy for the work, and were much in demand; there was at least one banquet a day now, often two, and afterwards the mothers would be fed in the kitchen on the scraps. Unfortunately fathers weren't needed, but they somehow managed to smuggle food out for them, even though they were searched afterwards.

The cult of the mother was all part of the crooks' image as honourable heroes who refused to kill, even though everyone knew they had strangled their mothers at birth. They were marked for life by this trauma and considered themselves orphans, hiding their secret and singing about their mothers who would wait for them and forgive all their sins.

The mother's chair was moved to the centre of the stage, and Glum came up behind her, moaning, "Sorry Mum, forgive me, I've been bad!" The song described how even when he was in nappies Glum had hated injustice and she had defended him, but now the cops had separated them, and he was sitting in a camp in Siberia surrounded by cruel guards, gazing at the sunset and thinking of her. Marik was overcome with emotion and beat his head with his fists, and Glum's voice filled with tears. "You cry-y at ni-ight whenever I wri-ite!" he wailed.

The old woman sat in a pose of stone immobility, representing a mother's unwavering trust, as he sang how he would never nark on his mum. An exhausted tear trickled down her cheek, and Marik sobbed.

"And I miss your wrinkled old fa-ace!" Glum finished, smothering her in a long kiss. There was something almost sensual about it, she was organic matter after all, and edible. She widened her eyes and backed away from him in her chair, and he finally tore himself off her and bowed to the audience. They roared their approval and the chandeliers came on, then the waiters carried in Cecile's speciality, "Feathered Miracle", a masterpiece of Varangian cuisine: an elk stuffed with a pig stuffed with a goose stuffed with a carp, which was stuffed with coins, with each cut wrapped in a sausage.

"Enough with the tears, let's drink to our soldiers!" cried Marik.

"Don't stand up," Gromov ordered Voronov through clenched teeth, and he obeyed.

"Each of us, we should thank God, has a mother," Marik said. "But as well as this mother, we have another, the same mother for all of us, and she's our Motherland, and our little soldiers here serve her."

There was suddenly something of the local government official about him; the successful crook clearly needed a boundless capacity to reinvent himself.

"We each of us have our interests," he went on. "I have mine, Glum has his. Ruslik has big ones, and needs something big to satisfy them with!" The hall laughed cautiously. "But we all have a common interest in our Motherland. I propose a toast to her, long may she live, and to the soldiers who serve her and make sure we've got something to eat, God give us health!"

The guests rose from their seats and clinked glasses, and loud-speakers blared out a patriotic medley by a popular Blatsk bard who was singing at another party and couldn't be present. There followed a series of messages for Marik. An official from the Blatsk mayor's office, spherical from his daily gorging, sent greetings from the Mayor. In fact there had been no mayor in Blatsk for a long time, although many still believed in him as they believed in Santa Claus, and even hung portraits of him in their offices. Each was different, since no one could agree on a single image of him, but in all of them he was expensively dressed, in a smart tie with a diamond tiepin, and they all resembled different film actors – stern shaven-headed Vitorgan with his wolf's eyes, Dzhigarkhanyan with his wolf's smile, neurotic Smoktunovsky with his weak mouth and wolf's ears – and everyone agreed on one thing: that the Mayor of Blatsk was the biggest criminal of all and the king of kings of the criminal world, who had passed through all the prisons of both hemispheres.

After more toasting and schmoozing, messages were read out from the boys in Moscow in senior positions, and special greetings from the Birch Tree folk-dance troupe; Marik loved its girl dancers, and one had been sent to him as a present with the message.

Gromov had eaten almost nothing but he had drunk a little, and his head was pounding. Meanwhile the high point of every Blatsk gathering approached, the reason he and Voronov had been invited to the table – the ritual game of hunt-the-schmucks. If they hadn't been there, Marik would have sent for some orphans, but the soldiers were more entertaining. Gromov realized what was happening the instant before Marik pulled a gun on him. As a front-line officer he was in his element. Pushing Voronov under the table with his left hand (remembering he was answerable to Gurov for his life), he whipped out his revolver with his right hand and aimed it at Marik, hoping he wouldn't have to use it. He clearly wouldn't have stood a chance with him.

"Son of a bitch!" Marik howled, lunging from his chair, and his bodyguards on either side of him leapt up and aimed their guns at each other and froze.

"Sorry, we're just off!" Voronov said, poking his head from the table, assuming as usual that he must have offended someone and it was all his fault.

"We're off, are we, boy?" Marik guffawed. "Stand up, Federal dreck, I'll send you off!"

"Stay where you are," Gromov ordered Voronov, who put his head down and lay flat under the table. "You'd shoot Federal soldiers, would you, Marik? That would be bad. Put your gun down."

Marik could have shot Gromov there and then, but he wanted more fun with him first. He took aim, and the bullet whistled past his right ear, but Gromov didn't like games and fired back and didn't miss. Marik crashed to the floor, and his bodyguards instantly started firing at each other, and there was a pandemonium of gunshots. Voronov crawled out from the table with his head down, and the Blatsk police rushed in, with their long experience of catching visiting schmucks; they didn't bother with the residents. The shoot-out continued and Gromov was fired at from all sides, but he was well trained in the tactics of escape, and luckily the others all seemed to have a grudge against each other. Out of the corner of his eye he could see the old woman gesticulating at him from the stage, nodding at the door to the kitchen.

"Keep down, Voronov, follow me!" he shouted, still firing.

One of Marik's surviving bodyguards shot at him, but the bullet merely grazed his hand. Voronov ran after him, crouching and clutching his stomach, and they hurled themselves into the kitchen. The cook looked at them with childish joy, pointing to a door that led to an inner courtyard, but Gromov knew he was a Blatsk cook and couldn't be trusted. "Where's the exit, jerk?" he said, putting his gun to his ear.

"There!" The cook pointed again to the courtyard.

"Bastard!" Gromov spluttered, realizing it was a dead end, where the surviving guests would surround the three of them and slaughter them.

For the brave soldier a sort of third eye opens at such moments, while for the cowardly both remain firmly closed. Gromov fired past the cook's head, and at that moment the mother ran into the kitchen. "Over there! Over there!" she shouted, pointing to another little door at the end of the corridor. He had an urge to blow the cook's brains out, but restrained himself and threw him aside like an old sack; everyone in Blatsk carried weapons, but fortunately the cooks at Cecile's had theirs removed as a courtesy to the customers.

The little door led to another narrow corridor, at the end of which was another door. Voronov followed panting, and Gromov heard the roar of the chase behind them. The door swung open to a steep staircase, and they ran down to a pitch-black cellar smelling of mould. "They went that way!" he heard the frightened cook howl. He flicked on his cigarette lighter and saw ahead of them a low narrow tunnel – like the tunnel to the underworld, he caught himself thinking. But there wasn't even a glimmer of light from that other world, just an eerie sense of something ending, as if his soul was leaving his body.

"Follow me!" he whispered to Voronov, and threw himself into the tunnel. He bent double, stumbling and running deeper and deeper into the blackness, and heard Voronov gasping behind him; the boy was hopeless at running, he couldn't think why the army needed him. They reached a sharp bend, and he lit his lighter again and saw an old brick arch covered in moss. Water dripped from the ceiling and cold wafted from the walls, then a smell of river dampness cut through the smell of mould and he saw a little light in the darkness. His lungs were bursting, and Voronov was barely alive.

"It's all right, Voronov, it can't be worse than dying," he told him.

He was no longer sure he was alive himself, in fact, however much he pinched himself. It was as if his soul had kept a phantom connection with his body, and just imagined it still had arms and legs. Ahead of them appeared a staircase with jagged brick steps, and a weak light streamed from somewhere high above them. He checked his watch: four o'clock. The bus from Konoshi had left, but it hardly mattered now.

"Shall we go up?" Voronov gasped.

"We've nowhere else to go. I'll lead the way," Gromov said.

* * *

They stood on a wide green slope that dropped down to a slow-moving grey river, yellow at the shores. He looked around. Above them were the ruins of Blatsk's medieval kremlin, which had survived three sieges in the wars with the Poles. It was a classic Varangian fort: the natives never built them – all ancient towns had been fortified by these Varangian or Khazar structures, which were practically indistinguishable. The narrow embrasures of a half-destroyed wall gazed down at the water, splashing against the shore, and between a rotting planked footway a flat-bottomed boat dipped and rose in the waves.

"Do I see people?" called up the surprised peasant at the oars. He had a grey beard and was dressed all in black, like a monk, with a little skullcap on his head.

"Will you take us?" Gromov panted.

"Of course I will, that's why I'm here!" he said happily. "Father Nikolai said people had come out of the tunnel, and I said how could people rise up from the earth? No one's come up for a hundred years!"

He quickly rowed to the shore, and Voronov jumped in. Gromov landed heavily and some water slopped over, but the boat quickly righted itself.

"Let's go, good people."

"Where to?" asked Voronov, suddenly afraid they were being taken somewhere no less terrible.

"Over there." The peasant pointed to a distant island in the middle of the river. "Danilovsky Monastery. Have you heard of it?"

"No, I haven't," Gromov said.

"Let's go," he repeated, leaning on his oars.

Chapter Four
White Power

The Governor had been cut off from his funds. He wasn't down to his last rouble yet, but he was running low, and it was no comfort when Asha told him her people would look after them and that the Wolves wouldn't abandon them. There was nothing he wanted less than to take money from a Wolf, as if living off the natives wasn't bad enough; he couldn't have imagined it in his worst nightmares. And he was worse than a native, because they were guilty of nothing and weren't bringing about the end of the world.

Their escape had cost much more than he expected. Food was the least of their expenses. Asha ate almost nothing, and in all the turmoil he had lost his appetite. But there was a toll to be paid in every town, and their bed and board in the villages where there were no Wolves, and money for taxis, because there was virtually no public transport. Clothes were another problem. They had left with only what they had on, and although Asha impressed him with her resilience, she kept shivering, and needed warm things. In short, he was getting through his money at an alarming rate and had no chance to sort things out, travelling all the time. They had already covered over half the distance to the mysterious Degunino, where everything would be decided. For Asha at least: he knew in his heart that his own fate didn't depend on whether the Wolves let the baby live or not. He knew too that no one could influence the Wolves, even a whole choir singing "Not alone in the field, little road".

It had shocked him on this journey to discover how little he knew, and how little skill was required to govern Russia. But it was unlikely he would ever work again. Despite the prevailing chaos, he was being hunted seriously now, with road blocks up and identikits of him in all the towns, and a press campaign accusing him of fraud and debauchery, which would make him a laughing stock with any of the natives who could read. No, getting his job back now was out of the question. He had committed the worst sin – he had broken the unspoken agreement with his caste, the government class that was so hard to enter and no one wanted to leave. It was just as he feared. Someone who entered the state system had no way back from it, like a dying man, and must never speak of it. The Governor was dangerous, and he knew it. He had seen the system from the inside and had stepped outside it, and discovered that the chest he had been guarding was empty, a total Torricellian vacuum. While he was part of its inner circle it had seemed to him a model of intelligence, and of higher, more unselfish thoughts. But now all these official abstractions seemed sterile and vanishingly remote, and he knew he had no hope of being rehabilitated. Mixed up in the same pot with the common people, he had submitted to their laws, and had come to value simple things, and the basic animal need for food and shelter. Asha, against all his expectations, remained calm and didn't cry or complain, her whole being focused on the task ahead.

* * *

He wandered around the market checking the stalls, listening to the natives' complaints about people swindling them. He had seen the same dirty clamorous natives in the Asian republics he had visited during his probation period as Governor, with the same selection of dirty goods, the same well-rehearsed complaints, the same speculation, which they saw as normal, since they knew no better. In Asia too he had seen the way they would instantly forget a customer, after haggling and begging and cursing him; the customer would leave, and the record simply stopped. A little yellow threadbare man at the market had jabbered and beseeched him to buy his sour, unripe apples, then stared impassively into the distance the moment he left. The government was right when it said these people would never learn anything. It was pointless trying to educate or even heal them, since wood healed itself, and at best you could give them work, and at worst charity.

In the ancient wooden cottage where he and Asha were staying with some distant relatives of hers, primeval chaos reigned, and was strictly maintained. The dishes were never washed, the room they occupied had greasy net curtains and a loudly ticking clock, and the hostess hadn't even changed the sheets. Shameful to say, as someone who had once held power over the natives, the Governor had never set foot in one of their cottages before. Why was there that gap running along the wall above the skirting board? Why did an enamel jug of water always stand in the corner of the room? Was it for house spirits? Why did they scatter a handful of buckwheat on the table every night, always in the same messily shaped mound, then sweep it carelessly on the floor in the morning and scatter it again at night? The house was full of invisible beings to whom they seemed to make elaborate sacrifices, and it made the place filthy and there was no rhyme or reason to it; perhaps they imagined it would stop their decrepit hovel falling down.

He bought only pickled vegetables at the market; there was nothing else to buy. The natives ate nothing but seeds, seeds, seeds, noisily cracking the husks with their teeth and smacking their lips, but he found them bitter and unpleasant.

Asha was out when he returned, and for the first time he felt guilty that everyone was working while he was loafing, a government official cast into the abyss of everyday life. But the guilt quickly passed, since they weren't doing anything either, or if they were, it was invisible. His elderly hostess sat motionless at the table, perhaps having a silent conversation with the crops, while her husband was crushing things under his shoes, apparently "chopping fritters", although to the Governor they looked like cigarette butts. Even the boy chasing the hens round the yard wasn't guarding them, but "sweeping" them – whatever that meant. Despairing of the natives' laziness, he went to the bedroom and switched on the TV.

White Power was on, a political education programme presented by a man called Toptukhin from the Russian Party, designed to further the government's national objectives. The Governor saw the need for such programmes, but Toptukhin's world was full of Russophobes who wanted the end of Russia, and he was always looking for ways to whip up people's patriotism. The Governor himself had belonged to the Russian Party all his life, but to its more Western wing, and he had no time for extremists like Toptukhin, who saw insults everywhere to Russia and the Russian spirit.

The subject of his programme today was the struggle of the Russian nation against the Khazar invasion, a sort of holy war that would end only when the last enemy was defeated and the truth could finally shine through. Khazardom was probably older than Varangianism, and there was something almost Khazar about Toptukhin's ontological hatred of them, although if anyone told him this he would have died of a heart attack. And the more he raved, the more the Governor realized that this naked nationalism was now official ideology.

Toptukhin was fat and bearded, like all true Varangians, and spoke in a deep gravelly voice, gasping and pounding his fists on the table.

There was something menacing about his breathlessness. Look what the enemy has done to a good man, he seemed to be saying, it's hard to speak, yet speak I must, and afterwards he would be given valerian drops and cups of tea. All the studio hated him: he was terribly sweaty. "A regular spiritual bashing!" Archpriest Posysai, one of his regular speakers, would say admiringly of his shows. Children were made to watch him at school and they hated him.

The Khazars weren't like the Varangians. None of them, apart from a few fanatics, now believed the country to be theirs. Russia was alien to them, even though they gave it a good name whenever they ran it, and promoted art, science and trade. But it was as though they were too good at it and had to be thrown out, with the silent connivance of the natives. And according to Toptukhin they didn't need "their" land anyway, since they believed the whole world was theirs, and would never be satisfied with just a small part of it.

Loud music played, and grey flames flickered across the screen (the television was black and white, and buzzed when the titles came on), and a Jew writhed in the blaze. The Jew was depicted in the manner of an old peasant painting, and for some reason was carrying a Shield of David: they were probably made to hold them as they were hurled into the fire.

Toptukhin dealt at length with the Khazar heretics and their sorcery, which they called praying, and eagerly enumerated their various groups and gatherings. "Men of the North, brothers!" he trumpeted. "Today, as Russia wages its final battle against Khazardom, the greatest battle in our history, all compromise is weakness. The power of the North, the White Power, must finish once and for all with the cosmopolitans and bloodsuckers who want to destroy our White God!"

Borozdin switched off and lay on the bed smoking, trying to gather his thoughts. There was nothing Toptukhin said that he hadn't heard before, but not as official doctrine. This was why they were hounding him. He had been cut off from the capital in Siberia, and it was clear to him that the "patriot animals", as he called these aggressive, stupid, endlessly offended people, were running Russia now and were responsible for his downfall. They hadn't gone for him because of Asha: it had nothing to do with her. The state, rushing headlong into a military regime, had to destroy everyone who didn't suit the needs of the moment: in other words anyone who could think.

What had Russia come to, he thought, lighting another cigarette, even though Asha had forbidden him to smoke indoors. Of course, he was their target, not her, and if he hadn't loved her they would have found some excuse to get rid of him. The reason he hadn't been arrested in Moscow was that they were checking to see if he passed the test for this new mobilized state, by renouncing the only woman he had ever loved. But he hadn't, and he no longer suited the needs of this state. He had imagined getting his job back, by hook or by crook, but he already knew this was impossible. (At that moment his hostess was busy washing sheets in the yard, not in water but on the dry earth, pounding them with a sort of hooked wooden crook: a native custom apparently, which Russians knew nothing about.) But what appalled him most wasn't the state's cruelty, it was its stupidity. It was only now he saw this, and it hurt him deeply. He had been a part of it for so long, and he couldn't reconcile himself to its sudden leap into lunacy.

He threw his cigarette through the window and switched on the television again to see if Toptukhin had finished. He hadn't, and was just winding up.

"It helps us little that we are brave and righteous," he concluded in a breaking voice. "The Russian people have no recourse against injustice and sorcery, and our enemies are busy infiltrating the state. Yes, there are those in government who instead of toiling for the glory of Russia have been driven by their insatiable greed to join the Khazars. I must tell you with unutterable sadness that in our upper ranks we have vile traitors. You will now see one of these traitors, brothers."

In the half-second before he saw his own face on the screen – the official portrait from his credentials – the Governor already knew he was an enemy of the state, slandered by this stupid nonentity as having joined the Khazars. How hard he had worked, virtually on his own, to give his government lustre and authority and a human face!

"Let anyone who sees this turncoat remember his mother's heart and his father's pride!" Toptukhin thundered. "Neither he nor his mistress" – Asha's face flashed on the screen – "must walk unpunished on our Russian earth, or drink Russian water, or breathe the air of our Fatherland, or tramp the sweet fields and the dusty roads! This traitor is worse than the Khazars! Do not let the traitor through!"

The Governor made his decision in an instant; in extreme situations he always thought quickly.

"I'll join them. I'll be a Khazar!" he said out loud. "That'll give the bastards something to think about!"

Chapter Five
The Pentameron

Vasily Ivanovich and Anka had been travelling for a month now, and in that time she had learnt a lot about his people. There were many different native tribes, he told her, although in reality there was only one, since they didn't recognize boundaries between them. The differences between those who lived in the steppes and deserts and on the coasts were merely geographical, and they looked different so people could tell them apart, but there was no distinction between them, and they had all lived together peacefully in the era before history, harvesting the fields and the seas, and no one fought for the right to be called leader. They were born farmers, Wolves or leaders, and didn't aspire to be different.

This pre-history era had lasted a long time, and they didn't need history, because they had always lived this way and the purpose of history was to divide people. But then things changed. Perhaps it was some genetic mutation, or the result of the Great Freeze, but other races came to the natives' lands. They might have been there all along and lived separately, or maybe they were a new branch of evolution, but one way or other the pre-history era ended and the era of the Occupiers began.

Some occupied with violence, some with cunning. Some cut the natives down to the last man, some enslaved them, others drove them out, and many tribes were exterminated. There were those who escaped to live underground or under the water, like the Picts and the Atlanteans, hence the legends about underground people and drowned races, but Vasily Ivanovich didn't know if people had actually lived under the water, just that no one from Atlantis had survived.

Anka asked him about Kitezh, the Russian Atlantis, whose sacred lake was said to be a symbol of redemption.

"I've never been there," he said tentatively. "It's not all our land. Maybe they were another tribe and it's just a lake."

She found it hard to believe that the true natives were the Joes. She could have understood if they were the Gastarbeiters, who flooded the country before the war, but the Joes? Why had they let themselves get into this state? Was it possible these helpless tramps were the only ones left? And if not, where were the others?

"Yes, there are a lot of us," he said. "Wolves and Joes, and we used to have fighters, but they were all killed. Fighters aren't born to us often now, because our people respect honour, and the others fight without honour and have no rules..."

"So why did you never stand up to them, Vasily Ivanovich?"

"We prefer to keep out of their way. They grabbed our land, but there were so many of us, and they came and went and didn't stay. It's better when these two are fighting each other, it gives us a rest."

"But what if they both joined together against you?"

"It'll never happen, Anka," he said simply. "They're the same in every way, but they never come together. It's their fate."

"And why can you never go straight ahead, Vasily Ivanovich? I see your people in Moscow all the time going round on the Circle Line, but why?"

The fact was that although she was now one of them herself, going round Russia in circles with him, she still didn't understand the circles.

"We like it, Anka, we think better that way. It's like our ring dances. We always dance in a circle, it's the others who brought in these new ones." Vasily Ivanovich disapproved of the waltz, the foxtrot and the gavotte, and considered them indecent.

In the time she had been travelling with him, Anka had learnt what cold and hunger were, and to see the world through the eyes of an abandoned child. But she had always had these feelings, and they didn't surprise her. Everyone carries in their soul the child lost in the city, because no one feels at home in the city, and it was easier for her now that she could finally acknowledge this.

She missed her parents and cried for them every night, and she phoned them the day after they left. But she had no money for the call and had to hang up; they barely survived on what good people gave them. There turned out to be a surprising number of these good people. They found them in most of the towns they passed through and they helped them, but there wasn't much they could do for them, and they were constantly on the run from the police. The Joes were being rounded up in earnest now. It was all part of the government's drive for "efficiency", and the Joes were "inefficient", and there was to be no more charity for them.

They travelled mainly at night, hiding by day in attics and doorways, and sometimes with good people. When their hosts left for work Vasily Ivanovich would sleep quietly, with his mouth hanging pathetically open, and she would watch television. There was never anything interesting on, and the Joes weren't mentioned directly, but it was clear to her what was happening; fugitives have a special ear for such things.

She phoned her parents two or three times a week now. Her mother sobbed and pleaded with her to come home, and her father shouted that the police were looking for her. But there'd been three teenage runaways of her age on the news, and she realized the police would rather catch Joes, who looked unmistakably like Joes and never got away.

She promised to return home after delivering Vasily Ivanovich to safety, and by now she was exhausted from looking after him and was desperate to leave. He had let himself go as soon as they left, and stopped washing and changing his clothes, and said a pilgrim had no need to wash. At first she found him revolting and was embarrassed to be seen with him. And his comrades, whom they met in the towns and in the unlikeliest places, were even dirtier and smellier than he was, with yellow faces caked in wounds. But you couldn't change them; they were the guardians of knowledge, and it came at a price. And she soon stopped being revolted by them and was sorry for them and bandaged them up, and her hated first-aid classes at school finally came in useful.

By now she was fifteen and was too old for his fairy stories, and he would tell her about the natives' history, which she hadn't learnt at school or from television. They had carried their secrets with them under the water and the earth, and by a miracle some had survived who still knew them, living in the peaceful valley between the river Volga and the Don. They submitted to the Varangians and Khazars there and watched them destroy each other, and despite suffering at the hands of both of them, they managed to keep alive the fabulous legacy of their golden age before history.

"It all worked out for us," he would say. "Yes, it all worked out!"

He told her Socrates too had suffered from being a native, one of the quiet Hellenic people colonized by the Greeks, who had also colonized the peace-loving Trojans. The story of Helen was just another of their lies, he said: how could there have been a war over a woman for ten years? She never existed, there was nothing about her in Homer, and why wouldn't Homer have mentioned a beautiful woman?

"So why do you think the colonizers don't like you, Vasily Ivanovich?" she asked him once.

"Who's to say?" he sighed. "They probably liked us to begin with, then saw there was nothing to be done with us and hated us – the Northerners because we wanted to live, the Southerners because we worked our way, not theirs, and they don't like people who can work."

He told her about Degunino and its endlessly fruitful earth and its magic stove and apple tree, a little way off from the village in the forest. "Degunino will sort things out, you'll see," he would say, and although he couldn't be more specific he seemed to know everything would be settled there.

He had enough stories to last the whole of their long journey, all the Joes told them. At first she didn't believe him when he told her the country was ruled by two aggressors, but as the weeks passed she realized she had known it all along. Perhaps it was some birth trauma that made people want to split in two, and now this final split meant bloodshed. Before the war everyone had been friends and had drunk tea together, but now that both of them were setting up their governments she realized his stories were true, even if the Joes had just made them up to justify their lives. The newspapers of course told nothing but lies about them. It wasn't true that they were all thieves and ex-prisoners, and almost none of them were drunks. Alcohol was bad for the Khazars and Varangians and made them violent, but it induced a gentle dreamy state in the Joes, and made them see wonderful things. They drank heavily, but it did them no harm. What harmed them was their dangerous life and being attacked by the police, and as for the rest, they could have gone round in circles for ever.

Many of them were in fact going nowhere, hoping to sit things out in the forests or the outskirts of the towns. Vasily Ivanovich was highly regarded by these Joes. They would listen respectfully to him and ask his advice, and they respected her for being with him. He could even make a few decisions, unlike the Joe Kolya, for instance, whom they were thrown together with one night in an abandoned dacha, who dithered for hours the next morning at the crossroads between two highways, unable to decide which way to go. He took a few steps along one and turned back, then tried the other and returned, and finally gave up and stayed where he was.

By now Anka knew that Vasily Ivanovich would never have reached the town of Alabino without her. He frequently tried to return from the one they had just left and go round in a circle, and when she asked him why, he replied guiltily, "It's not easy for us, you see, Anechka, all at once—"

"What do you mean, all at once? We're going in circles as it is," she said wearily.

"I know, I know," he mumbled. "We're circle people, Anka, we don't go straight ahead…"

Because of his age and frailty he had been sent to the shelter, but before that he had spent twenty years cutting circles around Moscow and the Moscow region. Apparently he had decided to become a Joe one day when he left work and suddenly knew he couldn't go home, and he promised to tell her what happened as soon as he could remember.

Another thing she learnt was that the mobs of homeless children on the streets of the towns generally weren't child Joes, but the children of the new arrivals, who were so sick of everything in this alien land that they saw even their own children as a burden. The child Joes were the ones they had expelled from their gangs, and these gangs were the Joes' main enemies and would attack them at night. The Joes had no one to defend them, and Anka was terrified of these street children; the adults still had a few vestiges of conscience left, but they had none.

"What about me – am I a native?" she asked him once.

"I don't know, Anechka," he said shyly. "Would you like to be?"

"I'm not sure," she said. She didn't much like this life, travelling on local trains with him through holiday villages and abandoned settlements to the mysterious Alabino, and there was often nowhere to wash and she caught colds. There was nothing good about being a native like Kolya, standing for hours at the crossroads scratching his head. But there was some power in Vasily Ivanovich that made the journey bearable for the delicate Anka, and there was a magic in his stories that made her feel very close to him, closer than she felt to her parents, and she still pitied and wept for him.

One night they made a fire beside a rubbish dump outside Tambov, where there were no good people, and three Joes and a Mashka joined them and each told their story, and each was different. The fire blazed, and a cosy dacha smell drowned out the smell of the dump and wrapped it in warmth, casting fantastic patterns on their faces, so their scabs and wounds could have been mistaken for shadows.

The first to tell his story was Mikhail Egorovich.

* * *

Mikhail Egorovich had lived quietly for twenty-seven years, until early one morning in June he received a phone call summoning him to the organization people feared more than any other. The organization was run by the governments of the Varangians and Khazars in turn, who were equally ruthless with their enemies, and despite the new freedoms since the collapse of the Union, the call promised nothing good. But there was still a lot Mikhail Egorovich didn't know; he wasn't a Joe yet, and thought things would work out.

He was told to go to an anonymous five-storey building with no sign outside. He had passed it a hundred times on his way to work, and thought it might be a government clinic. But it was the headquarters of the previous district administration which was now being wound up.

When he arrived at Room 402 as instructed, someone was already in there before him. He waited in the corridor, and after a while a bearded man came out with a battered file clutched to his chest. Throwing Mikhail Egorovich a brief terrified look, he rushed to the exit, and Mikhail Egorovich entered apprehensively, where a nondescript man with colourless eyes handed him a file. The master of Room 402 was smartly dressed and exquisitely polite, like all ill-educated people whose job is to take stock of others' faults; well-educated people speak simply, and have no need to hide their feelings. He explained to Mikhail Egorovich that the organization they had both worked for was being restructured in line with current changes, and that their project had been terminated. He was completely free now, and on the orders of the new democratic government he was being given his personal file to do with as he wished.

"But what are your complaints against me?" he asked distractedly.

"Complaints?" the man shrugged. "The reorganization, you see, the new programme—"

"May I ask what programme?"

"You'll find all you need in your notes," he said, giving him to understand the interview was over.

He rushed out like the bearded man, clutching his file to his chest, and read it on the trolleybus home. There was an unsmiling official-looking photograph of him, but he couldn't remember it being taken; he must have been caught with a hidden camera. There was a long form too, filled out in his name but in someone else's hand, and as he read the rest of his documents it became clear that the entire story of his life and every happy and unhappy event in it had been directed by some alien will, for some obscure malevolent purpose. They described his nursery school and his school, and a little girl he had been friends with there (although in fact she hadn't gone to this school; he had known her at nursery school and they had quarrelled and hadn't seen each other since). It was an elite English-language school, and his work was excellent, but thanks to a phone call from the organization he hadn't got a place at university to study Maths and had studied at the Institute instead. Even his wife had been specially chosen for him, although she didn't know this of course; they had simply pushed an invitation to the party where they met under her door at work.

There was much more of it, and for a long time he didn't know what to do with this life that had been constructed for him, and he had no one to discuss it with. The mighty structure he had worked for, with its incomprehensible aims and outcomes, had melted away, and when in a torment of doubts he revisited the white building that looked like a clinic, he found it being redecorated and no one there. He wondered for a long time whether to tell his wife about the file, and finally burned it on a bonfire at the dacha. But he was increasingly haunted by the idea that the whole of his life up to then was a script written by others, and he had been given it as part of some secret plan. He began to imagine things – passers-by gave him odd looks, a letter accidentally falling in a drawer contained a secret message, the entire purpose of the war was to drive him out of the country to stay with his Ukrainian uncle on his mother's side. And so on.

He was sick of living someone else's life, he wanted to live his own, but to do so he had to break with his old one. He left his wife and child and moved in first with a friend, then his mother. But with her too the plan did its work; according to his notes she had wanted an abortion on medical grounds when pregnant with him, but the doctor refused to perform it, and so Mikhail Egorovich was born. He left his mother's, and after losing his job he couldn't rent a flat. It hadn't been his work anyway, and he no longer knew who he was and what was the spider's web of someone else's imagination. Anka could relate to this, since she didn't know these things either, and his story had its own logic; it would be easy for someone who didn't know what they were living for or who they were to think everything was a conspiracy.

He went through a series of jobs, but wasn't himself in any of them, and he soon realized even his country wasn't his. And the worst of it was that he could never complete anything, as if everything he did had its own predestined outcome and was part of the plan. He spent more and more time trying to break the plan. His secret overseers would wait for him to turn left, and he would suddenly turn right. Anka understood this too; she had read about a prisoner in a concentration camp where once a week one in four of them would be shot. They didn't shoot him, and he survived, but he lost his mind when he got out, and believed the whole world was a plot against him, but that he could break it. For instance, all citizens of the Soviet Union had to leave their slippers at night with the toes facing away from the bed, so he would leave his with the toes facing inwards, imagining that this tiny gesture could break the whole structure. Convinced that all his actions were predetermined, Mikhail Egorovich could always switch on his free will just in time. Once he invited a woman he liked back to his room, but at the last minute he put the light on and said he had to work. She left baffled and angry, but he was happy, and it only occurred to him later when he was alone that this change of plan must be part of the plan. This was why they had given him his file, so he would never carry anything through to the end.

Finally one night he went to the bus station and boarded the first bus that came along, deciding to leave town and go wherever the headlights shone. Realizing that going to the terminus might be part of the plan, he got out at a stop in the middle of a field where there had once been a village. He stood in the black desolate emptiness and imagined living here to the end of his days, the landscape of his freedom, but he had to find somewhere to sleep. Two lights flickered in the distance, and he took the path to the right, then turned back and went left, and knocked on the door of a grey cottage at the edge of the abandoned village. An old woman let him in without saying a word, then went back to spinning an endless skein of yarn and singing an endless song in a language he didn't know. Or rather the words were familiar, but they were put together differently, and he understood only the line "Not alone in the field, little road".

As the song went on, more and more epithets were piled on the road, and it soothed him, and he knew that no one here could hurt him. Something bothered him though, a sense that someone was looking at him, although the old woman had turned away from him and was busy spinning. His eye was drawn to the corner of the room, and he saw a gloomy bearded man sitting on the bed, very thin and dirty, and he recognized him as the man who had rushed out of Room 402 before him clutching his file.

Mikhail Egorovich met his eye and nodded. He too had come here where he needed to be, and from that day on they had both wandered the empty landscape, seeking some higher plan than that of the all-powerful organization.

* * *

The next to tell his story was a shy Joe of about thirty-five called Sasha.

Sasha's problems began when he started to be replaced. Perhaps he wasn't being replaced, and it was the first signs of Vasilenko Syndrome, as the Joes' gift was called in medical circles. But whether or not he was being replaced, he could no longer get on with people.

First the girl he was in love with and planned to marry asked to meet him one day in Moscow, and told him out of the blue and for no reason that she was leaving him. He lost all dignity and wept and howled and pleaded with her, but it was no use, and at first he explained the changes around him in terms of his suffering; he imagined people were looking at him with contempt, as if only the love of his fiancée had made him acceptable in the eyes of the world, enveloping him in a cloud of happiness. But he couldn't explain losing his job as a result of losing her, and perhaps the chain of replacements started then. The boss simply called him in a week later, just as he was beginning to pick up the pieces, and told him his services were no longer required.

He analysed opinion polls for elections, a solid career with good prospects, although deep down he knew anyone could replace him at any moment. His work involved standardizing the results and adjusting them slightly, but at the time the end had seemed to justify the means, and he would discuss the results of his polls on television, with little political commentaries about human rights and personal freedom. But now something else was needed.

"The rules are different, don't you get it?" his boss asked him almost sympathetically. "You're carrying on as though nothing's changed, we have to talk about other things now."

"Such as?"

"Such as the campaign against illegal immigration, and I don't think you can do it, so it's best you leave. I've signed your last pay cheque for two hundred dollars."

At this Sasha finally recovered his dignity and yelled at him and didn't ask for his job back. He grabbed the money and ran, and later he would see his colleagues whom he used to smoke with on the stairs talking on television, and he didn't recognize them. The replacement had happened so quickly – they were the same people, but their words were different. He wondered if maybe things hadn't really changed at all – an actor could play an angel or a sinner, but he was still the same actor. And in his usual way he blamed himself, deciding the world was still normal and it was he who had changed. Perhaps he was having a mid-life crisis and was feeling vulnerable, and he would get over it and everything would be fine.

He was truly alarmed though when he went to the bank to change a hundred bucks he had saved for emergencies. Pushing the money under the window with his passport, he waited three minutes while the security guard stared suspiciously at him, then asked the cashier where his money was.

"What money?" she said.

"The money I gave you with my passport."

"What passport?"

The guard tapped his shoulder. "Something wrong, mate?"

"I just gave her a hundred dollars, you saw it!"

"No, I didn't, I was standing here and saw everything. Clear off!"

The guard kicked him out, and he ran in a panic to the nearest police station and explained to the officer, with little hope of success, that the bank had taken his passport.

"For lost passports go to the passport office," he said. "You want to join that lot?" He pointed to two drunks and a noisy prostitute in the cells, and one of the drunks winked knowingly at him and said something he didn't understand, or rather he understood the words but not what it meant, something about a "string of bubbles on a roundabout". Sasha was still young then and didn't understand things, but he took it as a sign.

He renewed his identity documents six months later, after they were lost three times at the passport office, but by then he was no longer sure he had an identity any more.

Soon after this he got a job at a school teaching History, and a seventeen-year-old girl called Svetka used to hang on his every word, as if he were speaking exclusively to her. One day the head had called him in to tell him it wasn't the time to talk of civil liberties, and that he must emphasize the historic role of the great Leader, and she was waiting outside when he came out.

"He's a halfwit, don't listen to him, or you'll end up like him," Svetka said.

"How dare you, mind your language! Go home to your parents, they're waiting for you!" he said.

"No, they're not. We can't stand him, but we like you, you're the best teacher we've ever had."

He wanted to say he probably wouldn't be for much longer, but he held his tongue, as he often did these days.

They would meet and talk, and he clutched at his conversations with this pale, clever little girl, because we all like people who like us, and he began to like himself when he was with her, and to feel confident and unafraid of the world. She kept their secret, and at school no one suspected anything. She even lied to her parents once and spent the night with him, and he was surprised to discover he had something to learn from this new generation.

He couldn't help noticing though the way she would change sometimes, and a strange absent expression would cross her face and she would seem to forget where she was, then pull herself together and nod. It all ended in the winter. Her absent moods were becoming more frequent now; the eager attention she used to give him had vanished, and he couldn't understand why. Once she didn't join him in the little park where he used to wait for her after school (they always left separately), and the following day he forgot caution and went to her at break time to ask where she had been.

"I couldn't come. I'll tell you later," she said, but she didn't.

They spoke for the last time a week later outside her flat, where he had been waiting for her.

"Please, won't you tell me what's happened?" he begged her, and when he looked at her he didn't recognize her. A stranger stared back at him, wearing the same round knitted white cap and the same ring on her third finger, but her eyes were blank and her glossy blond hair was dull and dark with grime.

"Nothing's happened," she told him.

"But why do you keep avoiding me? Is it your parents?"

"They have nothing to do with it. Nothing's happened."

Forgetting about the passers-by, he grabbed her by the shoulders in a frenzy and shook her. "Why are you like this? What have they done to you? Tell me, Svetka! For God's sake, tell me!"

Something of her old self flickered across her face, like the outlines of an old portrait showing through new paint, and he saw her struggle for a moment, as if she wanted to say something. She looked down, and when she looked up again there was the same blankness in her eyes. "Nothing's happened, Alexander Olegovich, you shouldn't shake me."

He left her and went home. But he had no home, because there was a snowstorm and he was drunk and had lost his street. He stumbled around swigging Bulgarian beer from the bottle, not feeling the cold, asking people where Filyovsky Park underground station was, and respectable dog-walkers stared at him with disgust.

He plunged into a station and set off on a line he didn't know, falling asleep with no idea where he was going, and waking at the last stop, which someone told him was called Bitsev Park. But there was no Bitsev Park, he knew that. He caught another train, going he didn't know where, and slept again, and when he came to, he was on an empty platform. It was late, he had been travelling for four hours. He sat on a bench, and a woman passed with a red flag.

He asked her what station it was.

"New Dead End," she told him.

"But there's no such station!" he said.

"Yes, there is, young man, on the new Preobrazhensky Line. It opened yesterday – are you from Mars?"

Afraid she would call the police, he stood up and waited for the last train, and on the wall of the carriage he saw an underground map showing the new Preobrazhensky Line, a wide maroon stripe crossing the Circle Line, starting in the remote outskirts of Moscow and cutting through the centre, vanishing in a maze of suburban stations. He didn't know of this line, but by now he no longer knew anything.

For weeks he sat alone in his room, drinking to forget himself. He was no longer afraid to watch television, the programmes just sickened him, especially one called Young, Pregnant and Alone. He had watched the show it was based on some years ago in the States, sympathetically helping schoolgirl mothers with their new lives. In this local variant, a large crimson-faced woman in a white hat, who looked like a collective-farm cook, yelled at the pregnant girl in an apoplexy of rage. "Dirty dropout, no one will want you now! How can your parents bear you! Who needs you!"

She raged for ten minutes, stamping her foot and splashing the girl with spit, and a man who looked like a farm manager tried to calm her. "See what you've done to this good working woman!" he said to the girl. "Don't bother with the slut, Klavdia Timofeyevna."

A model family was then paraded across the screen, a proletarian father and his enormous wife at the stove, with their proletarian son and baby grandson and its mother in a dressing gown, all shouting in chorus, "Hang yourself! Hang yourself!"

This was their message for those sick, alone and unemployed.

There were long queues at the shops again, and the saleswomen could be as rude as they liked. Even the foodstuffs had been replaced, and once instead of the Moscow cheese he asked for he was given a strange hard block of something that tasted of soap. The last straw was when he went to the vegetable market that spring to buy potatoes, and saw a pile of misshapen bright-green tubers on the stall that looked nothing like potatoes, covered in freakish horns and spikes like hedgehogs.

"Where are your ordinary potatoes?" he asked the man.

"What are you talking about, these are Vietnamese potatoes, we get them from Vietnam as food aid, where have you been?" he said.

He was unable to answer this question, and wasn't surprised when he asked a passer-by the time and was told, "Ton to few."

"What?" he asked mechanically.

"Ton to few," the man repeated and hurried on.

Either he had forgotten the language or the language had forgotten him; he could barely even understand the newspapers now. He had to get away, perhaps it was only in Moscow that things had been replaced, and elsewhere life was going on as normal. He sold his furniture and bought a train ticket to Gelendzhik in the Caucasus, where he had friends, and they were happy to see him and welcomed him and fed him – he felt safe with them in their well-ordered life. Their house was just five minutes from the sea, but he was too exhausted to see it that evening, and they gave him his usual room, which belonged to their son, who was in Moscow. The bed was in a different position, with the head facing the door – he distinctly remembered it facing the wall. But what did it matter where he lay his head, and after his first proper meal for many terrible months he fell asleep the moment it touched the pillow.

Next morning after his friends left for work, he made his way to the beach, and froze. The sea was red. It was more than he could bear – they couldn't have replaced the sea! He rushed up to where there was a market, and shouted to an old woman selling olives, "What's happened to the sea?"

"It's industrial waste," she told him placidly. "It washes ashore sometimes, but you can swim in it, it's not poisonous."

"But it's all along the coast, as far as the eye can see!"

"It's clean further off," she said. "Wait a while and the waves will wash it away."

It was a few days later that he forced himself to return to the beach and get used to this new world around him. He found a secluded spot and sat looking at the red water, and realized suddenly that the sky was dark, although it was just three in the afternoon. He looked up, and glimmering in the green sky the colour of a Vietnamese potato was a bright-blue sun that didn't hurt his eyes. An old man passed with his head raised to its blue rays, and his face looked dead.

"It's blue! Can't you see?" he shouted at him.

"I can't see anything," the old man smiled, and he saw he was blind and had a guide dog leading him.

He sat on the pebbles and closed his eyes and shook his head, then looked up again. The blue sun was at its zenith in the green sky, and he knew then that he would never be afraid of anything again, and a fierce healing rage burned in him that was stronger than his fear.

"To hell with you, you can do what you like, I'm the same as I always was and I'm not changing!" he said through clenched teeth, and at that moment the true language woke in him and he set off to look for the true sky and the true sea, but he still hadn't found them.

Anka had read somewhere that mixing up colours was a symptom of Vasilenko Syndrome, like a sort of Daltonism of the spectrum, and Sasha had told the story in the native language since he had already almost forgotten Russian, but she had understood it.

* * *

The third Joe to speak was Fyodor Stepanovich, who woke one morning from a long dream in the Arbour of the Winds, a secret place in Crimea and a place of healing, said to contain an opening into another dimension. The winds sang in many voices there, and the grass grew as tall as a person; only the locals knew it, outsiders never visited.

Fyodor Stepanovich had been living nearby in Gurzuf with his elderly mother, and was a chauffeur. He had been unhappily married and was divorced; he no longer expected much from life, and his dream was as lifelike as if he had actually slipped through to this other dimension. In it he was living in a town somewhere in the North, where he had lived all his life, with a different father and mother and, more importantly, a different wife. They lived at number 5 Great Communist Street, flat 32, and they had two children – a son and a daughter, named Kolya and Olya. His son collected little balsa-wood planes with elastic propellers, and his daughter played the piano and sang in a choir, and Fyodor Stepanovich was a bus driver on route fifteen, a wonderful route starting at a park on a hill high above a big slow river, and ending in the stunted outskirts of town, where new houses were being built. Beyond them was a flat expanse of open countryside which reminded him of the sea, but the real sea he had lived near all his life wasn't in his dream, and he didn't miss it.

He would sleep and dream for days on end in the Arbour of the Winds and forget himself there, and in his dreams he lived with his new family and he remembered everything that happened to them – his daughter's graduation concert, his son's broken arm, his wife's new job – more vividly than his life in Gurzuf. He felt amazingly happy with his new family, who loved him and never criticized him, and he was so close to them and his wife was so kind to him that he would wake in tears and sob.

His old life and job became unbearable to him, and he started spending all his time and money travelling the country looking for the town with the big river and the park on the hill and Great Communist Street, although there were such streets in most towns. He vaguely remembered a Decembrists' Square there too, which made him think it might be somewhere in Siberia, where the Decembrist plotters had been exiled.

One day he decided not to return to Gurzuf, and sent his mother a telegram saying he had moved to Blatsk and remarried. He went on looking for the town and his new family, and he was still looking for them to this day. Sometimes he would glimpse the face of his grown-up daughter in the street, or the back of his son's head, but would lose them in the crowd, and he was forever making little sketches of them on scraps of paper. He couldn't bear to think of them missing him, and couldn't think why he had lived for thirty dreary years in Gurzuf when he should have been with them. All he knew was that the spell would only be broken when he found the flat and his wife Larisa and his children Olya and Kolya, and they would come running out to meet him.

"It's a good story," Vasily Ivanovich said. "It's about homelessness."

* * *

Mashka Varka was next, a woman who could have been any age, with matted hair and watery slits of eyes, but an astonishingly rich, beautiful voice. She cleared her throat and announced, "Abandoned. A folk ballad."

The men sitting around the fire nodded approvingly as she launched into a soulful recitative: "When I was a little girl, I lived on white bread and cream, I wanted for nothing and my life was a dream. Then men came one day and sent my Papa to jail, and Mama loved a train driver on the iron rails. He beat me and threw me outside in the snow, and my travels started many years ago..."

The rest of Varka's life unwound in a series of couplets. She enumerated her various husbands' jobs (all ending in "-ist"), and her illnesses (all ending in "-ism"), and the towns she had stayed in (all ending in "-ovo"), and she ended with an "epilogue". Anka had observed that while conventional ballads ended with an epilogue dedicated to some patron or benefactor, the Joes would end by begging for food, and each of the men sitting round the fire honoured the tradition by throwing her a brass copeck.

"Was it like that for you, Vasily Ivanovich?" Anka asked cautiously.

"Exactly!" he smiled, proud of his people's artistry.

"But nothing in the ballad's true!"

"Of course not, Anechka, it's just a ballad," he nodded. "We've our ballads and we've our stories about how we left."

"So why did you leave?"

"It's obviously different for everyone," Mikhail Egorovich said loftily. "We don't tell each other everything."

"You mean you don't trust each other?"

"Of course we do," said Varka. "We trust each other and look after each other, we just don't all talk about it. Talking takes a lot of our energy and we need it for other things."

"So won't you ever tell me what happened, Vasily Ivanovich?"

"Why not, by and by," he said thoughtfully. "It's time to sleep now, you're already nodding off."

"No, I'm not!" she said angrily.

"Yes, yes, time to turn in," Sasha said. "Look at the stars."

"Sing her a lullaby, Varka," said Vasily Ivanovich.

Varka propped herself up on her elbow and gazed at the fire, and sang in her low sweet voice an old song that Anka seemed to know, although she hadn't heard it from her mother or father:

"Sleep baby, sleep,
Your rest the angels keep.
The little lamb is in the barn,
Its snowy fleece so soft and warm,
Sleep baby, sleep.
The stars shine bright as day,
The birds are resting far away,
To sing again at break of day.
Sleep baby, sleep…"

She sang on, and Anka looked up at the roof of the stars above them and felt the stillness of the night. I'm home, she thought, no one can send me away from here, and she fell asleep.

Chapter Six
The Monastery

"It's been a long, long time since anyone came to this shore," said the bearded man in black as he led Gromov and Voronov up the hill to the heavy gates of the monastery. "What brought you here, soldiers?"

"Well, we got lost, you see, and ended up in Blatsk and had to escape," Voronov gabbled, euphoric after his second miraculous escape, and despite Gromov's exhaustion and his brush with death, he felt irritated by his happy garrulousness.

"No one comes here from Blatsk," the monk went on. "Only a few of them know about your tunnel, from the days when it was a normal town. Come, dear friends, you must meet our Father Superior, we have a rule that all visitors must meet our Father Superior."

Out of the frying pan, thought Gromov. What sort of monastery was it, on this island he had never heard of? It must be a cult. It wasn't surprising sects and cults were thriving nowadays: the Father Superior might turn out to be even more dangerous than Marik. Well, they would see.

"We're on our way to Koposovo. We need to be there by midnight," he said pointedly.

"It's a long way to Koposovo," the monk said. "One of us can row you there tomorrow. Not tonight though, it's over twenty kilometres upriver and there's rain in the air."

They were trapped, Gromov thought. Meanwhile Voronov was prattling away without a care in the world and admiring the landscape, and there was plenty to admire. Blatsk was barely visible from here – it didn't seem possible they had been rowing for so long, it must be just a trick of perspective. And now they were on the island, a steep hill crowned with high white stone walls, behind which rose turrets of golden domes. A storm was brewing, and the sky above the river was swaddled in silver-grey clouds lit with little flickers of lightning the colour of faded nickel, but so high up that the thunder was barely audible. Far away on the Blatsk shore he could see dark lashes of rain, a low clump of trees and some haystacks, and a sprawling village with red roofs.

"That's Chivirevo," the monk said, unlocking the heavy bolt on the monastery gates. "In we go."

Gromov stepped through with Voronov behind him, and they followed the monk past some two-storey wooden buildings to a little house that looked like an ordinary dacha, surrounded by a fence. There was the sweet smell of flowers in the air – tobacco plants, calendulas and big tea roses.

The Father Superior came out to the porch to greet them, a tall middle-aged man with round metal-framed spectacles on his nose. "Welcome!" he beamed. "You've come from Blatsk?"

"We didn't mean to go there, it was an accident," Voronov assured him hastily.

"People come from all over the place, even Blatsk sometimes," he shrugged. "Not the locals of course, and we don't go there ourselves these days. I've a feeling Blatsk won't be around for much longer."

"What do you mean?" Voronov asked.

"Their days are numbered, young man. Come inside and we'll have tea."

Inside too the house was like an ordinary Moscow dacha, full of creaking old furniture and icons, and even the icons were the kind found in ordinary homes. Gromov knew nothing about religious painting, but noticed many cheap paper reproductions among the old wooden ones, such as were sold by tour guides in churches.

"There's going to be a storm," the Father Superior said, rubbing his hands as if hoping it might drown Blatsk. "I'm Father Nikolai, by the way."

"Captain Gromov," Gromov said.

"Lyosha Voronov," said Voronov. Gromov didn't bother to correct him for not presenting himself properly by rank. His uniform was a disgrace too; some people definitely weren't cut out for the army.

"Splendid. Were you in Degunino by any chance?"

"I was there recently," Gromov replied, not wanting to reveal the position of his unit.

"Who has it now, the Federals or Khazars?"

"When I left, it was the Federals."

"Ah well, not for long. It's a remarkable village, I haven't been there for years. We don't go out at all these days, this war has brutalized people. Both sides hate us, you see."

"Ours don't, we have priests in all our regiments," Gromov objected.

"Yes, but what sort of priests are they? They've nothing to do with Christianity, it's just Varangian nonsense. They hate us more than they hate the Khazars."

It's definitely a cult, Gromov thought, although he had never heard of a cult running a whole monastery.

"You're probably out of touch," Father Nikolai said kindly. "It's not surprising, most people are. Would you like some vodka? I don't drink myself, but I have some for guests."

* * *

"It's so good here," Voronov said a little later, gazing out at the rain. "It smells like the country, and it's so cosy."

"You like cosiness?" Father Nikolai smiled, and Gromov imagined there was a hidden hostility in his question. In fact there wasn't, but for some reason he wanted him to like him and was afraid he liked Voronov more, and it was such a shameful childish feeling he tried to suppress it.

"Yes, I do," Voronov said eagerly. "I remember as a child I used to lie in bed imagining I was flying in a little aeroplane lined with felt, like a felt boot, and it was all warm inside and I was cut off from the world looking out at the stars."

"Yes, we're cut off too," Father Nikolai nodded. "We prefer to keep our noses out of things."

"But why?" asked Gromov. "I know the Khazars hate Christianity, but as far as I know there are quite a few converts among them."

"I don't know which of the two I dislike more," Father Nikolai said thoughtfully. "Probably the Khazars, although many of us here say the Varangians. If it was a matter of principle we'd have had a schism by now. The Khazar faith claims to have a human face, as if there's anything human in them. First they target our ceremonies, then the Church itself, all with that false passion of theirs. For them Christ was a sort of dissident who liked a drink with his disciples, an inventor of aphorisms. The Khazars are geniuses at wisecracks and aphorisms, they should stick to being comedians. For the Varangians though He's an absolute dictator who shows no mercy. For them the superhuman is the ideal, and for Khazars it's the subhuman, and they both hate humanity and they're both wrong."

He paused to light an old oil lamp. "The Varangians have perverted Christianity with their wars and duty, and impose a military discipline in their monasteries. But why? A monastery is a place of joy, where fellow thinkers can gather to study interesting things. Those who are bored leave and go out into the world, and those who grow bored of the world return. They're all ours. Christianity is a language in which the most different people can speak together and agree and achieve miracles. It was Christians who built that tunnel, priests and hermits and virtuous women, and they saved you!"

"I don't really believe in such things," Gromov said as tactfully as he could.

"Well, it's up to you. But anyone who enters a monastery will sooner or later find Christianity, because his life outside has become unbearable to him, and he'll decide to stay and he'll be happy. You may not agree with me, but I believe monasteries aren't an escape from life but an escape into life. Only the Varangians could turn them into schools of punishment, with their worship of violence. Everyone's guilty before God the Commander, who conscripts them into His army. What good can come of pure duty?"

"Plenty," said Gromov. "I've seen what happens without it."

"Yes, well I suppose the absurd samurai notion of heroism for heroism's sake has a right to exist, but where's the joy in it? Christianity is based simply on a correct understanding of human nature, and that's all there is to it. Your heroism is necessary sometimes, but no one can endure endless self-sacrifice – over the years it grows into a hump that cripples you. And the saddest thing is when you forget your harsh life for a moment and meet a girl, the absolute ideal, a pure angel, the reward for all your years of denial, whom you worship as a paragon of virtue and raise to unimaginable heights. But not many girls can live up to it I'm afraid, and it's a sorry sight. Although better than some, of course—"

"Well, obviously we're all different," Gromov said curtly, trying not to show his irritation. "Not everyone believes in stories from beyond the grave."

"I know!" Father Nikolai said fervently. "It's quite possible there's nothing in them, and if there is, it's a bonus. It's even possible there's no God."

"There was a captain on our training course who was a psychologist too, and liked to convince us with counter-arguments," Gromov grinned. "He said we didn't have to fight, and would paint dreadful pictures of our poor defenceless country."

"Because he wanted to keep you in line, whereas I'm doing nothing of the sort," Father Nikolai corrected him gently. "We have our Bible-bashers and our websites and our aggressive marketing – who needs it? You know your motivations, I'm only trying to explain mine. It's possible there's no God, but without Him the world would be a lonely place without purpose or pleasure, with nothing but death at the end. Unless we build this dome over us we're cold and vulnerable and exposed to the rain. That's the picture of the world we've created so that we can live in it according to Christianity's precepts. The Buddhists have theirs, the Khazars theirs. Of course the Khazars don't believe in immortality, and nor do the natives. They live like vegetables. Well, let them—"

"Which natives?" put in Voronov. "The ones in Chivirevo?"

"Everywhere, young man. We realized there was nothing for us in the world, so we decided to find immortality here in this one, without movement, endlessly staying in one place. But the day will come when it all ends and we can leave here. Meanwhile we spend our time pleasantly guarding our faith until we can preach it to the world."

"But why can't you preach your faith to the world now?" Voronov asked, puzzled. "I've often seen wandering monks in Moscow, and no one persecutes them."

"Because in Moscow the war has dulled people's senses. They just want a preacher in a cave to absolve them. A man rapes a girl and she kills herself, and he goes to confess – forgive me Father Tikhon, I've sinned! I can't explain anything to you, I'm not God, just a monk, I can only tell you why I live this way. But the fact is that no one will listen to us while these two are killing each other, and almost no one wants to wear the habit these days. They'll need us though when the engine breaks down."

"The engine will break?" Gromov tried to pin him down. "You can see that from here? So who'll win?"

"No one will win."

"I thought you'd say Christ would!" he grinned.

"Well Christ won long ago, but military victories aren't our business. I'm not saying there'll be the Kingdom of Truth, but the Kingdom of Lies will end. No one knows what will happen next, which is what makes it so fascinating. We'll show you what we do at our devotions tonight, unless you'd prefer to sleep?"

"Not me, I'm not tired," he said.

"Nor me," Voronov chipped in.

"There's a room for guests here. Lie down and rest and I'll wake you later," Father Nikolai said.

* * *

Gromov and Voronov woke from a brief refreshing sleep under quilts in a large covered veranda, on pillows stuffed with sweet-smelling herbs. A little light streamed under the door of Father Nikolai's room, where he was evidently preparing for the service.

Gromov sat up in bed. Nothing of the place reminded him of a monastery, and it brought back memories of weekend parties in his student days, cooped up with his friends in someone's dacha.

He heard footsteps, and saw an elderly monk with a glass-domed lantern knock on Father Nikolai's door.

"Yes?" he called out.

"Brother Nikodim to see you, Father Nikolai."

"Hush, you'll wake our guests."

"We're not asleep!" Voronov said.

"Good, it's time for our devotions. I hope you find them interesting," he said, coming into the veranda. The monks filed in one by one and sat at a rickety table and greeted their guests warmly, while Father Nikolai poured everyone glasses of sweet-clover tea.

"Forgive me, Captain, didn't I meet you in Voronezh?" a shy young monk asked Gromov.

"Not me, I've never been to Voronezh," said Gromov.

"Me neither," nodded the monk. "It must have been two different Christians!"

Gromov smiled with the others to be polite, although he had never liked Zen jokes.

The monks chatted quietly among themselves, and he couldn't help suspecting a plot and trying to eavesdrop; he liked it too much here to drop his guard.

When ten monks were assembled, Father Nikolai turned up the wick of the lantern so it shone more brightly, and asked those present to speak. Everyone fell silent, and for a moment Gromov was afraid they were going to hold hands for a spiritual seance. But luckily this didn't happen: they all put their hands on the table in front of them, and Father Nikolai clasped his fingers like a steeple. "So what do we see, brothers?" he asked in a matter-of-fact voice.

What followed reminded Gromov not so much of his regimental meetings, as of the late-night radio shows he used to host long ago in his other life. He would take phone calls and read poems, and never before had he felt so connected to the world, alone at night in the Ostankino studios. People on night shift would call in, or from frontier checkpoints, driving alone on the empty highway or sitting by someone's sickbed. They didn't know each other and wouldn't have recognized each other by day, they just had to be awake at night, and this brotherhood of insomniacs, who had nothing to do with defending state interests, seemed in a strange way to guarantee humanity's survival. On those nights it was as if he saw the whole of his life before him, and he would remember waking as a child, sitting at the window in his nightshirt trembling with a sense of mystery and the feeling he was part of something big and important. A Sputnik would travel across the sky, and the Sputnik too would be part of the mystery, and he would go back to bed and fall happily asleep…

"Brother Nikon at the Varsonevsky cloister is poorly," a stocky monk with big hairy hands was saying quietly. "His ailment is not life-threatening, but disabling. It seems it's his joints."

"Is there any cure?" asked the monk sitting between him and Voronov.

"They're treating him with herbs. Perhaps we can send ointments."

"Let us pray for Brother Nikon," said Father Nikolai, and all were silent for a moment, thinking of their distant brother and his joints.

"Brother Andrei in the Turukhanovsky cloister has lost his way and may lose his faith," said a tall thin monk in a muffled voice, coughing into his hand. "It seems to him this business will never end and there's no purpose in the world."

"Quite right too," observed his fat neighbour with a nose like a potato and few teeth. "They're the normal thoughts of an intelligent Christian."

"You shouldn't enjoy those thoughts too much though, Brother Georgy, or it means it's the end," put in Father Nikolai.

"Isn't it temptation, Father?" asked the shy young monk. "Isn't it one step from thinking that the worse things are the better?"

"And aren't they?" Brother Georgy persisted.

"What about compassion for others?" said the stocky one. "If you want everything to burn, what will be left for us? We should live decent lives and not wish ill on the world."

"And will we survive?" intoned a monk sitting some way from the lantern, whose face was in shadow.

"Maybe it's best we don't," Brother Georgy said. "I wouldn't want—"

"Well, it's early days," said Father Nikolai. "You'll definitely survive, Brother Georgy, there's nothing wrong with your health."

"Or his appetite," the tall thin one added spitefully.

"As for Brother Andrei in Turukansk," Father Nikolai went on, "tell him, Brother Boris, that to see no purpose in the world is undoubtedly a good thing. There would be nothing for us to do if the world had purpose."

Brother Boris nodded and closed his eyes, and everyone fell silent again.

"I've told him," he said after a while.

"And what did he say?"

"He said he'd think about it."

"Brother Igor in the Novosibirsk cloister tells me he has succumbed to the sin of boredom," said a spectacled monk who reminded Gromov of his old Physics teacher.

"Tell him the following, Brother Vyacheslav," laughed Father Nikolai. "That whenever I succumb to boredom I feel a great joy, lying in my cell by the open window, smelling the sweet smell of the monastery meadow and staring up at the cracks in the ceiling, and their patterns carry me away to our distant cloisters, and I either fall into a healing sleep or think of something amusing. Tell him to do that, and the cracks will be a cause of great joy to him."

Brother Vyacheslav concentrated again. "I've told him," he said.

"And what does Brother Igor say?"

"He says the ceiling in your cell needs painting," Brother Vyacheslav squeaked.

"Brother Igor has succumbed to the sin of being tiresome," said Father Nikolai. "Tell him he should read *The Marriage of Figaro*, and I can deal with my own ceiling."

"Brother Vladimir in the Starovolga cloister wants me to tell you there were battles there with many casualties, and he asks your blessing to treat them," Brother Vyacheslav went on. "When the Federals left, they quartered their wounded with the natives."

"But how can he leave the monastery?" asked Brother Boris.

Gromov didn't understand the question.

"Tell Brother Vladimir I applaud his impulse. Perhaps he can let the natives know they can bring the most badly injured to him to be treated." Father Nikolai said, adding after a pause, "It's not for us to decide, but it's worth a try."

Gromov saw Voronov give him a questioning look and shook his head; he didn't understand either.

Father Nikolai and the brothers discussed various topics – one was unwell, one had received sad news from home, Brother Mark in the Biryulevsky monastery had fallen in love and wanted advice. The monks sniggered and offered advice, each suggestion more indecent than the last, and Father Nikolai silenced them severely and advised Mark to go to the object of his desire as soon as possible and, if it didn't work out with her, to pray hard. There seemed to be some connection between all these monks that Gromov couldn't understand, without mobile phones or phones of any sort, and the only thing that linked them was the monasteries.

"So what else do we see?" asked Father Nikolai at last, when monastery business was concluded.

"I see the old man and his wild girl going South," the tall thin monk said sadly. "It's hard for the girl."

"Can she hear us?"

"Sometimes."

"We must give her strength, if we can."

"We'll try."

"Can the old man hear us?"

"No he can't, but he knows."

"I don't like the old man," said the fat monk flatly.

"And he doesn't like you – what's the difference?" interrupted Father Nikolai. "What's he doing?"

"He's escaping to Degunino," said Brother Boris. "Someone was sent to kill her, but he didn't get there in time."

"He won't catch them," Father Nikolai said firmly. "There are the army's schemes and there is God's scheme."

"He's so disillusioned he wants to defect to the Khazars!" sniggered the fat one.

"I'm afraid for him though," said Boris anxiously. "Something bad will be born, and he won't survive."

"Follow him. And what about our forester?"

"He's left to look for his girl."

"And how is she?"

"It's not known to us. It's hard for us to see in those places, Father."

"And is she alive?" he asked anxiously.

"Yes, she is," said the monk whose face was in shadow. "For now, anyway."

"Remember, Brother Mstislav, you see further than the rest of us," Father Nikolai told him sternly. "Ah, the Inspector, the Inspector. We're waiting, but we're not waiting for him."

"So who are you waiting for?" blurted Voronov.

"You've good survival skills, young man," Father Nikolai nodded. "It was clever of our mutual acquaintance to give you to the Captain, he won't be lost with you to protect him. The natives have a wonderful knack for avoiding danger."

"But I don't want it," Voronov said dejectedly.

"What's foretold is foretold. You mustn't be afraid. The girl's not afraid, and the little girl with the old man's not afraid. Your Captain was going to kill Heaven knows who, and he wasn't afraid, even though he's never shot a civilian in his life. And he won't do it now anyway, because they've left Koposovo. So you'd have put her to death, would you Captain?"

"How do you know all this?" Gromov could barely speak, and no longer understood anything.

"And how does he know things?" Father Nikolai nodded at Voronov. "We just do, that's all. Tomorrow you'll leave in peace and take him to Moscow, then you'll go where you need to go. You want to see Moscow?"

"How do you mean?" Gromov said childishly, half believing him.

"Like this." Father Nikolai shrugged, and suddenly Gomov saw Moscow pulsing away far in the distance, and an ambulance racing across the city and getting stuck in the traffic. He knew it would get there though, and nothing mattered to him at that moment but the siren wailing in his head and the paramedic biting his fists with impatience. He was a good paramedic, not one of those who drove to emergencies at the last minute; he cared about his patient and he wanted to get there, and Gromov knew he would. He realized he could do nothing about the traffic, but that he could somehow reassure the man and tell him things would be fine, and he did reassure him, he knew that.

"Well well, I'd never have imagined it," said Father Nikolai. "I honestly thought... Aren't you interested in the war?"

"I already know about that," he replied mechanically, then pulled himself together. "What, you saw it too?"

"Maybe," replied Father Nikolai enigmatically. "Or rather I sensed it."

"We can do that," Brother Georgy assured him.

"So have you any questions, Brother Captain?"

"Plenty," he said. "But first, why can't Brother Vladimir leave his monastery?"

"He's a solitary monk," Father Nikolai explained. "Some take a vow not to leave until your confounded see-saw ends. They don't choose to be hermits, but every monastery must have one, and at Starovolga it's Vladimir and he's a doctor."

"And who is your hermit here?"

"Brother Mstislav," Father Nikolai sighed, pointing to the monk whose face was in shadow. "He can't even go to the river until it ends."

"Not allowed to, or doesn't want to?"

"It's the same for us," said Nikolai. "But even if he wanted to he couldn't."

Gromov glanced at Mstislav, who, as if guessing his thoughts, moved closer to the lantern, and he saw a man of about fifty, with fair hair and green eyes and the sad gentle face of someone resigned to his fate.

"Never mind, it won't be much longer now," fat Brother Georgy reassured him.

"It's not in our hands," said Brother Mstislav.

"Well, we'll know when it happens," concluded Father Nikolai briskly. "I thank you, brothers, you're free to go."

The monks left, talking quietly together, and Gromov was silent for a while.

"I won't ask how you do it," he said at last.

"But you did it yourself as soon as you believed you could," Father Nikolai reminded him.

"Yes, but I don't understand how. Are all these messages to do with the monastery?"

"Not at all," Father Nikolai said, looking surprised. "We discuss monastery matters, but we see further, almost everything in fact, a bit like you and your theatres of battle. Some places like Blatsk are too sickening for us, but I'm sure nothing important's going on there."

"And you see the future?" Voronov put in.

"Only in general terms," Father Nikolai said modestly. "I don't want to distress you, you're a fine young man, your people know what they're doing and who they send on assignments. But there's another power that can't be known – you arrived here and you didn't arrive there, obviously the good Lord has protected you." He turned to Gromov. "Who knows, maybe you'd have killed her, for absolutely no reason."

"And what do you know about it?" demanded Gromov.

"About the girl and the official you mean? Not much, just that there's an old curse that if a native loves a Khazar or a Varangian they'll have a child who'll be the end of the world. It sounds absurd, but absurd things can happen. For me it's all wrapped in mystery. Christianity demands so much of us that we've lost all our old mystical knowledge, all the pagan deities and magic. But people knew many things before Christianity, and in some places they still do. There are prophecies and spells and all sorts of nonsense, and it's quite possible your Gurov has some understanding of them. But he's just an ordinary man, and he's not looking in the right places."

He poured more tea and went on, looking at Gromov with respect and compassion, like a doctor bravely exposing himself to a patient with a serious but fortunately curable disease. "If you put yourself in the hands of the Lord, He'll arrange things according to His plan. But if you rely on yourself you'll fall – it's like Newton's law. Gurov planned everything down to the last detail, and gave you your route and someone to travel with who could get you out of any difficulty, and look what happens. The girl's not there, the person he sends to kill her takes the wrong route, and even if you'd arrived in time and put a bullet through her head – and you're a conscientious soldier and always carry out orders – it would have been pointless, because the girl has nothing to do with it. So she goes her way and you go yours, and you'll doubtless arrive wherever you need to be."

"I don't understand," Gromov said impatiently. "I'd like to ask you, as an honest priest, if you've the slightest evidence for God's existence. I don't mean just some mystical experience, unknowable, unnameable and all the rest—"

"No, of course not!" Father Nikolai threw out his arms. "If we did, we wouldn't have God, but a military leader. I yearn for proof, but there's none, just an empty space, and the yearning for it is so great in me I have to find something to fill it."

"It sounds like cowardice," Gromov said.

"Possibly, possibly. Cowardice and stupidity, and only you are good and right, and no one appreciates you. If they did, your heroism wouldn't be heroism. It's the military equivalent of the religious spirit. For your army priests, Christianity's a superman philosophy that renounces humanity. You have a top-secret mission to deal with the man and the girl, and you defend your secret fiercely. But being superhuman can only be achieved through violence. You know why we have so few preachers these days? Because we're tired of preaching the obvious. Sleep, dear friends, you're tired, I'm going to read a little longer."

He made the sign of the cross over them and went to his room, taking the lantern and some magazines from the shelf.

* * *

Gromov woke in the night from one of the sad dreams that had plagued him recently, and went outside for a smoke. He was glad to see the light still on in Father Nikolai's window, and hoped he would come out. At night our defences are weakened, and in the first minutes of waking we long for a friendly word. During his army training they would be woken at dawn for their three-kilometre run, and weren't even allowed to use the lavatory first, so that this dose of army cruelty would be with them for the rest of the day.

And at that moment, since all wishes at the monastery were granted, Father Nikolai came out. "I couldn't sleep," he said, as if knowing he would feel embarrassed by his sympathy.

"Me neither," he said gratefully.

The second cocks had crowed, and music blared from the far shore as people in Blatsk gambled the night away at the Tsar's Crown Casino. All around the monastery the grass rustled, the smell of mud rose from the river, and the water splashed, with a solitary buoy bobbing in the distance.

"On thinking about it I approve your decision, if it's of any interest to you," Father Nikolai said.

"Which decision?" Gromov was on guard.

"To join the army. A wise choice, otherwise you'd have gone to pieces. I knew a man – I might even say that man was me – who at one point began to destroy everything around him, a most unpleasant experience."

"Yes, it was something like that," Gromov nodded.

"No, it was exactly that, I remember it well. You could say I joined the army too, in a way, although it's nothing like yours of course. I suppose you've decided to see things through to the end – duty's duty, the more unpleasant the better. Very debilitating. But at some point I knew if everything around me was collapsing I must share the blame for it. I get a job, and six months later the firm folds. I fall in love with a married woman and her marriage ends, and my own doesn't last long. I knew even then that we weren't alone in the world, and felt I was the Lord's weapon and He had chosen me to settle some unfinished business. Someone had to do it. So I joined the Church, and that didn't work, and I joined another monastery – not this one – and that didn't work either. But I was just playing at it. I realized," he continued in a confiding tone, "that we must either tear everything up by the roots and make something new, or prolong the agony, because people want at all costs to live. I chose the first, but hadn't the stomach for it, I was still alive unfortunately. So I decided it would be better if I left. Blatsk is far away now. The Lord guided me here in His own way. The problem is that if people like you and I leave the world so as not to destroy it, it will be destroyed even sooner!"

Gromov knew what he was talking about, and would have thought the same thing if he hadn't forbidden himself to think.

"All the destruction we've brought about is because people have no system to guide them," Father Nikolai continued. "Some are incapable of doing anything and everything collapses around them, but if just one stick remains in the ruins, we can build something around it. And now there's a whole mountain of sticks and no one knows what to build. That's why I approve your choice, and I'm glad you're still alive in the world – you and another person who interests me greatly."

"Gurov?" Gromov asked. It was clear Gurov was twisted up in some way with everything that happened; he was a mysterious man, and clearly a lot depended on him.

"No, he has nothing to do with it. He's a fairly ordinary person, with his own rather childish logic, tapping rivets in the cauldron. No, there's another person, very consistent and clear-headed. Consistency's a most important virtue, I believe. I don't so much know of her... this person's existence... as feel it. I can almost physically feel this person moving across the earth to the place where people's fate is revealed. We don't leave the island, you see, and it sharpens our senses. They're particularly acute in Mstislav, who can't go out at all. He told us yesterday you were coming, by the way."

"Is she the woman I was meant to kill?"

"No, not her. I don't know about you, but I've never been keen on paganism – it's not a faith, it's just a mess of frying pans and oven tongs, with a god for this and a god for that. It doesn't interest me."

"I agree," Gromov nodded. "But can you honestly deny that your religion is just the same?"

"No, I can't," Father Nikolai shrugged. "But there's been nothing else for a long time, and it's a good system."

"Why?"

"In every faith there's a step everyone must take on their own. I can lead you as far as this step, because I know the way well, but the next part you must do alone. Some may discover their faith after prayer or a miracle, others are moved by the beauty of creation to give thanks, others find God through reason and logic, but no one can pass through this threshold without Him. How it will be for you I don't know, most likely your life will bring you to Him."

"How?"

"You'll see you can change, like the actor who must make people laugh and arrives at the theatre in a bad mood, so he shuts himself in his dressing room and smiles at himself for an hour in the mirror and becomes happy. You live like a monk anyway, why wouldn't you find your faith in such a life? You've probably found it already and are just waiting for the final proof." He yawned, and turned back to his room. "It's time for bed now, you must rest for the journey tomorrow."

Gromov stood a while longer on the porch, then returned to the terrace and fell asleep immediately.

Next morning they walked down to the river with Voronov and Brother Artemy, who was rowing them to Koposovo.

"By the way, who did you mean yesterday by 'the natives'?" Gromov said as they stood on the jetty. "If you mean the Russians, why not say so?"

"Because the Russians aren't the natives, I thought you knew," Father Nikolai said, surprised. "Didn't they tell you in the army?"

"In the army we know it's us."

"And the others think it's them. The ones it belongs to are the ones who are happy here. The alarm goes and you're driven from place to place – you're not happy on this earth, you're like a soul in the wrong body."

"You're Russian though, aren't you?" Gromov said, annoyed that Voronov was listening to this defeatist talk.

"I don't remember. Maybe once, but not now of course. I suppose according to you I've deserted to the monastery."

"I didn't say that."

"It's what you think, though. Any living person is a deserter for you. The true natives are the ones who are happy everywhere, but you're a foreigner everywhere." He smiled at him. "I didn't sleep last night, I was thinking about the proof you asked for, and there's one, a counter-argument. I see the Devil's work too clearly, and the fact that he's not victorious makes me believe there must be a divine hand in things. The ideal for us is to be in communion with God. But since there's no material evidence of His existence, it seems He has divided us into two sexes to create life, whereas the Devil, the proud angel, has divided us to destroy each other. Christianity exists to overcome divisions, hence the cross, the vertical intersecting the horizontal. But you're a soldier, and your samurai notion of duty is to fight on the side you were born into."

"That's not duty."

"But why is it your duty to overcome the gifts you were born with? By fighting on one side you help the Devil's plan. God isn't on the side of the big battalions, He thinks long-term. If you understand what I'm saying, what more proof do you need? But enough, I've succumbed to the sin of preaching. Think of it at your leisure. Go in peace."

Gromov and Voronov climbed into the boat, and Brother Artemy took the oars.

"Well I doubt we'll meet again. Good luck, young man," he said to Voronov. He looked at Gromov. "And you too." Then he turned on his heel and walked quickly back up the hill to the monastery.

Chapter Seven
The Gates

1

As Zhenka left Zhadrunovo station and headed for the village, she had a sense of something distorted in the landscape. The train had stopped only for a minute, as if anxious to get away as soon as possible, and no one else got off apart from her and Gurion's escort of five men. The other passengers looked strangely at them.

At first glance the place seemed ordinary, even quite pretty, but little by little, she didn't know how, it was as if she was seeing things in a dream. Her head spun, the air quivered, the edges of things blurred and the proportions changed, everything seemed to shift fifteen degrees and back again. Sometimes this happens even in our own familiar environment, then someone we know passes, or we think of something ordinary and reassuring and hang on to it, and the sensation passes. But sometimes this doesn't work, and we're sucked into a place from which there is no return. She tried to banish the feeling. But surely something must have happened to Volokhov, otherwise why would she find it so hard to walk, and feel this dizziness and breathlessness in the flat, slowly shifting landscape.

Great love gives people the power to communicate across any distance, to dream the same dreams, to sicken with the same illnesses, and far away in the village of Solomino, Volokhov could sense what was happening to her, and knew it was irreversible, but strangely not fatal. He hadn't sensed her like this in his old life, because of the distance between them, but the past month, when he had been with her every night, had made the physical connection between them unbreakable. She mustn't weaken, and he had to make sure she didn't – and he was on his way there to be with her. He avoided the word Zhadrunovo, feeling a little more life go out of him each time he thought of it, but he knew she was crossing some frontier, and that although he couldn't stop her, he could make the crossing a little easier for her. Yet surprisingly he didn't feel afraid. He knew something incomprehensible was happening to her, but what he was feeling now frightened him less than the world he had lived in before.

At that moment she was walking across a hot flowering meadow a little ahead of Gurion's escort, who were completely useless, she realized. Crickets chirped, and the air smelt of honey and dry earth. For some reason she could see patches of snow on the brown earth against the horizon, and even smell the spring smells of damp earth and melting ice – yet it was summer, there couldn't be snow. There was no sign of the mutinous garrison. She walked on as if wading through warm water, with that sense of dislocation between her thoughts and movements she sometimes felt after smoking grass. Gurion's men walked behind her, slowing down and falling further and further behind. She looked back, and saw a copse behind them and a pylon and the wires of the railway line, slightly blurred but still clear. The burning Zhadrunovo air quivered around her.

In the middle of the meadow stood a large gate, two posts like goal posts, smooth and white as dry bones, with a brown crossbar on top. The path led straight to the gate, with no barrier there or to the sides of them, and it would have been easy to walk round. But it seemed to her for some reason that she must stay on the path. She slipped to the left – and nothing happened, no one stopped her – and saw a football lying in the grass. As a child she had loved going to football matches with her father; then she and her mother had left for the Kaganate and he had stayed behind. She approached the posts, noticing their slightly rough surface, and kicked the ball through. Goal.

She looked round. Gurion's men stood far behind her, looking full of guilt and sympathy, as if lined up to pay their last respects to her; Gurion had told them in Grachevo to go only as far as the gates.

"What are you doing? Follow me!" she called back, and they looked even guiltier. She decided she would shout at them only if they disobeyed her, then fire her gun as a last resort. What she would do after that she had no idea.

They stood in silence for a while, then turned and walked slowly back to the station, and she noticed suddenly that the station and the line of cables behind the copse were no longer there: they had simply vanished. She knew of legends about magic places where things vanish, but all this was just a punishment for cowardice. She had approached the gates safely and the men had walked away, and it was unclear what would happen to them.

"Come back!" she shouted. "You'll be lost!"

They didn't look round and seemed not to hear her. She unbuckled her holster and fired her revolver in the air, but it didn't stop them and it made a frankly pathetic noise, like the pop of a champagne cork or a fart. A humble salute to passing into this new state of existence.

She headed for the gates, thinking some secret power might stop her this time, but the secret power didn't stoop to such cheap tricks. She looked back again, and already none of the men were there; it seemed cowardly soldiers didn't last long in this place. The copse was still there though, and the meadow and the flowers. Nature was still nature.

There was nothing she could do, she knew that now, and she knew it in such a literal sense that for a moment she felt a mortal sadness. But not allowing herself to weaken, she strode firmly through the gates. She would have to find the garrison on her own, without her escort of deserters.

The deserters stood and watched in horror as the Commissar's silhouette melted away until nothing was left of her, then they exchanged glances and stumbled back to the station, soaked in sweat. They felt ashamed, but under the shame beat the hot guilty joy known to every soldier when the bullet whistles past his head and misses him.

The village of Zhadrunovo stretched ahead of her in a flat dark line, thickening into a row of low cottages as she approached. It was a large village, she realized, larger than any she had visited before. In the yard of the first cottage she passed, she saw a pretty young woman with smooth dark hair and her mouth half-open in a sort of smile. "Hello, could you give me a drink?" she said. She was hot and terribly thirsty, and had already unbuttoned her tunic.

The woman went into the cottage in silence and returned with an earthenware pitcher of milk in one hand and a mug in the other, and poured the milk into the mug. She went on pouring as it spilt over the top and overflowed onto the dry earth, and she didn't stop and the milk didn't run out, and spread in a puddle in the dust. Zhenka laughed good-naturedly at this local trick and put out her hand, and the woman reluctantly stopped pouring and handed her the full mug. The milk tasted of milk.

"Thank you," she said, wiping her lips. "Can you tell me where the garrison is, please?"

"There's everything here. It's good here," said the woman in a low voice.

At that moment a young soldier came out of the cottage in an unfamiliar uniform, or rather she had seen it before but couldn't remember where. Russian soldiers had worn something similar in the early days of the last war, before peg stops were replaced with shoulder straps and so on. The garrison must have made themselves these old-fashioned tunics during the rebellion. He seemed to have just woken from a siesta, and his belt hung down to his bollocks, as they say in the army.

She greeted him, and he raised his eyes to her and nodded. "It's interesting," he said impassively. "They say there's nothing here, but there's everything here."

"Where's the garrison?" she asked him.

"Are you hungry?" he said.

"I said, where's the garrison?" she repeated. She felt bad about snapping at him after they had given her the milk, but their dimness was beginning to annoy her.

"Wait," he said, looking frightened, and went back to the cottage. She waited, tormented by the heat, and the woman went on smiling with her half-open mouth. A minute later he returned, and handed her a brightly coloured newspaper. "Here," he said with a guilty smile, "it's all there is."

She looked at it, and saw it was the children's comic *Pussycat* from the Seventies, with happy children on the cover playing in the snow on toboggans.

He was either the village idiot or was just pretending to be, and was wearing his soldier's uniform as a joke.

"Have you been to the dump?" asked the woman. "Go to the dump first. You have to pass it to reach the garrison."

She pointed across the field at a large pile of rubbish some two hundred metres from the village, which she hadn't noticed before. The garrison couldn't be there of course, but she turned and left these dimwits for the dump, which suddenly seemed much closer now; all distances were oddly foreshortened by the heat. The air ruffled and her head spun.

There was a surprising assortment of objects on the dump – a shoe, the sleeve of an overcoat, a ballpoint pen, a *Guide to Elementary Geometry*, a compass, a child's plastic sword, a two-handed saw, an old gramophone horn – all scattered without any apparent order, some things still quite useable. She realized she must throw something there to get past. She went through her pockets and pulled out a photograph of Volokhov and put it back. She had nothing else, apart from a few crumpled banknotes, but it seemed they didn't throw money here, and they probably used a different currency. Tearing a button from her tunic, she threw it on the pile, and immediately the air stopped quivering and she could think more clearly. She didn't think of death, because death would have been an unforgivable vulgarity. She was alive, even too alive. Her fingers ached from tearing her button off; she was still thirsty and wanted to live, and she could remember everything.

She left the dump and headed towards more cottages, and sitting in the yard of the first one she passed she saw her old friend Lieutenant Gorovets, mending a radio. She had had no idea he was in the Zhadrunovo garrison. He had worked for the Khazars in counter-intelligence and had been wounded in the battle for Zaveryukhino, a small village of no strategic importance which the enemy defended ferociously for some reason; his unit had retreated and left him in the cottage where the hospital was stationed.

"Hi, Gorovets!" she said. Something about him troubled her. He was shaggy and unshaven, with burs in his hair – and he was mending a radio, for God's sake. It wasn't possible. She knew he couldn't even fix the chain on his bike, he would ask a neighbour, and it was pure idealism that made him join the army.

He raised his head and squinted at her. "Good afternoon," he said uncertainly.

"Don't you recognize me, Gorovets?" she said, and for the first time since she arrived she felt afraid. She had known him since before the war, when they were teenagers; he hadn't joined the army then, because he hated sports and war games, but in the Kaganate all the young people had known each other.

"Of course, I do," he said, flinching slightly from her.

"What are you doing here?" she demanded.

"Well, it's nothing special, you see," he told her. "Although on the other hand it's not all at once."

There was the same fifteen-degree shift in the way he spoke as in the rest of the slowly shifting landscape.

"It's good though," he said. "When you look at it first you want to avoid it. Sometimes you do, sometimes you don't. There are seven stars here and seven stars there."

She was glad she didn't understand him; if she understood this language she would become like him, and she didn't want that. It occurred to her that the longer she stayed here the more her own vocabulary would change, at first by fifteen degrees, then forty-five, then ninety, and eventually each word would take on a completely different meaning. She closed her eyes and tapped the tip of her nose.

"It's no use, your childish skin can't grasp it," he said sincerely, and for a moment she heard his old voice that she knew so well. But it was as if he was less sorry for her than for himself, struggling to express himself in a language she would understand.

"Go," he said with an effort. "Go, and it will be different."

"What will?" she asked him.

"Well, why not?" he replied.

She left him and crossed the field. There were masses of bright-yellow wild flowers that turned fluffy after flowering, whose name she couldn't remember now, and she saw a group of soldiers training. They marched five paces forwards together and stopped, then marched backwards five paces; perhaps she was suffering from the state you fall into in extreme heat, but if there was a word for it she had forgotten it, and it didn't bother her. She tried to translate what Gorovets had said, but she had already forgotten what it was – it probably wasn't important. It was becoming harder for her to think in the dead language she had always taken as the living one, and her thoughts were spiralling into the true language, which seemed to take over the endless expanse of the landscape.

She heard a cuckoo cry, "Cuck-oo, cuck-oo!" then backwards, "Oo-cuck, oo-cuck!" But it didn't surprise her, it could sing as it liked. Everyone here did as they liked, and she must get used to it.

The soldiers marched backwards and forwards, endlessly repeating the same movements, as if hoping after the thousandth time they could turn round, but they didn't. She saw a little girl with red hair watching them, who turned from them as she approached and stared at her with cold transparent eyes, and the longer she looked at her the less Volokhov could sense her. It was like a wound healing over after a painful injury, and he realized that without this wound there was nothing to sustain him.

2

He was so consumed by this new sensation and the sudden deafness that had overcome him that he didn't notice Gromov burst into the collective-farm building where his Guards were quartered on their way to Zhadrunovo.

"Who's in charge here?" Gromov called in a hoarse voice.

Volokhov raised his head. "No one. Make yourself at home."

Gromov nodded to Voronov to follow, and they entered a large room with brown walls and a brown floor and rows of broken beds with mattresses covered in brown stains, on which lounged Volokhov's Flying Guards.

"What the hell is going on?" Gromov said in disgust.

Until that moment Volokhov had been with Zhenka at Zhadrunovo, with the cottages and the field and its strangely drifting proportions, and it was only now that he took stock of his surroundings, and saw with a sudden cold clarity the cracked floor and window frames, and the view of rusty wheels and farm machinery outside.

"Who are you?" Gromov demanded.

"Major Volokhov," he replied tonelessly.

"Major who?" Gromov said.

"Volokhov. What's the matter?"

Gromov burst out laughing, and Volokhov and Voronov exchanged worried glances.

"I don't believe it, the brainchild of our wise commanders!" he said through his laughter. "You know, Major, a week ago I was supposed to liaise with you under cover of darkness!"

"What?" Volokhov stiffened.

"I'm telling you, I was ordered by Zdrok – remember Zdrok? – to liaise with you in Degunino for a joint operation under cover of darkness. You're the Flying Guards, aren't you?"

"Well, yes," Volokhov admitted reluctantly.

"There! So we've liaised at last!"

"To hell with you, what operation?"

"God knows. I'm on leave now and on my way to Moscow to take this Private home. To hell with Zdrok, you mean, frankly you've no right to be offended with me."

"Fine, I'm not," Volokhov nodded calmly. "And who are you?"

"Captain Gromov, Commander of the Ninth Unit of the Sixteenth Battalion of the Thirty-fifth Guards Division," he saluted. "So Volokhov, why were you never seen? Is it an invisible detachment?"

"It's a good detachment!" cried fighter Dyldin from his bed, where he was cuddling Nurse Anyuta.

"I see." For some reason Gromov was no longer outraged by this shambles, as if the closer he came to Moscow and his leave, the less he cared about barracks morale.

"You don't see a damn thing, Captain," Volokhov said morosely. "I've heard of you, you're a tooth, aren't you? Slogger Gromov, servant of the Tsar and the soldiers' friend."

"Well, not only that."

"What's the difference. You're a tooth, and you don't understand you're going round in circles like a dog chasing its tail. You think you're doing your duty, but no one needs you, you're just playing a barrel organ. Have a drink. I can't talk to you sober."

* * *

"So how do you plan to do it? Start all over again from scratch?" Gromov asked him an hour later, after they had got through most of a two-litre bottle of vodka.

"No," Volokhov said thoughtfully. "Not necessarily from scratch."

His face was flushed and he was already very drunk, and in the flickering light of the candle his shadow on the ceiling was shaggy and enormous. Voronov sat quietly beside them.

"It's all very simple," he said firmly. "You just need a hundred men who believe in something apart from their bellies, and they'll stop going in a circle and live by human laws, and there'll be a fifth season of the year, and a sixth, and a tenth—"

"And how do you hope to achieve that?" Gromov asked cautiously.

"By keeping moving," Volokhov explained.

"In a circle?"

"No, of course not!" He smiled a mad crafty smile. "Not in a circle! I'm an Alternative, you see, I've studied all the alternatives. A nation's generally formed by war, but in a civil war there can be no victory. It ends, then what? The flight from Egypt was one solution. But if I'd led this lot over the border they wouldn't have wanted to come back! How could anyone lead their people for forty years? Four is enough. And why should I lead them through the desert when we have our forests, our Russian forests! You can see the results! By the second year of our journey they've already learnt some discipline and responsibility..."

The man was clearly insane, but it was pointless trying to argue with him, and Gromov wanted to hear more. "And you've planned your itinerary?" he said.

"What itinerary? It's a long time since we've known what's ours and what is theirs. The main thing is not to go in a circle."

"So what about the legendary Flying Guards? Was it all a lie?"

"Yes, that Zdrok's crap," he grinned childishly. "He's no fool. The son of a bitch knew the best detachment was one that didn't exist, it's very Varangian."

"And Volokhov, the scourge of the Khazars? Aren't they offering a million for your head?"

"You're a freak, Gromov." There was no malice in Volokhov's voice, and he sounded exhausted. He poured himself another glass of vodka and downed it in one gulp, and Gromov took a sip of his. "Why did Odysseus sail for ten years? He had to return to serve Ithaca as its king, and where could he go to in the Mediterranean? There's a lot of it, but ten years? No, it was something else entirely. Why are we stuck between Scylla and Charybdis, Captain? Because we've no Ithaca to return to, it's been occupied by Penelope's suitors! She finishes her weaving and unpicks it, and we weave and unpick, weave and unpick. We must tread our own path there, like treading grapes to make wine. Odysseus wasn't stupid. The reason he didn't turn back when they'd almost reached it was because he knew they weren't ready to return! What could they do after the Trojan war, Captain? People had forgotten the rules, and killed without honour or reason. He had to work out the new rules of life in his wretched tub, before he could return and drive out the suitors. See, Odysseus is Moses! They're the same!" He crowed with laughter. "And Penelope weaves and unpicks, weaves and unpicks. I'm travelling too to my Penelope through the forests and mountains... I've seen her, by the way."

"Who?"

"Zhenka. For Heaven's sake, don't you know her? The Khazars' chief Commissar, Zhenka Dolinskaya, the woman I love?"

"No, I don't."

"Well, I do. Five years ago I almost married her."

Gromov peered at him for a while and said nothing.

"You should have married her," he said at last.

"Yes, well, she was crazy then. Although I must say we had some wonderful battles together. The last time was just a week ago, although she warned me it would be the last. 'It's the only time my spirit has yielded to the flesh,' she said. And it all went on on Russian territory – well, they call it that, but it's no one's of course. I dreamt of us living together in Russia, but in the end we lived together secretly every night for three weeks. Days and nights ran together in the madness. She's a fire woman, I tell you."

Gromov lit a cigarette. "Why didn't you strangle her when you had the chance?"

"You've got a point. But you think they'd have gone home without her? No, old chap, it's all very serious with them, you're either for them or against them. So many times I wanted to break it off with her, and she didn't strangle me or betray me, and she could have, you know. Sometimes it's best to do the decent thing. A dirty victory's a bad start for a nation. I'm a historian, so I know."

"Tell me what she's like, your Penelope."

"Zhenka?" he dragged dreamily on a cigarette. "She's a redhead, and she's hot – she's a hot, hot woman, fuck it. Her temperature's always two points above normal, and she does everything fast. She thinks fast, and she comes fast too, which is a great virtue in a woman, and she never stops coming. She's like a fire that never goes out. She's tall, with grey-blue eyes, and she gets angry – God, she gets angry. And then she calms down instantly. Either she's trained herself or she's just playing at it. And she doesn't walk, she flies. She's twenty-seven, and her tits are something else! And the amazing thing is she loves me! She moans and cries and tells me she loves me, the slut, and it's all a bloody disaster. Be my guest, I tell her, kill me when you win, but you can't kill everyone. You'll be in power for a few years, then the nation will have its say."

"And what does she say?"

"She laughs and cries. You're my beloved fool Vol, she says. She'll be OK if her own people don't kill her. Trust me, Captain, I'm a historian, people like her are usually killed by their own people. As soon as they like someone they kill them, just like that, the bastards."

He poured himself more vodka, gulped it and sighed, and seemed to sober up briefly.

"They're two viruses, Captain," he continued in a hoarse whisper. "Two virus races, two exterminators. They've sharpened their skills on us and we've made them like that. They should have set off like us and kept travelling, like gypsies."

He paused to scratch his chin.

"Your northern friends want to build an empire. There's plenty of positive empire-building in history, but there's no truth or justice with these ones: their imperialism is about smashing others and grabbing for its own sake. Our Khazar friends aren't building an empire of course, oh no, they're building a corp... corporation, and a corporation has one simple principle, to be eff... efficient, that's it. I can't get the words out but my brain's still working. The fewer people there are, the bigger the killing. But they don't kill us, they just want to banish us from life's blessings and let us die quietly. They're not killers, Captain, they're hopeless fighters, alas. If they don't need you, why destroy you? They just say thanks and boot us out."

He paused again.

"And what if these eternal opposites came together and produced a third option, the killer and the bloodsucker in one? The bastards have learnt something after fighting each other for two hundred years – or maybe two hundred thousand, I forget. The time will come when there'll be no one to defend us and we all have to escape to the forests. The forests, Gromov, the forests! Or the steppes. I love the steppes," he went on dreamily. "Especially in the evenings. A lone horse gallops by looking for a new rider. I've never seen one, but there are songs about them…"

Gromov nodded, having long ago stopped listening to his ravings.

"Thank God there's so much of Russia and no one will find us – am I right, Captain? I, Volokhov, commander of the Flying Guards, shall raise my people like chicks in an incubator, mark my words!"

By now Gromov was frightened, and he felt Voronov sitting beside him stiffen. Volokhov was terrifying, he was so drunk he no longer listened to objections or questions. Gromov didn't want to be part of this war between two viruses. He knew what his duty was. His duty was to take Voronov to Moscow and be on his way to Masha.

"Do you know what they're like, Captain?" Volokhov continued, slurring his words. "They're like your Private here. Hey Private, stand up when an officer addresses you!"

Voronov jumped up.

"I was joking!" he hissed. "*Assieds-toi*, Private. Were you given him to look after you, Captain? Aha, Inspector Gurov takes care of his own."

"We're on an assignment," Gromov said curtly.

"Yes, we're on an assignment, comrade Major," Voronov repeated eagerly.

"Shut up, Voronov," Gromov said. "You've no right to address Major Volokhov without permission in the presence of a superior. How many times must I tell you—"

"Teach him, teach him," Volokhov said with a malicious smile. He seemed to have sobered up again a little. "Teach your Private. You haven't grasped yet that most of them are unteachable. Or us,

I should say. We're a surprising race. Maybe five per cent of us are capable of something, the rest go round in circles and talk to trees. They exist in their own landscape, and you can't take them out of it, understand? They're safe there, that's why no one will ever stamp them out, it's terrible how alive they are. But until they change, nothing will start. And the only way for them to change is to keep moving, keep moving..."

Gromov stood up. "Right, Voronov, we're off," he said.

"Why? It's the middle of the night." Volokhov looked up. "Stay here and sleep."

"We have our assignment. Goodbye Major, best of luck."

"Do you know the way? It's a big station, you'll probably get a lift across the field."

After Gromov left, Volokhov felt a strange sense of relief, and even his drunkenness seemed to have evaporated. With the exception of Zhenka, he felt uncomfortable with the Khazars and Varangians, like a foot in a new shoe, but he could talk frankly with Gromov, and perhaps even lead him. He was a Varangian, but he was smart, and he understood military duty. He could have taken him with him, even with that fool of a boy, although he liked Gromov more than he liked his fellow native. But Gromov had his own agenda. What the hell, so did he. Maybe in four years he would reach Moscow and would have learnt along the way who to serve...

3

As Gromov and Voronov walked across the damp dark field, night birds fluttered and twittered in the grass, as if looking for somewhere to settle for the night but unable to find the right spot. Perhaps they too had to keep moving or they would change into something else, Voronov thought, which was why they sounded so sad.

Ahead of them the first muddy streaks of dawn were appearing in the sky, and suddenly a horse galloped past. It disappeared, drumming the earth with its hooves, and the ground shook for a long time afterwards. The horse too had to keep moving and realize its destiny as a horse, not a Varangian or Khazar horse, but a wild native horse of the steppes.

Everything moved at night, Voronov realized, it was wrong to think of night as a time of rest. In July, when the nights were light and the long green dawns lit up the fields of central Russia, the world secretly migrated. The partisans moved along the railway tracks laying explosives, and the natives moved along the same tracks mending them so the circle wouldn't be broken. Hedgehogs and grass snakes rustled, mosquitoes buzzed, and the riderless horse cut across the translucent landscape. The monks locked in their monastery came together for their nightly prayers, cars drove who knows where, soldiers regrouped from one village to another, and clouds raced across the dark sky, and in the gaps between them the stars changed places to confound the astrologers' predictions. This was how the world seemed to Voronov, and he didn't notice his sore feet or his tiredness. He could even hear the mice squeak as they led their dances across the field, and he felt part of all this movement, without sense or purpose. As a city dweller he had never walked in a field at night, and it intoxicated him, like a dog driven crazy by new smells.

Gromov strode on, swatting mosquitoes, and perhaps he heard things Voronov couldn't hear. Constantly alert to danger, he followed the horse and the night birds and the subtle movements of the air, and three months' army training and two years of war didn't teach these things. But he was a poet, and the poet is closer to a soldier than many realize. And at that moment he seemed to sense that they were approaching some frontier beyond which unimaginable things might happen, as if the horse was a messenger from another dimension.

It wasn't too late to turn back, but his duty led him on. There was no sound from the station, and it seemed deserted, with just a row of posts marking the tracks and a spider's web of wires, black against the reddening sky. He smelt the smell of grass and gunpowder for some reason, as if there had been a recent battle here, and he knew and loved this smell. But what battle? Who had been here?

There wasn't a living soul at the station. A timetable hung in a wooden frame next to the door, showing trains to Shabalino, Zabava and Vasyatino. There was one Moscow train that appeared to have just left, and the next was due at five the next morning. He didn't fancy waiting a day. Maybe they could get there on the local ones. But judging from the neglected state of the place none had passed for a long time. There were just a few rusty carriages on the track and a decrepit steam engine ahead of them, and there seemed little chance anything would stop.

"No one's here, are they?" Voronov said, forgetting he wasn't supposed to open his mouth in the presence of his superior.

But there was someone there: Gromov could see a light behind a window on the first floor of the dilapidated station building.

"Wait here, I'll go and see," he said.

He entered the empty waiting room, with its broken ticket-office window and rows of broken chairs, and heard a tapping noise above, like the sound of someone typing with one finger.

He felt his way upstairs in the darkness with his torch turned off, so as not to alarm the invisible typist, and pushed open a heavy metal door into a long corridor with a little light streaming through another door, which was half open. He went in, and saw an ancient telegraph machine such as he had seen in the Museum of the Revolution and, hunched over it, a soldier tapping out a message, wearing the pointed felt helmet of the old Bolshevik Red Army cavalry. Beside him on the floor lay piles of yellow paper, evidently with the replies.

He had to step out of the room and pinch his elbow hard, and when he returned the telegraphist was still there, tapping the keys and moving his lips as he read the tape pouring from the antediluvian machine, then throwing them on the floor and tapping away again.

Deciding he must have lost his mind, he ran down to Voronov, who was waiting obediently at the door. To hell with subordination. "Quick, Voronov!" he whispered with a dry mouth.

They went up the stairs together as quietly as possible, and found the telegraphist sitting in the same place, tapping out his endless messages.

For some reason Voronov seemed to find it quite natural and wasn't surprised at all. "He's a telegraphist – what's wrong, comrade Captain?" he whispered, and his calmness shocked Gromov more than the spectacle of this phantom.

"You mean he's been sitting here all these years?" he asked in horror.

"Well it's just, I heard..." he hesitated. "Apparently a lot of people have seen these cavalrymen from the Revolution, it's like the Flying Dutchman, only they're real. They're still fighting, because the Civil War isn't over for them yet. When it is, they'll be demobilized."

"Goddammit," Gromov said, trying to get a grip of himself and not let the madness take over. Perhaps someone was making a film, or the fellow had no uniform and had been given this old one. He stepped decisively into the room and tapped the man's shoulder, and felt the real nap of his real army greatcoat under his hand.

"Yes?" The man turned and looked at him with red, swollen eyes. "Are you the new shift, comrade?"

Not likely, thought Gromov, with visions of himself sitting there at the telegraph desk like Hercules holding up the sky for Atlas.

"No, I'm not. I've an urgent message for you, comrade."

The man looked disappointed. He might have been twenty or forty, and his face was covered in stubble, one of those baked yellow peasant faces stamped with endless exhaustion. "They're attacking us everywhere, see. I've no time, no backup—"

"Send this message for me please, to Seventh-Level Inspector Gurov of the General Staff," Gromov said, surprised by his composure. "'Mission not accomplished stop. Take full responsibility stop. Bound for Moscow stop. Captain Gromov.'"

"You're going to Moscow?" The man tore himself from the keys. "What's the news from Moscow?"

"I've no idea, I'm just going there."

The man tapped out the message, and somehow seemed to know where to send it and the address of Gurov's unit.

"It's sent. Will you wait for the reply?" he said.

"If possible. What are they writing about?"

"All sorts of things, the retreat from Kharkov, the famine on the Volga, mutinies on the Don, the bastards. There'll be a train taking coal to Moscow soon, platform three. Wait, comrade, here's your reply."

Gromov froze, prepared for anything.

"'Never mind stop. Proceed Moscow stop. Will sort it out stop. Inspector Gurov,'" the man read slowly. "'PS Idiot Captain even though tooth stop. Take care.'"

"Well, well," Gromov said, stunned.

"If you pass through Kasimov, tell them I'm working hard and not to expect me back," the man said.

"And your name?"

"They'll know it." He waved his arm, and the machine spewed out another message and he returned to his tapes.

Gromov slipped out of the building with Voronov into the July night, and the leaves and grass of the great damp earth seemed to be signalling to each other that it was summer and they were alive.

The steam engine puffed on the tracks, attached to five ancient carriages, one of which was open. Gromov climbed in first. There was no coal there, just two bundles of hay, as if put there specially for them. Voronov stretched out on one and fell asleep instantly, and Gromov lay with his hands behind his head, staring at the dark ceiling and out at the dawn.

The train set off and slowed at a hill. Summer lightning flashed and another horse galloped by, and as the sound of its hooves died away in the distance, he smelt the damp grass and looked out at the stars. It was good in the no man's land of the steppes, in the Civil War days of the Revolution.

Chapter Eight
"Vasilenko Syndrome"

There had been a nuclear power plant once in the town of Alabino. Then at the end of the last century there was an accident. Either it was caused by an earthquake – although there had never been earthquakes there before – or it was the managers' carelessness, but the whole area had been sealed off, with guards on all the roads and barbed-wire security fences, and the five thousand inhabitants of this young scientific centre evacuated who knows where.

After the catastrophe, the collapse of Russia soon followed, and maybe the catastrophe was the first sign of the collapse. Ten years passed, and visitors were allowed in, and it was always claimed such places weren't dangerous, but no one knew anything for sure. The nature and consequences of the accident were shrouded in mystery, and those who came close to explaining them either did away with themselves or vanished without trace.

Anka knew very little about the place, and to be honest she had thought they were going to some other Alabino, but when they had to crawl under the fence stretching all the way into the forest, she realized Vasily Ivanovich had brought her to the prohibited zone.

"We shouldn't be here, Vasily Ivanovich," she told him reproachfully. "I've heard it's contaminated for two hundred kilometres."

"No, it isn't, outsiders don't know what it's like. You can see where you've brought me, then go home. I'll be safe here."

They walked for a while through the forest, then the trees began to thin out, and through the shafts of light between the birches and maples she could see some tall white tower blocks. From a distance they looked quite smart, but as they drew closer she could see they were peeling and dilapidated, with smashed doors and windows.

The stadium in the centre of town was overgrown with trees, and Joes lay around on the grass. Alabino was their place. Ordinary people were afraid to go there, and Geiger counters showed ten times above normal radiation levels, but it didn't bother the Joes, and they came to no harm there.

Anka was afraid too, but Vasily Ivanovich reassured her and was even offended. "It's a safe place, I wouldn't let you take me somewhere dangerous."

They were all happy to see him, but asked him nothing about himself – it wasn't the done thing with them. They hardly talked to each other at all in fact; they all knew each other too well and didn't like to be inquisitive.

"So why doesn't everyone come here?" she asked him.

"Some think the round-up will be over soon and they'll sit it out where they are. I've warned as many as I can, but you can't force them to leave if they don't want to."

On all sides the elements had taken over, and the blind ungovernable force of nature had burst into the town, with trees springing up in the yards of the buildings and the children's playground, and suckers breaking through the asphalt. Visitors didn't come to the town itself, only to its distant approaches, to fish in the river Alabyanka for mutant fishes. They didn't catch them to eat, just to look at, but they caught nothing abnormal, just the occasional normal roach.

Anka swung on the creaking swing in the playground, and it reminded her of the old playground at home, and she had to stop before she burst into tears. In the Park of Culture and Rest a big wheel turned slowly in the breeze, and the child Joes meekly peered up at it with smiles of amazement. There were things here for the children, but they were all rusty and broken, like the children themselves. Anka wandered around the kindergarten, where the Joes had moved in. They hadn't touched or damaged anything, and the little cupboards full of dolls' clothes were still there, with a newspaper on the wall from the day before the accident. But everything was terribly neglected and shabby, and the paddling pool outside was thick with sedge, where a plastic toy goldfish with a crown floated in the mud. Such toys weren't made now: the new ones were all guns and soldiers and little models of oil-workers.

She didn't know much about the changes in Russia that had started before her birth, but after reaching Alabino she realized it was possible the whole country suffered from Vasilenko Syndrome. It no longer had a past or a future, and its history and plans had crumbled like a rotting papyrus – people just did things and went here and there, and seemed to have forgotten why.

The Joes had picked the Alabino zone long before the purge. It was their heaven, where no one shouted at them and no one went anywhere or did anything. They sang their ballads and lay on the grass, or wandered along the overgrown roads and the banks of the river and through the empty scientific institutes, from which all the apparatus had been removed, and they made their homes in the abandoned flats and built makeshift huts for themselves in the forest.

Here, in this place that belonged to them, they returned to their old pursuits. They had kept moving because they didn't want to farm someone else's land, but the Joes in Alabino could talk to the earth and things grew wonderfully for them, with five-headed dandelions and potatoes as big as a child's head. A group of researchers had visited in protective suits with a mass of precautions, and concluded that it was all due to radiation. But it had nothing to do with radiation, the Joes simply left the earth in peace and it flourished for them.

It would be wrong to think though that no one was in charge in Alabino. Ekaterina was in charge.

Ekaterina was their Guard, a large powerful woman who had worked with Joes for a long time, because her heart moved her to it. She bandaged their wounds and found jobs for them and kept relative order in the town. The occasional Joe might stay put, but there weren't many permanent residents and most tended to wander off, since wandering was in their blood, and all those who came to rest and recuperate called it "going to Ekaterina". She took everyone in, and was strict but fair, and she enjoyed living in this little sliver of Russia that was the last bastion of Soviet life. She had visited from her native Petersburg once and had stayed, moving into a tower block with a rusty sign saying "Glory to Labour!" on the roof.

"Now then, we'd better see Ekaterina," Vasily Ivanovich mumbled after they arrived. "We've this rule that everyone who comes must go straight to see her."

Anka walked reluctantly through evening Alabino, past abandoned cars and overflowing skips. She didn't want to see Ekaterina, she wanted to lie in the grass and warm herself in the sunset and doze, and not worry about the police. More than anything she wanted to go home. She had brought Vasily Ivanovich here out of harm's way, and he didn't need her now and could look after himself.

On the door of Ekaterina's flat was a clumsy drawing, like the giraffe at his shelter, of a strange creature that looked like a woman at a stove, holding some things like saucepans and a white roll of what could have been lavatory paper or a bandage, with "Ekaterina" scrawled at the bottom in careful childish letters.

He knocked, and a powerful voice called, "Yes?"

"It's Vasily Ivanovich, Ekaterina," he said, beckoning Anka inside.

"Who's with you?" she called from the kitchen, where – to judge from the smell – she was boiling fish. There was more than enough in the river to feed the whole town.

"She can see through walls!" he whispered excitedly.

Ekaterina came out, very grand and imposing, with greying hair pulled back in a tight bun.

"You've brought your granddaughter?" she demanded.

"She's come with me, Ekaterina Nikolavna," he gabbled. "See, I lived with her family for two years, a good family, and when the round-up started I decided to leave, and she wanted to come with me, so I wouldn't be on my own. I didn't want her to, I said she shouldn't, and now she's brought me she can go back—"

"You wanted to help the old man, did you, dear? And I suppose you'll tell people everything when you get back?" Ekaterina asked her with an unpleasant smile.

"No no, you don't know what she's like, she saved my life!" Vasily Ivanovich said, looking scared.

"I can see what she's like," she said. "Come to the kitchen then, I've made fish soup."

She was boiling it in a huge vat on a gas stove converted to run on wood – Anka had seen a stove like this from the last war, at the Museum of Moscow Life. There had been no gas or electricity in Alabino since the accident.

Soon Joes had gathered at the window, and Ekaterina poured bowls of soup for them and passed them through. They ate gratefully, some with spoons, some gulping straight from the bowls. There was no salt in Alabino, but visiting Joes would sometimes bring a little, and she would pick some up when she went home every winter for her annual inspections.

"So why did you run away with him, little girl?" she asked when Anka had finished. It didn't taste nice, but she was grateful for something hot.

"I thought it would be dangerous for him to travel alone," she wavered, scared of this severe woman who seemed to be accusing her of something.

"It's dangerous for you too though, isn't it?" Ekaterina said in a quiet, unfriendly tone. "Aren't your parents worried about you?"

"Yes, they are," she said. "But we couldn't hide him at the dacha: they'd have found him. He had to leave Moscow."

"And where will you go now?"

"I'd like to go home, if you can tell me the way."

"Of course I can, but I don't think they'll want you."

"Why?" She was aghast.

"They might arrest you for helping a Joe escape: the police have probably visited your parents already and reported you as a little vagrant. You'd better stay away if you don't want to go to jail."

Anka hated the revolting diminutive "little vagrant", and there was something menacing about Ekaterina's large soft arms with their dimpled elbows.

"There's nowhere else for me to go," she said. "I don't want to leave home for ever, and my father will make sure I don't go to jail."

"Nonsense," she said. "Your father can't do anything."

"Don't talk about my father like that," Anka said firmly. She didn't know why she was angry with Vasily Ivanovich for bringing her, or why she was saying these things, and guessed it was because she enjoyed being the only benefactor in town and was jealous of her for making a far greater sacrifice, despite her age.

Ekaterina stared at her in silence.

"Anyone would have done the same," Anka said. "He's so helpless – sorry, Vasily Ivanovich…"

"Fine, we'll sleep on it, morning's wiser than night."

She had always hated it when her parents said this, because like all anxious children she could never sleep, and her head would swarm with terrible visions of earthquakes and the painting *Madness* from her children's encyclopaedia.

"I'm not tired – can I go for a walk?" she said.

"Of course you can, you're quite safe here," Ekaterina said. "We need to talk, Vasily Ivanovich."

* * *

In the old sports stadium a young elk thoughtfully threw back its horns to gaze at the new moon. It wasn't afraid of people, perhaps because it realized they weren't real people.

Anka strolled in the cool of the evening past Joes singing folk ballads round fires – she didn't understand everything, since they sang mainly in their own language – then she went into the forest and turned back feeling frightened. The whole of Alabino smelt of tree bark and wet earth, like the forest, and she stayed out as long as she could to avoid going back.

As an honoured guest, Vasily Ivanovich had been given a room to himself in Ekaterina's shabby four-room flat. She kept it clean: there was a piano and some furniture and a few bits and pieces the Joes had knocked up for her, and they could even wash there. Anka was given an old patched inflatable mattress to sleep on, and could hear her in the kitchen talking to Vasily Ivanovich in the candlelight. She picked up snatches of what they were saying and wanted to go to the door and listen, but the floorboards creaked and they would have stopped. And soon her tiredness got the better of her and she fell asleep, and dreamt of pale transparent people in a dead Alabino, stretching out their thin hands to her and begging her to help them, but she couldn't, it was too late.

"Why did you bring the little girl, Vasily Ivanovich?" Ekaterina was saying quietly.

"I didn't bring her, she brought me, Ekaterina. Didn't you hear what she said?"

"She wouldn't have gone with you though if you hadn't wanted her to. Tell me the truth, Vasily Ivanovich, is there something between you?"

"Listen to you, she's like a daughter to me!" he said, horrified. "I had a daughter once like her, a wonderful little girl, I've forgotten her name—"

"You've forgotten everything, Vasily Ivanovich. A woman's soul is a mystery. If she left with you she must love you. Don't you know the girl's a Khazar? You can't fool me, I'm a Guard, it's my job to know these things. Didn't you notice anything when you lived with her family?"

"How can they be Khazars, Ekaterina Nikolavna? They all left Moscow when the war started – and our Guard in Moscow met her!"

"Gurov? When did Gurov meet her?" she frowned.

"He came to the flat to warn me to leave, and spoke to her parents."

"What was he thinking of? She's obviously a Seventh-generation Khazar, he should have spotted that you're a couple!" Ekaterina snapped. "It's all wrong, Vasily Ivanovich, the earth can't take any more. You know a Khazar can't travel with a Joe. Haven't we guarded against it for a thousand years? You should have seen it coming."

"I've seen everything, Gurov set off the falcon," he said with inexpressible sadness. "But I swear to you by the stove and the apple tree that it won't be because of me."

"Well, she can't stay here. You must take her to Degunino and let them take a look at her there."

He froze. "But why? She's only just come, let her rest!"

"There's nothing for Khazars here. You must go to Degunino tomorrow, and if they say she's no threat she can go home."

"But there's fighting in Degunino. I don't care about myself, but what about her?"

"You know quite well that there's been no fighting for a long time and things will soon go back to normal, so long as you don't go out with Khazars."

"But I'm not!" Vasily Ivanovich repeated; anyone else would have become angry long ago, but Joes didn't know this emotion.

"Stay out of it and I'll talk to her tomorrow. It's time for you to sleep."

But he couldn't sleep. If it wasn't for Vasilenko Syndrome he would have done away with himself long ago, but the Joes didn't know how to do this either.

* * *

"Vasily Ivanovich can't stay in Alabino, he has to go to Degunino," Ekaterina told Anka the next morning as kindly as she could. She found it hard to talk to Khazars. She really did have an infallible instinct for them, and there was no way she could like them, but she did her best not to show it and even smiled at her.

"I've heard of it, there are battles there."

"Battles don't worry us," she said brusquely. "What worries us is if something happens to our stove and apple tree, and Vasily Ivanovich is our specialist, he knows how to talk to them."

"That's right, Anka," he nodded. "I have to look at the stove or Degunino will perish."

"And the apple tree," she reminded him. "After that he can continue his journey on his own and you can go home. I've no one here to send with him."

"It's best if we leave, Anechka," he said.

"Of course, Vasily Ivanovich, we're obviously not wanted here," she said.

"Very wise, Anka, he's made the right decision," said Ekaterina.

She wanted to tell her he had never decided anything and she took all the decisions herself, but she didn't want to argue with her.

"You can leave after breakfast," Ekaterina said. "It's about five hundred kilometres. You must catch the train to Koposovo, then take a boat down the river or walk through the forest."

Anka wanted to refuse breakfast, but she swallowed her pride; they had a long journey ahead of them, and as they set off along the concrete road through the prohibited zone into the trees, she felt a strange sense of relief known to anxious people for whom home was always temporary, and only the road was theirs.

Birds warbled and the forest was full of woodland smells and berries. Vasily Ivanovich panted behind with his rucksack. "It's better here, isn't it, Vasily Ivanovich?" she said. "'On through the forest in the morning dew, the sun's so bright and the sky's so blue!'" she sang, and he followed in silence. It wasn't his song.

Chapter Nine
Family Day

1

The building where Gromov had lived as a child overlooked the cabbage field of a collective farm, beyond which was the ring road, and between the field and the road stood three tall chimneys. The chimneys might have been a cement factory, but he didn't want to know, because they would have lost their magic if he knew. From the balcony on the seventh floor he could see the whole of this quiet suburban area, and the mysterious L-shaped construction of the farm elevator glowing in the sunset. Moscow had ended here in those days. He loved to watch people returning from work, and for some reason it was always spring in his memories. It was probably one particular spring evening he remembered, with the sharp smell of dust and bursting buds, and all his other memories had blended into it. It's always one winter morning we remember, and the icy walk to school, or one spring evening on the balcony, or one hot June day, with a blessed draft through the blinds cooling our burning skin.

A railway line had run past the building, and the trains would puff across the cabbage field to a level crossing. The iron controller's voice would waft to the balcony, and the engines would travel slowly, dragging behind them two or three big freight wagons – it was easy to jump in. Some boys from the building had hitched a ride one day and disappeared for good, and it was discussed in whispers in the building. No one knew where the line went. Once, when he was ten, Gromov decided to find out and jumped on, and the train crossed a little railway bridge that looked as though it would collapse under its weight, then wound past fields and a wood, and on to some heavy concrete gates that opened as it approached, ending up at the freight station, with white lights in metal cones. Where the train had come from he didn't know, and he guessed that one day he would find out.

He realized the whole of his country was tangled up in this vast network of tracks, with its unpredictable crossings and destinations, and that if you boarded this train it would take you to wonderful places. The great iron and steel machines operated by their own laws, and would reveal your destination to you when you got there. You could set off north or south, and the track would lead you there. He had been given a toy train, but never played with it – he preferred real ones, and he thought about them constantly. He imagined the mysterious unsleeping controllers keeping watch at the crossings in their cosy cabins, sleeping in brief snatches during the day on wooden trestle beds. Some things absorb years of human tiredness; sometimes during his army training he would accompany the battalion's duty officer on his trips, and would rest on the bed where he had slept and feel the tiredness soaked into it. The railwayman on duty would sleep for a few hours, but asleep and awake he would dream of engines, points and signals, drinking glasses of black tea in iron railway holders, nibbling railway sugar and pressing buttons. Anyone who jumped on one of the trains clanking past Gromov's building would slip from one dimension into another, and it would take all responsibility from them. Time would be ruled by timetables. Everything would be decided for you, and you could stop thinking of pointless things such as where to go or stop, and concentrate on putting your hands behind your head and being rocked by its movements.

Gromov knew that when he returned to Moscow on leave he would arrive by train, but he didn't know his flat would be in another part of town. Moscow had changed, and was now divided into the upmarket areas, the quiet ones and the slums, and the building where he had grown up was now far beyond the pockets of its old residents. The farm had been sold off to private property developers, mainly former oil magnates who had been investing in property since the collapse of oil prices, and the field was now the "Golden Keys" development, one of Moscow's most prestigious districts. His parents had had to leave the flat and move to one near the ring-road, and it was an hour's journey by bus and underground from the station where he and Voronov arrived on the old train from the Civil War days.

"Here we are then: good luck, Voronov," he said, shaking his hand. "You can find your own way home, I wasn't told to drop you at your mother's."

"I can find it, comrade Captain. The comrade Inspector said I wouldn't be needed until further notice!" Voronov said happily, still unable to believe he was in Moscow.

"I don't expect you'll go back to the army. It's probably for the best, the army doesn't need someone with a brain. Well, I've no complaints about you. Thanks for helping me, take care of yourself."

"Thanks, comrade Captain, I'll phone you," Voronov jabbered pointlessly, because he didn't have his number. But in his heart he was already home now, and as he walked to the bus stop he forgot Gromov and never thought of him again.

He was free, Gromov thought, with a slight feeling of contempt, turning his back on him. He straightened his kit bag and cap, breathing in the smell of dust and wet asphalt, then set off in a light drizzle for the underground. So many times he had imagined returning and breathing this smell, and now he felt nothing. He hadn't returned from victory: he had nothing to celebrate, and his return made no sense. He wasn't returning anyway, he was on leave, and he had the long journey to Central Asia ahead of him. He hadn't heard from Masha for months, and wasn't sure he wanted to stop with his parents rather than travel straight on, but he had to check out Moscow first.

The rubbery smell of the underground was the same, as were the blue-and-white trains on the Circle Line, but there were no Joes in the last carriage now, and for some reason even the pretty girls in summer dresses clutching folded umbrellas didn't cheer him up. He probably hadn't acclimatized yet from the Red Army telegraphist and the strange railway carriage to normal Moscow, and he felt angry with it for being so normal, while they were spilling their blood for it at the Front. They had crawled through mud, sat in trenches, senselessly captured and abandoned village after village, and it was as if none of it had happened or was needed here. They played out their roles as Muscovites, he played out his as cannon fodder, and the strange thing was that he had chosen this role for himself because he was sick of being a Muscovite.

He got out of the train, deciding to walk the rest of the way. Perhaps walking would calm him. He hadn't phoned his parents; he still couldn't believe he was home, and he wanted to surprise them.

* * *

They were alive, thank God, although existing in a barely human state, and he couldn't accept it. It was always hard for the soldier on leave to adjust to being home, and he was reminded of the poem he had read when he still read poems, about the returning soldier putting on his pre-war clothes and finding an old phone number in the pocket. It was easy for the soldier of a victorious army to fit back into civilian life after his hardships; Gromov had learnt to endure these hardships, and even found a strange pleasure in them. But his return now from that world to the normal one was almost unbearable.

In battle he didn't ask why he scrambled up muddy hillsides, slept with his clothes on, kicked his men into battle, jumped up at three in the morning and marched them through the rain. The army was the army, and he had joined up because war gave purpose to his life, and duty and courage were their own reward. But he only had to come back and sit at the table drinking soup with his parents for the stuffy hell of his old life to engulf him. To enjoy the soup and his parents and the roof over his head he needed to have achieved something, but he had achieved nothing, and couldn't justify it with poetry. He couldn't bear his parents' wretched existence and their kindness. They would have loved him however he acquitted himself, just as his dog threw himself at him without caring about his achievements, just as they earned their pathetic money so they could eat their soup. Their lives dragged endlessly on without purpose, and what had no end had no purpose, and what had no purpose had no end. Wasn't this what the crazy Volokhov was talking about?

"Eat some bread with your soup, dear." His mother gazed at him with adoring eyes, touched to see him eating, just as it touched her when he yawned or sneezed. They simply loved him: that was the most terrible thing, that was what he had run away from. All his childhood she had told him to eat bread with his soup, convinced for some reason that it was good for the digestion. His father sat looking at him, knowing he should ask him about the war, but knowing nothing about it, because it wasn't on television. They seemed to think he had simply served in the army without making any contact with the enemy, even though he had written to them a few times in the first year, when there were battles, terrible battles. But they just believed whatever they wanted to, and couldn't worry about their son. They had lived through the Soviet era, then everything had collapsed into ruins, and now the ruins too were collapsing, and they thought they had a right to a quiet life and their healthy senile egotism.

"You'll have to register, you know," his father said.

"What do you mean?"

"Didn't they tell you? There's a new law, everyone has to register now, it was on the radio," his mother explained. ("On the radio" clinched every argument for her.) "You must register at the passport department of the Commanders' office today, or there'll be problems for us. And you need a certificate from the clinic too."

Gromov had stopped being angry and almost laughed. "What certificate?"

"You need an X-ray, otherwise they'll take you off the housing register and they might take us off too. Your father knows someone at work who didn't get his X-ray and his family was almost evicted." (Her stories about their friends and neighbours always ended with some happy miracle.)

"But don't they know I'm in the army?"

"You're in the army there, here you're on the register," his father said didactically. "The Kapoviches' son moved out to a flat in the centre and registered himself and his wife there, but he had to have his X-ray here. The house captain told them he was living there, but he still had to register in both places."

"So why don't you tell us what you've been doing? You never tell us anything," his mother said, putting a pan of fried potatoes on the table.

She didn't want him to tell her anything of course, and was terrified it would break their cocoon. Asking him about the war was simply a ritual, and everyone from government officials to Joes needed rituals. Perhaps in a thousand years' time people would describe it as a sort of heroism. A father would say, "Serve, son!" and describe his experiences at the Front, and the son would say, "I serve, Dad!" and warm his old heart, and his mother would weep.

"What can I say – practically nothing's happening now," he said.

"You're a skeleton – are they feeding you?" she said. "Skeleton" was his grandmother's word, and at her memory she shed a few tears. "Why do you never write?"

"I'll write when there's something to say, Mum."

"By the way, did you hear Shelaputina's divorced?" she said. Shelaputina had been in his class at school and her family had lived in their old building; he had no idea what she looked like now.

"Really?" he said.

"Yes, she just left him. Her mother told me, I met her on the bus. Her parents moved here. Most of the parents from your class are here now, and the children are living in the centre."

"It has the infrastructure, you see," his father said solemnly.

"But we've got the shops on our doorstep here, and a nice clinic," his mother added.

Gromov didn't know what to say next; a minute later he might have asked them about the weather.

He left the table to do the dishes, but she stopped him and did them herself with exaggerated enthusiasm, and he caught himself feeling like a character in a computer adventure game, where you had to perform one task in each room before leaving, although of course you could stay in the same room for ever. You knew what you had to do to complete your task and go to the next room, and do something there. He had done everything that had to be done in the kitchen. He had talked to his father, he had talked to his mother, and they seemed to be waiting reproachfully for him to go to the next level and visit the Commander's office.

His mother saw him off in the lobby. The flat was a shabbier version of their old one, and the mirror was smeared with grime.

"Look at you, brush your hair!" she said fondly.

Lord, he had nothing to brush! His hair was cropped almost to the skull, as required in the Russian army. He was a regimental commander, a fighting officer, who had buried his comrades, led his unit into battle, endured his superiors' curses, the Cossacks' shindigs and his subordinates' laziness. So many times he had almost died, eating nothing for days but a half-nibbled biscuit and forgetting what it was like to sleep in clean sheets – and she still told him to brush his hair, as she used to when he left for school. And he should have been touched, but to his horror he felt nothing but a dull irritation.

"Mind how you go," she said as he left.

* * *

The district he walked through back to the station, after just two hours at home, was as rundown and shabby as the flat. Even the people were old and shabby, and the only young one he passed was a huge fat boy he used to see in their old district, shopping with his mother at University Market. The market had long since closed, but he remembered his tiny mother loading the boy with the bags: she had to buy a lot of food as he never stopped eating.

There were the usual long queues of old people at the shops and clinics, registering for every possible event in life, and he thought of the Commanders' office almost with relief. The whole thing was pointless, but at least military pointlessness had its own rules, rather than the unacknowledged pointlessness that seemed to be creeping into every corner of life here. What he hadn't reckoned on was that the Commanders' office was part of Moscow life too, and was far from the war.

It was in the administrative district, not far from the Red Gates. All government institutions had gradually migrated here, and moved into the Stalinist buildings from the early Thirties which had run the military, penal and legal departments of the Stalin empire. The only non-administrative feature of the place was the children's playground opposite the Commanders' office, perhaps to inspire the children with the soldiers' example so they would follow them into the army. There were just five old residential buildings, all occupied by officials, who would leave for work every morning with their flasks and sandwiches. They could have gone home for lunch, but this way anyone looking in during the lunch hour would see the official eating, and the look of disgust on his gobbling face would make them retreat in fear and wait outside until the sacred ritual was over.

Gromov knocked on a door saying "Registration of Personnel", but everyone was on a break. The next door he tried was locked, but at the third one he was shown into an office where a civilian official fastidiously examined his uniform, measuring the distance between the stars on his shoulder, and examining the stripes on his trousers. He felt like a horse being examined by a gypsy at a market. He drew the line at removing his cap and dropping his trousers, so the man could check he was wearing the regulation underpants, without patterns.

"I came to register, not for a check-up," he growled.

"Who are you to give me orders!" the man said in a coarse market-woman's voice. "If I tell you to spread your buttocks, you spread them! If I tell you to march on your arse, you march on it!"

"How dare you insult an officer, you rat!" Gromov asked quietly.

"I know you're an officer!" the man shouted. "Fighting officers, spilling your blood – we know how you spill your blood in bed with your tarts! That's where you're fighting!" He jabbed a finger at a map covered in little red-and-yellow flags. "No one knows what's ours and what's theirs! I'll put it in your file that you refused to remove your trousers!"

Gromov could have knocked him senseless with one blow, but he didn't fancy a fight in the office. He went out, and the man didn't follow him; he wasn't interested in punishing his odd visitor, just kicking him around a bit.

This time the Registration office was open, and sitting inside was a bent old woman with glasses on her bent nose.

"I've come to register," he said.

She said nothing.

"I've come to register!" he repeated more loudly.

She raised her head and looked at him as a soldier looks at a flea.

"I heard you," she said, jumping from her chair and straightening up; she barely reached his belt. "The lord and master of creation wants to register! You call yourself a Russian officer! Russian officers weren't like you in my day! Leave immediately and come back when you know how to address a lady!" She stamped her foot. "A lady stands before you and you don't offer her a seat! Our wonderful army abandons position after position, while our old people and children in the rear wear their fingers to the bone making you coats!"

The door opened and a plump colonel came in, and Gromov sighed with relief at seeing someone in uniform.

"What are you doing here, Klavdia Ivanovna?" he asked her wearily.

"I came for some papers," she told him. "You weren't here, and this suspicious young man—"

"Don't mind her, Captain, she's our archivist. She's very patriotic but completely crazy."

She went out, weakly banging the door, holding her nose as she passed Gromov and spitting at him.

"You see who we have to work with, Captain?" he asked. "She's lost her mind and we can't get her locked up, and she works in the archives writing people's registration documents. I told them to send someone younger, but there wasn't anyone! What's your regiment?"

Gromov handed him his documents.

"Tomorrow you must go for your X-ray," he said. "You need to pay fifteen roubles first at the accounts office. Door seventeen."

"But I'm only staying two days," Gromov said, hoping to persuade the officer not to ruin his leave for nothing.

"Two days, three days, what's the difference," he replied. "Pay the money and get the receipt and your X-ray and come back with them. Don't drag it out, Captain, you're supposed to register on the day of your arrival, but I'll give you extra time because of Klavdia Ivanovna." He winked, and Gromov saluted and left.

It was drizzling, and the playground opposite smelt of wet poplars. He didn't feel like going home yet. The town had known better days, and he could remember them well. The smell of wet asphalt and poplars every summer would remind him that the dull two-coloured poetry of winter had ended, and it was time to think in other words and move in another rhythm. So many times he had dreamt of returning to Moscow and breathing its smells, and now there was nothing to return to. Even the smells smelt ersatz; everything was fading, even though it was only July, and he realized that anyone who left would discover they could never return. Yet being free of this last illusion made it no easier.

He cast around for somewhere to go, and made his way to the city centre, where there was a club he used to visit in his old life called the Birch Twigs, whose signature dish was a cheap salad topped with a bunch of parsley to look like twigs. He had to see if it still existed – not to wallow in nostalgia, but to find people there who might respect him.

* * *

A friend had written that the club had moved from Prospekt Mira to the New Arbat. All of Moscow's restaurants, casinos and night spots now huddled in the Arbat, spilling through its maze of side streets and onto the New Arbat highway, turning the sky gold at night and glittering in the wet asphalt.

There were no cheap student clubs now, since there were no longer any poor students left. Almost all education had to be paid for, and was the preserve of the lucky few with large incomes. Two free places in every faculty of Moscow University were offered as prizes in a TV quiz show, but that didn't require brains, just smartness and sex appeal.

The area around the Red Gates looked as if it had been hit by a tornado, with damp tents flapping in the wind and twenty-four-hour food stalls. There were no kebab stalls now that most of the Caucasians had been thrown out of the city, but he bought an appetizing-looking pasty. He took one bite, and it tasted sour and mouldy, and he spat it out; that would teach him you couldn't buy anything edible for fifteen roubles.

On his way to the Arbat he didn't pass any Joes, just a couple of cops dragging a beggar from the underpass. He walked on, with a growing sense that his life had nothing in common with this life here that Father Nikolai had described. But in the end hadn't he been fighting for happy children and beautiful women here? Unfortunately he didn't pass any happy children or beautiful women, and everywhere he looked he saw how polarized it had become. Khazars used to live side by side with Russians, and the rich next to the poor, and although the poor weren't as smelly as the Joes, who knows, maybe new bands of them were gathering in the outskirts and becoming partisans. Gromov had obeyed the stratifying law of war, like a giant separator, but no one in the army wanted to avenge the poor; their existence merely continued on another plane.

The Birch Twigs was now in what had been the old Arbat grocery, where he used to buy pies and grape juice as a child. He had loved the cool of the place in summer, and its grey marble floors and big transparent cones of juice. Now, however, the burly security guard refused to let him in, explaining that people came here to relax from the war – as though they spent the rest of their time digging trenches around Moscow. Cursing to himself, he was about to turn away when his friend Luzgin from the old days rushed from the depths of the building and grabbed him in a hug, then had a word with the guard and pulled him inside.

The club was just the same as it had been on Prospekt Mira, with the same roughly painted underwater scene on the walls and red-green fish and seaweed, and the same Shurik singing the same light songs Gromov had long ago forbidden himself to listen to. He used to come here and hear Shurik sing when he was with Masha, and had drunk with him. He loved those who didn't cling to life, and there was a freedom and lightness about his songs. Maybe the boys and girls he was singing about had never existed, but they were about happy people living happy uncluttered bohemian lives. He had never been like this, but had always wanted to be, and Shurik represented the type in its purest form, fluffy as a dandelion, with his slender neck and mop of blond hair. He seemed to recognize Gromov and nodded at him, as he nodded at everyone, and was genuinely happy for anyone to come and hear him. And as he sang, Gromov thought of courtyards on summer evenings and people in big old Moscow flats, from which everyone had been evicted...

"What are you up to, Grom?" Luzgin tugged at his arm. "What are you doing here – have you been demobbed?"

"There's a war on, Luzga, how could I be demobbed?"

"It's still going on, is it? God, you weren't wounded, were you? Or are you on leave?"

"I'm on leave."

"You always were a laconic bastard. Take a break, go wild! There aren't many of us here today, you've seen them all. So where's that girlfriend of yours? She was tall, I remember—"

"She was evacuated."

"But why? They evacuated everyone at the start of the war, of course, but it was just a false alarm, she could have stayed."

"She had to leave, her building burnt down."

"Yes, but she'd get a flat if she came back, and so would you as an officer. So tell me, when will it end? Will we break them? Or is it a military secret?"

"We'll break them all right."

"And are you still writing there?"

"No, I haven't written for a long time."

"That's good, I suppose you're collecting ideas so you can write them up afterwards like Babel's *Notes of a Cavalryman*. What rank are you, by the way?"

"Captain."

"I can't see a damn thing in the dark, but you haven't changed a bit, Grom, I'd recognize you anywhere. Wait, let me read you this I've just written."

Luzgin read. He was in the habit of showering people with his poetry, and it horrified Gromov to remember doing the same thing, reading his latest poems to anyone who would listen. Luzgin's was the poem of a good Moscow boy on the wrong side of thirty, witty and ironic and with a slightly histrionic ending, which somewhat reduced the effect. There was nothing of him in it, which was just as well, since he and everyone else knew it was best not to examine themselves too closely these days, and he had a large baggage of quotes at his disposal instead.

"Good work," Gromov said. "Well done."

"What do you mean 'good'? It's my best work! *New World's* publishing a selection of my stuff in August, I'll send you a copy."

"Yes, do," he nodded. Luzgin had always wanted *New World* to publish him. Gromov couldn't think why it would matter to him now, he hadn't even realized the magazine still existed.

"Cheredinsky's going to read soon. He's something else. He wasn't drafted like you, he went to the Front for the glory of it."

"I wasn't drafted, Luzga, I joined up."

"Fine, whatever you say. The girls all scream when he reads. People say he's gay, but don't you believe it, he's living with Marfa from the church choir. Do you remember her?"

Gromov remembered Marfa Popova, and hadn't thought of her once during these past years. She wrote poems of a religious, erotic nature,

355

and it was strange to think he used to listen to her read them and even discuss them with her. Two nights ago he had been with mad Volokhov and the mad telegraphist, he had travelled on an ancient steam train from the time of the Revolution, and now he was listening to Luzgin's chatter in the Birch Twigs. He couldn't bring these two worlds together; they could go on separately, but never coexist. Times when different worlds coexisted, during revolutions and proper wars, were the most fruitful and the most frightening. For a brief moment there would be a glimpse of some common world, in which the poetess bandaged the wounded and the peasant wrapped his feet in aristocratic velvet instead of foot-cloths, and at these times it seemed God's plan would be revealed, and heaven and earth would speak together. But now nothing of the sort was happening, and he realized more clearly than ever that this war was just one of the endless levels of the game.

"Cheredinsky's only good when he reads, he's no good on paper," Luzgin was saying. "But like it or not, Grom, and I know you don't, the spoken word will replace the written one."

"It's war, Luzgin, how on earth would I have heard of him?"

"Yes, of course," he said. "You know, I used to envy you. But when they discuss this war on television, you think, what the hell's it all for? It's not cowardice, you understand Grom, but it's not my war. I can't fight for this government, and my conscience won't let me fight against it – it's still my country, and our country's a sort of prejudice we can't live without. I won't go until I'm called up. If I'm called up, I'll go."

Gromov knew quite well that Luzgin's age group had already been called up. And what sort of call-up was it anyway? They only mobilized one in five at most, mainly thick peasants, the chronically malnourished and the children of alcoholics. Luzgin was wrong though if he thought he blamed anyone. According to Tolstoy, the righteous person decided to lead a righteous life the same way he would save himself from a burning building; he didn't blame those who wouldn't save themselves: he sincerely pitied them.

He looked around. The Birch Twigs hadn't changed, and its main feature was nostalgia. It was noticeable in most writers' and artists' clubs in Moscow now, this hankering for the jazz age and early Hollywood, and the imitation glamour of Sixties Moscow. Already on their second visit the boys and girls would be drawn into the process and would miss the first time, when the crowd had seemed livelier and the atmosphere more fun. All these clubs lived in this permanent state of regret for past, or rather passing times, and nostalgia was a powerful drug for those who needed something to gild their wasted lives. But it had survived when so much of Gromov's old life here had changed. One thing had definitely changed in him though. In the past two years he had never stopped wanting the native girls, and had slept with them in Degunino and the other villages and on his free nights in the towns. But he could barely remember them now, and all the girls here were so different, and he couldn't imagine drinking and flirting with them and going to bed with them.

At that moment Cheredinsky bounded onto the stage to a chorus of female squeals. He could equally have been eighteen or thirty, and was tall and fragile, an eternal boy, wearing nothing but a pair of skin-tight crimson silk trousers. Draping himself round a steel pillar like a striptease dancer, he began in a high exalted voice to read some verses consisting of ellipses and snatched phrases, whose meaning Gromov couldn't grasp. There had been nothing to say for a long time in Moscow, and even four years ago it was the fashion to imitate some violent emotion in these half-phrases, as though in a breathless rush. He threw back his head, shook his long curls and read:

"Touch me like the first time, I won't tell, I won't tell,
Tear off your yashmak, let me under your veil.
A little bird flies to the light.
Death will come soon, maybe tonight!"

"Well?" Luzgin whispered.

"It's all right," Gromov said.

"He's brilliant! Imagine him reading with a writers' brigade at the Front!"

"It'll never happen."

"And that little bird is me-e-e!" Cheredinsky trilled, turning his back on his audience, then, whipping off his trousers, he threw them behind him and ran behind a curtain.

There was a little skirmish around the trousers, and a plump, florid girl grabbed them and waved them triumphantly over her head. The others screamed, and she clutched her trophy to her face and sobbed.

"Well, what do you think?" Luzgin asked, looking slightly embarrassed, wanting Gromov either to share the shame or absolve him. People went crazy here in the Moscow trenches.

"Look, Luzg, isn't that Bakharev over there?" Gromov said.

"You're right, he's recognized you," Luzgin squinted at him. "He's a high-flyer these days, he works for the government and writes speeches and books. He's working with Myshastikov on a multicultural project."

Gromov had been made to read Myshastikov's writings on his political education course – high-flown poeticisms in which a wispy idea would wrap itself round some anchoring phrase, like Cheredinsky around his pole – "the great steppes", "the corridor of passion", "autonomy for whites", "plastic barbarism", "Northern orientation".

Bakharev had swelled up a lot in the past two years, and sat morosely smoking a pipe in the corner, evidently in the corridor of passion.

"Come on, you haven't met for ages, I'm sure he'll want to hear about the Front! Bakhar, look who I've brought to see you!"

They jostled to his table, where he was sitting alone without comrades. Visitors to the Birch Twigs would generally gather in a respectful circle around him and not bother him with their greetings. He shot Gromov an odd, uncertain look; at the age of just twenty-eight he was still striving for gravitas. He knew he should say something encouraging to a serving officer, but he knew too that someone of his rank couldn't simply chat with his old schoolmates. He had changed, and must subtly make this clear. Bakharev was sure Gromov would ask to get him released from the Front, and Gromov knew Bakharev was afraid he would expect some favour, and both knew there was a very narrow corridor for any conversation between them.

The reason Gromov approached him now was that long ago at poetry readings he had a few times said some surprisingly clever things. He had smoked a pipe then too, to give him solidity, but he didn't think in Myshastikov's strange clotted constructions. His work now consisted of thinking up these anchoring phrases. They had never made any sense, the government just needed a poet for all this symbolism that somehow imitated sense. Bakharev took a scatter-gun Rambo-like approach to his "verbalisms", as he called them, and Russia's political scientists, who all lived on Kremlin rations, filled these formulae with their own arbitrary meanings which they explained to the population on television.

"Hello there, Gromov," Bakharev said carelessly. "Where are you serving these days?"

"The Degunino Front. Hello, Slava."

"How's the men's spirit?" he asked with an ironic smile, knowing like any intelligent official that he had to ask these foolish questions.

"They run out of that in the first year," Gromov said. "Couldn't you make it simpler for officers to register? We've ten days' leave, two weeks' maximum, and we have to waste half of it on damn forms and X-rays."

"It's not my area, I'm afraid," Bakharev said coldly. "Won't you sit down – why are you standing?"

Gromov and Luzgin pulled up chairs.

"What are you drinking?"

"I'm not," Gromov said.

"We can't have that, an officer not drinking!" Bakharev snapped his fingers at the student waitress and ordered a bottle of the new non-alcoholic White Power vodka, which cost three times the price of normal vodka. "I'll mention it, of course, they listen to me up there." He glanced at the ceiling. "But don't get your hopes up. And you definitely need the X-ray. Did you see the programme on TV about people smuggling drugs in their stomachs?"

"Mother of God, I watched it, it's a complete fantasy!" Luzgin burst in.

"I assure you it's the complete truth, I was personally involved in the making of the programme," Bakharev observed gravely. He turned to Gromov. "Sometimes something seems absurd, but when you examine it more closely it makes sense, like your Rulebook. I serve the army too in my way, so don't imagine..."

For some reason they were all convinced Gromov thought badly of them. They had long ago stopped being embarrassed with each other, but seemed to develop a sudden inferiority complex in the presence of an officer, which of course made things much easier for him.

"Well, if you can't cut the paperwork, couldn't you at least make our leave longer?"

"I'll mention it to them," he said in a slightly irritable tone.

Gromov recalled Bakharev interviewing a certain well-known poet and being photographed with him, and asking him some apparently challenging but deeply flattering questions, such as whether modern readers wouldn't find his new collection too profound. He would show everyone the ancient *maître*'s signature on his copy, and boasted of having painted the fences of some old poets living at the writers' village of Peredelkino, for which he was paid in modest meals. He claimed to be caring for the old – and writers got no privileges these days – but clever Bakharev knew the staying power of poetry, and that it wouldn't be long before he came into his own.

"Yes, you do that," Gromov said.

Bakharev was silent for a moment. He had done the officer a favour, and must now impress him with his knowledge. "Incidentally, there's a rumour it'll be over soon."

"What will?"

"The war, obviously. We've achieved our main aims, full state control and the mobilized economy. They're tired, frankly. You think they want it to drag on for ever? They know it's pointless to go on fighting such a crushing enemy."

"So what will happen?" Gromov asked. The conversation had taken an interesting turn.

"Nothing. We'll probably have to surrender some of our territory, and there'll be a small Russian Kaganate somewhere in the Caucasus."

"And they'll go there? Have you spoken to them?"

"Oh, they'll go, we're speaking to them all the time," he said with a little smile. "Sorry, Gromov, but modern warfare's not in the trenches now, it's conducted over good meals with good wines. In the post-industrial world the trench is just a prop, most of it goes on up there." He nodded again at the ceiling. "They're writing the new plans right now. The world must move on or stagnate – we need new scenarios!"

"And you're writing them, I suppose?" Gromov asked.

"Sometimes it's me," he said significantly. "You see, at a certain point we need a new stage for our dramas. Both of us are writers – you wanted to make literature in war, I in politics," he said, pleased finally to have found a formula that made him Gromov's equal.

"So my drama in the trenches is pointless, because you've already decided things?"

"No, not pointless! The point is it means something to you."

"And when will it end?"

"Soon, I think," he said vaguely. "I'd have liked it to end sooner, but the ones up there were afraid. Nationalism can turn against itself, our guard dogs are straining at the leash. Have you seen the patrols on the streets?"

"And who are they arresting?" Luzgin cut in. "Who's left to arrest? The Khazars have all left, and the Caucasians…"

Bakharev glared at him and didn't deign to respond. Luzgin wasn't a serving officer and didn't merit any democratic favours.

"It's enough though, we've been fighting too long. No one wants to join the army now, and forgive me, but there've been no significant victories. The generals are straining for power, and we don't want that: they can't even command at the Front. Don't spread it around, I'm telling you this as a friend." He dropped his voice. "It'll be over by autumn."

"A lot can happen before autumn."

"Such as?"

"A lot of people can die. You haven't thought it through – war's not that simple."

Bakharev tensed. "In what sense?"

"It changes people. Moscow has been protected from it, but it's going on everywhere else and it won't stop just like that, it'll move to the streets as it has in Chechnya. You can't leave a war half-finished, people must either win or lose. They need something to hang on to, or they'll beat their wives and smash up their flats."

"Who said we wouldn't win? There'll be victory, we'll drive the enemy from our land!"

"And back to our land?" grinned Gromov.

"We'll set up as a sort of reservation for them, a Pale of Settlement if you will."

"And how will you suppress radio, television and the Internet?"

"We'll take care of that." Bakharev had no idea how to suppress radio, television and the Internet, and hadn't even thought about it. The government was incapable of thinking even one step ahead now, and knew only that if the war wasn't settled by dividing up territory there would soon be nothing left to fight for. And the Khazars knew it too: the new peace signals were practically moving to meet each other.

"It won't be a truce. There'll be a final battle, and the generals on both sides will win," Bakharev said.

"When will that happen?"

"Soon, soon. Don't worry, you'll be back by then, they won't start without you."

"And you know the result already?"

"Not entirely, but it will be a good, effective conclusion. We've given a lot of thought to minimizing casualties. Only this isn't for others' ears, you understand Gromov."

Bakharev was suddenly frightened by his candour. Why was he so desperate to impress this officer?

"What if you've miscalculated this battle of the generals, and the men see it differently and turn their guns on them?" Gromov said slowly.

"I don't think they will. And then what, would they kill each other?" Bakharev smiled. "You're a trench officer, you must see they don't want to go on fighting. We'll send them home as heroes, with all sorts of privileges. Have you considered what you'll do next, by the way?"

"We don't think about that," Gromov said. "You said yourself this isn't like other wars, no one thinks it will end soon."

"So what do they think? I'm interested."

"They don't think anything. They say among themselves that it's not a proper war, just a big training exercise. The enemy's hiding and it seems they don't want to fight. We take some villages, they take others, then we change places. Sometimes actors and writers come, sometimes they show films—"

"You see," sighed Bakharev. "It's time to end it. Don't worry, we've already planned our 'Demobilization Project'." He had in fact only just thought of this, but he knew those above would approve. "Also our 'Border Project', defining our frontiers."

"And has anyone asked the people living in the places we give to the Khazars if they want to live under them?" Gromov asked.

"We'll evacuate them. We'll find somewhere for them, and Moscow will be rebuilt. There'll be our 'Housing Project'." Even Bakharev couldn't help sniggering at this.

"It'll never end, Slava," Gromov said. "Discuss it with your bosses if they listen to you. And my leave too, OK?"

He stood up and left the Birch Twigs and escaped into the warm damp air of the Arbat. The rain had stopped and a light mist hung over the streets, and from all the buildings a trashy ballad was playing on the radio, and he could have been back in Blatsk. Why hadn't he shot Bakharev? It would have been easy, he was flabby and unfit. He would have yelled, "You swine, playing games and writing your poems, while twenty of my best men were killed in the first year of the war, and that was just in my unit. Not to mention the Khazars who died!" But he hadn't, because it wasn't Bakharev who ordered the killing, he was just a pawn and would be one to the end. Gromov could never be an ideologist for this war. Yet he had chosen the soldier's life, he had fought and killed... Volokhov was right, he was Odysseus without his Ithaca.

"If the army's wound up, I'll go to the monastery," he decided. "Father Nikolai will take me."

He took a deep breath, and set off on foot towards Borodinsky Bridge.

2

He walked slowly through night-time Moscow. Lord, was there anything sadder than a Moscow night? People had forgotten the meaning of the word "sad". Something had happened to the language, people had forgotten it and invented another, and even managed to write poetry in it, knowing that nothing could be expressed in this artificial language. Somewhere there were real words, as they were spoken in Degunino. "Sad" was one of those words. It wasn't something rough or frightening, it was bright and unbearably sharp, a feeling that everything was over and nothing was left, and that this was the sum of every life. "In the side streets in the mist where we stopped loving…" Why did he suddenly remember this song after all this time?

He must call his parents. He didn't want to go home, he wanted to wander. He dialled their number and told his mother he was staying the night with Luzgin.

"Take care – don't forget the curfew, will you?" she said. "The patrols are out after midnight."

He hung up, spitting at their curfew. A curfew was all he needed. A man arrived from the Front and couldn't even walk round Moscow at night.

He set off again, wondering why Bakharev had so shocked him. It was strange he had never really grasped the spuriousness of this war before. He was a big boy, he should have realized. When Volokhov and Cherepanov said everything had been agreed in advance, he thought it was just drunken raving, but now even the Caucasians were returning to Moscow. In the first days of the war there had been organized attacks on them by gangs of skinheads, and they were evicted ruthlessly. They had gone off somewhere mysteriously close to the city, and six months later they were already digging in around the suburbs, and it wasn't long before they were appearing at the markets again, and no one beat them up, as if the whole thing had blown over. Moscow had swollen unhealthily in that time. The farms in the outskirts had been sold off to the new elite housing developments, and in the large unpopulated areas little Caucasian and gypsy settlements had sprung up, like a Caucasian belt around the city. In the Caucasus itself the usual border clashes went on, but the Caucasus had always lived its own life and hadn't bothered Moscow for years. The idea of giving the area to the Khazars was ludicrous: the Caucasians had no liking for them, and it was a difficult border area, full of Dagestanians. The intention was obviously to set them against each other. And what if the Khazars started seizing more territory?

He walked down Lenin Prospekt, through this Moscow that was the same and not the same, and heard the roar of approaching cars. He had never known the city so empty at night: in ten minutes no traffic had passed, and now a cavalcade of jeeps tore past at terrifying speed, many with foreign number plates. He guessed these car chases were now the chief entertainment of Moscow's youthful elite. Of course no one ever saw them at the Front, and they risked their lives on the night streets of Moscow instead. He would have gladly strangled the lot of them, and if the soldiers returning from this spurious war had turned their guns on them, he would have joined them with pleasure. But unfortunately, the world they built would be even worse than this one. And what sort of peace would it be? More old people would be thrown off the fields, and a new elite of former generals would race through the city in tanks, desperate for some excitement after the war.

"In the side streets where we stopped loving..." No, this wasn't sadness. Sadness was the withered five-pointed maple leaf blowing across the cracked asphalt to the pavement, desperate to survive. It was strange, he had rarely been happy in love, and had brought even less happiness to the women who had loved him, yet he remembered these times as the best ones, which merely confirmed his general view that this life was worse than the old one.

He reached Kravchenko Street, and walked past rows of empty trolleybuses at the depot with their windows open, like people sleeping with their mouths open, and at that moment he heard whistles and thundering feet from the courtyard of a block of flats. The patrols must be arresting someone. He flattened himself to the wall of the next building. "Come out or I'll shoot!" a voice yelled, and a shot rang out, and a window above him flew open.

"Come inside, idiot!" a voice whispered.

Without stopping to think, he pulled himself up to the ledge and scrambled inside.

"Have you lost your mind, hanging around at night?" the voice said. "They'd have blown your legs off."

He peered at his unexpected saviour. A young man evidently, with the shaven head of a new recruit. He strode to the window and closed it, dropping the blinds, and in the light of the street lamps Gromov saw it was a girl – tall, thin and big-nosed – and he thought he must be dreaming. It was Katya Stein. She was the last person he expected to see in Moscow, this girl from his old life who had written poems, a Khazar, still in the city despite the war.

"Katya," he whispered.

She came closer to him. "Gromov?"

"Yes."

"You've escaped from the Front?"

"No, I'm on leave."

"That's me done for then," she said under her breath.

"What do you mean?"

"You'll report me, of course."

"Why would I do that? Have you lost your mind?"

"What will you do with me then? You're an officer, you've taken the oath, haven't you?"

The patrols thundered and whistled outside.

"Hell Katka, but you're—"

"Yes, what am I? Go on, Gromov, say it," she said sharply.

This prosecutorial tone was new in her. She must be twenty-six now. He hadn't liked her poems, and he hadn't liked her. She was from a typical Moscow Khazar family. Her father was a urologist, her mother a former beauty in the oriental style, and her little sister Lorka danced and did drawings and everyone was in ecstasies over her talents. They were a smug arrogant family, and such families often produced girls who wrote poems imitating Brodsky and Mandelstam. He had been invited to her birthday party once and he hadn't enjoyed it, but had stayed out of a morbid curiosity to observe this alien environment, like observing insects under glass.

"What are you doing here?" he asked her.

"Where else would I be?"

"Well, in the States for instance."

"I was born here. It's my country and I'm not leaving," she said in a challenging tone.

"But it's dangerous for you," he said gently, feeling an unexpected respect for her.

"I know. Ask away, Federal, will you turn me in at once?"

"I'm a serving officer. I don't turn in civilians," he said, tight-lipped.

"How touching. But you'll kill me anyway."

"I only kill in war."

"What's the difference?" She waved an arm and turned away.

He smoked in silence, looking at her. There was nothing in her now of that annoying girl, and he liked her. He tried to guess the reasons for her insane stubbornness in staying, but he couldn't discuss them with her and didn't know what to say to her; he had completely forgotten how to talk to people.

"It's my country and my language, do you understand? I've as much right to be here as you do."

"I agree."

She stared at him. "You know Gromov, I always liked you."

"Well, I'd never have thought it."

"I was rude to you out of embarrassment, and I was an idiot."

"And I was rude to you too."

"No, you weren't, you didn't stoop to it, you kept your mouth shut. You were a good writer too, I liked what you wrote. If your poems were all that survived of you, you'd have achieved a lot."

"Well, there aren't any poems now."

He was as awkward and clumsy as his country, he thought, a big awkward man who hadn't known how to live with people but had written some good poems. And now he couldn't live with people or write poems.

"What's happening in the war? Have you killed many of ours?"

"Not many. It's trench warfare now."

"If we had an underground movement in Moscow, I'd have killed yours, but there aren't many of us left, Gromov."

"I know, you're the first I've seen."

"It's Volodka Usov's flat, remember him? He gave me the keys when he was called up."

Volodka was a half-crazy poet – why on earth would the army want him? The healthy young oafs stayed at home, tearing around Moscow in their jeeps looking for excitement, while penniless Volodka, who could do nothing but scribble his endless poems, was at the Front.

"It's a quiet neighbourhood, there aren't many patrols yet, but there soon will be." She sat at the table and smoked. "It's a miracle none of the neighbours have reported me. See, I shaved my head hoping no one would recognize me. They will in the end, though."

"Tell me what you're doing here, Kat," he said carefully.

"Why shouldn't I be here? You think we should be chucked out so you bastards can have it?"

"Why didn't you go to the Front then?"

"Because I don't want to kill people, I just want to live here."

"Yes, but see how it's turned out, the town doesn't like you."

She waved her arm again. "Thanks a lot, Gromov. Before the war you're all lovely, then the Gestapo come and throw us out of our homes and send us to our ghetto, and you say the air's fresher and doesn't stink of garlic."

"Katya, have you no arguments apart from the ghetto?"

"Plenty. I should never have let you in. I was sitting on my own and saw a living person standing outside like an idiot. Someone saved me once when I went shopping. I was all wrapped up, but a cop asked for my papers and I ran. A man on a bus pulled me on, and if he hadn't, I'd have been arrested and shot."

"Nonsense, of course you wouldn't."

"How do you know? It could happen. The neighbours are good, but there aren't many places left to hide. Everyone has to be careful now, I don't want to burden them."

She smoked, and told him her father had died and her mother had been desperate to get Lorka out. "I told her I was getting married here, and she believed me. She had no time to think about anything. You remember what a rush the evacuation was."

"Yes I do. But I don't understand. If it was a passionate love affair it would be different, but you're alone."

"You think a woman needs a man to make her decisions for her, Gromov?" She tipped her head to one side and screwed her eyes up at him, and he was sorry he couldn't see her properly; they couldn't switch the light on, as the flat was meant to be empty.

There was nothing he could say to this, and he didn't want to, and at that moment he admired her very much. "No, of course not, why should I? Have you enough to live on?"

"I'm fine, Mother left me a bit."

He didn't believe her. It was unrealistic to think anyone could live on their savings for two years in these hard times, especially now the dollar was no longer legal, and he realized she must have good people who helped her.

"I make a bit too," she said defiantly. "Children still need to be coached for university and yours don't know Russian and never have. I've a couple of kids whose parents won't hand me in, and I don't charge much."

"That's good." He paused. "Perhaps I'll go now, Katya. The patrols have left."

"Stay here for the night and leave in the morning. Tell me about the war."

"Nothing's happening, we're just running away from each other."

"I never understood why you left."

"Well, it's... complicated." He was grateful for the chance to formulate things he couldn't say to himself, and realized he did need someone to talk to after all. "You know yourself, you're a poet, there are times when you can't write, and when you do you develop a mass of complexes you can't live with. You begin thinking everything around you is a lie, even the landscape, and you grab at any truth going. Well, you have to work, or you die or go mad. So I decided life in Moscow wasn't for me, and I discovered it was no more sickening at the Front. And the main thing is there's no time to think or ask myself why I can't write."

"Can't you?" she asked him with lively interest; she knew what he was talking about, they had this in common. "Perhaps you shouldn't have left?"

"Perhaps. But something's happened to Moscow, it's as if all the life's been wrung out of it. Some become soldiers after an unhappy love affair, but not me. I just couldn't look at people, I didn't know what interested them any more."

"'At times in my sleep I wonder why they live and find no answer'," she sang in a half-whisper.

"Yes, something like that. 'And I couldn't forgive them for living without you...' Some people can live and not write, but not me. What else am I good for? There's nothing to replace it..."

"Yes, yes, nothing can replace it, even love. If I fell in love and stopped writing, I'd have the feeling... I don't know, of living in a cardboard box... I'll make some tea."

She lit the gas under the kettle in the kitchen and returned, and they talked.

He told her about the first year of the war, and she told him about the patrols and round-ups and the endless precautions she had to take when she left her hiding place, and something of the lives of the few

Khazars who had stayed. They seemed to believe computers would solve everything, and were busy with what they called "diversionary tactics", chattering on the blogosphere and telling the truth about the battles – which meant taking the official communiqués and writing the opposite. They did no harm of course, but they were hunted like Young Guards.

"By the way, do you know what they've agreed?" he asked her with a smile.

"Who?"

"Your people and mine. I heard it from Bakharev, he's a big wheel now. He says the end of the war has already been agreed."

"It's impossible. Yours might agree, but not ours," she said, with such passion he felt ashamed of his flippancy.

"Why not? Yours would do it for idealistic reasons, ours would sell the country for a copeck."

"Our people are all sorts, good and bad, but they'd never make peace," she said. She wanted to say more, but there was always a barrier Khazars couldn't cross when talking to others.

He stood up and moved closer to her. "And can't there be a law that we must find a way to live together? I honestly don't know Katya, I'm asking you."

"No, there can't," she said flatly.

"Why can't you and I live together?"

"We've lived together for two hours, but that's just two of us. And we won't make poets of everyone, will we? I'll get your bed ready, it's time to sleep."

She made up an old mattress for him and he lay looking at the light of the street lamps through the blinds and the shadows of the branches on the walls, listening to the distant roar of the night racers on Lenin Prospekt.

At six in the morning he woke, left her a note to thank her and climbed through the window, quietly closing it behind him.

* * *

"The rent for the flat is due," his father said.

Gromov had a strange relationship with his father. Once it had seemed to him they understood each other perfectly, without needing to speak, with that special male wisdom of mutual understanding and friendship, and now it turned out it had all been a lie, and the reason they didn't speak was that they had nothing to say.

369

"I'll go to the housing office and pay it," he said. "Don't bother, Dad, you rest. I've got to register anyway and go to the idiotic clinic."

"There are queues everywhere."

"Never mind, I'll wait."

"You know, you shouldn't be so quick to judge us," his father said after they had sat for a long time drinking tea in silence. "We live shabbily, I know what you think, but you'll understand when you're our age." (Gromov noticed the "our"; his father was seven years older than his mother, but it sounded worse if expressed as an unbreakable total.) "You probably judge us for moving – it was your flat too..."

"Don't, Dad, it's fine."

"No, wait. You haven't been here long, I've forgotten how to talk to you. It's better for us here, it's handy, the pace of life suits us."

He nodded mechanically, gulping his weak tea. Did they really have to economize on tea? Didn't they get extra supplies for their officer son?

"We don't do badly," his father continued hurriedly. "Your mother's job is nearby, and we've put a bit aside for you..."

"You needn't have done that!" he said.

"Don't be angry with me, I just want to say you... you shouldn't criticize our life."

"God, Dad, I don't."

"Go out, meet your friends, why should you bother with the housing office?"

"I don't mind, it's on my way."

The way of all flesh, he wanted to say, a journey to a place where nothing mattered but your own physiological condition. His father was telling him he too would become like this, and would live in a suburb built for old people, where even time was old and everything was in the past and no longer believed in itself. He would end up there and realize he shouldn't have judged them, only it would be too late by then to tell them. Every old person consoles himself with the thought that the young will eventually repent; it was the only comfort left to them. His father wanted to say all this, heaping his old person's sadness and tenderness on him, and he no longer had the strength to resist it or anything else.

In these suburbs the old people were swept up in an endless programme of events, with barely time to eat their meals. Life here was so organized that they slipped smoothly from one queue to another as they arranged their little affairs. There were queues for their cheap, fat-free curd cheese at the dairy, queues for their pension forms that had to be handed in once a month, queues for the shabby clothes distributed by social services, which they took gratefully and didn't complain. The queues were their meeting places, their clubs, where they affirmed their right to exist, and Gromov noticed how slowly they moved. In the queues for their check-ups they had time to describe ten illnesses; in those for their pensions, the ingratitude of their children; in those for bread, the high cost of living. And this was how they spent their days.

He stood in one such queue at the local housing office, where he had to fill out a form saying how many metres his parents' flat was, and whether they needed more space for their son, and if they did, he would have had to go to another office for another form explaining that there was no free space in the district, and he would be compensated to the tune of thirteen roubles twenty-nine copecks, to refuse which would incur a fine five times larger than the compensation.

Two aunties sat drinking tea at the desk, wearing mohair cardigans, big hats and winter boots despite the July heat, occasionally stopping their tea-drinking to attend to someone. At one o'clock he received another form to fill in and take to the nearest bank. But the bank had an insane timetable, and was open in the mornings on even dates and in the afternoons on the uneven ones, and in the first half of the month the lunch hour was at one, and in the second half at two, so he had to sit smoking for an hour on the see-saw in the children's playground under a fine drizzle. A little girl with a face like an old woman's pushed herself round a creaking roundabout with her leg, and some bright-orange cats lurked around the skips.

He reached the bank ten minutes before the end of lunch, but the old people there for their pensions had already collected their tickets an hour ago, and he was fifteenth in line. Each old person would go to the window and humbly rustle their crumpled documents and inform the cashier that they were invalids. This was what he had defended, this was what he was fighting for.

He waited his turn at the bank, returned to the housing office, queued for another form and learnt about the health of five old women slumped under an anti-alcohol poster, and at half-past six he joined the queue at the passport office. At five to seven a dusty policeman closed the window.

"Come back in two days," he said.

"Two days? Why not tomorrow?" he gabbled.

"What do you mean? That's how it is."

"But I have to register at the Commanders' office."

"So what? You should have come here on time. You're holding me up."

He turned and left. He had known he wouldn't register. Moscow had turned into a place for boy racers and old people going in circles like the old roundabout in the playground. He caught a trolleybus back to the flat. It travelled slowly, grinding and shuddering, for slowness was power, and he felt cramped and stifled. Life here went on so slowly, and when it was over it would turn out to have gone too fast.

There weren't many passengers on the bus. A youth of about eighteen, a pimply type in a black leather biker's jacket, was bawling at a fat girl in heavy make-up wearing a blue-and-red striped dress. She wept and grabbed his jacket, and he punched her in the tits. She went on pleading with him, sobbing wildly. "Fuck off, bitch!" he shouted, and punched her in the face. The other passengers looked on indifferently; there was nothing like it on TV.

Suddenly the spring that had been coiled in Gromov all day and perhaps for the whole of his life snapped and, leaping from his seat, he flung himself at the youth in one bound and began pummelling him so hard that at first he could see nothing through the red mist in his eyes. The youth howled in a thick womanish voice, and this enraged him even more and he went on beating him, breaking his arm and throwing him face down and smashing his head on the floor. Somehow, despite his broken arm, the youth managed to grab his hair and shout for help, and Gromov felt the girl drag him off.

"He's killed him!" she screamed. "The bastard's killed him! Call the police!"

He stared stupidly at her, and it dawned on him that she was defending her beloved.

"But he was beating you," he mumbled.

"No, he wasn't, no one saw anything. You started it!"

The bus stopped and Gromov got off, and the last thing he saw through the window as it moved off was the youth raising his head and the girl bending over him lovingly.

He stood at the deserted bus stop, and at that moment he saw a train in the distance, travelling slowly like everything else here. Above it a pale moon hung in the pale-blue sky, with pink stripes floating across it. The train was going east. He raced off, and a minute later he had reached the tracks. The train was running between some tall grey buildings, and was long, with a lot of carriages. He jumped into one, which was open as if to welcome him, and saw another bundle of hay in the corner. He had no idea where it was going, but he had dreamt since childhood of leaving on the train that passed his building. There was nothing he had to do now but lie on the hay and look out of the half-open shutters, as the train travelled past more buildings, then through some grey steel gates and further on, away from the city.

* * *

He sat on this train through the outskirts of Moscow, past schools and clinics, garages and gardens, factories and dumps that were slowly becoming one with nature; past stations and signals and elevators and fences, and little bridges across rivers; past unpainted barns and freshly painted barracks and half-finished houses – and between all of them the train, the golden mean, travelling with its cargo along its road of iron. If he sat on this train, he would escape to some intermediate realm between himself and the world, of wanderers and silences and speculations, where the railwayman sat in his cabin and the controller was in charge. And having passed through this realm he would enter another, where there was nothing but the sky and the wind and the mocking cry of the stormy petrel, and grey storks and herons and night grasses. And further east the howling winds of Central Asia and thin camels where the steppes became deserts.

If he sat on this train, he would see Ashkhabad, Samarkand and Bukhara, their arches and minarets sharp against the bright-blue sky, and the fire-spitting sky of the Caucasus, and the swarming children of the South, who had no hearts but an abundance of fruits. If he sat on this train, he would fall off the world, a soldier on leave, thundering along the rails in the dark carriage away from the war.

Chapter Ten
Treason

"Here's Degunino, do you like it?" Asha asked. They had been travelling for almost a month, and for most of it she seemed close to tears, but now her eyes were shining with pride.

They stood on the railway embankment overlooking a wide path that dipped down to a meadow of sweet grass, beyond which some low cottages stretched in a dark line across the horizon. It was a large village.

Their pictures were everywhere now – people looked suspiciously at them at the stations – and they had decided to get out and walk the last fifteen kilometres along the tracks. There had been no passenger trains here for six months, only troop trains carrying soldiers, equipment and front-line artists' brigades to the Degunino cauldron, and only one other train had passed them; the war was dying out.

The smell of hot diesel and metal from the line mingled with the scent of honey and wild flowers wafting in the warm air from Degunino. Asha ran down to the meadow as if she wasn't four months pregnant and hadn't been travelling for four hours, and was almost lost in the grass. It was almost as tall as a person after the rains, and far away in the distance five specks of people were slowly mowing it and singing, although the Governor couldn't catch the words. All around him was the happy drone of bumblebees, and a butterfly fluttered to his shoulder; he could have sworn it laughed as it flew off.

"Lord, this is the life," he said out loud.

Life seemed made for pleasure here. The air was filled with a smooth contented laziness, one of those hot late-summer days when nature rests from resting and lets things take care of themselves.

"I'm home," she said, walking ahead of him on the path. "What a place! You don't see flowers like this anywhere else."

They finally reached the village. No military commander could have planned this maze of twisting, intersecting side streets, and he had the odd sensation they kept slipping away from him and the houses were moving. Degunino played terrible tricks on its guests' imaginations.

"That's the river Dresva over there," she said. "It starts here and flows far away."

"So you know where your aunt's house is?"

"Of course I do, I know every fence here!" she said proudly.

Dogs lazily scratched themselves in the yards and came to greet them wagging their tails, and she whispered affectionately to them. They met a few people on the way, and she nodded at them and they nodded back but didn't speak; there was a smell of fear in the air.

Her aunt's cottage was no different from the others, apart from the thick ivy clinging to the north wall, with a mass of flowers in the front garden, mainly blue cornflowers and huge golden dahlias like globes.

"Auntie!" she called.

"She's not answering," she said a minute later, more to herself than to him. She pushed open the gate and he followed. There were sounds of movement inside, but no one came out to greet them.

She called again more loudly. He hadn't expected this. On the way here he had imagined the flowers parting for him in horror and the earth sinking under his feet, not wanting to bear his weight, but in the hazy August heat of Degunino it had seemed nothing could possibly go wrong.

No one came out, but he could sense frightened eyes fixed on him from behind the window, or perhaps it was just the flowers and the butterflies staring at him.

She turned to him, and the joy in her eyes had turned to despair; if no one was coming out to meet them, it must mean there was no hope for her here.

"Perhaps nobody's in?" he said.

"There's always someone in!" she said, refusing to be consoled, and at that moment the door opened and a tall middle-aged woman appeared in the porch, wearing a dark dress and a frayed lilac kerchief on her head.

"Come in," she said quietly.

* * *

"Which of them has Degunino now?" Asha asked her.

"The Southerners I think, we can't tell them apart."

"The Mad ones or the Iron ones?"

"What's the difference, the wagon's on the roof and snap, they're in."

"Auntie, what am I to do?"

375

Asha sat with her head in her hands without crying, and the Governor was afraid to break the silence. An untouched cup of some dark willow-herb infusion stood before him, mixed with various strange roots and herbs.

"What were you thinking of?" her aunt turned to him. "She's just a girl. But you?"

"I want to marry her," he heard himself saying. It felt strange to be justifying himself to a native, but he knew everything depended on her.

"You should have asked her what race she was. Do your people just take someone and marry them without asking?"

"Usually," he confessed.

"How could he have known, Auntie? Where is it written?" Asha said.

The woman didn't frighten him: what frightened him was his sense of utter powerlessness. Asha had come here to decide her fate, and now it seemed nothing would be decided.

"Everything's fine, nothing will happen," he said.

"Fine? Nothing's grown this year. The Dresva roars day and night and there's no fruit on the apple trees, and did you see the grass? You should have seen how tall it was last year! Marfa's cow never stops mooing, and Akulina's starling has stopped speaking..."

Asha dropped her head in her hands again.

"You can't stay here, and it's the same in the mountains. It's all apples and ceilings."

"We'll leave," Asha said. "We'll rest here for two days, then we'll leave."

"Where will you go? They're looking for you everywhere." She nodded at him. "I've seen him on television."

"They won't find us, I'm joining the Khazars," he told her. "They'll hide us."

"The Mad ones? They can't save you." She waved an arm at the window. "I'll call the women round tonight. We won't hurt you, Asha, you know that, we'd never raise a hand against you, but I can't help you..."

"He's just a baby!" she cried. "What harm can he do to you?"

"Everyone knows what he'll be like. They say he'll be born with teeth and hair, and he'll kill his mother and father, and everyone else—"

"That's impossible, how can a baby kill its father?" the Governor interrupted.

"This one can, and there's nothing you can do," she said, frightened. "The Guard came and told me you were coming, and that I should take her to him, but he hasn't come back."

"And will you hide me if he does?" Asha challenged her.

"Of course I will, but you can't stay here, I can't help you!" She embraced her niece for the first time and clutched her head. "Oh, what a misfortune, Asha, what's to be done? Sleep now, rest from the journey. I'll wake you when the women come."

* * *

When he looked back on that evening with the women of Degunino, the Governor understood better his feeling of powerlessness. It wasn't that he was afraid of them: they were afraid of him, and he realized that in all his years working with the natives he had never understood his powerlessness. It was impossible to discuss the future with them: their lives were an endless present, and all questions about tomorrow would be met with: "As God wills." There had never been a time when tomorrow hadn't come, so why worry? But whenever the future impinged on the present, it horrified them. Asha carried something terrifying in her that was growing in her every day, and they hid and huddled and hadn't the power to stop it.

These Wolves of Degunino, priestesses of their half-forgotten faith, weren't big murky vestals, but tiny round old women, twittering and squeaking and smiling shyly at them, finishing each other's sentences like Ryakin and Streshin, as if they were dancing in a circle around them.

"His voice will be soft, and he'll be white with brown eyes—"

"And teeth!"

"Yes, teeth, big teeth!"

"He'll make trouble—"

"He'll make trouble and he'll kill you—"

"As soon as he's born he'll kill you—"

"I know all that," Asha said. "And what if I leave?"

"You can't leave," the women wailed.

"He'll still be born if you leave!"

"Ay, he will."

"He'll be white and his hair will be black—"

"And his eyes will be brown—"

"The oven won't bake and the apple tree won't fruit."

"It's bad, it's bad!"

The Governor felt himself being dragged down into their silly childish helplessness, and he couldn't bear another minute of their wailing. After travelling for a month he still hadn't lost his masterful manner.

"Enough!" he cried. "Explain to me in plain Russian why this baby is so dangerous."

There was a sudden silence, and they exchanged anxious glances.

"Sorry, Gublinator."

"We don't know."

"Knowing's knowing, but if knowing's not given to you—"

"It's not known and not to be spoken—"

"Fine, we're leaving tomorrow," he cut in.

"They won't let you!"

"They're looking for you!"

"Never mind about that. The Khazars are in Degunino now, aren't they?"

"The Southerners, the Southerners," the women started again.

"They're staying in our homes."

"They're not bad to us—"

"They're polite to us—"

"Where's their HQ?" he demanded.

"At Galya's!"

"The fifth house on the third street!"

"Well, that's where I'm going," he said decisively.

He would have gone anywhere to get away from these kind old women whose meek lives would be destroyed by the birth of his baby. Degunino was in the hands of the Khazars now, and he was going to the Khazars.

He walked along the dusty street, past cherry orchards and neat allotments and fences twined with bindweed and mad cucumbers, and imagined everything looking at him as if he was a mad dog, doomed but dangerous. He had come here to wreck Degunino's peace and comfort, and he had to get away as fast as possible. There was nothing more for him here; he had brought trouble and he was leaving. Maybe the Khazars could use him and send him and Asha somewhere.

The fifth cottage in the street was low and spacious. The sentry outside asked him his business.

"I'm a Russian Governor," he said. "I want to come over to your side."

* * *

378

"So I hope with all my heart that I can be useful to you, as someone with some experience of government work…" he finished.

"Undoubtedly, undoubtedly, we're most grateful," his interviewer droned, rolling up the cameramen's wires and cables.

The Governor hunched conspiratorially over the table, trying to blend in with his surroundings as his colleagues in Siberia were so good at doing, and he realized he had always hated them.

The awkwardness he was feeling came from the knowledge that he was utterly redundant. Defecting to the Khazars was the biggest step he had taken in his life. He had committed treason and repented on television, and could be shot for it. But they wouldn't even waste a bullet on him. It would be better if he simply cleared off.

"Well now, Alexei Petrovich, let's go to my room and chat," Everstein smiled.

His kindly tone disguised the power of a tyrant. The Governor knew all about this: he had been a tyrant too once. There was nothing in Everstein now of the idealist who had greeted him two hours earlier, showering him with friendliness, giving him tea and phoning the TV crew to film his confession. And now he was being kicked out.

"More tea?" he asked solicitously.

"Fine," the Governor shrugged.

"So what will you do now?"

"I don't know. Work for you – fight for you if necessary. There's no way back for me, you see."

"That's been the case for a long time."

"True."

Everstein scratched his nose. "Well, we couldn't let you fight for us of course."

"I understand, you don't trust me."

"No, dear Alexei Petrovich, it's because you aren't a Khazar. You conscript anyone who comes your way, but not our army, if you've noticed. Yours is large and bulky, ours is small and mobile. And you're over forty, I understand – we don't need a man of your age. Added to which, you have no useful skills, Alexei Petrovich."

"I don't know what you're getting at," he said irritably, wondering if he was supposed to strike a bargain with him and define terms. Yes, he had switched sides, yes, he had repented, but he was a person too, and a former government official… He had no idea what would happen next.

"You thought we could use you as an organizer," Everstein went on in the same kindly tone. "I'll be frank with you, Alexei Petrovich, there's nothing more we need from you, your mission is completed with this interview. You're free to go wherever you like and live as you wish, my friend."

"But you don't understand, I've nowhere else to go," he replied angrily. "I came to you because I can't stay on the Russian side!"

"I do understand," he suppressed a laugh. "You thought we were desperate for a repenter in our ranks. It would be different if you were some sort of specialist, but, hand on heart, you've nothing we need. You've done just one simple thing all your life, and now you're suffering for it. You kept the natives down, for which thanks very much, but you showed no mercy to the Khazars either, did you? You've belonged all your life to this delightful caste to which you owe your career, and in any other environment you'd be a fish out of water. Did you really not see it coming?"

The Governor would never have guessed it would turn out like this two hours ago, when Everstein practically threw himself at his neck, and he was obviously enjoying his power over him now and spinning it out. He looked affectionately at him. "It's the mistake you officials always make when you switch to the winning side – not that there've been many of them. I can't deny their instincts are sharp, but love has blunted yours and something human has appeared in you. You shouldn't have switched sides, Alexei Petrovich. I might have welcomed someone else, but you still have the oppressor's instinct, you can rule no other way."

The Governor said nothing. Never in his life had he hated anyone as much as he hated this man.

"I'm not an animal. I know you're being hunted and you won't have long after this interview. I advise you to go further south. Go to Krasnodar, go to the mountains, our Chechens are fighting there. They don't need you either, but at least they'll hide you and help you get out of the country. Somewhere in Asia perhaps. What you failed to see, Alexei Petrovich, was the one little thing we have and you don't, which is that we're chosen by God. Every Khazar is a part of the world's soul, only we have value for the Almighty. That's why we'll win and why you can't join us, do you understand?" He looked at him compassionately, clicking his tongue and shaking his head, as if to say: "Poor Governor, it hasn't worked out, has it?"

"Go south, as far south as possible. You can pick up thirty silver coins from the accounts office tomorrow before you leave."

The Governor left without saying goodbye. He knew what he had to do before he left.

Chapter Eleven
The Final Battle

1

At the General Staff in Moscow, the generals were putting the final touches to their budget for the Final Battle.

"As ideological backup we'll have prayers said first by Priest-General Gundoskin. Colonel Kozyaev will be in charge," said Lieutenant-General Kolesov, a flabby, swollen man who loved steam baths, couldn't do press-ups, and wasn't big on charm or looks, as befitted a Varangian warrior.

"Present!" Kozyaev jumped up, clicking his heels.

"Then the parade-ground ballet," he continued, reading from his notes. "Drill, one-two-three, presenting arms, victory march past the tribune, welcome speech by Lieutenant-General Kolesov – that's me. Then at twelve hundred hours the shooting of malingerers picked by Smersh, co-ordinated by Major-General Tyutyunin of the Central Smersh administration."

"Present," stiff, spectacled Tyutyunin said coldly, without standing up. Smersh men didn't bow to the commanders, and were answerable only to Smersh.

"Will you carry out the shootings yourself?" Kolesov asked, with sudden interest.

"If circumstances require," Tyutyunin replied, even more coldly. He wasn't obliged to share his top-secret business with the "greens", as Smersh contemptuously called the fighters.

"Fine, don't go into details. Is the battlefield ready?"

According to the Varangian rules of garrison and sentry duty, the battlefield must be prepared carefully in advance, like an ice rink before a figure-skating contest. In fact the so-called fieldwork involved simply sending in a couple of regiments to trample the earth and sweep it. But a large part of the budget was allocated to this and was traditionally pocketed by the General in charge, economic planner Major-General Kabluchny.

"The field is being prepared," Kabluchny reported anxiously. "In the process a hill was discovered and is now being flattened."

"What are you saying, Major-General Kabluchny, you couldn't find a flat field in Degunino? You couldn't find a relief map on the Internet?" (In Kolesov's mouth, "Internet" sounded like a foul obscenity.) "I've the Final Battle in two days with the advanced forces of the Khazars – do you take us for children? You'll flatten the hill or I'll have you shot, Major-General Kabluchny. I can toss you aside like this!" He stood up and threw his chair across the room.

Kabluchny stared at the floor in silence. He knew the ritual.

"You'll eat shit, Major-General Kabluchny, and I shall personally ensure it's runny!" The other generals laughed obligingly. "You're an agent of the enemy, General Kabluchny. Or rather Colonel Kabluchny. Or rather Warrant Officer Kabluchny."

With each demotion Kabluchny lowered himself further, and at the point he became Warrant Officer he was sobbing and grovelling on all fours at Kolesov's feet.

"Enough," Kolesov puffed. "If the hill isn't flattened tomorrow, I'll stick the British flag up your arse and cover your eyes with it."

He retrieved his chair and sat down, becoming slightly calmer. Both he and Major-General Kabluchny knew there was no hill in Degunino. But it was important to stage these blow-ups for the younger generals and for correspondent Colonel Tutykhin from the *Red Star* newspaper, who was attached to the General Staff. Legends were born of such scenes, and of generals driven by a holy rage to pick up a spade and work alongside their men clearing hills. Tutykhin knew any such activity by the General Staff was unthinkable, and that they would all collapse with hernias. He made a note to remind himself to mention the hill.

"Accommodation for the press pool, supervised by Major-General Zubikov."

"Present!" Zubikov jumped up eagerly.

"Show me your list," Kolesov demanded.

Zubikov put before him a list of names: twenty men from the *Red Star* and television channels One and Two, and three journalists from other newspapers, who were being punished for various misdemeanours by being sent to the Front, where they would report directly from the trenches. Three gallant reporters from the "Special Correspondent" programme, known as the "Three Fatties", would watch the battle from the generals' enclosure, and were accredited to shoot prisoners.

"Fine," Kolesov said shortly. "Other expenses – a performance by a Moscow theatre workshop of 'The Dawns Are Quiet Here'. What the hell is this?"

"It's for some relaxation after the battle," boldly explained Major-General Koromyslov, the General Staff's Ideologist-in-Chief.

"What relaxation, Major-General Koromyslov? The soldier has just escaped death, his adrenalin's buzzing, and you want to shove the quiet dawns down his throat? You'll use the people's money to feed your bawdy old actresses? I'll deal with you, Major-General Koromyslov!" Kolesov bawled, but without the ferocity with which he had demoted Kabluchny.

He cut the money for the show and took it himself, and having finally divided the budget between the ideological, quartermaster and rear services, with just twenty per cent for the battle itself, he rose heavily and left for his office, with its stained-oak carvings of Russian birch trees and humble virgins waving handkerchiefs at departing soldiers. Then he sat down at his huge desk and put a call through to General Strotsky, Commander-in-Chief of the Khazar General Staff, and a flirtatious conversation began.

According to a secret agreement between their two governments, the Khazars would be given the Krasnoyarsk region and part of Rostov after the battle, and the Khazars would live in clover behind an impassable wall in the southern part of the old Kaganate, whose full restoration turned out to have been an impossible dream. The governments had planned that the Final Battle would be continued to the death of the last soldier, but their generals had secretly agreed with them to sabotage these plans. The Varangians still hated the Khazars, however, and didn't believe a word they said, and the Khazars trusted no one, and these three vectors formed a complex tactical game which Kolesov and Strotsky played with consummate skill and ingenuity. Everything was determined by a multitude of factors in the world. It was just that the factors and everything in the world was shit, and neither of them trusted each other or knew what determined what.

Both generals were supposed to report back to each other what was said at their secret meetings, but they would do so in a garbled arbitrary fashion, and the reality of the battle slipped further and further from their grasp. Kolesov told Strotsky it would start at midday, although he had arranged for it to start at eleven, and Strotsky, knowing the Varangian was lying, decided to be there by ten. Kolesov said it would take place outside Degunino, and for some time both armies had been stamping around the village, the only one with any food. But Strotsky didn't believe him, and decided it would be outside Baskakovo, where the Varangians had their HQ. Finally, although

Kolesov had no intention of using nuclear weapons on his territory, he told Strotsky that he would, and Strotsky said that he would use his too, and chemical weapons too, to be on the safe side.

Having arranged the battle to their mutual satisfaction, the generals hung up and rubbed their hands.

* * *

Major-General Paukov too was busy, organizing the disposition of his troops. As a strategist he knew these dispositions were all on paper and had no relevance to the battle. He couldn't anticipate the enemy's plans, and neither could he inspire confidence in his men or sense their mood, but his dispositions were expansive and inspiring:

"Column One (1st Battalion) to advance to the northern extremity of Degunino," he wrote, sticking a big blue arrow on the map, "and not sparing their blood, reach Hill 23 (quadrant 2569). Column Two (2nd Battalion) to advance to the southern extremity of Degunino and dig in along the river Dresva, cutting off the enemy. Column Three (3rd Battalion) to advance on Degunino in a wide pincer movement from the direction of Baskakovo and demoralize the enemy. When the enemy withdraws its forces, Column Three will turn left and advance to the eastern extremity of the above-named village, and at 13.18 hours march in decisively with reinforcements. The Fourteenth Unit, under Captain Funtov, then moves to the western extremity of Degunino, and at 15.32 hours Column One is replaced by Column Two, and the Fourteenth Unit strikes at the enemy's rear, sowing panic in its ranks..."

Paukov knew his dispositions made no sense, and simply involved his columns dashing from one part of the Front to another and replacing each other in a circle around Degunino. But as a general he realized that the purpose of military commands wasn't for the troops to occupy this or that position, but so that several thousand overfed men could regulate the flow of soldiers without any risk to themselves, at a safe distance from the fighting. Adding the last flag to the circle, he returned to his chair and slapped his thigh. There was something special about him, as that old tart Guslyatnikova had discovered.

* * *

Meanwhile, in Baskakovo, Gurov was busier than all of them. He had to be everywhere at once and had no one to help him, and he was exhausted.

Gurov possessed no special powers, and seemed powerful only compared to the rest of his people, few of whom now remained. And there would have been even fewer of them if it hadn't been for the five per cent who had somehow avoided Vasilenko Syndrome, or rather the national character.

The natives possessed a variety of talents. There were the poets and prophets, and the apparently useless tender-hearted survivors like Voronov (these delicate boys were always invulnerable: the hard ones broke, the soft ones merely bent), and there were the Wolves like Volokhov who were obsessed with a single idea. But the poets and prophets were incapable of fighting, the survivors thought only of surviving, and for some reason the Wolves had recently become defenceless against love. They fell in love, and this became their obsession, they were good for nothing else. It had come to the point that Gurov had to have his own people liquidated if they didn't obey him. He had sent Volokhov's Khazar girl to Zhadrunovo, but the Wolf girl was bearing the child of a Varangian, and somehow he had been unable to stop it. Voronov had failed to meet her and convince her to get rid of it, and now it was up to him. It was late, she was in her fourth month, but he was stronger than she was, and he had no doubt he would succeed. He had already visited her aunt in Degunino, and knew where she was hiding. The village was under the Khazars now, and as Gurion he could have gone there right now. But despite the Wolves and their prophecies, there were things he had to do here first. He was a Guard, and must protect his people in the coming battle.

At one point he thought they'd had it. If Gromov and Voronov hadn't carried out their assignment, it must be because the earth didn't want it, and he trusted what the earth told him. Then he came to his senses and realized it was telling him he must deal with Asha himself. Even the most powerful native couldn't avoid their ban on killing, which meant he must persuade her, and he knew he could. He had no choice.

He knew the dark vitality of his race, and that none of his countrymen could kill even if they wanted to. He didn't share their morbid attraction to travelling in closed trajectories, and he himself would have liked to change things long ago, but he knew this was impossible. He was one of a small number of natives whose wills hadn't been paralysed, but in every other way he was of this race. All his adult life, making his career in Varangian circles and shining in Khazar ones, playing a double agent's game and being himself in both of them, he had sought pure-bred members of his race, untainted by alien blood. Some he discovered through instinct, in others he sensed an unconquerable will to survive; some he would ask a simple riddle, and it would seem to them they had heard it before, not at school or on the street, but from some deep genetic memory of their language. But it was better in a way if they didn't – round the well, the apple and the falcon and so on. He was word-perfect in his language, and had learnt it from his parents without dictionaries or textbooks, and it contained the whole life of his people. Most had the sense not to write or publish in it, apart from a few mad novelists and poets, but he knew thousands of native songs and verses by heart. He didn't recite them, just used them as a sort of password, sometimes murmuring to himself, "Not alone in the field, little road." What was the song about? It was about the land, criss-crossed by a network of roads that led nowhere. You set off in one direction and were led in another, and it was impossible to predict where you would arrive. He himself had a sort of agreement with the earth and could go wherever he liked, but who knows what the girl would say to him? He wished he could ask wise Vasily Ivanovich, but Vasily Ivanovich was travelling around Russia with his saviour and hadn't been in touch for a long time.

Of course he felt sorry for the baby, he was sentimental like the rest of his people. But didn't they remember history? How in Judea the native virgin had carried the child of the aggressor? There was the Slaughter of the Innocents, but she was cunning. It had nothing to do with angels, she herself had known what she had to do, marrying a husband who wasn't the father and escaping with him to give birth in a stable, and Judea couldn't stop the baby being born. And where was Judea now?

Gurov disliked Christianity. He felt a certain admiration for their monks, but they should sit in their monasteries and stay out of things. He knew what his people needed, and they didn't need these children of mixed-race unions, who brought with them the terrible spirit of history. Let others pray to history and put their faith in progress. What was progress? The path of death. The rest of the world had Phlogiston, the breath of history, but Russia didn't need it. These people of mixed blood became wandering preachers who would turn the world into one great Zhadrunovo, where the makers of history were sent.

He could sense Ploskorylov some way off in the distance, and a moment later heard him puffing outside the door. He tapped discreetly like a welcome guest, and came in.

He lifted his eyes from his writing. "Yes?"

"Priest-Captain Ploskorylov to see you," he murmured.

"You'd better sit down then, as you're here," Gurov said with an unfriendly smile. "Have you come on business?"

"I could say it's business, yes," he said in a teasing voice, pulling out a chair.

"Well, get on with it," Gurov said.

"I've come to remind you of my Initiation, Petya," he murmured. "You promised it would be at the end of July."

"You can put that right out of your mind, Priest-Captain, you should be thinking of the battle now."

"I am, of course I am!" he said. "But anything might happen to me, Petya, and if I were to… If I were to die without experiencing it…"

Gurov smirked. He had already planned Ploskorylov's Initiation ceremony in vivid detail, and thinking about it would always put him in a good mood, even when he was up to his ears in work. He planned to adopt the Varangian ritual everyone had to pass through to work for Special Services – checking denunciations, arresting plotters and provocateurs – and it consisted of the banal act of buggery. It taught men not to switch sides, since if anyone ran over to the enemy, Smersh would publicize the names of all those he had practised his perverted love with, in the most passive and degrading way. The Varangians even had a special Initiator, the legendary Gunka, who was fed extra rations for the job. Every interrogator who had broken iron heroes had been initiated in this way by Gunka, and Gurov had just the man for the Priest-Captain, that stupid brute Korneyev. Maybe he could get him to do it right now, just for the pleasure of it. But this was no time for pleasure.

"You'll have to wait," he frowned. "You must prove yourself a hero in the battle before we can even consider it. And if they kill you, well you'll know everything and won't need to be initiated, will you?"

Ploskorylov flushed. "No, of course not… But you see, Petya, if I'm to acquit myself properly I'd like to know more about what it involves, they didn't tell us at the Academy. The Sixth Level – well that was different. Tell me, if we win the battle – and I don't doubt we will – what happens next?"

"We fight to the last Khazar," Gurov shrugged. "As stated in the Book of Church Festivals by the Anchorite Akaky…"

"Yes, yes, of course," Ploskorylov interrupted. "But what will follow the final victory? Will there be the Kingdom of Ice?"

"I doubt it," Gurov shook his head. "You know Varangianism won't stop until only the last worthy men are left."

"Yes, I know, complete destruction – but please tell me, Petya, what will these last worthy men do?"

"How dare you at your Fifth Level ask an Inspector such a question when he's considering the fate of the battle!" Gurov said in a thin terrible voice, rising from his seat. "You're asking about things known to only a very few at the Seventh who are capable of drawing intelligent conclusions!"

Falling to his knees, Ploskorylov reached for his hand and smothered it in kisses. "Forgive me, Petya, forgive me…" he whispered, only realizing then to what depths he had sunk.

"Get up and leave," Gurov said heavily. "You have shown unforgivable insubordination, and in view of your ignorance of the duties of the Orderly—"

"I've learnt it, I've learnt it! The Orderly is a soldier of war, whose chief duties are to supervise, monitor and report—"

"About tu-urn!" he bawled. "Get out of my sight! Prepare for the battle! Wash your socks!"

Ploskorylov was blown away, and Gurov's mood improved slightly. He took a childish pleasure in kicking this tub of lard, although he hadn't worked out yet what would follow the Initiation. Dances around the ice crystal to Father Frost? Group copulations in endless positions and combinations? He was free to imagine what he liked. The problem was that the Khazars and Varangians had no eschatology, and this was the first symptom of the virus race. Their dreams extended only as far as exterminating each other, and if asked what would follow they would shrug their shoulders. They were both waiting for the Final Battle with no idea what they were fighting for, and at times he felt almost sorry for them.

But he knew there would be no apocalypse. The world wouldn't end, because his people were immortal, and if he kept his wits about him the circle wouldn't be broken.

* * *

Far away, at the dead of night, a bubble was growing deep under the ground.

Other gases were mined from the black-green mole tunnels of roots and decaying organic matter and rotting flesh, but no sooner had the body left the soul than these transparent bubbles of emptiness formed. They lay like stones, as if the earth had forgotten them, and around each of them grew a lacuna, an expanse of emptiness. Everyone knew matter made more matter, but from emptiness came Phlogiston, the dancing blue gas of happiness.

It was as if someone with four-fifths of their life predetermined – a trip to the dentist, a chat with an unfriendly boss, interviewing someone for a job – finds the dentist is sick, his boss has been sacked, or the person he has to interview has taken fright and left. In the packed timetable of this busy man a bubble appears, a half-hour gap. He can go for a walk and look at the sky, which he hasn't done for a long time, and he smells the poplars and sees the children leaving school and buys himself a bun, and dancing inside it is a little spark of Phlogiston. A beautiful woman passes, and he realizes she is telling him to leave his jealous girlfriend and go off with someone else, and in the place of this joyless, long drawn-out affair there's a blessed vacancy, in which anything is possible. These empty moments are the ones that change life, and the gap is filled by Phlogiston, the gas of emptiness and free time.

At such moments the pure spirit rejoices, and the most interesting things happen. People love matter and produce endless quantities of it from themselves, like a spider spinning a web from its entrails. There is always something in the granaries, the world is stuffed with people and things, and the gas has nowhere to go. But when it escapes, free of this world and its productive relations and forces, there history can begin. Marx, the dull bookkeeper, believed history was made by the evolution of matter, but history starts where matter disappears and there's a half-hour space to do nothing. Leisure is the midwife of history, and in these blessed gaps the gas accumulates and little blue flames burn at night. Nature's gases, the flatulence of the earth's bowels, are no match for Phlogiston, whose formula is unknown and probably doesn't exist, for Phlogiston is the pure power of the imagination, the promise of all possibilities. The best engines are powered by it, and cars spitting stinking petrol can never catch up with the ones that run on it, and they go to fantastic places. And now the bubble was growing and the emptiness was widening, and the first sparks of Phlogiston were flickering over Russia, like solar flares over the mud.

2

The day of the Final Battle was warm and sunny, although neither side was in any mood to appreciate the weather.

By seven that morning the Varangian regiments were lined up on the square, listening to the patriotic folk-rock groups Bread Basket and Little Windmill sing their war songs and hymns to Perun. Their body movements were aggressive, and the troops stamped their feet. They had grown so used to inactivity in the rainy months that they were completely unprepared for battle, and were afraid it would be endless fighting from now on.

Lieutenant-General Kolesov strode to the square to lead the battle in person, or rather shout at the commanders taking his place. He delivered a mild dressing-down to Paukov, a serious one to Zdrok, and a terrifying one to Captain Kukishev, then had a few orderlies shot for leaving a dead fly under a mattress. Only Major Evdokimov from Smersh made a good impression on him, and Priest-Captain Ploskorylov, evidently not a fighting man but an experienced demagogue.

"Soldiers!" he bawled. "Today some of you will die. Dying is our business. I might even say half of you will die. Take a good look at each other – you may not see each other again. Who can say who will die? But if you don't, your mother and your sister will be raped, and your father and your brothers..."

He enumerated in detail all those who would be raped if they didn't die. The soldiers tapped their feet as Little Windmill played 'Onwards to Perun!', about elves and runes and the path to the North, and a lone horseman with his golden-haired companion.

Then it was Ploskorylov's turn. He intended to talk about geopolitics, and Degunino's role as the historic crucible where North and South met, and how nature rejoiced as she sent her sons off to battle, and much more besides. Before him stood hundreds of about-to-be-dead soldiers, and he wanted to bless them all and felt a sweet choking sensation in his throat and a sweet swelling sensation in his trousers. But something quite unexpected was happening. As a result of the General's telephone conversation, the Khazars had entered Baskakovo an hour early, and now along the great field picked for the battle, so they could all spread out comfortably, the first Khazar detachment was advancing slowly under the command of Captain Zeldovich.

"Muck your fother, what's this?" yelled Kolesov. "Major-General Paukov, was your reconnaissance asleep?"

"To your columns!" Paukov shrieked.

The officers dashed to their battalions, and the musicians stood clutching their useless instruments with no idea what to do next.

The First Column, in accordance with Paukov's dispositions, trudged reluctantly to the north of Degunino, with the new recruits in front wearing plimsolls – the ones in plimsolls were to fall first. But the Khazars' General Strotsky had made good his promise to Kolesov and had set off a gas attack at the northern edge of Degunino. Smelling the gas, the First Column swerved east, where Ataman Batuga's Cossacks galloped up on their sleek horses and crushed the recruits in plimsolls. The rest of the First Column retreated in panic from the superior forces of the united Cossacks and arrived at the Dresva, which the Second Column was meant to be defending. But the Dresva had burst its banks in the rain, so they were forced to dig in near the village, under the noses of the Khazars. The Khazars, who had started the battle, were waiting to be attacked from who knows where, but not from the Dresva. Strotsky quickly regrouped his forces to save lives, and drew off his advance troops from Degunino to the village of Chumkino, from which the unsuspecting Third Varangian Column was now marching towards Degunino. And they trampled all the wheat.

The Khazars' Vengeance Shock Brigade appeared from the village, driving before them their usual crowd of old people, women and children, the Khazars' favoured tactic in arguments and war. Bringing up the rear was a soldier with a megaphone shouting: "Look at the old people, women and children! The criminal regime no longer pays old people their pensions or mothers their benefits, and shoots old people, women and children! They prefer death to this life. March, old people, women and children!"

"And we baked pies for you!" shouted the women.

Part of Batuga's detachment hurled themselves at the old people, women and children and crushed them as an example to the others.

The Khazars looked on and took photographs, and a journalist from the magazine *Daily Week*, whom they had engaged to report the battle to the West, tapped into his laptop: "It can't be said saving hostages is a priority for the Russians."

The Vengeance Brigade watched Batuga's cavalrymen crush the old people, women and children, then set off in the direction of Baskakovo singing 'Peace to You'. And they trampled all the clover.

Seeing the enemy on the horizon, Paukov's Third Column turned north in a panic and were stopped by the forest. Seeing the Third Column on the horizon, the Khazars turned south and were stopped by Batuga's men, who galloped to the Dresva, from which they headed for Degunino, intending to expel the Khazars with one blow.

Discovering that the Khazars' main forces had already withdrawn from the village, Batuga decided to occupy it and met no resistance. "We've cucumbers and apples for you, boys!" said the women. But it wasn't long before a column of cunning Khazar fighters jumped out of the forest to the east of the village and started firing at them with sub-machine guns, driving them out. And they trampled all the rye.

"We've pies and pickled cabbage for you!" the women said to the Khazars when they arrived.

Meanwhile the Second Column, which was defending the Dresva just outside Degunino, heard the shooting in the village and left their trenches, realizing no one would try to cross the river. But as the exhausted infantrymen scrambled up the muddy hill, they met their own Third Column coming the other way and began firing at them, not realizing who they were.

At that moment Batuga galloped howling from the village with a slashed face, pursued by the Khazars. And they trampled all the oats.

"I'll kill you, filth!" Batuga shouted.

The Second Column pondered his words, then scrambled off to Degunino, just as the Khazars' tanks rolled out of the forest, raised their turrets and took aim.

"We've potatoes and tomatoes for you!" the women shouted at the tanks.

They spat fire, and several shells sailed over the bewitched village and landed with a thud in the other forest, where Paukov's Third Column was hiding. There were anguished shrieks.

Realizing the forest was exposed on all sides, the Third Column ran off in all directions, but noticed something strange had happened. A minute ago they had been running on flat land, but now they appeared to be at the bottom of a deep crater, as if the earth had suddenly reared up and swallowed them. Their boots stuck in the mud.

"Crater!" shouted their captain.

At the same time something inexplicable had happened to the Dresva. The floods had spread wider and were inching closer to the village, until its muddy depths almost reached the cottages, and the whole of the Second Column was now sinking into the water. The tanks had stopped firing, and they too were sinking, up to their caterpillar tracks, then over their turrets, until they disappeared completely. The crews managed to jump out and tried to run away, but it was as if the earth was grabbing them by the legs and dragging them down.

Shaken by what they had seen, the soldiers of the First Column crushed by Batuga scattered in disorder across the field to Degunino, dashing through the streets with their eyes on stalks. "We've bread and radishes for you!" cried the women.

The Khazar forces realized by now that they couldn't retreat, advance or perform any manoeuvres at all. The earth was parting like the Red Sea, and the river had already swallowed up two entire battalions and unceremoniously spat them out twenty kilometres from Degunino, filthy, soaking and demoralized. And they trampled all the sorghum.

Paukov's dispositions had had nothing to do with it of course, but roughly two per cent of his dispositions in the battle had performed correctly, which according to the Varangian strategy and tactics manual was par for the course.

3

Asha sat by the window and felt afraid. The baby hadn't moved yet, but it wasn't that, and it wasn't the war that frightened her. War couldn't hurt a Wolf, and the shells had missed the cottage and simply flown over the village. Yet she could feel the danger moving closer to her, rolling like a big gingery ball across the field to her hiding place, and she could see the Guard, but couldn't escape from him or stand up. Her legs seemed stuck to the floor.

"Would you like some sour cream?" Galya asked him at the door.

"Later," he said, and went in to Asha.

Gurov had already visited her aunt a week ago, and had now entered Degunino on horseback with Batuga's Cossacks and was one of the first to arrive. She saw him darkly through a fog, but he saw her clearly, and the baby inside her.

An outsider would have understood little of the conversation that followed: the words they spoke were the same as the aggressors', but their meaning was different, for they were speaking in their own language.

"Green widow," the Inspector nodded. "The hills are walking?"

"The mound is closed," she said, bowing her head.

"The mound's open, the stream is behind."

"Pour it for me," she sighed.

Anyone who knew their language would have heard:

"Hello my beauty, we meet at last. Do you know who I am?"

"No, I don't."

"Don't be silly, I'm sure you know why I've come."

"Yes I do," she confessed.

"So will you do it?" he asked her gently.

"Never, you'll have to kill me first!"

He sat down on the bench, realizing it would be a long conversation, and heard the battle raging in the village.

"Why kill you?" he said without animosity. "There are so few of us who can float, and now they're torturing our pilgrims."

She raised her big eyes to him. "I know. And soon there'll be none of them left." She spoke so quietly that her words were drowned by the din outside, and he had to lip-read. Then suddenly everything fell silent; it seemed the Khazars had been driven briefly from the village and the battle had moved to the field.

He jumped up from his seat. "You could have had a child with anyone, and you had to pick this one! Didn't you know who he was?"

"How would I know? I know the earth."

This was quite true. Her people in Siberia were renowned for their skill at thawing it and making vines grow in mud and potatoes on rocks. Yet as far as the future was concerned they were blind and deaf. They knew their prophecies, but didn't appear to believe them.

"Don't lie to me," he said. "You know quite well what will happen."

"Yes, I know the earth's rising," she replied, and in the silence her words sounded powerful and terrible. He peered at her. She might be trying to trick him, but if she wasn't, things were worse than he feared. He wasn't descended from a long line of peasant farmers as she was, and he must have missed something. If the earth was already rising, it meant the time was near and she was irrelevant.

"It can't be, don't try to pull the wool over my eyes," he said.

"Haven't you noticed? Haven't you heard it hum?"

"It's always humming, pregnancy just sharpens the senses."

"No, this is different, I can feel it quivering at night."

"Maybe you're quivering at night! You know this baby can't be born! It's what I do, making sure nothing happens, like you make the bushes grow and the snow white, it's my job. It's no fun for me tormenting my people, I'm not a Northerner or Southerner," he said more quietly, calling them by their ugly native names, the ugliest words in their language.

"Well stop doing it if you don't like it."

"If only I could. Don't believe me then. But I know what I'm talking about, and that there'll be nothing left, not even you—"

"Enough. Either I have the baby or you must kill me."

"I can't, you know that. I'd kill your Northerner though."

He thought this would shock her, but either she was good at hiding her feelings (Siberian Wolves were known for their self-discipline), or nothing mattered to her now but the fate of her child.

"You won't find him," she told him calmly.

"Don't play games, I know he's here with you."

"He was, but he's left," she said. "He's gone over to the Southerners and asked them to hide us. His people will never forgive him."

"They won't take him."

"Well they have, he was on television. He's gone with them and I'll follow him. They said I must leave Degunino."

"How could they, they're not Guards!" Gurov shouted. "You think you can just go somewhere else to have the baby and nothing will happen?"

"The earth's already rising. If something happens it won't be because of me."

"Fine, I won't argue with you," he said. "But if it's rising, it's already too late. I see I can't frighten you, but aren't you sorry for people here?"

"What, the women who give everyone cucumbers? The men who build roads that go in a circle? Who's to pity? Do you pity them?"

"Yes, I do," he said.

"Well, I don't. We live like grass and we don't see the light, and there's no end in sight."

Beyond the village the field thundered. "You see how desperate it is," he said. "The Northerners sold out their own side long ago, but there are still some of the others left. They're educated boys and they've no pity for anyone."

"I'll keep the baby and we'll leave. Don't worry, Guard, I know the words."

"Why should I worry? I know words you've never even heard of!"

"Try me!" she said. "If I say the word there'll be a road from here to the mountains and I'll get there."

As she said this, the earth was parting before the Khazars three kilometres from the cottage, and the river had already swallowed up two of their battalions and washed them away.

It wasn't that Gurov felt nothing: he felt a lot, but we are given free will to control our feelings. He had underestimated the little girl's strength – that was Siberia for you – and she was growing stronger every minute from this baby in her. He must deal with her fast, with a final killer blow.

"The earth will be a dead place if it wakes, aren't you sorry for it?" he asked her.

"Yes, I am," she wept, but there was no weakness in her tears, and he knew he wouldn't move her.

"We shouldn't have met like this, Asha, we could have done great work together," he said sadly.

"No, we couldn't," she said. "I wouldn't want to do your work, setting them against each other and dragging things out."

"But you've no one to defend you. I've been keeping an eye on you here in Degunino."

She looked away, and he knew she wouldn't budge, and that there was nothing either of them could do about it. She was a serious girl, and like a clever Wolf she had given him the choice of killing her to save their world, but he couldn't. He had a gun, but, terrible to say, he had never used it.

At that moment there was a flurry of footsteps outside, and Ploskorylov burst in, waving a hand grenade, excited by the chance to show Gurov he was fighting in the front ranks.

"Inspector! Are you in danger?" he cried.

Gurov threw him a look that would have crushed a more observant person to dust. "What are you doing here, Ploskorylov?" he asked him quietly.

"Your life, Inspector, I've come to save your life! You're in danger, the Yds are on all sides!"

"Fuck off!" Gurov roared, and a gust of wind hit the village like a big cold bird.

"But Inspector..." he stammered, and was about to scuttle off when someone behind him grabbed his shoulder.

"Not so fast, Priest, no hurry. Let's talk."

It was Everstein, who had suddenly appeared from nowhere.

He turned to Gurov. "Gurion, what a surprise! Counter-intelligence is always ahead of us. Keep your hands off him, though, he's mine!"

Ploskorylov shuddered and broke into a sweat.

"Amazing, how did you catch him?" Everstein jabbered. "We catch their soldiers, but their patriots are always in the rear! Give me that hand grenade, Ploskorylov – you don't know how to use it, and it won't work, it's just a dummy."

"No, it's not!" Ploskorylov shrilled.

"Throw it then. I'll show you what works." Everstein whipped out a beautiful little Khazar pistol, an officer's dream, and pointed it at Ploskorylov's stomach. Ploskorylov handed over his grenade, flinching from this contact with a Khazar.

"That's better," Everstein said, still aiming his gun at his stomach. "So why did you go into battle? I saw how your men covered for you; they're terribly fond of you – weren't you afraid they'd shoot you?"

"What do you know about my men?" Ploskorylov shrieked. Everstein had obviously decided not to kill him at once, and wanted to kick him around first. Perhaps he wouldn't kill him. He had learnt at the Academy that if they were going to do it they normally did so immediately.

"I know more than I need to. An extraordinary race. I can never understand why they don't turn their guns on their officers, but that's by the by. So you're sitting out the battle in the cottages, Ploskorylov?"

"I'm guarding the Inspector!" he said defiantly.

"Marvellous, thanks, Gurion's our man."

Ploskorylov had been white before, but he now turned grey.

"Petya, is it true?" he gasped.

"Of course not," Gurov said stiffly. "You should mind your language in front of him, Misha."

"Well he won't have the chance to tell anyone, will he?" Everstein smiled. "You don't know me, Gurion, I've been watching him since before the war. I wept when I read what he wrote about us Yds, it was a sort of poem about stringing us up on Red Square, and how he'd personally tear us to pieces with his teeth! So here we are, Ploskorylov, what should we do with you? Pray to you or offer you money?"

Ploskorylov trembled, his eyes darting between the two of them.

"The village is ours of course, you lost the battle brilliantly," Everstein threw at him. "The earth can't stand you any more, the Dresva's become an ocean in broad daylight."

"Round the well?" Gurov asked Asha quickly. ("Was it your doing?")

She shook her head.

"Well, it wasn't me!"

"I told you!"

"What is that, what well?" Everstein demanded.

"It's just a saying," Asha said.

"And who's this beautiful prisoner? I haven't seen you here before."

He moved closer to her and peered at her, his gun still trained on Ploskorylov, although he needn't have bothered: the Priest was paralysed with fear and no longer understood anything.

"So I was right, you didn't leave!" Everstein exclaimed happily. "And where's your beloved Governor, our illustrious defector? It's all gone wrong, hasn't it? How did you break them up, Gurion? You weren't even here when they arrived!"

Gurov said nothing. It seemed best in the circumstances.

"A brilliant operation, and on such a grand scale! We call the fellow a criminal and he runs over to our side, which makes you wonder about his state of mind, and he arrives in Degunino just before the Final Battle. A Trojan Governor! And now in the battle for the village we discover a Fifth Column." There was a plot to be exposed. He turned his gun on Asha. "Well? Where is he?"

"I'm here!" cried the Governor, leaping into the room with an old Khazar rifle in his hands.

Well well, Gurov thought, wishing he hadn't been so scrupulous and had shot him earlier.

"I wondered when I'd find you, Everstein, and here you are!" the Governor said.

"Hands up!" said Everstein, who was used to people obeying him.

"What, to you?" The Governor sneered. He could barely restrain himself when Gurov was threatening Asha, but he hadn't understood most of what they were saying and had kept out of it. It was Everstein though who was to blame for his treason, and he had vowed to hunt him down, and the fact that the Khazar was now here before him revealed the hand of destiny. He wasn't planning to shoot him at once: first he would tell him in detail exactly how much he hated him. But as he was thinking all this, his finger slipped on the trigger and his rifle went off.

The ensuing pandemonium resembled the chaos of the Final Battle. Everstein ducked, but managed to fire his pistol, and the Governor crashed onto Gurov. Ploskorylov rushed to save the Inspector, and Everstein fired at Ploskorylov, and when the smoke cleared Everstein was wounded in the rib, the Governor in the stomach, and Gurov was finally and irredeemably dead. Ploskorylov hadn't suffered a scratch, and stood in the middle of the room gazing around him in panic.

Everstein lay unconscious on the floor. The Governor gasped for breath, with blood bubbling from his lips. Gurov lay face up – Everstein had shot him clean through the head. Asha didn't move, and Ploskorylov knew now that no one would tell him the true purpose of the war, and that his Initiation, the reason he had joined the battle, would be indefinitely postponed. More importantly, he had failed to save the life of an Inspector of the General Staff, who had died before his eyes as a consequence of a chain of incomprehensible events.

"Aahh!" he shrieked, waving his fist at Asha. "Bitch! Whore! It's all your fault!"

Galya put her head round the door, looking frightened. "You want cucumbers? Chickens?"

Asha stood silently clenching her fists, then bent over the Governor and tensed, as if summoning all the power of her will to return him to life.

"Not him! Don't save that one!" Ploskorylov howled.

"You won't save the other one," she said in a low voice.

"Witch!"

"Oh get..." she said without looking at him, and a cold north wind burst into the room as she said the word, and some supernatural force lifted Ploskorylov into the air and over the cottage, blowing him across the river and the blue forests, far away and out of our story, from which we see that in the Final Battle some people got what they deserved.

* * *

When Everstein regained consciousness, he didn't understand at first who or where he was. Some stranger's cottage, smelling of burning gunpowder, for some reason. Perhaps the woman had cooked it for lunch and it had run over. But why gunpowder? As if they hadn't enough to worry about, and now lunch was spoilt. It was impossible to control the world, things were always running over and becoming something else. Then he remembered everything and groaned with pain. Turning his head, he saw Asha kneeling by the Governor, bending over the wound in his stomach and whispering something to him, as if drawing death away from him. Everstein lay there pale and still, with his eyes closed and his hair soaked in sweat, and felt the life leaking out of him, as if it was being dragged from him. He knew his wound wasn't serious, and that a decent Khazar doctor could have him on his feet in a couple of days, but something irreversible was happening now and it was too late. The native girl was taking his strength and giving it to her Governor, like a blood transfusion. Blood could be poured back though, but you couldn't return strength, and the place in his body where his strength had been was covered over with a sort of connective tissue like gristle, and he couldn't move. With a weak hand like macaroni he reached for his pistol, which had dropped beside him, but his fingers wouldn't obey him. And the worst thing was he couldn't speak. His tongue obeyed him, but it had nothing to say, and he knew he was going to die from a stupid spell by some stupid native girl, who if he was fit and well would have had no power over him at all. He was dying at the end of the Final Battle too, which they hadn't won, because the Varangians had simply run off and abandoned Degunino, a shameful outcome. It wasn't shameful to die taking his knowledge with him – and how much he had! – but to die without knowing what it was all needed for. They had almost won, and now the new stage of God's plan would surely be revealed, but he wouldn't live to see it. He couldn't resign himself to this, and started resisting, and for a moment his life seemed to stop ebbing away.

The Governor moaned, and Asha stopped whispering, realizing the operation was being obstructed. Then she fixed Everstein with a steady, empty gaze, and in the blankness of her eyes he knew that the next stage of God's plan consisted of the disappearance of Everstein and all future Eversteins from the earth. The whole insane adventure to speed up history had simply speeded up the journey to the fathomless emptiness, and all the Khazars' plans to formulate the amorphous were drowning in porridge. Everything they had achieved with the natives and the world in general led to one thing, to disappear into the girl's empty eyes, and faced with the absolute nothingness of life, he sighed and stopped resisting.

"There, that's better," she whispered to him. "Lie there while I take the rest." She turned to the Governor. "That's it, you can get up now. We'll go to the mountains and spend the winter there. I'll have the baby in November and no one will find us."

Chapter Twelve
The Village of Degunino

Things began to change in Degunino soon after the Final Battle. At first it seemed nothing unusual – the earth had opened during the fighting and the river had swallowed up the soldiers, but such things had happened before: the Khazars and Varangians merely hushed them up to focus on their military achievements. The natives worked for the earth though, and they knew it was helping them. So often it had helped them, hiding them or opening up under the others, and those who watched television would say wars couldn't be won without it. This was seen as rank blasphemy by the Khazars and Varangians, who relied on suffering and sacrifice and shock brigades, but people in the villages knew their land, and that if it had joined the war it must be the end. It just wasn't clear whose side it was on. It was probably sick of both of them.

And before long, desperate times came to Degunino. It started towards the end of August, when its famous apple trees started to wither and drop their leaves and the fruit turned yellow. Their main tree, hidden from outsiders in a clearing in the forest, which had given them their seeds and cuttings and would flourish all year round, bearing frozen Ryazan apples in winter, had for days given out a barely audible moan, as if apologizing that it couldn't feed them. The old stove next to it that had tirelessly baked them its tasty pies – they could never predict the fillings: one day it would be rice or apples, the next cabbage – at first began producing them soggy and half raw, then stopped altogether, staring broken and empty at the shocked villagers. Even in the harshest times, when other villages were dying from one invader after the other, Degunino's stove and apple tree had fed everyone, and they survived. But if the stove and the tree refused to work, it meant they couldn't go on either. They continued living as they always had, strangers to killing and robbery, generously giving away all they had and dancing in a circle in the clearing that was the temple to their god, and the men would hide in the forests to escape being mobilized and return to their wives in the lulls between battles. But it was as if the soul had gone out of the village. People knew they had angered the god Give, and that this had happened when their Guard was killed in the cottage of Asha's aunt.

Not that the Guard was their main authority. There weren't many Guards, and some even thought they didn't need one at all, and the village could survive without him. But the older and wiser of them knew it was no coincidence he had been killed, and without him there to stop Asha and watch over them they would have to face the disaster on their own. She had left Degunino with her barely upright companion, followed by dark looks. What did it matter to them how far she went into the mountains? It made no difference where she had her terrible baby, who would be the beginning for them. The village grew cold and quiet, and people stopped singing and wept.

* * *

Galya touched the cracked bark of the apple tree in her garden and wept: "Apple tree, apple tree, what did I do wrong? Forgive me, little stove, be strong, be strong!"

She could sense the tree and the stove in the forest summoning up all their strength to reply, clinging with their roots to the cold earth to produce just one apple, one pie, to comfort people. But their only response was a pitiful moan. The villagers knew that the stove and every cottage and soul in Degunino had roots that drew their strength from the earth, but now all the moisture had been sucked from the earth and their roots had dried up. The cottages cracked, doors creaked, walls groaned. The roof of Asha's aunt's cottage collapsed, and her neighbour Frosya's window was broken. Things had been leading to this for so long, yet no one had seen it coming. There was evidently nothing eternal in the world.

People in Degunino were afraid of death. They didn't think of it and didn't allow it. What went into the earth didn't die, it became grass or a tree, and the circle went on. They hadn't realized that the earth must eventually dry up, and if they didn't escape this circle into a landscape fraught with dangers, there would be nothing left of them and they would vanish into thin air.

"Apple tree, apple tree!" the women wept in the gardens. "Stove, little stove!"

There was a separate lament for the ivy and the fences, and for the dahlias that had flowered so wildly that year, and their laments filled the village of Degunino.

* * *

The first frosts were early that year, and it was then that Anka and Vasily Ivanovich arrived in the village.

"Is this Degunino, Anka? Have we come to the right place?" he whispered, listening to the moans that grew louder as they approached, like the telegraph poles wailing in the damp autumn meadow. "It's just as our Guard Katerina prophesied: something's not right, can you hear?"

Anka couldn't hear, but she knew something was terribly wrong.

All the Joes would pay a few visits to Degunino on their travels, and Vasily Ivanovich went straight to the cottage of Asha's aunt, whom he had known for many years.

"Why didn't you come before, Vasily Ivanovich!" she wept when they arrived. "Come, I'll show you the tree."

Some small round women tumbled out of her collapsing cottage and surrounded the withered apple tree in the garden, without glancing at Anka. "Look, look, Vasily Ivanovich, why has it happened?"

"What a calamity," he said, kneeling on the ground. "Seems you didn't tend her, her roots are dry—"

"How can you say that, Vasily Ivanovich? I covered my darling to comfort her..."

Anka didn't understand the rest, as the women had switched to their own language. They had to dig deep into their memory when they returned to it, and it caused them almost physical pain, and they would use it to discuss the most important things that had no analogy in the language of the aggressors.

"Did you store the little box?" Vasily Ivanovich asked sternly.

"Ay, I did."

"And you spelt the corner?"

"That I did."

"Maybe you didn't voice it?"

"Ay, I did!"

At any other time Anka would have laughed at this mumbo-jumbo, but from their voices she knew something serious and terrible was being discussed, and Vasily Ivanovich seemed almost more upset than they were.

"It's the first time, Vasily Ivanovich!"

"It never happened before, Vasily Ivanovich!"

"Little stove, little stove!" they chorused, and hurried back into the cottage with him. The tree looked no different from the ones at the dacha at home. She went to it and stroked it, and a few withered leaves fluttered down, and some yellow resin leaked from the trunk like tears.

"Come Anechka, we must go to the forest," Vasily Ivanovich said, hurrying out with the women again. "Lord, what have we done?"

"It's the same in the forest, it started in the forest!" the women wept.

In the middle of a perfect circle of trees stood an old spreading apple tree, and beside it a cosy little stove that looked as if it had been there for ever. Perhaps the wind had blown the seed of a stove there, picking the roundest clearing it could find and dropping it off then flying away, and the chimney poked through the earth and grew and grew, until it produced its first harvest of pies for passers-by. And after that the village was built around it, because where a stove took root was a good place for a village, and it had blessed it.

The tree hadn't died completely, and there was still the odd leaf on it, but the walls of the stove were laced with sinister wide cracks that no amount of clay could fill.

"What's happening, Anka!" said Vasily Ivanovich in tears.

She went to the stove. Now after her two-month journey with him, she believed in its powers. So many times she had saved him from hopeless situations, and she had grown used to looking after him and already considered herself to be stronger and even older than he was, and it seemed to her that here too she might be able to help. She touched it, and something rumbled and stirred in its depths and the door fell open, and she pulled from the warm coals a single pie. It was all it could offer her, and it was hard and stale.

"Eat it, Anechka, it'll do you good," Vasily Ivanovich whispered.

"I can't, Vasily Ivanovich, it's saying goodbye," she said.

She put it back. There was no knowing where it had been.

* * *

"Where are you going, Vasily Ivanovich? Why are you leaving us, Vasily Ivanovich?" the women cried.

He stood on the street, bowing to all four corners of the village. "You know where I'm going," he told them.

"No one comes back. You can't go there, Vasily Ivanovich, you can't!"

"I must," he mumbled. "I must ask Give to help us."

"Don't go, don't go, Vasily Ivanovich!"

"No, my darlings, I must. You think I'm not afraid? I'm very afraid. Just wait, maybe I can put things right."

"Where are we going, Vasily Ivanovich?" Anka asked as they trudged along the dusty road back to the station, followed by the wails of the women, the apple tree and the stove.

"Don't ask, Anechka. Go home now. I must go there without you."

"What are you saying, Vasily Ivanovich? I can't leave now, we have to save Degunino."

"You don't need to save it, it's not your village."

"Are you getting rid of me, Vasily Ivanovich?"

He stopped in the middle of the road. "Listen Anechka, you can't come with me, no one ever comes back from there!"

"Well, maybe that's because people like it so much."

He grew angry. "Why are you so stubborn! Catch a train and go back to your parents!"

"I won't!"

"What am I to do with you, Anechka," he cried, wringing his hands. "You've seen for yourself..."

"Yes I did, and I can't leave," she said firmly. "We have to do something."

He felt her calm strength and submitted to it. Joes had no immunity against other people's strength, and happily gave in to anyone who made decisions for them. "Well then, let's see what we can do," he said.

"So where is it?"

"It's a place I know. I'll tell you about it on the way," he said evasively.

Chapter Thirteen
A Tale of Three Towns

"You can come out now, it's all clear," the Governor told Asha, peering cautiously round the corner. The grey provincial street was empty, apart from a flaking silvery statue of Lenin pointing reproachfully at the Victory cinema. The cinema had closed and become a clothes market, then the market closed and it showed films again, mainly patriotic ones that no one wanted to see, so it closed again. There had been a new-age fair selling occult artefacts and natural remedies, then a Russian Orthodox festival, but now the building was empty, apart from the local youths who broke in at night to drink cheap beer. As in every town in this part of Southern Russia, things were forever closing and opening as something else, always with a slight but marked deterioration. There had been a cathedral, painted in the nineteenth century by the kind merchant Chunkin, a self-taught artist, large, pink and chubby, whose pink chubby angels carried people's prayers directly to the throne of the Lord and were always answered. Merchant Chunkin was later ruined, and abandoned the cathedral he had painted in better days, since someone who painted chubby angels could hardly prosper under the Khazars or Varangians. Then, during the Bolshevik Revolution, the cathedral was knocked down, along with its angels, and a food store was built there instead. But such was the power of the place that the milk was always the freshest, the curd-cheese the tastiest, and the salesgirls the kindest. They were pink and chubby too, and smiled at the customers, who were all happy in their personal lives.

During the next revolution the shop was knocked down and another cathedral was built, in the Gothic Varangian style, but the parishioners felt uneasy there and an evil spirit lurked in the corners. The milk in the shops was sour, the cheese was tasteless and the salesgirls Gothic, like Varangian warriors, despising the petty needs of others, and nothing good ever happened in the town. And now everything had collapsed. First Cathedral Street had been renamed Rosa Luxemburg Street, then Cathedral Street again, and was now First Patriotic Street. There wasn't a Second Patriotic Street, because our country was one and don't you forget it, even though there was almost nothing left of it now.

All the streets had been renamed three or four times, and it was no fun to walk on them. It was a lousy town, frankly. It was built near the river Purr, named long ago for its peaceful purring sound. The Varangians had come and turned the place into a fortress, the fortress was destroyed during the time of Ivan the Terrible, the Khazars came and rebuilt it, the Varangians returned and burnt it down and rebuilt it, the Khazars came again and destroyed it and rebuilt it in stone, and after being rebuilt and destroyed every hundred years or so the town had become terribly bored of it all. First the river Purr was renamed the Red, because of the endless slaughter, then the Gum, because the Khazars' leader had dropped his dentures in it, then the Spoon Bait, because the First Secretary of the Regional Committee liked to fish with spoon bait there, and now the Spring, to match the bright patriotic spirit of the times. But none of these names caught on, and for the townspeople it was simply the River.

Having checked that it was safe, the Governor led Asha out, and they walked slowly and decorously like a normal couple along National Resistance Street, formerly Lenin Street. They had only just thrown off their pursuers, dodging and hiding for a long time in a cellar, and walking was difficult; the very air seemed to resist them. The street was crossed by National Drill Street, curved in a hump as though from all the drills that went on, and at the end of it stood a policeman. The news reports on television were all talking of the Governor's defection, and their pictures must have already reached there, and even though by now he was unrecognizable, thin, unshaven and unwashed, the policeman recognized them from the aura of hopelessness they gave off: he had an infallible instinct for these things. He sniffed the air as they approached and sprang into action, deciding to have some fun with them.

"Run!" the Governor shouted to Asha, ducking into a side street as the cop dashed towards them. A dusty heat flooded the town, and it was hard to run. Asha was five months pregnant, it was the ninth month of the year, and the first month of autumn. A crowd of people gathered behind them and the Governor clutched her limp hand, knowing they had nowhere to escape.

"Run!" cried a happy drunk sprawled by a gate. "Run, grab 'em, run!"

"Run!" roared his enormous wife, the house captain of Number 6, National Anger Street. "Grab 'em, run!"

The Governor had to drag Asha along, and they ran slowly, but the crowd didn't speed up, wanting to prolong the pleasure and trying to decide what to do with them. It would be no fun stuffing them in sacks and drowning them in the river: they wanted to see them suffer. Perhaps they could stuff them in sacks and turn it into a sack race, then kill them.

"Catch 'em!" shrieked a cat running across their path, black with anger, grey with dust.

"Kill them, kill them!" the crowd chanted. It didn't matter to them who they were killing or why. Things had changed from one thing to another so often that they had forgotten who they were, and felt nothing but a dull hatred for themselves and everyone else. As the Khazars and Federals arrived in quick succession, National Street was renamed Kosher Street, and all the ancestors turned in their graves. Then Kosher Street became National Street again, and the ancestors turned back in their graves, the earth stirred in the graveyards and the tombstones fell down. People said it was vandals, but it was the ancestors who did it.

From General Paukov Street, so named in Paukov's lifetime because he was born here, a small detachment ran out armed with staves and tore after them.

"Run!" shouted one crowd.

"Run! Kill the Antichrist!" shouted the other.

Asha tore her hand from the Governor's and fell. "I can't go on," she said.

"The wind! Call the wind!" he begged her, his voice breaking.

"I can't, I've no strength, there's no wind here."

The mob shrieked and gobbled and slowed down; they didn't need to hurry now.

"To hell with it, it's been three months, I'm sick of running," the Governor said.

Asha stood up, and they stumbled towards their pursuers hand in hand, and at that moment the first bubble of Phlogiston that had gathered under the earth exploded in the air with a deafening crash, separating them from the crowds by a deep crumbling abyss. People stopped terrified at the edge and backed away as it widened, and the transparent, colourless gas shot up into the sky.

"It's an earthquake!" they whispered.

The Governor and Asha, unable to believe their heavenly salvation, stood rooted to the spot.

"Did you do it?" he asked her.

"No, the earth did it. It's the beginning," she said tonelessly. "If it's risen it means it has no strength left and can't survive."

He sat on the shattered asphalt clutching his head. "You mean it's the end of everything because of us, Asha? Because of the baby? I'll believe anything, but not that."

"I don't know," she said. "But if they want to kill a baby, this world deserves nothing better. Let's go."

* * *

In the next town they came to, N+1, there were almost no people, as most of them had left for Moscow while there was still something left. There were rumours that it would be closed soon to outsiders; all the fields for two hundred kilometres around the city had been built on, and it wasn't made of elastic. But people were still being allowed in to do the dirty jobs, and they had to hurry.

The town of N+1 had a large number of churches and two-storey buildings, which were slowly filling with water. It wasn't from the stagnant little river N-ka, trembling with wasps and dragonflies, but from some deep underground source, possibly a mineral spring, rising from the bowels of the earth and spilling over the town. Its citizens had committed no sins and hadn't deserved this punishment, but there was no point seeking moral causes for physical events like floods and earthquakes. They happened not as retribution or a lesson, but because the earth had been neglected. When the town emptied of people it had turned to mud, and the mud didn't dry up and had become a lake, and now N+1 was disappearing under water. In places it was already waist-deep, like a new Venice, and it had been a wet summer too, there wasn't a dry street left. There was only one shop open, where Asha and the Governor bought some rock-hard spice cakes, and a museum of local handicrafts, whose directress and tour guide, Maria Semyonovna, grew water-loving vegetables in her garden.

Maria Semyonovna was tall and had once been beautiful, and was wrapped in a shawl, the uniform of all educated women in the provinces; the shawls were made by the natives, and if they didn't have the fabric they made lace instead. Most of these women who were the upholders of the national culture – the librarians, teachers and museum directresses – had a one hundred per cent Varangian concept of culture. They kept meticulous records, lifted their little fingers when drinking tea, said please and thank you – Varangian passwords that had nothing to do with good manners – and they liked to read Varangian romances in which stern Varangian girls looked down their noses at their feeble male admirers. Of course there were true intellectuals and good people among the provincial librarians, teachers and museum directresses, and Maria Semyonovna was one of them. She loved her shabby merchant town and her tiny museum with its local handicrafts, mainly mushrooms, made from wood and clay and any material that came to hand. Mushroom patterns would be woven into the shawls and lace, and a table decoration of mushrooms had been sent to the President, who learnt for the first time of the town's existence. A huge variety of mushrooms used to grow there too, nourished by the underground waters, when they were still peaceful and buried.

The Governor and Asha went into the museum because it was the only place they found open, and were welcomed by Maria Semyonovna. "Come in, come in, I'm glad you're interested in the history of our town!" she said.

She took them round the rooms, done up in the style of a merchant's house from the early nineteenth century, with fragments of family archives under glass on tables – high-school essays, excerpts from a private correspondence in which everyone thanked God they were alive, and a page of an essay entitled 'Forest Fire', by the writer and well-known terrorist Kislopryadilshchikov. On the walls hung portraits of local merchants and their children. The merchants were beetle-browed and stony, and it was clear a merchant's word was unbreakable, and their children's faces expressed a secret horror that they too would grow up to be stony and their merchant's word unbreakable.

"Here is a musical box," said Maria Semyonovna. "The rolls were found in the house of former merchant Prokofy Zhvakin. His musical box was damaged during the Revolution, and children used the rolls as target practice for their bows and arrows, but one was found in his attic that plays 'Waves of Amur'. Then one day his musical box turned up at the inn of former innkeeper Prushkin, and was repaired by former odd-job man Zobov. It was kept for a while by Commissar Steinman, who in 1937 became former Commissar Steinman, and our museum's founder, Boris Pavlovich Feklygin, a former schoolteacher, found the roll and put it together with the box, since the roll would be of no use without the box, or the box without the roll. And now we'll listen to the beautiful music."

She inserted the roll and turned the handle, and the spring released it and it whirred round, and wheezing through the apertures came the muffled sound of bells playing the 'Waves of Amur'. Asha looked out at the town. The water had already risen to the window of the museum and was leaking through cracks in the varnished floorboards, rippling with little Amur waves. "Amour" meant love, and the water seemed to be fluttering with love for its vanishing town.

"Thank you for your attention," said Maria Semyonovna, adjusting her spectacles. "We must now continue our tour by boat."

She quickly pumped up an inflatable dinghy and opened the window, letting in a gush of water, and jumped into it and helped Asha and the Governor in.

"Beneath us we see Semyonovskaya Street, and the house of former Merchant Kuzin, who donated three thousand roubles to our library," she said, rowing efficiently between the drowned houses and the church steeples rising out of the water. "Here is our remarkable Church of St Nikolai. It seemed tall and long-necked to me when I was a child, and I named it the 'Ballerina'. And here is our lovely Church of Paraskeva Friday, which seemed to me round and fat so I called her 'Granny'. We have a very nice town – I'm sorry you find us temporarily inconvenienced."

The water swelled unstoppably, and the boat rose higher, until soon only the crosses of the churches poked above the water. In the distance was a steep rocky shore, where the Caucasus mountains began.

"Thank you for visiting us. Our tour is now over," she said, mooring the boat to a rock.

The Governor and Asha scrambled ashore and tried to help her out, but she firmly refused. "I must get back to our museum. I hope you enjoyed it," she said. "There's a path through the mountains which will take you to people. Goodbye, don't forget our town."

Then she cast off and grasped the oars, and rowed briskly back across the smooth pink-grey water.

* * *

In the next town lived proud mountain warriors and numerous defenders of the law, who had escaped the cities and taken refuge in the Caucasus. It might be thought that these people would run off with the Khazars, but unlike the Governor and Everstein's naive Vova Sirotin, they were clever enough to know that the Khazars would at best thank them and give them a certificate. No one needed them abroad either, and the mountain people appreciated the PR advantages of their presence.

The mountain people weren't that interested in the rest of the world, which no longer made wars with them now they didn't need their oil. But they had their own website, mountainpeople.ru, with its Caucasian verses and suicide-bomber ballads, similar to those in soldiers' demob albums, and the houris too were depicted in roughly the same way.

Every day at four in the afternoon, Field Commander Said, who the Russians hadn't caught for a long time and no one else could be bothered with, would appear on his website praying to Allah and denouncing Unbelievers.

"We wash our feet five times a day, but the Infidels don't wash their feet," he would say portentously. "The Infidels wear stinking undergarments, but we wear no undergarments. The Infidels eat unclean food, the unclean pig, phoo. We don't eat pig, we despise pig. The pig doesn't wash, the pig is a dirty infidel animal. The Infidel is a pig, and must be cut like a pig."

So saying, Said would cut down an Infidel directly on camera, then say a prayer of thanks, and the Infidel's place would be taken by a defender of the law, who would describe the proud mountain people's struggle for independence. Their struggle had been successful, since no one cared about them now, sitting in proud isolation in their mountains. It was becoming harder to cut down Infidels, as they rarely went voluntarily to the mountains and it was risky to kidnap them in the towns. There was a small tour business, "War in the Mountains", which ran trips to show tourists the local culture and throat-singing, taking in a visit to the ruins of an old monastery, a wine-tasting and being kidnapped then released, after a ransom was paid (the sum was agreed in advance and was included in the price of the ticket). But Said couldn't help cutting down one of these hostages sometimes, and it was having a bad effect on business.

Since the world stopped going crazy for oil, the warring Caucasus was quietly turning into a heritage site, visited by academics and lovers of antiquity. The suicide bombings were generally unsuccessful now. The bombs were carelessly made, and one bomber had survived and written a book about it, but it hadn't become a bestseller. This region, assumed until now to be Russian, was to be given to the Khazars in the peace settlement. Although they didn't want it, they had little choice but to rely on the mountain people as their allies. The mountain people weren't keen on the idea either. They hated the Khazars, and weren't interested in fighting Russia: there was too much of it, and they had confined themselves to seizing the foothills of the mountains and parts of the Kuban. Moscow lived its own life, and in the rest of the country the war had exhausted itself.

On that day, as the Governor and Asha trekked through the mountains towards the shores of the Caspian to sit out the autumn and quietly await the birth of their baby, the mountain businessmen hadn't had any tourists for a long time, and Field Commander Said was cutting down a woman defender of the law instead. He sat outside the town on a narrow path overlooking a ravine, washing his feet with water from a special jug, accompanied by a short sermon about the virtues of foot-washing, then he allowed the woman to speak.

She was an elderly woman, who knew the customs of the mountain people and what would happen to her, but she still hoped that if she spoke well, Said might slaughter a sheep instead: sheep didn't wash their feet either. Staring at the camera, she described in a trembling voice her love for the proud people of the Caucasus, these ambassadors for peace, going to the school at Beslan to give the children Coca-Cola and chocolate and decorating the hall with fake explosives, begging the then-President with tears in their eyes to stop the war, not forgetting to wash their feet five times a day. These ambassadors of peace, she repeated, these doves of peace...

"Enough!" Said said, telling the camera to move in for a close-up, then deftly slit her throat and threw her down the ravine. "See what happens to those who insult the Prophet," he said to the camera, and prayed.

The Governor and Asha froze with terror on a nearby rock as he rose, nodded at the cameraman to follow, then went off to feed the rest of his defenders of the law. It was his favourite pastime. He would let them out of the shed where they lived and hurl them a turnip, and watch them fight in the dust for it.

"Are these people?" he addressed the camera. "They're dogs, praise Allah!"

Apart from this brief burst of activity at four in the afternoon, Said didn't do much. He would have enjoyed catching a couple of new hostages, but the truth was he was lazy. In the cold night, under the big green stars, Asha and the Governor crept under the barbed wire and crossed the unpatrolled frontier.

Chapter Fourteen
The Village of Zhadrunovo

As Volokhov and his Guards travelled deeper and deeper into the heart of Central Russia, he discovered that, like the rings of the trees they worshipped here, its structure too was concentric. Its enemies could drive a wedge into the wood, but they would never reach its core, and at its core was Zhadrunovo, to which they were heading.

His destiny was to create a nation, leading them through the fields and forests for four years, or for as long as it took, and the more he travelled, the more he understood the scheme of things of which he was a small part. It had seemed to him once that finding Zhenka was more important than any nation, and he still wasn't sure if he could create one. Then he realized that the two weren't incompatible, and perhaps his journey in search of her would produce a detachment of true warriors and living souls.

Yet his path kept being knocked from the straight to the spiral, and he was exhausted by the earth's current, as powerful as water. Sometimes there were no direct roads between the towns, or they had to skirt rivers flooded by the rain, and when they came to the railway line that had taken Zhenka to Zhadrunovo, they found it had been blown up by partisans. He approached Zhadrunovo slowly but steadily, cutting through the narrowing circles. Deeper into the centre of the spiral he went with his people, knowing there was no direct route to the place where they were going, and that everyone had their own route. Some went straight ahead, others faced insurmountable obstacles, some found a bridge, others a ford or crossing, others a whirlpool. Some, like Zhenka, reached Zhadrunovo instantly, others would circle it for months, and for everyone the path was different. The land itself decided where they should go, and Volokhov trusted it to get him there. He had been travelling for three months – why wouldn't he find her?

It had been a hot, beautiful summer here, and he knew with his new knowledge that it would be the last one. He knew too that there would be life after it, but that it would be quite different, so unlike the old one that he couldn't even see its pale outlines in the future. Now everything flourished for the last time, as if a shroud lay between it

415

and the approaching autumn. He walked with his Guards through warm fields smelling of dry grass and dust, and empty pine forests and translucent birch groves, and stayed in settlements of strange people who had forgotten who they were and what they were called. He travelled on, surprised by nothing and thinking of nothing, keeping sight of his goal and coming closer to it all the time, like a satellite falling to earth. And the closer he came, the more he understood that even beyond the village of Zhadrunovo there was life, but he lacked the power to imagine it.

He didn't so much feel Zhenka now as sense her presence. He no longer dreamt of her, and she didn't speak to him in his thoughts, but he was picking up strange signals from her, warning him and directing him to the right path. He knew the Zhenka he met in Zhadrunovo wouldn't be Zhenka, but a vision of Zhenka, like Faust in heaven meeting not Gretchen but some poor sinner who had borne her name. Yet part of Zhenka's soul was eternal and was in a complex relationship with his, sending him her distorted signals like a voice from the other side. He heard distant calls from beyond the mist, growing louder as he approached, and he already knew she wouldn't be as she had been before, and perhaps they wouldn't even recognize each other.

Another strange sound came to him that he heard all the time, awake and asleep: a single note, insistent yet unobtrusive, like the song of the wires over the plain or the whistle of the wind, or snow blowing across the flat green ice. It wasn't a moan or a complaint, but a flat gentle hum, enticing him and engulfing him. The earth seemed to be singing to him, and he took this too as a signal, telling him he was going the right way. Or perhaps, best of all, it was just humming to itself, like a child quietly playing alone, oblivious to outsiders. There was a strange tenderness and joy in the sound, like a smile of love and welcome. It seemed to be slyly encouraging him, telling him things would be nothing like he expected. He was hearing it more clearly now, and he knew he was on the right road and it helped him to orientate himself.

Once he came with his Guards to a lake in the forest, black and flat as a plate, which the local people called Lake Echo. As they approached, they heard a high girlish voice call "Cooee!" across the water, and another call back from the other shore. The voices went on calling to each other with childish joy from one side to the other, bursting suddenly at odd intervals from unexpected places. One called just behind them, and when they looked round no one was there. Then they started again – "Cooee!" "Cooee!" – as if an invisible party of friends had scattered to collect nuts or mushrooms and had become separated. But no one appeared and nothing moved, apart from a slight ripple passing across the water.

"We mustn't go there," Volokhov said. He wasn't afraid, but he knew they had fallen into an opening, and that it was dangerous; it was open to them now, but it was intended for others. His Guards rose regretfully from a short rest and headed away from the black water, edged by contorted birches and hovering dragonflies, and the voices called sadly after them, then fell silent.

There were many of these openings, and in the months he had been travelling he had learnt to recognize them. He knew now that the whole of Russia was crossed by tunnels of air that led directly to difficult, inaccessible places, and it would take only a few days for someone to walk through such a tunnel from one end of the country to the other. The land hid these little passages and bridges in unpredictable spots, and he could detect them now, because after travelling for so long the Wolf had woken in him, whose true nature Gurov had described to him. But he barely remembered Gurov now, and he had forgotten what he said: it was more interesting to look around him.

Many miracles happened to them on the way. They spent the night once in a lonely cottage in a forest that carried them twenty kilometres to another forest in a place they didn't know. They sat in a silver moonlit birch grove where some heard singing, some a string orchestra, and others a marching band. They heard bells floating over a river, yet there were no bells to be seen. But when you travel for a long time you believe anything, and surrender to it. He had chosen good people who didn't tire of walking, yet strangely the longer he walked with them, the more different their visions became, and soon one was seeing a field and another a forest. When he thought about it, he realized that in travelling they were finally discovering their true selves, and since people were all different, there was no reason they would see the same things. At one point Shmakov, the leader of their choir, had seen some raspberry canes as a trolleybus, and he disappeared behind them and sat on it and went home. The others went into the canes and heard the trolley wires clicking and cars hooting somewhere far away where Shmakov was, but they didn't grieve for him, and knew he had gone where he needed to be.

* * *

Volokhov travelled on with his Guards, putting up in places no enemy had reached, and in each of them people asked about the war.

"You killed the German, did you?" asked a shaggy old beekeeper, treating them to fresh honey and cold milk from his cellar.

"What German? We've already killed the German, Granddad," said Yakov the Carthorse.

"Aha," he nodded. "We live deep here, we don't know things. News doesn't reach us, and the radio is silent. It spoke before, but now it's silent. Did you kill him long ago?"

"Over seventy years ago, Granddad."

"That's good. He didn't come here, there's no way he can get here, we don't know things."

Yakov the Carthorse mended the old man's fence and did some hammering in the shed and plastered his walls – the old man complained he hadn't the strength for it. The hives were three kilometres from the village, which was half empty, like most Russian villages now. Some had left, others had died, but life still went on there in its well-structured way.

"So everyone's leaving?" Volokhov asked him.

"Some leave, some stay," the old man said enigmatically.

"Commander," said Yakov, taking Volokhov aside. "I'm sorry for him on his own, I could help him with his hives and catch up with you later. I like it here, Commander, don't be upset if I stay. I never wanted to stay anywhere before, but I feel at home here."

"Stay," said Volokhov expansively. "I can see it's the right place for you. Like should cling to like if the end is near."

And Yakov stayed.

They travelled on without him and came to another village, where a girl of about seventeen in a spotted red dress ran out to meet them.

"Oh no, it's soldiers!" she cried. "Brave soldiers, have you fought the German?"

"We fought him years ago, my lovely, didn't you hear?" Mikhail Motorin answered for all of them.

"No, we didn't," she shook her head. "They say the German has tanks and europlanes."

"We call them airplanes," Motorin replied, moving closer to her and caressing her with his eyes.

"And gases too," she said. "When the German sets off his gases, everyone falls down."

"Not at all, gas is forbidden," he explained. "Maybe we could have a bit of kvass or some milk?"

"It's a long time you've been fighting, Granny's father left years ago, and there's been no word of him," she said shyly, and Volokhov realized, to his horror – then not with horror at all but with a happy smile – that she was talking about the First World War, before the Revolution.

"We'll survive now, we're going home, we're going home," said Motorin. "What's your name, darling?"

"Good people call me Xenya," she giggled.

"Well, Xenya, let's drink to victory!" he said, and they all drank to victory.

There were five old men and six old women living in the village with Xenya, whose parents had left long ago, also to the war – why else would anyone leave? – and she was a granddaughter to all of them. There was no end to their fascinating tales about the war. Her parents had sent a letter from there calling old Pryanishna to come, but Pryanishna was too old for war and went nowhere. If the German came, she would attack him with her oven tongs, but it seemed unlikely. No one ever arrived and stayed: a commissar visited during the Revolution and had spat and left.

"Don't be upset, Commander, but I feel an attraction for the girl," Motorin told Volokhov after they had eaten. "If I have your blessing I'll stay."

He was already speaking the local way and it was infectious, and the village smelt wonderful, of honey and tar.

"Stay," Volokhov blessed him, and after a comfortable night in the hayloft, he set off next morning with his dwindling detachment.

They travelled on, and came to a village where a lonely old peasant lived with a boy. The boy was dumb and the peasant was deaf, and he kept talking about the "Crenchman". They also had a speaking dog, although it was shy with Volokhov and his Guards and didn't speak, just looked at them as if it might at any moment.

"We beat the Crenchman, boy!" said Volokhov. "Explain we beat him long ago and he needn't be afraid."

The boy explained to the old man in gestures that the Frenchman weighed no more than a bundle of hay, grabbing a pitchfork and tossing some in the air to represent the Frenchman. The old man understood and nodded.

"Forgive me Major, but I'm staying with them," nurse Anyuta said with her usual directness. "It's hard for them alone without a woman."

The boy, although deaf, nodded that it was, and the dog nodded to say he wasn't lying. It was both a listening and a speaking dog, the most valuable kind, but it didn't know how to get its own food, since after acquiring the miraculous power of speech it hadn't the strength to kill defenceless animals. And so they lived, looking after each other, and they couldn't do without each other. Anyuta was to crown this symbiosis, because when people and animals look after only each other, it's a dull life. There has to be someone there to admire it and enjoy the fruits of their work, and so she stayed.

They travelled on without her, and over the next twenty villages Volokhov lost the rest of his Guards. He wasn't sorry, they had all found their places in the world and perhaps this was the purpose of their journey, for these good people to scatter in the villages and fertilize the inert Russian life there. Everywhere he visited, people were happy to see him back from war, and in one he was asked if he had beaten the "Lyakh" – the medieval word for the Poles. The Russians had come and mustered their levies, they said, and all the boys went off and none of them had returned. Volokhov explained that the Lyakh had been beaten centuries ago and the boys couldn't have been killed, they must have stayed in Moscow. That's it, the old men said, they stayed in Moscow; if they died, they would have come back. People had to come back at least every three hundred years, or there would be no one left. Everyone was dying, more were dying now than were being born, where would the Lord find them? They told him the dead rested then rose from the earth, and they showed him the cemetery from which they returned. An old woman was sitting by a gravestone, waiting for her husband who had drowned sixty years ago, and if he didn't get up soon she wouldn't live to see him.

Having seen the village where the dead fought, rested, rose and returned, Volokhov guessed he must be close to Zhadrunovo. He was alone now, and it became easier for him to walk.

* * *

The clouds moved and the dawn was crimson and the cranes were flying... It was a good poem, and he had known it by heart once and had forgotten it, because here in the heart of Russia everything incidental is forgotten, and he knew then that he was a true Wolf, who had learnt to see things properly, connecting with them and not looking for meaning. The landscape lay around him like drawings in a fairy tale, with its white-hot stones inscribed with worn messages, its half-empty villages where lonely old men put him up, its dusty roads and fields of ripe grain and pine forests and poignant sunsets. He walked steadily across the fields, approaching Zhadrunovo from the forest, happy at heart and knowing he was close to his goal, as if the place was saying: "Forgive us, dear man, that we didn't let you in before. Not everyone is allowed in, but if you are, it means you're not our enemy and we can help you. Come and find your girl, take her away if you want, just don't look back."

No, that was some singer, or was it a Greek myth? His story would be different though. He would go to Hades and it would be nothing like he imagined, and perhaps he wouldn't want to come back...

The clouds moved and the dawn was crimson and the cranes were flying...

The clouds were low and blue and moved in mysterious circles, and even the wind here blew in a circle. So the dead left and came back – and it must be true, how else would new people be found? He was surprised he had never realized this before.

The cultivated earth ended, and he walked through a field of tall grass scattered with convolvulus and some blue bell-like flowers. The grass grew taller, reaching to his waist, then his shoulders, and soon he disappeared into it over his head; it was like walking into a house without knocking, and people would ask why he had been gone so long and what news he had and who was hunting them. And he would say no one was hunting them, and he had been gone so long because it had taken him all this time to find them.

The rain started and stopped, and he plunged on through the grass, until he came to the edge of a forest. It was of many colours, a mixture of conifers and oaks, and grew thicker and darker as he pushed on, not noticing that it was dying. First it was green, then a reddish colour, and soon it was completely brown, with just a few shrivelled saplings growing in the mud. The needles snapped under his feet. He sat on a stump and scratched his head, and the wind blew golden rays of light through a spider's web. I've come far, he thought, I've never come so far.

Just then he heard a rustle at his feet and a little squeaking sound, and he looked down and saw a mouse. Standing on its hind legs, it asked him with its front paws to bend down. He put out his hand and it jumped up. "Good morning, Uncle," it said. "Give me some bread and I'll give you good answers."

421

"You clever thing," he said, pulling a crust from his bag, given to him by the old man in the last village. He crumbled it to suit its mouse capabilities and, after munching delicately, the mouse stood on its hind legs again, looked round to make sure no one was listening, then whispered in his ear the answers to certain riddles.

Volokhov thanked it and set off and, as the wise mouse predicted, he soon reached a flat plain with six trees. In one sat Finist the bright-winged falcon, in another the Phoenix, and in the third Sirin, the bird of joy, with the head and chest of a beautiful woman and the body of an owl. In the fourth sat Alkonost, the bird of paradise, another half-bird, half-woman; in the fifth sat Gamayun, the prophetic bird of wisdom, with a large woman's head; and on the sixth a chattering sparrow. He had never seen such birds before, but the mouse had prepared him well.

"Good morning, young man," said Sirin. "What time do you stamp the flax?"

He replied as the mouse had told him: "In the middle of the privy."

Sirin flapped her wings and took flight, which meant his answer was correct.

"Hello!" Finist screeched happily. "Before Dmitr the maiden was clever, and afterwards?"

"Even cleverer," he replied, and Finist flew off satisfied.

"Your good health, friend," said the Phoenix. "Round the mound, touch the ground – what is it?"

It tensed, ready to lunge at him and peck his eyes out with its golden beak, hunching its wings like a robber hunching his shoulders before whipping a knife from his sleeve.

He concentrated, and repeated what the mouse had told him: "None of your business."

"Splendid!" sang the Phoenix, rustling its green wings with an encouraging sound and shooting vertically into the dark-blue sky.

"What will it be now?" Alkonost asked Volokhov in a deep contralto voice. Her plumage was cobalt, like shot silk, with a collar of pure gold.

He replied correctly: "I don't know."

"Well, I do," Alkonost said, pushing her head under her wing, and fell asleep.

"Well done, young man," Gamayun said condescendingly. "Now tell me the answer: who he sees he deceives, who he loves he destroys, who she forgets will die."

Volokhov paused and scratched his head so as not to seem a know-it-all, then replied: "The answer is lost."

"Good," Gamayun nodded. "Now listen to the sparrow."

"Oh, oh, oh!" chirped the little sparrow, fluttering fussily on its branch in an excess of emotion. "How good life is, how much happiness there is! You wake in the morning and you eat and it's good! How cleverly the world is arranged, how ungrateful we are to grumble at God! Even winter is lovely, like a white canvas sparkling with diamonds! How pleasant it is to sit with friends and talk. You say something clever and they go, 'Aah!' But I'm sad without mother, I miss my mother!" It sat on its branch and wept, sweetly folding its wings.

Volokhov knew he must depart from the formula and repeat the improvised response he had learnt: "Fly away while you're still alive."

"Ah, how delightful," it murmured, suddenly losing interest, and turned into an owl and flew to a hollow tree, from where he could hear it saying, "You're a fool, brother, a fool!" It must have been a sort of password, like on a SIM card, because the tree opened and he saw ahead of him a pale-green night sky over a huge tree, and a little girl with red hair and transparent eyes coming to meet him. She took his hand and led him through swirls of mist, and he felt nothing special, just a slight sense of anticlimax.

"Listen, is Zhenka Dolinskaya with you?" he asked her, clutching her small cold hand.

"Who he sees he deceives, who he loves he destroys, who she forgets will die," she told him.

"You mean she's forgotten me?"

"Yes, you are a fool," she said. "Aren't you alive?"

"Yes, I am," he said uncertainly.

"Look, she's over there, washing clothes," she said.

From far off at the river he could hear sounds of splashing and laughter, like the laugh of a water nymph, and in the middle of the water winked a green buoy. There was nothing surprising about Zhenka deciding to wash clothes in the middle of the night. She had probably been busy all day, and wanted him to find her at this peaceful domestic task which was so alien to her.

"Why can't I feel her?" he complained. "I used to feel her all the time, but I can't any more."

"That's not true," the little girl rebuked him, and he knew she was right: he could still feel her, only in a different way now. That steady encouraging note that had sung to him as he crossed the concentric Russian plain with his thinning detachment was her voice, but he had never heard it like that before. He had known her angry, sad, joyful and tempestuous, but not this quiet deep current he had always searched for in her. He thought suddenly how good she was. He had never been sure he could love a blood enemy, but she could, although her blood told her not to. He remembered how little she spoke of her love for him, how she tolerated his clumsy monologues and forgave him, how sometimes when he was in Moscow she would phone him at night, forgetting the time difference, knowing he wouldn't be angry at being woken, to tell him she couldn't help it, she just had to hear his voice – and he realized how stupid it had been to fight her, and how truly and for ever she had loved him, and how steadfastly she had defended this love before and during the war and on their travels. She didn't want to trick him or fight him, she wanted nothing more from him than who he was. Yet at the same time she wanted him to know himself and to be complete, as she was. He remembered their quarrels on those hot stuffy nights in the Kaganate, losing his temper with her like the worthless fool he was, and she would flinch from his cutting words and look at him with such childish dismay that he would grow even angrier. It was only now he remembered all this about her, and her boisterousness, her endless hunger for activity, and her sudden moods of sadness. Lord, what had life done to them! They were so used to being harnessed and harassed at every step that they didn't believe anyone could just love them.

Yet a cold clear voice in his head was telling him he shouldn't torture himself. In the end perhaps it was she who had found him and had loved him and come for him – but what did it matter, they were the same now.

A fresh still night lay over Zhadrunovo. Laughter bubbled from the river and the buoy winked, and the whole world was winking, saying yes, yes, my beloved fool, what did you think! A blue mist came down and wrapped him in a soft blanket, smelling of grass and river silt, and the river laughed and sighed. It was the way people laugh from sad, distant shores when someone floats past and is carried far away and can't stop, and he was at the shore of the river now, and someone was floating past and waving.

The little girl looked at him and waited.

"I remember reading a story once about people going into a garden and finding peace," he told her. "In the garden was a house, and in the house they would have a beautiful life, and at that moment the house crashed to the ground leaving a sad, empty place. Because nothing should ever be taken from its rightful owners. And I think, what if…"

"Who are you talking to? Come on, let's go," said the little girl, and the blueness descended on him.

Chapter Fifteen
The Soldier on Leave

Gromov's journey to Makhachkala took ten days, and he had just five left of his leave. The trains had been few and far between, and he heard vague rumours on the way that the war was over, or at least the fighting was over. But there was nothing definite, and he felt duty-bound to go back and face the music with Gurov for failing his assignment. His oath was his oath.

As he travelled further south, the landscape changed to flat steppes, salt marshes and stagnant mudflats, through which poked clumps of dry grass. The sky became flat and colourless, and he could smell the Caspian. The long dry steppe stretched to the shores of the sea, and the elements of land and water were in complete harmony. One was dry, the other wet, and there was no place for human beings in either of them; they could visit and look around and admire them, but would only be tolerated here for so long.

People had been evacuated to Makhachkala at the start of the war, when things seemed serious. They were mainly the destitute, urban middle class whom the war would have hit hardest: the elite wouldn't suffer, and the rock-bottom poor had nowhere lower to sink and nothing to lose. They had packed only their essentials: the evacuation was rushed and chaotic, and there was nowhere to stay. New houses were being built for those with money, and rents in Makhachkala were almost as high as in Moscow. Masha had written little of all this, but Gromov knew from talking to people how things were.

The train stopped fifteen kilometres outside the town. Every train he had travelled on here had stopped before the station; something strange had happened to the timetables, and it was as if no one wanted to reach their destination. He climbed out and strode along the tracks, not thinking or looking back. It was better this way: the walk would prepare him for their meeting. It was for this meeting that he had asked for his leave, and he had waited two years for it and thought of little else. There had been nothing else in his life, if he was honest – apart, of course, from his duty.

He walked across the steppe that smelt of the sea, towards the sea that looked like the steppe. Some big birds fluttered around him and swooped off, squinting at him with their round golden eyes, and Makhachkala rose ahead of him like a mirage. He headed for the docks, past dusty grey buildings and children playing in courtyards, and leant his elbows on the parapet and smoked, looking out over the flat green water. A dark-skinned little boy came up and peered inquisitively at him, and he asked him where Akhmetov Street was. The little boy pointed right, and he stumbled through a maze of slums and narrow alleyways looking for a street sign, but he couldn't find one, and became hopelessly lost. He was about to give up when he heard a voice calling him, the voice he had been waiting for and the reason he had come.

He turned round, and how she ran, how she ran to him! It was worth everything for this, all the hardships and fighting and the death and despair, and the trains that didn't arrive. She was very brown, wearing a short cotton dress that he remembered, and her hair was bleached from the sun. She threw her long sunburnt arms around him and buried her face in his chest, and he understood two things at that moment with exceptional clarity: that he had arrived, and that he would soon leave. It was as if she carried with her this sense of imminent loss, and somehow he needed it to be this way and he couldn't understand why.

* * *

"So tell me everything," he said.

"What's to tell, you know what the evacuation was like."

"Not really, only what people wrote."

"No one wrote anything. It's as if they started this war just to clear us out of Moscow."

"How can you say that, Mash?"

"No, really, they needed the sick and the weak out of the way. They'd have done it by force if they needed to, but we were already so broken. Did your parents leave?"

"No, they stayed."

"Thank God. Mother almost lost her mind from all the hysteria on TV about the Khazars. We just got rid of everything, sold the piano for a few roubles and left. It was an army train, it was all very military and stupid. You know, Gromov, I sometimes think the war's a big game they're playing. So many people have been able to cash in."

"Nonsense, you remember how it started."

"Remember what? They'd been leading up to it for years. War takes care of everything, silly Gromov. Do you know how many flats in Moscow have been grabbed? Our flats have all gone. You didn't visit Medvedkovo when you were there, did you?"

"No, it was too sad."

"You should have. There are different people living there now, the building was knocked down to build smart new apartments. Lizka wrote and told me, she stayed. They had to get rid of idiots like you and me. Idiots like you went to the army, and idiots like me went to Makhachkala, so the idiots Moscow belongs to could have it. I'd have run off to the Front if there was something to fight for. No, don't…"

He had moved towards her, wanting to hold her and comfort her, but she misinterpreted his gesture and moved away. They found it hard to be physical with each other, as they lay on the bed, painfully trying to catch up and get used to each other.

"And can you make a living here?" he said.

"I've made all sorts of livings here, Grom, everything short of selling my body, and that's only because they like plumper ones. I worked in the propaganda office putting out army nonsense – writers were evacuated at the start, all the writers' and artists' unions. Half of them went to the Front, and the older ones came here. Then I stamped permits for farming businesses and had meetings with the locals who don't know Russian. Mother works in a shop, sometimes as a cashier, sometimes as a cleaner. Once I worked in a hospital, but I was sacked and the job went to a local. We live from hand to mouth. I'd have left long ago, but where would I go? There's nowhere to live in Moscow now, I've heard Moscow's closed."

"I'll find you somewhere. I heard that too, but it isn't."

"And have many evacuees returned? Of course they haven't. We'll never be allowed back, Gromov, they don't need us. That's what you're fighting for, my handsome."

He said nothing.

"So tell me how the fighting's going."

"It's stopped," he said. "In the first year there was real fighting, and it's not pleasant when a soldier spews up his guts. They tell you you'll get used to it, but you don't, no one gets used to it. Then there were lulls between the battles, and the lulls dragged on, and at some point it was obvious neither side had the strength to fight, but they were ashamed to demobilize."

"Why should they? They don't need you to go home, they need you to fight. At first I didn't understand why people didn't turn their weapons on their commanders, the revolutionary way. But if they had, then what? They're destroying themselves as it is, it's a dead end on all fronts. And you went off to destroy yourself too, don't deny it."

"I won't."

"Because it's your duty, your duty."

"But it's always been like this. We're not allowed just to live: only thieves and murderers can just live. If you join the army, at least you're clean."

"Really. It must be wonderful to have nothing on your conscience."

"I know what you're thinking, Mash, you're thinking I should save you instead of saving myself."

"No I'm not, I don't want you to save me, if you did I wouldn't love you. I don't want some fat draft-dodger setting me up in Makhachkala. Mother's relatives here have given us this room and I'm grateful to them."

Gromov already knew about her relatives, who had given her the little room where they were spending the night, on the first floor of a crumbling barrack block practically indistinguishable from the one in Medvedkovo. Her mother was guarding the shop all night and would be back in the morning, and tomorrow they would have to find somewhere else to sleep.

"So you'll stay here?" he asked her.

"I don't know, maybe. You can move here with me if you'd like, but I know you wouldn't. You'll go back to the Front, won't you?"

"I have to. I can't get out of it, or I'll be court-martialled."

"What court-martial? Who'll look for you here? It's fine, I like it this way. Gromov, Gromov, I could never live with you."

"Why not?"

"I don't know, I don't think I could live with anyone, everything nauseates me. I can't bear people in Moscow, because they're the same as me but they're strangers to me. I can never live in Moscow again. It's simpler here, it's more honest. Everything's foreign – the language, the people."

"So am I a stranger to you?"

"No, but you would be if we lived together. I probably shouldn't say this to a soldier, you need something to hope for while you're fighting, but it's easier for me to love you when we're apart. And you know it's the same for you. I love you so much, Gromov, but for me to love you, you have to be somewhere else."

"I don't mind, you were always honest."

"I'm a freak, you mean, I can't be with people. I'd kill myself, but it would be so cheap. And there's Mother…"

"And me."

"Yes, of course. Maybe you've softened me a bit, you hurt me a lot when you joined the army, you know."

"Really?" He propped himself up on his elbow to look at her. "I never knew, I thought you wanted me to go."

"Why would I? You left me alone in the war."

"I thought you'd never forgive me if I stayed."

"That's stupid. I'm a woman, not a Valkyrie. I didn't want you to go."

"You should have said!"

"You wouldn't have listened."

"How do you know?"

"I know you. And I'm used to being alone now. We've five days together, maybe in five days I'll have grown used to you. Don't be hurt. I should be happy to see you – and I am, I'm terribly happy, but I don't know what's going to happen, Gromov."

"What will happen is that I'll finish fighting and come for you."

"I don't know, Grom, I don't know. Sleep now, you're exhausted."

"I don't want to sleep." He put his arms round her and kissed her neck, and she stiffened.

"Not yet, it's been two years, I've forgotten how…"

"I'll show you then. I love you, Mash."

"Don't say that, it doesn't mean anything! You can't love when war's a death camp! You were right to leave. Stop it, I don't want it!"

He made her remember what it was like, and realized finally that there was no return from war. A burnt-out man had come to a burnt-out land that had once flourished at the sight of him and was bright with flowers, and now everything had to start again from nothing. Even the returning conqueror is out of his depth with women at first, but the soldier on leave, returning from the war to a ravaged place where he isn't a conqueror, has nothing to hope for. And they didn't grow used to each other, although by the end of the fifth day he managed to make her smile and laugh her old laugh again. People never get used to each other when they are on leave.

* * *

The station bustled around them, with people selling seeds, medals and stale watermelons, while an invalid played an accordion. There were only a few trains from Makhachkala: one arrived and one left once a week, and the station was like a stage set. It had been arranged to look like a station, but the play had ended long ago and the audience had nowhere to go, and the accordionist played and people sold their seeds, medals and watermelons at their old pace, perhaps even more animatedly than before. A few of the performers had already realized they were just extras, but Masha and Gromov had always known it, and it united them more deeply than love. Or perhaps love was just this, knowing the finality of things, and knowing the other knew it too, and perhaps beauty was simply the highest form of this, allowing us to feel more sharply, more clearly that everything would die.

The train hooted, and they waited, without tears or sadness.

"Well, goodbye, Gromov," she said. "If you were different I wouldn't love you, and if I was different you wouldn't love me."

"That's true," he said.

"We can't live together, you know that. What sort of life would it be for the hero and the beautiful woman? He fights, she waits, the dragon is killed, and they live happily ever after. But who knows what happens afterwards? You and I will miss each other happily ever after. You'll dream of me and won't be able to live without me, and I'll always love you and I'll sing and cry and sew, and you'll always leave the day before you get tired of me. And now you'll kiss me, so you'll remember nothing but this kiss for a year or two, and I'll remember nothing else too."

"That's true too," he said, and he embraced her thin body under her thin dress and smelt its fresh cotton smell, the smell of her sunburnt skin and the leafy scent of her hair, and he felt her exhaustion and fragility and her strength, as she crossed from youth to maturity. He kissed her and tore himself away, and stood still as she ran off, without waiting for the train to be announced, turning back just once to wave at him.

He boarded the shabby cut-price train laid on by the cut-price show, and sat by the window. The table was scrawled with obscenities. Passengers and new recruits going off to the Front knew with their native genetic memory the four-letter spell, writing it on tables, walls, fences and every available surface – pointlessly, since the magic word was already losing its power. The recruit wrote it on the wall of the carriage, but no wind blew in to save him from the army. The poor Joe carved it in the corridor with his knife, but the language of the wandering poet was forgotten now, and had gone deep underground.

The train moved off, and Gromov returned on the iron tracks to the war that no longer existed, to fight for his country that no longer existed. Only the railway existed.

Epilogue

High in the mountains in a cave above Makhachkala, where the Governor had made his humble home, Asha was about to give birth to the Antichrist.

They had walked to Makhachkala by a long circuitous route through the mountains, and there at last no one was chasing them, and they could breathe freely. Their pictures hadn't reached the town, and there was almost no government there, it lived its own life and didn't care about the new evacuees. They would have been lost without a place to stay, but Asha, with her usual infallible instinct, found a girl called Masha who helped them find somewhere. The girl so hated the world she wouldn't have minded if it was destroyed. She wasn't a native herself, but from that middle layer who were the majority in Russia – Varangians and Khazars who had lost all memory of their roots. But her hatred was strong, and she hated this world almost as much as Asha did. Asha didn't tell her the whole sad story of their escape, just that they had been driven from their home, that her husband had lost his job, and the police were after him and wanted to arrest him for nothing, simply because he didn't fit in with the new government. The girl Masha was one of the evacuees, the most defenceless people here, and was eager to help others who were as defenceless as she was.

The Governor got a job as a guard at the market, and until November Asha managed to hide in the town. She was looking forward impatiently to the birth. She knew her newborn would kill her, but she wouldn't be sorry to die to bring him into this world. She didn't want to die before he was born, but afterwards she didn't care what happened.

Then one day the Governor saw pictures of them at the market, and realized their pursuers had finally caught up with them. The man who employed him either didn't recognize the pictures or pretended not to – and he was unrecognizably thin now, after five months with almost no food. But the fact that they were still being hunted was worrying, so they moved to the mountains, where no one would find them.

The week before Asha was due to give birth, they moved to their cave in the mountains. Masha guarded her while the Governor was at

433

work, and he brought them food from the market. There was already snow on the mountains, but Asha didn't feel the cold, her whole being consumed by her terrible baby. She knew who she was bringing into the world, and what sort of baby he would be, and she was waiting for the birth as a sort of liberation.

"Are you married?" she asked Masha once. Until then they had avoided talking about such things and about the future.

"He's not my husband. He's in the army."

"Who's he fighting for?"

"Our people, against the Khazars."

"No one fights for us. When will he come?"

"I don't know. When the war ends."

"Everything's going to end," Asha said happily. "My baby will be the end of this world. He'll grow up and he'll avenge us all."

"Oh really," Masha said, deciding she must be suffering from some sort of pregnancy psychosis.

"Yes, really, I have to warn you. He'll kill me first, but you must look after him and stay with my husband and save him."

Masha couldn't listen to any more of her nonsense. Asha was a silly native girl, maybe a little mad. True, she had managed to hypnotize the women at the market to give them all sorts of tasty food, and she found her amusing to talk to. She was always making up strange stories about the natives and their heavenly village where there was everything, and a hellish one where there was nothing. She must have gone off the rails when her husband, an important official, was dismissed from his job. There were quite a few of these ex-officials nowadays, and new plots were discussed every day on television. But her madness was dangerous, she might harm herself or even die of fear, and Masha decided to have a word with the Governor.

That evening, when he returned along the secret paths to the cave, she seized the chance to take him outside. "You know Asha's afraid she'll give birth to the Antichrist?" she asked him.

"She's not afraid, she wants to give birth to the Antichrist," he said firmly.

"But don't you know it's insanity?"

"Because of this insanity we've been hounded across Russia. I'm convinced it's because of him."

"Listen, Alyosha, I know you've been through a shock, but you must get a grip on yourself. No one's giving birth to the Antichrist, it's madness and lunacy and you should talk to her about it."

"I will not talk to her about it. I want her to give birth to the Antichrist, or whatever they call him. I want our baby to destroy this world."

"I'd gladly destroy it myself, but I don't want her to destroy herself. She'll die if she thinks like that."

"Yes, but it's what she wants."

"And you? Do you want it?"

"Maybe. What must be must be, don't try to stop her."

"Goddammit," Masha said, and didn't return to the subject.

The day before Asha's labour started, Masha dreamt of the Antichrist, a huge handsome baby boy with teeth and hair. He crawled across the floor of the cave to where Asha was lying exhausted after the birth, and he didn't understand she was his mother, he just saw something edible before him and threw himself at her like a ravenous dog. Masha screamed in her sleep and woke, and her scream joined Asha's as her labour started.

The Governor sat outside and waited, rocking back and forth, with his fingers in his ears. He couldn't listen to Asha's shrieks, and he didn't hear his son's first cry. Masha did everything, and although she had no experience in such matters, people discover they know things when they have to.

"He's not the Antichrist, Alyosha," she told him after it was all over, staggering from exhaustion, and he barely managed to catch her. "Come and look at him, he's a normal baby. There was no reason for you to run away."

"I don't understand. Does it mean they're all mad?" he said.

"Of course they are. They must have been chasing you for another reason, and you're mad too. Admit it, you just made the whole thing up to explain losing your job."

"I'm not mad, I don't need to make anything up," he said sadly. "We've been chased thousands of miles from Siberia because of this baby. They wanted to kill us, don't you understand?"

"I know, she told me, and it's stupid. He's a normal baby and he needs to live – we all do. The world's not going to end. I wouldn't be against it, but it won't happen."

"Wait until he grows up, we'll see then," he said.

But he was obviously a normal baby, the Governor could see that, they must have got it all wrong. So would the earth be healed, even though it was clearly moving to its end? What if people had picked the wrong couple? What if he wasn't a son of Rurik at all, and Asha wasn't a Wolf?

Masha came to the entrance of the cave and looked out at the snow on the mountains and the brown town below. Sooner or later she would have to return to this town and somehow live on. The baby woke in her arms and squealed.

* * *

It was at this time, on a bright cold morning in November just before the first snow, that Captain Gromov was travelling in a military train to the South, where dispersed bands of Khazars were still said to be hiding. The war was over, but it still dragged on, and he knew he must see the show through to the end, and to be honest he was interested to see what the end was like.

The soldiers sang, played cards and scrapped from boredom. The army was hungry, and their autumn supplies still hadn't arrived. Colonel Zdrok had deserted and vanished without trace, and there were all sorts of rumours from Moscow, but Moscow was far away and almost unreal.

The train travelled past a black, leafless forest and a black field stretching into the distance, and approached a small station slowly, as if afraid to wake some secret force. And at that moment Gromov felt a sudden overpowering urge to jump out onto the platform and see what the village was like.

It was a perfectly ordinary station, but its name was familiar, and he remembered strange Inspector Gurov, who had died while he was away, saying he would send him to Zhadrunovo, and something about no sheep grazing there. It was just a saying of course, but the power that was pushing him out was almost irresistible, like the urge he used to have sometimes as a child to throw himself from the fifteenth floor of the flats.

He stood in the corridor, gripping the icy handle of the door, and he would have controlled himself and travelled on to fight in this endless war, but he saw a thin, dark-haired girl of about fifteen sitting on the asphalt with a bent old man, and there was something so lost and helpless about them that he jumped out, leaving his things on the train, and he didn't miss them.

He landed on his feet. The train was moving slowly, as if the driver had been expecting this to happen, and it picked up speed immediately and disappeared into the autumn distance.

"What are you doing here?" he asked the girl. She had a worn, exhausted face and thin red hands.

"We've come all the way to Zhadrunovo, you see, and now we've got here Vasily Ivanovich doesn't want to go on," she told him.

"Why not?" he asked.

"People don't come back," the old man mumbled. "What's there and how they live no one knows—"

"But we have to go, Vasily Ivanovich!" the girl said in a tearful voice. "You must persuade Take to make the stove and the apple tree better…"

"They'll never get better, Anka," he said. "We can't go there, we must go back."

"Please, Vasily Ivanovich, we've travelled all this way!" she cried. "I can't go in circles any more, we must stop somewhere, we must!"

"Wait, one at a time," Gromov said. "How did you end up here?"

"Vasily Ivanovich is a Joe who lived with us in Moscow," she explained. "When they were rounded up he had to leave, and I went with him so he wouldn't get lost."

"You mean you left everything and went off with him?" he asked her incredulously.

"I had to, he couldn't go on his own. First we went to Alabino, and they told us there to go to Degunino, and when we got to Degunino the stove was broken and the apple tree was dying, and now we've come to Zhadrunovo and he won't go there."

"We mustn't. None of us go there," he whimpered.

"But why Zhadrunovo?"

"To ask Take to mend the stove and the apple tree," the girl repeated. "Never mind, you don't know who Take is. And now he wants to leave, and the only road from here is to Zhadrunovo. If we've arrived, shouldn't we go there?"

"Of course you should," Gromov said. "Don't worry, I'll take you. We must make the stove and the apple tree better."

"That's good, you go, and I'll go back to Degunino," nodded the Joe.

"You mean you're getting rid of me, Vasily Ivanovich?" the girl asked in an anguished voice.

"But you're not alone now, Anechka, you've got your officer," he said. "You go, I'll be fine on my own."

"Go then," she said, and wept.

"Don't be sad," Gromov said. "Your name's Anka, is it?"

"Yes," she said. "What's yours?"

"Maxim," he said. He stroked her dirty, matted hair. "There's nothing to be afraid of – maybe it's for the best. You gave up everything to take care of him, and that's very good, Anka. Goodness and duty can do wonderful things together, don't be afraid."

"I'm not," she said through her tears. "But do you know how afraid I was when we were travelling? The police were after us and we had to keep moving and we'd nowhere to stay, and everything kept moaning and wailing as if the world was about to end but wasn't ready yet, like before it snows, and I was so afraid, Maxim, and so sad, and so sorry for them. They can't do anything and no one helps them, and what could I do?"

"Never mind, it's all over now," he said.

* * *

In the Danilovsky Monastery, the solitary monk Brother Mstislav knew his confinement was over, and he could go outside.

"Father Nikolai!" he shouted. "It seems I'm free!"

"That's interesting," Father Nikolai smiled. "I had an idea it might happen."

"Who could have done it? There were two couples, but it couldn't be them. One was separated just in time, and the other doesn't count, as it turns out the man's of quite a common race and his baby has no special powers."

"Aren't you ashamed to repeat the natives' stories, Mstislav?" said Father Nikolai. "What does it matter what race we are? What matters is that these two others have met, and maybe something will come of it. It's irrelevant that she's half Khazar and he has some native blood, just give thanks to the Lord that our monastery walls are cracking!"

"You mean the last thousand years and the whole history of our closed order was a mistake?" said fat Brother Georgy, coming into the room.

"No, because the longer we're enclosed, the greater the force of history that can burst forth," Father Nikolai said, radiating a quiet joy. "I can't promise you a new sky, brothers, but I can definitely promise you a new earth!"

Brother Mstislav left the monastery and walked through the gates, as if recovering from a long illness, and went happily down to the river.

* * *

438

"I'll be going then," said Vasily Ivanovich.

"Off you go, Vasily Ivanovich, look after yourself," Anka said, smiling through her tears.

He turned from her and dithered for a moment, and at first slowly, then more briskly, set off straight ahead along the rails and away from the village of Zhadrunovo, and the earth didn't resist him. And as he walked he sang the only song he knew:

"Not alone in the field, little road,
Not alone dreaming, not alone waking,
Not alone turning, not alone changing,
Not alone in the field, little road, not alone…"

Anka and Gromov stood on the platform and listened to the song receding into the distance until it fell silent, and the wailing that Anka had heard for so long fell silent too. Opposite the station, muffled happy voices rang from the forest, promising unheard-of things.

"Shall we go?" asked Gromov.

"Let's go!" she said, and they walked hand in hand to the village of Zhadrunovo.